Rough Hard Fierce

Skye Warren

Thank you for reading the Chicago Underground series! You can join my Facebook group for fans to discuss the series here: Skye Warren's Dark Room. And you can sign up for my newsletter to find out about new releases at skyewarren.com/newsletter.

Enjoy the story…

Rough

Prologue

I HUGGED MY knees and stared at the strip of plastic on my bed. A small part of my brain knew it was weird to have it on the comforter, something I'd peed on. The rest of me was too busy freaking out to care.

One night I'd rather forget. The word *no* said and ignored. A little plus sign in an oval window. The dominoes fell, one after the other, leading to this…

Pregnant.

"Maybe it's wrong," Shelly whispered, her eyes wide. It took a lot to shock my best friend, but this had done it. Her face was pale, body as tense and still as mine.

I shook my head. "I've missed my period twice now."

Her blue eyes questioned me. "I thought you two weren't…"

Of course she guessed who the father was. Andrew. He'd been my other best friend. And definitely the only boy I would have trusted with my virginity. Only, I hadn't trusted him. Or just hadn't liked him that way. And trust? That had turned out to be a mistake.

That was a lesson I'd never forget. Trust was an awful mistake.

"We weren't," I said, my voice hoarse. We weren't together, weren't dating. Weren't having sex, if you didn't count that one awful night.

"Then how?" she asked with a slow blink, uncomprehending. She didn't *want* to comprehend, and God, I wished I didn't have to live with the knowledge either. I wished it were a physical thing I could cut out of my skin. But it was just a memory—and memories lived forever.

I said nothing else as I stared at the plastic strip. As a tear fell down my cheek.

Said nothing, even when Shelly sucked in a breath.

She'd lived through her own daily hell. Maybe that was why she figured it out, when another teenaged girl might have taken my tears for regret. Or maybe she noticed too, how angry he'd become in the weeks and months before.

She hesitated. "Did he… did he force you?"

"No," I lied, my voice hollow. "Of course not."

Even on that night I knew I'd never tell anyone what had happened. Not Shelly. And definitely not the police. If they couldn't protect Shelly from her own father, how could they protect me? They wouldn't believe me. I'd take the words—the confession, the shame—and bury them deep. So deep no one could ever hear them. Not even me.

Shelly heard them, though. Her expression turned cold. "I'll kill him."

My heart clenched. I hated him for what he did. But I loved him as my friend, the one who'd hung out every afternoon and made me smile when my dad hadn't been back in months. Most of all, I understood him—more than I wanted to. I knew what went on at his house, even if he'd never actually told me. We were all broken, and we turned on each other with our fear and our fists. It was a cold way to live. A familiar one.

My hands curled into fists, grief and anger and anguish all at once. "He's gone."

Shelly shut her eyes, pain clear on her face. We both knew he'd skipped town suddenly.

I just hadn't told her why.

I'd never wanted her to know. Never wanted anyone to know about the choking terror of that night. And now there was a permanent reminder, a living memory of the worst moments of my life. A baby. I forced myself to think the words. There was a baby inside me right now.

What was I going to do with a baby?

Drop out of school. Get a job. Buy diapers. A sob escaped me, dry and hard.

The bedroom door opened. It took both of us a second to register. No one else was here. No one else was *ever* here. For one brief second, I thought it was *him*. Maybe Andrew had come back. Maybe, despite the awfulness of what he'd done, he'd find a way to help.

And God, I needed help from somewhere.

It wasn't Andrew. It was my father, back early from a long haul to California.

"You girls want some pizza?" His gaze narrowed on the white strip on the bed. "What the hell is that?"

I grabbed the pregnancy test and shoved it behind me. "Nothing."

My father stepped forward, his weathered face dark, eyes filling with rage. "That better belong to your friend there. She looks the type to get knocked up."

My jaw clenched. "Don't talk about her like that."

"Then it's yours?" He stepped forward. In the small room, that brought him right next to me. In a flash he'd twisted my arm. With a cry, I dropped the test to the ground. "Is that what you been doing in this room every time I'm on the road? Fucking around?"

"No," I cried, and it didn't matter that it was the truth. I'd never fucked around, not on purpose. Even that one time, when I hadn't wanted it, it hadn't been here. The truth didn't matter, though. Trust didn't matter.

He picked up the pregnancy test and stared at it.

I begged him, but only in my mind. *Try to understand. Support me. Please.*

I need you to be my dad now.

"Get out," he said, his voice low. "You want to spread your legs and get yourself knocked up? Get the fuck out of my house."

I stood there, frozen. Even when he picked up my lamp and threw it to the wall.

It shattered and fell to the carpet in a thousand pieces.

Shelly grabbed my hand and pulled me out of the room—and out the front door. The white strip of plastic came flying out the door after us. It landed in the dirt at my feet. I looked up at the house, knowing it would be the last time I was ever here.

Maybe the old manufactured double-wide wasn't much by some standards, but it was my home. And maybe my dad was gone more than he was here. But this had been my life. I hadn't wanted it to end. Hadn't been ready for it to be over. How was I going to live now?

I pressed a hand to my stomach. How was I going to support this baby?

I didn't know the answers. The only thing I knew was that I'd figure it out alone. Or with Shelly. But I would never again trust a man. I'd never give him the chance to hurt me or throw me out.

Never again.

Chapter One

There's a certain sultry walk a woman has when she's bare that can't be faked. No hose and no panties. The nakedness under my skirt was as much about keeping me aroused as it was about easy access.

I'd perfected the art of fuck-me clothes. A surprising number of men asked me out, even at a grungy club on a Saturday night. Cute little college girl, they thought, out for a good time. I saved us all time by dressing my part.

Tonight's ensemble consisted of a tight halter and short skirt with cheap, high-heeled sandals, bouncing hair, and bloodred toenails. The scornful looks of the other women didn't escape me, but I wasn't so different from them. I wanted to be desired, held, touched. The groping fingers might be a cheap imitation of intimacy, its patina cracked with rust and likely to turn my skin green, but they were all I deserved.

My gaze panned to the man at the bar, the one I'd been watching all night. He nursed a beer, his profile harsh against the fluid backdrop of writhing bodies. His gray T-shirt hung loose on his abs but snug around thick arms, covering part of his tattoo.

Dark eyes tracked me the way mine tracked him.

His expression was unreadable, but I knew what he wanted. What else was there?

He was hot in a scary way, and that was perfect. Not that I was discerning. I needed sex, not a life partner. There were plenty of men here, men whose blackened pasts matched my own, who'd give it to me hard.

A woman approached him. Something dark and decidedly feminine roiled up inside me.

She was gorgeous. If he wanted to score, he probably couldn't do better, even with me.

I tried not to stare. She walked away a minute later—rejected. I felt unaccountably smug. Which was stupid, since I didn't have him either. Maybe no one had a chance with this guy. I was pretty enough, in a girl-next-door kind of way. Common, though, underneath my slutty trappings—brown hair and brown eyes were standard issue around here.

"Hey, beautiful."

I glanced up to see a cute guy wearing a sharp dress shirt checking me out. Probably an investment banker or something upstanding like that. Grinning and hopeful. Had I ever been that young? No, I was probably younger. At nineteen I had seen it all. The world had already crumbled around me and been rebuilt, brick by brick.

"Sorry, man," I said. "Keep moving."

"Aww, not even one dance?"

His puppy-dog eyes cajoled a smile from me. How nice it might feel to be one of the girls with nothing to worry about except whether this guy would call tomorrow morning. But I was too broken for his easy smile. I'd only end up hurting him.

"I *am* sorry," I said, wistfulness seeping into my voice. "You'll thank me later."

Regret panged in my chest as the crowd sucked him back in, but I'd done the right thing. Even if he were only interested in a one-night hookup, my type of sex was too toxic for the likes of him.

I turned back to the guy at the bar. He caught my eye, looking—if possible—surlier. Cold and mean. Perfect. I wouldn't taint him, and he could give me what I craved. Since Tall, Dark, and Stoic hadn't deigned to make a move on me, I would do the pursuing. A surprising little twist for the night, but I could go with it.

I squeezed in beside him at the bar. Up close his size was impressive and a little intimidating, but that only strengthened my resolve. He could give me what I needed.

"Hey, tough guy," I shouted over the din.

He looked up at me from his beer. I faltered a bit at the total lack of emotion in his face and fought an automatic instinct to retreat. His eyes were a deep brown, almost pretty, but remote and flat. Dark hair was cut short, bristly. His nose was prominent and slightly crooked, like it had been broken. Maybe more than once.

He looked mean, which was a good thing, but I was used to a little more effort. Even assholes provided a fake smile or smarmy line for the sake of the pickup. There was a script to these things, but he wasn't playing his part.

My club persona and beer from earlier lent me confidence. Whatever was bothering him—a bad day at the construction site or maybe a fight with the old lady—I didn't care. He was here, so he needed this as much as I did.

I planted my elbow on the bar. "I saw you looking at me earlier."

He raised an eyebrow. I shrugged. He was making me work for it, but I found myself more amused than annoyed.

"Buy me a drink?" I asked.

He considered me, then nodded and signaled the bartender.

The beat of the club reverberated as I took a sip. "So do you talk?"

His lips twitched. "Yeah, I talk."

"Okay." I leaned in close to hear him better. "What do you talk about?"

He ignored my question—or maybe answered it—by asking, "What are you doing here?" Almost like he was asking something deeper, but that had to be the alcohol talking.

"I'm trying to get laid, that's what I'm doing here."

I pulled off a breathy laugh I was pretty proud of.

He didn't react, didn't appear surprised or even interested, the bastard. He just looked at me. "Why?"

I decided on honesty. "Because I need it."

He seemed to weigh the truth of my words, then nodded toward the exit. "All right, let's go." He got up and threw some cash on the bar.

His easy acceptance caught me off guard, just for a moment. But it shouldn't have surprised me, because...well, because men always wanted sex. That's what I liked about them—they didn't even bother trying to hide it. It was worse when I hadn't seen it coming, when it had sneaked up on me—Now wasn't the time to think of that. It was never the right time to think of that.

He tucked his hand under my elbow, guiding me. He used his body to maneuver us through the crowd, almost as a shield. The whole thing was so gentlemanly, given what we were about to do, that I wondered if he'd heard me right. Maybe he'd want to get coffee or something, and wouldn't that be awkward all around?

But he was a man, and I was a woman wearing fuck-me clothes—this could only end one way.

When we exited the club, I couldn't help sucking in several deep breaths. Even the faint smell of street sewage was refreshing, washing the stench of smoke, alcohol, and countless perfumes from my lungs. I never liked the crowds. The press of bodies, the mingling smell of sweat, the small bumps from all around. Tiny violations that were somehow okay since everyone did it.

As my heart rate settled, he inspected me as if he could read me. He couldn't. "What's your name?" I asked to distract him.

"Colin. Yours?"

"Allie."

"Nice to meet you, Allie. Your place or mine?"

I was comfortable again. I knew this play: horny girl who can't wait to get naked.

"We don't need to go anywhere. Let's get started right here." I let a soft moan escape me and clasped myself to the brick wall named Colin. Never mind that I was dry as a bone. He wouldn't notice. They never did.

He raised his eyebrows. "In the parking lot?"

"Or in my car. Whatever. I just want you to do me."

"I'm not fucking you in a car. It's forty degrees out."

I was hardly in this for comfort. I'd done it in colder weather just this past winter. "I don't mind."

"Well, I do."

"Fine." I was willing to give him so much. Why couldn't he take it the way I wanted? "Then we can go to the motel over there. You're paying."

He didn't look happy. I wasn't either, but I couldn't budge on this. Going to an apartment might be the norm for hookups, but my hookups weren't normal.

Going to their houses where they might do God knows what was out of the question. And I wasn't about to bring one of these guys home.

"Not there," he said. "I'll pick the place."

Chapter Two

I FOLLOWED HIS truck in my car to a motel about ten minutes away. When I pulled in, he waved me to a parking spot next to his truck and went into the office.

The place wasn't fancy, but the manicured shrubbery and freshly painted building proclaimed this was an entirely different kind of establishment than the dump by the club. No renting rooms by the hour here.

The sign out front advertised $119.99 a night. A typical price for Chicago, but I sweated the cost. The extravagance of my six-dollar drink from earlier paled in comparison.

What if it was too much money? I might not be worth it.

I kept watch on the frosted office door like he might disappear. Eight minutes later, he came out. My stomach clenched. He flashed a key and nodded toward the back before getting into his truck. I followed him in my car and pulled up beside him again.

It was dark back here. Deserted. The only light came from flickering, yellow lamps dimmed by tiny hordes of bugs. Scattered buildings slumbered around us like a nest of dragons, their snore the low drone from the appliances. It wasn't exactly safe. Technically that was what I wanted, but the allure of danger only worked up to a point.

He didn't come to my car. Instead he opened the motel room door and waited.

I could drive away. He probably wouldn't even come after me. Even if he could, if I drove somewhere safe—assuming there was such a place—there'd be nothing he could do.

But his solemn patience gave me the courage to open the car door and join him.

The stale air and harsh edge of cleaning supplies softened me. I'd ridden along with my dad in his 18-wheeler once. He usually slept in truck stops, but with me he'd gotten motel rooms. This was just an empty room, but it felt strange to use a place for casual sex that I associated with childhood memories.

Once inside the room, I set down my purse on the floral fabric chair.

Colin reached out and trailed his finger along my jaw. His eyes, almost black in the dark motel room, searched my own. I thought he was going to fuck me then, but he said, "I'm going to make coffee."

I blinked. Shit, coffee. "Okay."

He went to work at the coffeemaker. Unsure of what to do, I sat down in the chair, clutching my purse in my lap like I was waiting for a doctor's appointment instead of rough, dirty sex.

He poured a cup of coffee, adding the cream and

sugar without comment, and handed it to me. I took a few sips. It soothed some of the skittishness I hadn't realized I had. He didn't take any for himself.

Enough of this.

I set down the cup on the cracked countertop and stood to kiss him. I started off light, teasing, hoping to inflame him. This was all calculated, a game of risk and power.

He kissed me back softly, gently, like he didn't know we'd started playing. He held his body still, but his mouth roamed over mine, skimming and tasting.

It wasn't a magical kiss. Angels didn't sing, and nothing caught fire. But he wasn't too rough or too wet or too anything, and for me it was perfection.

I rubbed against him, undulating to a rhythm born of practice. His hands came up, one to cup my face, the other around my body.

I sighed.

He walked me backward, and we made out against the round fake-wood table, his hands running over my sides, my back. Avoiding the good parts like we were two horny teenagers in our parents' basements, new to this. I shuddered at the thought. This was all wrong. His hands were too light. I was half under him already, my hips cradling his, so I surged up and nipped at his lip. Predictably his body jerked, and he thrust his hips down onto me.

Yes. That's what I need. I softened my body, surrendering to him.

"Bed," he murmured against my lips.

We stripped at the same time, both eager. I wanted to see his body, to witness what he offered me, but it was dark in the room. Then he kissed me back onto the bed, and there was no more time to wonder. The cheap bedspread was rough and cool against my skin. His hands stroked over my breasts and then played gently with my nipples.

My body responded, turning liquid, but something was wrong.

I'd had this problem before. Not everyone wanted to play rough, but I was surprised that I'd misread him. His muscles were hard, the pads of his fingers were calloused. I didn't know how he could touch me so softly. Everything about him screamed that he could hurt me, so why didn't he?

I wanted him to have his nasty way with me, but every sweet caress destroyed the illusion. My fantasy was to let him do whatever he wanted with me, but not this.

"Harder," I said. "I need it harder."

Instead his hands gentled. The one that had been holding my breast traced the curve around and under.

I groaned in frustration. "What's wrong?"

He reached down, still breathing heavily, and pressed a finger lightly to my cunt, then stroked upward through the moisture. I gasped, rocking my hips to follow his finger.

"You like this," he said.

Yes, I liked it. I was undeniably aroused but too aware. I needed the emptiness of being taken. "I like it better rough."

Colin frowned. My eyes widened at the ferocity of his expression.

In one smooth motion he flipped me onto my stomach. I lost my breath from the surprise and impact. His left hand slid under my body between my legs and cupped me. His right hand fisted in my hair, pulling my head back. His erection throbbed beside my ass in promise. I wanted to beg him to fuck me, but all I could do was gasp. He didn't need to be told, though, and ground against me, using my hair as a handle.

That small pain on my scalp was perfection, sharp and sweet. Numbness spread through me, as did relief.

The pain dimmed. My arousal did too, but that was okay. I was only vaguely aware of him continuing to work my body from behind.

I went somewhere else in my mind. I'd stay that way all night.

At least that's what usually happened. Not this time. Instead I felt light strokes on my hair, my arms, my back. His cock pulsed hot against my thigh, but he didn't try to put it inside me, not in any of the places it would almost fit. His hands on me didn't even feel sexual. He petted me, and I arched into his caress.

"Why did you stop?" I meant it to come out demanding, but instead I sounded weak. I hated sounding weak, especially about sex. He may be the one with the cock and the fists, but I called the shots. I had to.

"Allie, shhh. It's okay." He was trying to soothe me, and it was working. He turned me back over and began to kiss me, still murmuring words against my lips. "I'll give it to you. Don't worry. Relax." More words than he'd spoken all night.

I was lost, my emotions all jumbled up from my arousal and my high and subsequent low, at the mercy of this stranger.

What's happening to me? I needed to get back to something I knew. I wanted him to fuck me, to be inside me, to center me. I whimpered, hoping he'd understand.

"Shhh." He arranged my arms and legs so that they were splayed open on the bed and then kissed his way down my stomach. I shifted restlessly, knowing what he planned to do.

I didn't want to say no, exactly, but I couldn't look forward to it. That would probably have sounded weird to some people, that I would have rather gone down on a guy than have him go down on me.

Giving head was a no-brainer for me. I loved cocks, the way they tasted and felt in my mouth. And just the invasion of it, the submission. It was a pretty gross thing to do when I thought about it. Maybe that's why women didn't like blowjobs, but they didn't understand about the power.

Colin, however, settled down between my open legs like he planned to stay. I felt too self-conscious to say anything at all, especially while he was focused on such an intimate place. I couldn't help but tense up.

He kissed the inside of my thigh, his fingers trailing the path of his mouth. He switched to the other thigh, and only when my hips tilted up slightly did he move closer to my center. He licked through my folds, the soft contact startling. His fingers played there too, but he didn't ram his fingers inside me or press my clit. He just licked and suckled and dipped his tongue inside to lap at the wetness pooling there.

It was almost like he wasn't trying to get me to come. In my experience a guy would aim for the good parts and try to get me off as fast as possible, if he even bothered. But Colin licked me like he had all the time in the world. He wasn't speeding up or pushing me on.

The room was silent except for the wet sounds from his mouth on me. The pressure of having to perform an orgasm eased with his leisurely pace. He didn't seem to be expecting me to come now, so it was okay that I didn't. I relaxed into the pleasure, luxuriating in this new sort of worship. God, was this why women loved getting oral sex?

Liquid released from inside me and slid out onto his tongue. He moaned. He actually moaned like...I don't know, like it tasted good. As if the taste of me had turned him on. Damn, that turned me on right back.

For all that I liked giving head, I'd never thought a man could really want to do it to me. He wouldn't like the taste or his tongue would get tired or he'd get bored, but Colin didn't seem to be thinking any of those things. The slow, languid way he licked me again and again spoke of someone who was enjoying himself.

And then, without me having to fake it, my hips rocked in a thrusting motion. He hadn't sped up, but the sensations of his mouth and his own appreciation of the act propelled me toward orgasm. I didn't want it to end.

Colin read my body's pleas and moved his mouth up to my clit. He sucked and slid his finger inside me, using the rhythm of my hips as a guide. So damned good. I couldn't help the moans that came out of my mouth. I'd heard the phrase "I'd die if he stopped," and I'd never understood it before now. I wouldn't have died if he'd stopped, but I just might have cried.

I'd had sex lots of times, but I'd never had a lover so in tune with what my body wanted. It was a conversation, one my mind was barely aware of, but my body knew instinctively.

He played me like he already knew me. He didn't tease me, not withholding my climax or any of that tantric shit, for which I might have had to kill him. But neither did he rush me toward climax. It was as if his entire purpose had narrowed to drawing out my moans.

My whole body went taut, muscles tight, hips flexed up to push against his mouth. My inner muscles clenched at his fingers, pulling them deeper. My breath stopped, and all I could do was make a choking sound.

I came and came and came; all I could think was that I'd found something I'd lost.

Colin stroked me through my climax. I jerked violently when his tongue flicked over my clit one last time, and he withdrew his fingers. I expected him to put his cock inside me. Instead he climbed up my body and lay beside me.

He wasn't going to do it.

I felt vulnerable right then, and he knew it. He was going to try to be honorable or something. I didn't want that. I couldn't believe in it.

His cock looked dark and thick and wet at the tip. Something softened in a deep, cold place inside my chest that he was willing to postpone his pleasure for my ridiculous personal shit. That he would even *know* I had any personal shit when this was just a random hookup.

But no, I wanted to please him. He let me push him fully onto his back. I climbed over him and teased him into an openmouthed kiss, ran my hands down his chest. I wanted to give him something, and this was all I had to give.

I'd thought he wanted to be submissive to me, from his gentleness, the way he had worshipped me during oral sex, and the way he was pliant when I pushed him over. It wasn't a role I'd have thought I'd like, but I found myself willing to go there for him. I already knew I'd go down on him. I was looking forward to blowing his mind, along with his cock.

But as I started trailing my kisses downward, my intention clear, he stopped me and shook his head slightly. I'd never had a man turn down a blowjob before. I'd never heard of it happening, not during sex, not when it was free. It flustered me, the way he could do anything to me but he chose to make me feel good.

He arranged me again, so that I was straddling his hips with my legs on either side of him, resting my hands on his chest. His arousal bobbed up toward my hanging breasts.

Colin reached across the bed to his jeans and pulled a condom out of his wallet. He slipped it on and maneuvered my hips onto his erection, then down, slowly. The tautness of his face spoke of urgency, but he held my hips still. We were on his time.

At last he rocked up with tiny thrusts. When I caught the rhythm on my own, he released my hips and smoothed one hand back along my ass. The other came up to my breasts, stroking them, tweaking them.

I could feel the difference in his touch from before. He wasn't trying to get me off now. He was playing with me for his own pleasure. I leaned into his touch, and he sucked my nipple into his mouth.

My arousal built, taunting me, and I tried to speed up.

His hand tightened on my ass. *No, not yet.*

I relaxed into the rocking motion as the pleasure between my legs grew. This was nothing like the sex I'd had before. It was more like a dance or even a meditation. I had no idea how much time passed, but when my legs got sore and tingly, he rolled us over.

He surged into me deeper, in an aggressive rhythm that took me faster and harder. I pulled my legs higher and curled my hands lightly on his neck, opening my body in supplication. I wasn't an active participant any longer. I couldn't help him or even react—I could only take it.

I came again, and this time it wasn't in a blinding explosion but a soft wave. Not a crest but a hum of pleasure, accented with each of his thrusts.

He buried his face into the side of my neck, groaning roughly as he came. His whole body rumbled at the sound, shuddered at his release. His arms tightened their hold on my body, and his hips pushed down into me, harder, deeper—*yes*.

He collapsed and rolled off me. He lay faceup, eyes closed, breathing hard. Colin looked beautiful to me, then. I might have thought he was handsome before, or maybe not, but it was an objective sort of observation. Looking at him now, knowing him—it was too much.

I stumbled off the bed and into the bathroom. I felt my own wetness sticky on the insides of my thighs, but I didn't bother to wash. I sat down on the linoleum and leaned my back against the bathtub, trying to get it together.

I'd thought his sweetness was weak, but that wasn't true at all. He was entirely in control, treating me the way he wanted, not the way I asked for it. And more than that, he seemed to know what I needed, giving it to me despite myself.

He walked into the bathroom, still naked, and sat next to me on the cold floor. I thought it was pretty silly and not totally clean. He put his arm around me and wiped away the tears I wanted to hide. I cried quietly for who knows how long while he held me.

I knew I'd feel stupid when I came back to reality, so I held it off as long as I could. Even after I stopped crying, I kept my eyes closed and buried myself into his side.

Then his stomach growled. We wouldn't be able to sit here forever.

I peeked at him. I wasn't sure what to expect, but it wouldn't be good. Anger maybe, or frustration, disgust, pity, or any number of bad things might be there, before he got the hell out of Dodge.

Instead his lips quirked up into a wry smile. "I'd like to see you again, but this doesn't bode well for my chances."

I laughed, the sound loud in the small space, because it wasn't at all what I'd expected. It could have just been my postorgasm, postbreakdown hormones talking, but if I were honest with myself, I was already falling for him.

That didn't matter, because I had other considerations. One, mostly, but she was enough.

"I like you," I hedged. The disappointment that flickered in his eyes said he read my tone correctly.

"But I don't think so."

He considered me for a moment. "Okay," he said. "That's not what we're here for, so I won't push."

He got up and offered me his hand. In the bedroom he handed me my clothes in between putting on his own. I averted my eyes, not because I didn't want to see, but because there was a formality between us now that we'd had sex but weren't going to see each other again.

"I'll drop the key off at the front," he said. "You can finish up in here."

"Okay."

He turned back at the door. "Listen, I own the Oasis Grill down on Kirby, okay? In case you change your mind. Just ask for me."

He paused and then added, "Colin."

I hadn't forgotten.

"Maybe," I said with a noncommittal smile.

"Bye, Allie. Take care."

I peered through the blinds and watched his truck leave the parking lot. So, that was that. Why did I feel a lingering sense of loss? He was a stranger to me. He had to stay that way. That's what this night was for—dirty, emotionless sex. Though this night had been distinctly less dirty and far less emotionless than I liked.

Chapter Three

I LEFT THE motel room, my mind blissfully blank as I drove through the sleepy Chicago streets. My apartment building loomed up ahead, its gray stucco walls and barred windows making it look more like a jail than a home. In Stone Park, that was an amenity. *Don't bother breaking in,* it said. *You won't find anything valuable.*

Within the white walls of my apartment, I took a quick shower to rid myself of the smoky stench of the clubs and the musky smell of sex. I didn't mind them, at least not tonight, but I didn't allow any remnants of my monthly date nights to seep into my regular life. Colin included.

I changed into my standard uniform, sweatpants and a tee. My flip-flops slapped the concrete stairs as I ran up to the identical apartment above mine.

Shelly answered the door. Her hair and makeup were done, though she wore jeans and a tank top. She had an appointment after this.

"So. How was your date?" The lilt in her voice made everything sound ironic, though in this case, the word *date* certainly was.

I hummed in response as I followed her into the living room and flopped down beside her on the couch. I accepted the ice-cream pint and spoon she offered.

"Uh-oh," she said. "What happened this time?"

"I didn't say anything happened." I took a bite. "This is chocolate. How can you eat chocolate this late? It'll keep you up."

"Don't change the subject. Spill."

I sighed and took another bite. "This guy. He wasn't like the others."

"What does that mean?"

"It means, he was…gentle."

"Oh," she said, knowing. "You should let me hook you up."

I shot her a dark look over the spoon.

"I'm just saying. If you're only in it for the sex, you might as well get paid. You can even charge extra to get roughed up."

"Right, so I can get put in jail for solicitation. No, thank you."

She rolled her eyes. "That doesn't happen. Hardly ever."

"We're not having this conversation." I didn't judge Shelly for what she did. I admired her strength. But I had to draw the line somewhere. Right now I was just a regular single mom with her rare date nights. If things got a little heated, who was to know? But accepting payment would change the score. Right now I was in control.

Or I usually was.

I passed the carton of ice cream back to her. "Besides, it wasn't exactly…"

It wasn't exactly bad. It had been amazing. *Real,* my mind whispered. That was what real sex was supposed to be like. It had been anything but bad.

"Allie?"

I looked up and found her watching me.

I smiled briefly. "Sorry. I'm a little distracted."

"I can see that. Curiouser and curiouser." Shelly liked to quote *Alice in Wonderland* to me. It was our secret joke, one I never quite appreciated.

"Don't be dramatic. It wasn't completely lame. That's all."

"I see." The teasing light extinguished from her eyes. "Allison, we have to talk."

Nothing good ever came from hearing my full name. "Bailey?"

"No, she's fine. But…it's related."

A knot formed in my stomach, threatening to expel the churning mixture of chocolate ice cream and alcohol.

"He called me," Shelly said. She was watching me, probably wondering how I would react. I wondered the same thing. I had the expected feelings: fear, revulsion. But maybe relief too, that the paralyzing wait had come to an end. "He said he just wanted to catch up. And…he asked about you. I told him I didn't know where you were."

"How did he find you?"

"Same number since high school." She put up her hands. *I'm sorry.* "Changing numbers is not a good business move for me. Still, I think we may have taken the hiding-in-plain-sight idea a little too far."

"I'm not hiding."

She raised her eyebrows.

"I'm not doing it well," I admitted. "He was the one who left."

Shelly didn't press me, thank God. We walked into her bedroom, where Bailey slept in the middle of the queen-size bed wrapped in fuzzy pajamas, her little fist against her mouth. I scooped my baby girl up, huffing a breath under the weight. Well, she'd be two years old in a few short months, not exactly a baby anymore.

Turning sideways through the bedroom doorway, I left Shelly's place and carried Bailey down to our apartment, depositing her in her own secondhand princess bed. Already in her pajamas, she slept on as I tucked her in under the sheet. I gave her a kiss on the forehead and paused to breathe in her scent. That turned out to be a mistake, because she chose that moment to wake. I calmed her as she fussed, singing my small retinue of nursery rhymes until my voice had gone hoarse and her eyelids stopped fluttering.

This was how I protected her, by keeping the darkness separate.

I couldn't give her a mother who was whole, unbroken. But I could be here for her, night after night, day after day. And if I went on an occasional date night, if there was a twisted side of me let out only then, she never had to know.

I padded into my own bedroom, convinced I'd made the right choice in not seeing Colin again. Men had one use in my life, and that was what the club was for. I wasn't in a good place for anything more than that, would probably never be.

Colin seemed like a nice guy, not like my usual dates. But I'd been wrong about a man before, hadn't I? So I'd made the right choice. Almost definitely.

When I lay down in bed, though, I thought back to the way he'd been with me, the way he had touched me. The way he had *licked* me. Jesus.

Most kids loved getting presents, but I hated it. After every present people would look at me expectantly, waiting for the gasp of surprise, the exclamation of how much I adored it, and the obligatory hugs all around. I worked at these happy displays, and if it wasn't up to par, I suffered the disappointment. It got to where receiving presents was associated with letting people down.

If a man gave me oral sex, I felt pressure to come quickly. Then it would be like I owed it to him to be properly grateful afterward. Even if I could get off, the stress wasn't worth it. And sometimes I couldn't even come. How could I relax with a stranger's teeth at my most vulnerable place? It wasn't a common problem for me, though, because picking up random guys at bars isn't usually conducive to finding generous lovers.

Colin had licked me, though, and it had been amazing. I had the oddest thought that I wanted him to do it again. That wouldn't happen, of course. But I slipped my fingers into my panties and dreamed.

Chapter Four

I STARTED LOOKING over my shoulder in parking lots, bundled into my thick jacket as if it were armor. Slowing down as I approached alleyways as if something might jump out at me.

Bailey wasn't excused from my insanity either. I crept into her room multiple times a night, making sure she was there and breathing. I even gave in a few times to sleeping on the floor near her bed, sharing the dim comfort of the night-light.

Colin was to blame, of course.

Shelly said it was Andrew—the call from him—but I didn't want to think he could still affect me like this. After all, we were safe from him. As safe as a woman and a baby could ever be from a man who wouldn't wish them well.

I told myself this was something far more basic. More base.

It had been a little over a month since I'd met Colin—since I'd fucked him. I had told Colin what I needed, how I needed it, and he had refused. He hadn't misunderstood—the brief display of force he'd shown when he flipped me over had disproved that possibility.

There was no doubt he was strong enough, but he'd been gentle, kind, almost...loving.

That's not what sex was about for me. Not anymore.

As Bailey and I entered Shelly's apartment, Shelly glanced at me with that blank expression she usually reserved for her johns and then peered back out her blinds. The boarded-up street front was hardly a pretty view. Besides, in our neighborhood, it was best to stay away from the windows.

"What's up?" I asked.

"That car," she said. "I don't suppose you recognize it."

I sat Bailey in the middle of the room, where it'd take her at least a full minute to get up to any trouble, and peeked between the slats. A dark car, probably black, sat out on the street that formed a T with ours, facing our apartment building. I squinted. Between the distance and the glare on the glass, I couldn't tell whether those shapes were passengers or merely seats.

"No," I said. "Why?"

"I saw it there last night. Kind of odd. When I got back from the store this morning, it wasn't there. Now it's back."

It could be anything out on the street. I wasn't sure why this particular car spooked her, except that it did look rather shiny—as in clean—for this area. And though I couldn't quite tell from the shape of it, it seemed somewhat new. Nice cars in a bad neighborhood spelled trouble.

"It's probably nothing," I said. "Or the neighbor in 6A. He's got shifty eyes."

"Yeah," she agreed. "Probably nothing."

It looked like I'd rubbed off on even Shelly. I didn't like seeing her shaken—that wasn't her—so I went for distraction. "Bailey has a new trick."

"Oh?" she asked, some of the scary flatness fading from her eyes.

"Bailey, catch." I gently tossed the large, soft ball to her. She pounced on the ball as it hit the floor, accurately guessing the arc if not quite catching it midair yet.

"Yay!" Shelly clapped. "Who's my good girl?"

Bailey giggled. Previously we had only played roll, so this was a whole new world for her. I left them to their new game so I could change and get to work.

THE BAKERY WAS a study in facades, the front of the shopping-strip building all brick, with fancy porticos and signage. Back in the employee parking lot, the cement was exposed, shorter than the brick wall. The contrast reminded me of a movie-set prop.

The inside was split too. The front room, where the customers came in, was spacious and tiled and clean. The back rooms were unfinished, the innards of the building exposed and cramped. Between the two, it was fitting that I was in the back. It wasn't pleasant, just where I belonged.

When I went inside, my coworker and slacker supreme lounged against the counter. I forced myself to smile at him as I clocked in. "Hey, Jeremy."

He glanced at me—my mouth, not my eyes—and then away. "Hi, Allie."

"So…what have you got for me?"

"Two wedding cakes in the freezer. Cupcakes on a timer. Rick took an order for tomorrow."

"Shit, tomorrow? What for?"

"Don't know," he mumbled, staring intently at the refrigerator beside me.

I managed a weak smile. "All right. I'd better get started."

He shrugged and went into the bathroom. His shift was up when I got in, so it'd be on me to make whatever order Rick had agreed to.

After washing my hands and checking on the cupcakes, I went in search of Rick. He looked up from his paperwork. Not bothering with his customer smile, he said, "We got an order for a birthday cake. Fifty people. Over-the-hill theme. Tomorrow."

"Jesus, Rick."

"Don't start with me. This is business." Yes, business. The business where I cooked the cake using my recipes, decorated using my ideas, and took home a barely legal hourly wage. I wasn't too bitter about that, but I didn't want to work overtime on top of it. Not when Bailey was home with Shelly, and Shelly needed me back so she could go to work and make much more money selling her body.

Meanwhile the Sweet Spot was billed as an authentic family bakery with an eye on modern trends. No, Rick wasn't my family. And judging by the covert looks he'd steal when he thought I wasn't looking, he didn't think of me that way either. But he didn't touch me, and that made this better than Shelly's job. Maybe.

"Fine," I said. "Is that all they said?"

"She wants it classy." He rolled his eyes.

I smiled slightly, commiserating. "Right. Over-the-hill, fifty people, classy. Got it."

The back was empty, bathroom door open, so Jeremy had already left. I got to work on the cake batter. In reality the decorating was the easy part. The painful part would be all the waiting that would happen while baking, then cooling, then the first coat, then the full-on decorating. I'd have to work past my shift today to get it done, for sure. Most likely I'd stay up late tonight, rolling out fondant pieces on my counter at home so I could apply them to the finished cake tomorrow.

I barely heard Rick's yell over the whir of the electric mixer. I flipped it off and listened.

"Allie. Phone!"

Only Shelly had this number; only Shelly would care to call. Well, I had to talk to her anyways, ask her if she could watch Bailey late today. Wiping my hands on my apron, I grabbed the plastic receiver.

"Shelly?"

Silence.

"Hello?"

I looked at the phone, then put it to my ear. Still nothing. I hung up. Poking my head out onto the floor, I called to Rick, "Nobody there."

He looked up. "What?"

"There was nobody on the phone. Was it Shelly?"

"It was a guy." Rick shrugged and looked back down at his work. "Asked for you by name."

"Huh." Weird. My dad? Not likely.

My heart still beat too fast, thumping erratically as if my body couldn't make up its mind whether to squeal like a teenage girl or to worry like the woman it had become.

I called Shelly just to check. It hadn't been her, but she agreed to watch Bailey late tonight. Only after I hung up did I think about using Call Return to call the guy back. Not that it was a big deal. Guys weren't exactly standing in line to talk to me.

That's what I kept telling myself. At least until I dropped the entire tray of frosted cupcakes on the floor.

Count backward from ten. Everything will be fine.

Chapter Five

By that night I was practically climbing out of my skin. I needed the release that my monthly date nights provided. They were rough, dirty, and more than a little unsafe—but they were on my terms. Without my fix I felt panicked and jumpy.

It must have showed, because Shelly took one look at me and told me to drop Bailey back off before her bedtime. I said no and took Bailey to the park, then to the library, anything to distract us both from the anxiety that threatened to tear me apart. In the end I gave in, tucking Bailey into Shelly's bed and singing her to sleep before heading out to the club.

As I entered the building, the stench of stale alcohol and sweat hit me. I took a deep breath, a drag. Unsteady on my heels, I wove through the crowd toward the bar. Without planning it, I ended up where Colin had sat last time, and I felt an irrational pang of disappointment to find the bar stool empty. I sat there instead, my ass where his had been, nostalgic over some dirty, cracked plastic.

I signaled the bartender for my usual, but it burned on the way down. I glanced around, feeling cornered, even though I was right in the middle. Everything—the bar, the people, the strobing lights—was covered with a film of grime and dirt and shame. No, that didn't make sense. It was me.

A hard body pressed against me from behind. Some part of my brain flickered with hope that it was Colin. But the body pressed harder, grinding its erection into my back, and I knew it wasn't him. Not that I could recognize his cock print, just that it was too cheesy of a move for him. Too aggressive.

The acrid scent of sweat wafted from behind me. I started to turn, but hands clasped around my waist and squeezed.

"Where do you think you're going?" a rasping voice whispered in my ear. Cold lips slid down the side of my neck, leaving a trail of wetness like a slug.

I shivered. He chuckled.

At the other end of the bar the bartender was serving a group. If I screamed, he would probably hear me, even over the racket of music. He'd help, maybe.

"It's okay, baby. I'm not going to hurt you." *A lie.* My skin prickled in warning. I wanted someone who could be mean, but I tried not to cross the line into outright crazy, and this guy was ringing all the warning bells. His hands were already so tight on my hips that they'd leave bruises. Without having seen his eyes, I knew they would be empty, lifeless. He would be more than rough—he'd be brutal, dangerous.

"Come outside and play," he said.

This was what I'd come for, but now that it was here, I didn't want it.

"No."

He yanked on my arm, and I toppled from the stool. I finally got a look at him. I looked up to angry eyes and a shaved head. His bulging stomach did nothing to negate the meaty muscle everywhere else.

His eyes looked like I'd envisioned, but with something else: a cruel amusement. Oh, he'd hurt me, all right, and he'd enjoy it. Chills raced through me.

He grabbed my arm and turned to leave, but the bartender called us back. "Hey, stop."

The man paused and turned. "What's up?" he said.

The bartender looked from me, to the guy holding me, then back at me. "You okay?"

I don't want this. Help me. "No, I..." Fingers tightened on my arm, cutting into the flesh. I cleared my throat against the thickness. "I'm okay."

The bartender narrowed his eyes; then he was gone, lost in the swirl of flesh and nylon as I was dragged through the crowd and out the door. The man pulled me over to the side of a building, toward an overflow parking lot, mostly vacant. The heavy beat of the music boomed even outside the club, but I could still hear my blood rushing through my ears. I struggled, but it didn't slow him down.

A truck was parked in the corner, against two brick walls.

He shoved me against the truck door, the metal

cold against my back. His body pressed into me as his mouth came down on mine. He tasted me, consumed me, pushing his tongue in deep. Thick, harsh hands groped me, squeezing my breasts and grabbing my bare ass beneath my skirt.

"You know you want it, you little slut. Let's see what you got." He yanked my shirt down at the draped neckline, ripping the fabric. The cold winter air kissed my breasts right before his hands grabbed and burned.

Oh God, I was torn. I'd come here for this. I should want this, but I didn't. I wanted to leave. I wanted him to stop touching me. I wanted to curl up and die.

"Don't be a tease." He squeezed hard. I gasped in pain but let him do it. Of course I did. This was what men did, and I was the girl who let them. The sick sense of triumph I felt every time I proved it was absent this time around.

"That's better, baby." He ravaged my body with his mouth and his hands. He was leaving marks on me, marks I knew from experience I would study later with revulsion and fascination.

Someone else kept intruding even as this guy assaulted me. It was Colin's tongue in my mouth, Colin's hand yanking my hair, Colin's cock pushing painfully into my pubic bone. I closed my eyes. Maybe that was the solution. I could get the roughness I craved, but my imagination would make it safe.

Two fingers shoved inside me. Dry. My eyes

snapped open. *Not Colin.*

He jammed them deeper, eliciting a whimpered, "No." I hadn't meant to say that. I told myself I wouldn't say no, not again. It didn't work, just made them angry. He was moving too fast and it hurt too much, but I could already feel myself start to slide into that place—the place where my mind slowed and none of the pain or the shame could touch me.

It didn't matter, because he didn't mind me. He'd do what he wanted. His lips twisted into a smile.

Abruptly he spun me around so that my exposed breasts were smashed against the door of his truck. His body shoved against mine stole my breath away, then more pain, in time with muted grunts from behind me.

Just as quickly there was nothing. No hard cock pushing against me or rough hands restraining me. Disoriented, I pushed off the truck, staggering back.

"…the fuck away from her," I heard. And shit, I knew that voice.

Not Colin turned into an entreaty in my mind. I slowly dragged my gaze up. *No, please, anyone but him.* But of course there he was, looking like he was leading the charge into a fight instead of just witnessing me in all my shameful glory. Maybe other people dream of being naked in front of a crowded theater, but I already knew this moment would be memorialized in my nightmares: me, half-dressed in a dirty parking lot, in front of Colin.

My arms flew to my breasts, covering them in a

futile attempt at modesty. My shoulders hunched as if I could curl in on myself. I envied those little pill bugs that could roll up into a ball. But my body didn't come with any built-in armor. There was just my almost nakedness, exposed by men and my own stupidity.

Paralyzed with humiliation, I could only stand there.

"It's not how it looks," said the man. His voice was loud but shaky. If anyone could recognize false bravado, I could. "She wanted it. She was asking for it."

Oh God. I had the most wildly inappropriate urge to laugh. It was true; it was true.

"Colin," I managed to get out. "It's nothing. It's okay."

Colin swung his gaze from the man to me. "Are you hurt?"

"I'm fine." Close enough.

"Come here." He opened his arm, and without thinking I ran to his side.

"Fuck, I didn't know she was with you!" The man was yelling now, almost screaming. "I didn't know. What the fuck? I wouldn't have touched her, I swear. I wasn't going to hurt her."

With his arm around me, I could feel Colin's muscles tense as if he might spring at any moment, but I wanted this to be over. I leaned into him, molding my arms around his chest in an embrace meant to comfort and restrain.

"Please," I whispered.

He glanced down at me, eyes blazing, but said to the man, "Get the fuck out of here."

The man, whose name I hadn't learned, got into his truck and sped out of the parking lot, leaving Colin and me in a haze of exhaust. We stood in that embrace, my bare breasts pressed against his shirt as if it were the two of *us* having an illicit encounter.

He pulled off his shirt, and my fucked-up mind wondered for just a moment if he would pick up where that man had left off. And how crazy I was; I'd let him.

Colin held out his hand with the shirt. I took it from him and slipped it on with a murmured thanks, unable to look him in the eye.

"Allie," he said.

"Just go," I croaked, looking at his shoes.

It was over, but my anxiety had only increased. He wasn't touching me anymore, and I could hardly blame him. I didn't want to touch my dirty skin either. I'd crawl out of it if it were possible. Just leave this dirty body behind and be someone else.

"What the hell were you thinking?" he asked.

Our roles seemed to have reversed, because I couldn't speak. He was supposed to be the quiet one, and I was supposed to act brave. I shook my head.

"I could understand you wanting to do better than me, but why would you pick that fucker over me?"

"It wasn't like…that." Not exactly and not for the reasons he thought.

When I didn't elaborate, he sighed. "Are you sure

you're not hurt?"

"No. I'm fine." If I kept saying it, maybe it would be true. But my breath was coming more rapidly. "I just want to leave, okay? Just go."

"Allie, stop."

"I said go. Leave me alone. I know you want to, so do it!" My words bounced off the brick walls, making his seem unnaturally quiet.

"I'm not leaving you."

Unable to face the intensity of his stare, I looked down, only to feel a warm, strong body encase me. I stiffened only a moment before relaxing into his arms, because I could only fight myself for so long. *Safe.* His chest hair tickled my face, but I rubbed my cheek across it like a cat leaving her scent.

After a few minutes Colin led me to his truck and bundled me in like I did for Bailey, snug and secure. We left the club and my car behind, driving toward my apartment without me having to give directions. The light from the streetlamps only served to make the dark roads more intimate, as if we were the only ones in the city.

It was the perfect mood for confessions, not that I wanted to make any. "How did you know where to find me?"

"The bartender."

I pondered that for a minute. "That guy. The one who… He seemed really scared of you."

A pause. "He just didn't want any trouble."

"It kind of seemed like he knew you."

He shrugged, keeping his eyes on the road. "I'm a mean son of a bitch."

"You're not mean, Colin. You're a good guy."

He smiled faintly. We drove the rest of the way in silence. Despite its inauspicious ending, the whole encounter accomplished what I'd needed. I felt relaxed, sleepy almost.

Even though he'd come home with me, I hadn't expected he would want to have sex. In fact, I would have thought he wouldn't, either out of disgust at what he'd seen earlier or a misguided sense of chivalry.

So I was surprised when Colin led me to my bedroom and kissed me, just a touch of his lips to mine. His hardness pressed against my stomach, announcing his purpose. My feelings were a jumble, but I wanted to give him something. A thank-you, an apology. If there was one thing I knew how to do, it was to let a man fuck me.

He pulled off my clothes carefully, his fingertips pausing at each bruise. I stood for him in the middle of the room, still in my mellow head space. He could have asked me to do anything for him, but what he asked was, "Will I see you again?"

God, please.

How did he do this to me? I'd told myself that men only wanted sex, and that they weren't above using force to get it. And that made a sick sort of sense, because Andrew was a man. A good one, supposedly.

One I had trusted, that was for sure. My friend.

When he'd raped me, it was easier to write all men off. The men at the club had only proved the point. They thought they were using me, but it was the other way around. Every slap, every insult, every pinch-of-pain thrust had only cemented the walls that had allowed me to move past the rape and live my life. Now Colin wanted to bring all that down.

I couldn't go back to that dark place in my mind. I'd do anything not to go there again.

So it killed me when I responded, "Yes."

Maybe it made me weak, but I couldn't give him up.

"What?" The little crease in the middle of his forehead showed he was as surprised as me.

"There's something I have to tell you first." I took a deep breath. "I have a kid. A little girl."

"Okay." He drew the word out.

What was the norm in a situation like this? I hadn't dated, hadn't thought about it. "Okay good or okay bad?"

"Okay, I already knew that."

"What? How?"

He shrugged. "Car seat."

I supposed that made sense. And now that I thought about it, there was baby stuff pretty much all over my apartment. More baby furniture than adult furniture. Only my room was spared, because it was empty but for my bed.

"And you're…cool with that?" I asked.

He scowled. "I'm here, aren't I?"

I had my doubts. This whole night seemed like a dream. A strange nightmare-turned-fantasy dream. That guy had been the worst, but then I always expected the worst. What I hadn't expected, what had never happened before, was being saved. Being protected, carried away by a freaking knight in a white truck.

Suddenly I needed a shower. What had been acceptable earlier tonight—that man's hands on me—now felt entirely wrong. Their very imprint defiled me, and by extension Colin.

"I need to shower," I blurted out.

Colin nodded like this pinball of a conversation was completely normal. "I'll be in the kitchen."

I wondered if he'd really be there when I got out. Maybe he'd think about my issues or just the fact that I came with a kid and bolt out the door the second the water started. The thoughts churned my stomach, but if he left, it would be for the best. Definitely for him.

The water shocked my system. *This is really happening,* it berated me, *so stop fucking around.* And I wanted this, wanted Colin, wanted so many things that I didn't have a right to. But no matter how little I deserved it, I could never stop hoping.

I threw on my softest T-shirt and sweatpants and shuffled into the living room, afraid of what I would find. What I found was Colin with practically a party platter at the kitchen table.

Deli meat and cheese, grapes, and crackers decorated a couple of plates. I recognized it all from my fridge, taken out of packages and laid out like this was a soiree instead of a crummy apartment in Stone Park.

"Thought you might be hungry," he said.

My stomach grumbled its agreement. "I have to pick up Bailey first. My daughter."

"Oh," he said. "Your car is—"

"She's just upstairs," I said. "My friend can take me to get my car tomorrow."

"I'll have someone drive it back. Don't worry."

And for some reason I didn't. Worrying was a well-worn shoe for me, but in the surreal dark of this night I accepted his word. I accepted him. He'd have someone drive it back. I shouldn't worry. I was safe.

Shelly was groggy when she let me in. "How'd it go?" she mumbled.

"Brought a man back."

Her eyes snapped open, full alert. "What?"

She'd been the one to teach me the rules. And by teach, I meant she'd drilled them into me, her lessons replete with stories of women who *hadn't* followed the rules. Even though most everyone at the club held their hookups at their apartments, it wasn't the safe way to play. And considering I had Bailey and also that my dates tended to be assholes of the first order, I played it safe. Relatively speaking.

"Well, he brought me back, technically. I think I'm going to"—what the hell had we agreed to?—"well, to see him again."

Shelly inspected me for a long moment as the suspicion faded from her face and a knowing smile bloomed. "You are, huh?"

"Shut up," I said, though I was more embarrassed than mad. "I didn't agree to marry the guy."

The light of laughter gleamed in her eye. "What's his name?"

"Colin," I grumbled.

She sang under her breath. "Allie and Colin, sitting in a tree…"

"Oh, great. You're in first grade." I marched into the bedroom to fetch Bailey, ignoring Shelly's tinkle of laughter behind me. And continued ignoring her smirk as I passed her on my way out, laden with a sleeping baby girl.

Shelly's soft voice followed me down the stairs before she shut the door. "Then comes Bailey in a baby carriage."

Back in my apartment, I slipped past the kitchen and carried Bailey straight to her bedroom, where she settled immediately. The faded pink toddler bed was old and used, but it had a certain charm. Something old-fashioned and innocent. As soon as I'd seen it at Goodwill, I'd spent too much money on it. It didn't fit with the rest of my sparse apartment, but it fit Bailey.

She was the only thing good and clean in my life. If I had to release the darkness inside me once a month in order to keep it away from her, I had never minded doing so. But now there was Colin, and presumably he would not be okay with me making solitary trips to the club for a quick, dirty fuck. Neither did he want to be rough with me himself. I didn't see how this could work out in the end, but I couldn't bring myself to let him go.

In the kitchen Colin had piled together a sandwich from the contents of the plates and poured a glass of milk for me. I sat down with this strange, achy feeling. Guilt, maybe. I'd never had someone take care of me like this, not ever. There'd been my dad, but I'd been the one who needed to make dinner if I wanted it done. It was the kind of thing a mother would do, but I'd never had one, at least that I could remember. Who knew Colin could be motherly?

"Thanks." *For everything,* I wanted to say, *not just for the sandwich. Not even for protecting me from the guy at the club. Thank you for seeing my flaws and wanting me anyway.* But those words hung in the air, just out of reach.

"You're welcome," he said, his face blank. He stood up, grabbed my keys from the counter. "I've got to go. I'll make sure your car is back by morning."

He rummaged through a drawer and shoved a piece of paper and pen into my hands. I scribbled my number on the paper and kept my eyes downcast as he plucked it from my fingers.

I was used to feeling competent. In my work and in my life. It wasn't a wonderland, but it was mine. Even the date nights were an extension of that control—they were on my terms. But now I felt bumbling, inept, unable to do basic things like date a guy.

"Hey," I said.

He paused at the door and turned back.

"Maybe we could go out. Tomorrow night," I said.

A faint smile turned his lips. "Sure."

And then he was gone.

I went to the closed door and turned the lock, then rested my forehead against the glossy white paint.

Shelly's voice rang in my ear. *"Allie and Colin, sitting in a tree…"*

Of course, Shelly had it wrong. Even if I were serious about Colin—and we were a far cry from that—I had a baby first. Another man's baby, at that. And love and marriage had nothing to do with this thing between Colin and me. It was sex and companionship. Friendship, maybe. Love was for suckers.

Chapter Six

"How are you?" Colin's eyes raked over my breasts as if checking to see whether any bruises from last night lingered.

Flowers. He was holding flowers. I accepted them, trying to look as if I'd done that before when I didn't think I'd even held a bouquet before. They were heavier than I expected. The smell of damp spring serenaded me.

"I'm okay. Thank you." I led him to the kitchen to hide my blush. "But I…I was hoping to talk to you about last night."

A muscle ticked in his jaw as he leaned his hip against the counter. "Go ahead."

"I know how it looked, but it wasn't like that." Maybe it would have been better to let him believe it was rape, to never talk about it again, but I couldn't bind him to me by pretending to be the victim.

"I heard you say no," he said.

I wiped my palms on the plasticky fabric of my dress. "I know I said that. But sometimes that's what I want. For someone not to stop. I know that sounds kind of crazy. I mean, it probably is crazy. I guess what

I'm trying to tell you is that I…have issues."

His face softened just a fraction. "I know. Can you tell me?"

My throat tightened. Actually, every muscle went taut as if the strength of my body could keep my mind from saying too much. It wasn't a choice, not talking about what happened. It was a physical impossibility. It always had been.

People seemed to think they could fix anything by talking it out. Afternoon talk shows and therapists and meetings didn't really help people. All they did was provide a forum for them to talk. Assuming a person *could* talk about it.

The only person who really knew what had happened that night was Shelly. And even then she had pieced it together from my babbling and bruises and, later, the positive pregnancy test.

The thought of telling someone, of telling *Colin*, about that night was…unthinkable. If I tried, my mind shut down, blank and helpless.

I didn't know how much time had passed with me frozen, but he pulled me to him. "It's okay," he said. "We all have issues."

I heard Shelly's voice in my ear, quoting the Mad Hatter. *"We're all mad here."*

His hands running along my back unlocked my voice. "Even you?"

He nodded.

My eyes searched his. "What are your issues?"

"That would be cheating."

I couldn't help but smile. His eyes narrowed on my mouth.

He leaned down and pressed a soft, almost chaste kiss to my lips. I felt his lips open, and I opened mine too. But he didn't plunge inside. Instead his lips fastened on my lower lip and tugged.

My eyes fluttered shut. I felt the soft wetness of his tongue, the scratch of his bristle, but oddly the most intimate was the touch of his nose against mine. I breathed in his exhales, and he breathed in mine.

"Promise me you won't go back to the club," he whispered against my mouth.

I kept my eyes shut. It was safer. "Okay."

This was just supposed to be a casual thing, a date or two, but somehow it felt like more with him. He tempted me to want more. He was like the male equivalent of the sirens I'd read about in high school, who promised happiness when disaster loomed.

"Would you do that for me?" I opened my eyes. "Give me what I need?"

He paused, and I knew he'd understood what I meant. The roughness. His eyes gave nothing away. "Maybe," he said.

Chapter Seven

Colin took me to a hole-in-the-wall Italian restaurant for supper, where we split a classic Chicago pizza. The couple who owned the place screamed obscenities at each other, so obviously colored by affection that it made my heart hurt just to hear.

Later, back at my apartment, Colin followed me to my door. I unlocked it, but before I could enter, he pulled me back and kissed me. I remained frozen that way, leaning away from him for only a few seconds before melting. He pressed me into the door, kissing me, covering me. Headlights flashed onto us from a car in the parking lot, and he broke away.

Colin turned the knob and eased the door open, guiding me inside. As soon as we were in, I pulled him over to the couch, unwilling to let this turn into another coffee session. He sat, and I climbed on top of him, straddling his erection through his jeans. The hardness of it was intimidating and thrilling.

As a young girl I thought of a boy's penis as a weakness, a vulnerability that could be exploited by a well-aimed kickball. But now that I was a woman, a cock was a thing of power, something that could give or claim or bruise.

Our mouths met in a kiss, both licking and exploring and biting. The line between taking and being taken blurred. If my stomach revolted at the thought of having sex, with the memory of that other man's hands still crawling on my skin, that only increased my need. I could do this. I'd prove that I could.

I rocked my hips, pushing my clit onto the ridge of his cock.

"Good girl," he murmured against my lips. I froze at both the humiliation and the pleasure of his words, then rode him over his jeans. Our kiss broke off from the force of my thrusts. He pulled off my shirt and bra to bare my breasts before he covered them with his hands.

The pleasure from my clit ricocheted through me. Almost, almost there.

If only I could stop thinking. *Does he want me? Of course he does; I can feel his erection. But any girl would do. If he wanted me, he'd already have fucked me by now. He wouldn't be sitting there, letting me do this. What is he waiting for? Come on, come already. I'm taking forever. He'll get bored, or worse. I'm doing it wrong. I'm not good enough. If you want me, take me. Please take me. Fuck me. Prove that you want me by fucking me.*

A sting on my nipple snapped me back into my body. Colin pinched the other one, and I gasped.

He slapped the side of my hip, the pain making my inner muscles clench. "Don't stop," he ordered.

His mouth replaced his fingers at my breasts, licking and sucking. I kept riding him. It hurt, what he was doing, but I knew I needed the pain and he seemed to know it too.

I hovered on the brink. Then he bit down, lightly at first and then harder. Too much. It hurt too much. I couldn't take it. My eyes fell shut as I shuddered through my orgasm.

When I became aware again, I was enfolded in his arms, my head resting on his shoulder. I looked up at him, expecting to see smugness or arousal, but instead he looked troubled.

Shit, I'd done something wrong. "I'm sorry."

"For what?"

"For…doing that. It's your turn."

I reached for his zipper, but his hand stayed me. "Wait."

Panic caught in my throat. He didn't want me. My skin crawled with shame.

But I could fix this. I'd make him want me. "Come on, baby. Put your hard cock in my mouth."

I licked my lips, and his fingers tightened around my wrist. "Please," I said. "Give it to me. I'll make it feel good."

I tried to tug my hand away. He opened his fingers one by one. Gratified to have my hand back, I unzipped his jeans. I'd told the truth. Whatever he felt or didn't feel for me, I'd make his cock feel good.

His cock sprung out, hard and eager. I grasped it at

the base and pulled. The softness of the skin was always a shock, too soft for something so hard and scary.

Sliding to the floor, I licked the tip, that faint salty flavor a tease for us both.

"Suck it," he said. My eyes flew to his and found them hot and insistent. I smiled. He'd certainly gotten over his reluctance. But I wouldn't gloat. I took his cock into my mouth, slid it on my tongue, and back toward my throat. When I pulled back, my body sucked in a deep breath, knowing breaths wouldn't come freely for a while.

I edged him deeper with each long suck, craving more even while I fought down a gag. This was what I wanted. A cock was made for fucking. Putting it in my mouth wasn't something that came naturally. I didn't have teenage dreams about being tenderly face fucked. But I did it anyway, with relish, because it felt good for him. It's a special kind of gift, debasement.

My jaw ached, but I welcomed the pain—I was pleasing him. I worked him harder with my tongue and lips and hands. His hands came up and grabbed my hair. *Yes.* He pulled me to him as his hips rocked up, less deeply but faster. I opened my mouth wider in acceptance, straining against the stiffness. He came with a grunt, spurting salty warmth into my throat, his hands stroking mindlessly through my hair.

He hadn't yanked my hair or choked me on his cock, but it was still good. I reveled in the sight of his sated expression. All that buildup, not just the blowjob or making out, but even the dinner—all so that I could give him this moment of peace. Without opening his eyes, he reached for me and pulled me up into the crook of his arm. I curled into his side, shutting my eyes against the sight of his soft cock lying outside his jeans, too raw a reminder of what I'd just done.

He sat up and straightened his clothes. I did the same, suddenly wary.

His face turned away, but not before his eyes darkened. "Allie…I have to go soon."

I looked down. "Oh."

"Hey. I just have to take care of some business. Nothing bad." His finger stroked my cheek and lifted my chin back to him. "That was great."

"Yeah?"

"Yeah," he said. "I'll call you later tonight, okay?"

"Okay."

He turned at the door. Pulling me to him with his hand behind my head, he kissed me, lingering. "I'm going to see you again soon," he said against my lips.

My lips curved against his. "Whatever you say."

"Damn straight." But his eyes were twinkling as he shut the door.

This entire night worked for me. I'd had a great time but wasn't ready for the implications of a sleepover. And I got to pick up Bailey while she was still awake, our dinner being so much earlier than a club visit. That may not have been everyone's idea of a great date, but to me it was almost like heaven.

Except for the cough. It was only a small, dry cough when I picked Bailey up from Shelly's apartment, but it quickly progressed into a full-fledged mortar explosion, complete with phlegmy shrapnel. As if that wasn't scary enough, her fever spiked from a low-grade 99 up to 102 degrees even with medicine.

Shelly had accepted a client since I'd gotten back so early, so I swiped her laptop to hunt online for advice, but all I found were stern call-your-pediatrician directives. Bailey's pediatrician was long gone from the low-cost doctor's office, and now the only option was the twenty-four-hour emergency clinic. She wailed and coughed and then wailed some more. I'd never seen her like this.

By the time I called the emergency clinic, Bailey was in full-fledged banshee mode. The receptionist gave me a scripted, "She should be seen," barely audible over Bailey's shrieks of pain and baby frustration. That meant spending a hundred bucks we didn't have, but I'd pull it from the rent money for now.

Fortunately, the clinic was not at all crowded for a Saturday night. In fact, after the last couple of people were called in, we had the dingy waiting room to ourselves. I filled out the paperwork and settled in to wait for Bailey's name to be called.

The night air had a calming effect on Bailey. If it wasn't for the nasty cough that intermittently racked her small body, she almost seemed well. But we were there already and had paid, and it made more sense to stay and be seen.

I almost didn't notice him. My attention was split between Bailey and the clock. But he stopped right in front of us, and I looked up. Even then I didn't recognize him right away. A big, scary-looking man who'd had the shit beat out of him, that's what I thought. Angry, red welts covered his face. His right eye was swollen and literally taped shut, with what looked like first-aid tape. My arms tightened around Bailey, and then I recognized him—the man from the club, in the parking lot.

The man who'd almost raped/fucked me and had only been stopped by Colin's threats. Apparently he'd picked the wrong girl to mess with this time, because he was wrecked.

Had he followed us here? Would he try to hurt us?

This was a public place, but I knew from personal experience that no place was safe, least of all a hospital. I glanced nervously around the small, empty room of plastic chairs. The receptionist was behind a frosted-glass sliding window. Probably the most I could hope for was that she would call the cops if trouble started. Oh, and we'd have speedy-fast medical aftercare. Great.

I had to get him away from us for Bailey's sake. There was no going along with it this time. I licked my lips, trying to think fast with an armful of sick baby.

He spoke, but only half of his lips moved, the other half busted up. "I'm not going to hurt you, I swear."

Right, that's what people always say when they have

no intention of hurting someone.

"I just want to apologize," he said, the last word slurring almost unintelligibly. He shifted his weight between his feet nervously, or maybe just in pain.

I didn't really care, so long as he left us alone. "Okay."

"I didn't mean anything by it."

"Okay. It's okay." I willed him to walk away, begged him with my eyes.

"I hope I didn't hurt you. Are you all right?"

All I could think of was how to get this guy to leave, but I didn't know what he wanted. If anything, he seemed to be getting more worked up. His breathing increased, but not in a menacing way—more like he'd fall down any second.

I glanced at the closed receptionist window again, wondering if we'd need her help for a different kind of emergency. "Umm, you don't seem so good. Are *you* all right?"

He jumped back. "No! I'm fine. I don't want any trouble."

"Okay," I said, more confused than wary at this point. "So..." I trailed off, glancing at the door suggestively.

"Ah! Right. Well, you take care. And again, I'm sorry. Very sorry." He backed away from me to the door as if I might lunge and attack him with the diaper bag. I heard him mumbling apologies even as the door shut behind him. My whole body slackened in relief that he was away from Bailey. She dozed in my arms, fitful from her sickness but otherwise no worse for the wear.

That call was too damn close.

We made it through the actual visit with minimal fussing. The doctor, who performed what appeared to be a cursory exam, said it was probably a virus but sent us home with an oral antibiotic "just in case." By the time I dragged us back home, it was already midnight. Late, but not that bad, considering all that had happened.

Bailey, who had been exhausted on the ride home, decided to wake up with wide eyes after I administered the antibiotic. Meanwhile my lids were closing. Not good.

My throat started to ache, and it felt so cold. I cranked up the heater, already cringing at the thought of our gas bill next month. I set Bailey up with some soft toys in the living room and then collapsed on the floor beside her, watching her play.

I jolted awake to the sound of my phone ringing. I took a quick inventory of Bailey, who seemed to have collected everything that wasn't nailed down and piled it in the middle like a bird's nest.

My hand fumbled for the phone. "Hello?"

"Hey, Allie." A few of my frazzled nerves settled at hearing his voice.

I glanced at the clock and groaned. It felt later than one o'clock. "Hey, you."

"What's wrong?"

I sighed. "It's nothing. Bailey's caught some sort of bug, and I guess I've got it too. She's wide awake, and I'm exhausted." I took a deep breath, in and out.

"That doesn't sound like nothing. What can I do to help?"

"What? Oh, no. We're fine." I rubbed my hand over my eyes, willing myself to stay awake. "I'm sorry. Did you need something?"

"No. I was just calling to… Well, it doesn't matter. But it sounds like you could use a hand."

"Nah, I'll figure something out. I've done it before, you know."

A pause, then, "Can I come over?"

I glanced at Bailey. "Uh, now? It's pretty late…"

"Yeah, I know. I'll just come over, and if I'm getting in the way, you can kick me out, okay?" He hung up.

The phone slipped from my fingers, as if maybe the conversation had been a dream. I drifted in a haze of discomfort as I watched Bailey use a block of Post-it notes as stickers on all the furniture.

Colin had to knock twice before I dragged myself to the door, holding Bailey. He held up a plastic drugstore bag. "I brought meds."

A burst of pleasure at his thoughtfulness was quickly doused by my exhaustion. I took the bag from him and led him into the kitchen.

"Here, I can take her while you do that." He

reached out his hands for Bailey, but his eyes were veiled as if he expected me to refuse.

I hesitated for a moment but realized I trusted him more than that tired doctor. I handed her over, awkward because I rarely did so. He was less nervous than I would've thought as he set her on his hip. She gave a token fuss before settling against him.

The picture of him with her made my heart thump. Apparently Colin had a horse-whisperer effect on both girls in the Winters household.

I hid the strange euphoric feeling by dumping the contents of the bag onto the counter. I sorted through the boxes casually as if men brought me gifts of kindness and health every day. "Wow, did you buy out the store?"

"I didn't know what you already had, so I just got everything they had."

I opened a few to take. "You didn't have to do this. Thanks, though. This is really great."

"No problem. Should I put Bailey to bed?"

Bailey examined Colin with undisguised curiosity, looking no closer to sleep than she had a few minutes ago. "Uh, sure. You could try that."

"Any specific thing she likes?"

"I usually read a few books and then sing to her. When she wakes up in the middle of the night, like tonight, I try to cuddle her back to sleep."

"Okay," he said and headed toward the hallway.

No one except for me and Shelly had ever put her

to sleep before, and I doubted Colin had tons of childcare experience, so I wasn't expecting success. Still, grateful for the reprieve, I leaned against the counter with my eyes closed for a few minutes.

I took a bunch of pills to help with various symptoms and then headed to Bailey's bedroom. The door was cracked open, and I peeked inside. Bailey lay on the bed with her eyes closed.

Colin sat on the edge stroking her hair and singing. *"In my thoughts I have seen rings of smoke through the trees, and the voices of those who stand looking…"*

Led Zeppelin! I clapped my hand over my mouth.

This big, strong man, wearing a muscle shirt and cargo pants, sang rock songs to a toddler in the middle of the night. I was so toast. Game over. And it was doubly terrifying, considering I had no idea how to make him stick around. He would leave and take his sweetness and his Pepto and our hearts.

Chapter Eight

In disgust at my own vulnerability, I stalked into the living room and started picking up Bailey's things. How was I supposed to hold myself emotionally aloof when he was being so damn sweet? But the truth was, he might be a knight in shining armor—but I couldn't be saved. I was too far gone for that. I'd been too far gone since I was sixteen. And now, three years later, I felt ancient.

Colin came in and leaned against the door frame. "Hey, I can do that. You can rest."

"Is she down?"

"Out like a light."

I closed my eyes again for a long minute, savoring the peace. "Thank you. Really."

"No problem."

"Here." I patted the couch. "Come and sit. Not too close, you don't want to catch this thing."

He rolled his eyes and sat. "After what we did earlier, I don't think an extra foot is going to help me."

I laughed, which kicked off a coughing spurt. When it was over, I groaned and rolled my head forward. Colin shifted closer and kneaded my shoulders.

"Jesus," I said. "Stop being perfect."

His hands froze. "I'm not perfect."

"Okay," I said, partly because I hadn't meant to offend him and partly because I wanted him to continue. His fingers, thick and calloused, started to move again, pushing away my knots. Those hands were strong enough to hurt me, but instead they brought me pleasure and now comfort.

God, this was better than sex. It was probably best not to tell him that, male ego being what it was, but it was true.

"So good," I managed to groan, to let him know I appreciated him.

"Shh," he said. Even better.

He rubbed my shoulders, my neck, even my arms, until I relaxed back into him—a puddle of sick, exhausted woman. My mind entered a slushlike state, dreamy. His arms wrapped around me, gently rubbing my hands. Who knew hands had tension?

At first I'd been so desperate for relief that I was content to be pampered, content to use Colin that way. But after a while, even through my fog I felt the oddness of the one-sided flow of pleasure. Normally I would feel guilt that I'd even accepted it, and maybe concern that he would demand recompense, more than I had to give. But with Colin it was different. There wasn't fear, only gratitude. I wanted him to feel good, as good as me. Of course, I also didn't want to move or even open my eyes, so that was a dilemma.

I turned my hands over. My fingers felt small and fragile in his large ones, like a bird's wings fluttering in a cage, but he wasn't holding me down. He let me explore, my fingertips tracing the calluses on his palms. I curved my fingers around to the backs of his hands. Rough skin, though not as rough as the calluses, and the soft hair of a man. My fingers inched up—it was coarse and…? My eyes snapped open, and I looked down to see open cuts on his knuckles. I stared at them for a moment.

An icy shiver ran down my spine, one that had nothing to do with my fever. I didn't know if I was slow because of the late hour or because I didn't want to see it. I remembered what the man at the clinic had said—that was the exact phrase Colin had used last night, that the guy just didn't want any trouble. Last night the guy had acted like he knew Colin, or at least knew *of* him.

I turned slowly in Colin's arms until I was facing him, still clutching his hands. "How did you get these?"

His face closed up, confirming my fears. And in his eyes there was knowledge of what he'd done. There was caution too, which I hated.

"Colin."

He looked like he might not answer me, but he said, "It was nothing. A disagreement."

"Who?"

He shrugged, not casually enough. "Someone

where I work."

"Right. Someone didn't pay the tab, so you beat him up?"

Colin shook his head, but his eyes never left mine. "The restaurant isn't the only place I work."

"Tell me." *Tell me you didn't do that to him. Tell me you aren't another violent man.*

"My brother. He owns a few businesses."

"Was it the man from the other night?"

"Why would you think that?"

"Gee, I don't know. Maybe because you tell me you have something to take care of. Then I see him with the shit beat out of him. And then you come around with—"

"You saw him? When the fuck did you see him?"

I flinched at his language, which was laughable considering my own dirty mouth. Still, this one was less like an exclamation and more like a lash.

"Did he come here?" he asked. "I swear to God, I'll kill him."

I pulled away from him and stood, wrapping my arms around my sides. "You did it, then."

"Yes, I kicked his ass, but it was a fair fight." He stood and paced away from me. "What? Did you like him or something?"

"No, I don't *like* him, but I don't want to see him hurt because of me. Jesus, Colin."

"You didn't do it. He started it, and I finished it."

I rolled my eyes. "I am not some stupid girl you

fight over, winner take all."

"I wasn't fighting to win you. I was teaching him a lesson. Now answer me. Did he come here?"

"No! Not that I owe you an explanation, but apparently you'll go homicidal if I don't tell you. I saw him at the ER where I took Bailey, okay? All he did was *apologize* to me. And he looked like shit. You seriously hurt him."

"Good. But he shouldn't have talked to you at all. I warned him what would happen if he did."

My eyes widened. "You're not going to do anything else to him."

He said nothing.

"I'm serious. I can't believe you even did that much. This isn't like the caveman days. Who does that? Crazy, violent people, that's who. You could've really hurt him." And then a thought hit me. "You could get in trouble. Even go to *jail*."

"If I do get sent to jail, it won't be for *that*."

"What does *that* mean? What other things are you doing?"

He gave a quick shake of the head. *Don't ask.*

"I swear to God, Colin, do not make me play twenty questions. If you are up to something dangerous and you are bringing it here into my house with my daughter, then I have a right to know."

Finally he looked ruffled, his cheeks pinking and his nostrils flaring slightly. "I'm not bringing anything into your house. No one will hurt you or your daughter, especially not if I'm seeing you."

"Is this supposed to be comforting? Because it's really not. What does that even mean? Who the hell are you? The mob?" I tried to laugh but choked on it when he shrugged.

"Nothing that organized."

I stared at him, dumbstruck. Out of the frying pan and into the fire, that's what had happened.

He sighed. "Can you please sit down?"

"I don't want to sit down."

"Allie. Sit."

I sat.

"You know I own a restaurant. But before that I worked for my brother. I won't lie and say everything was above the table, because it wasn't. It wasn't always legal and it wasn't always…good."

He looked at me resignedly, as if I would condemn him. I thought of Shelly, and I thought of Andrew. My own halo was much tarnished. No, I wouldn't condemn Colin for his past, but that didn't mean I had to accept it into my life. I had to think of Bailey.

"You aren't involved in that stuff now, right? I mean, now that you run your restaurant."

"Most of the time." His words were slow, too carefully chosen to be comforting. "But sometimes he asks for my help, and I do it. That's what I was doing at the club the night we met—meeting him."

"What types of things do you do?"

"Whatever he needs done."

"Violent things?"

"I never claimed to be perfect." His eyes focused on mine, his voice steady.

A small laugh burst out of me, the sharp sound bouncing off the walls of my bare apartment. "No, you didn't, but there's a long way from not perfect to violent criminal, don't you think?"

He said nothing.

"And if I asked you to stop doing those things, would you?" But I already knew the answer.

"He's my brother."

I wasn't angry. Not angry for whatever slight deception there may have been not to tell me this up front. Not for his past, whatever illegal or violent things he had done. Not even angry for what he had done to the guy from the club.

I was afraid.

Afraid that somehow, that world would intersect with mine, when I'd worked so hard to isolate myself. Even my club nights were carefully orchestrated and contained, incidents that never spilled over into my real life. Until Colin.

I was afraid I'd misjudged him, that he wasn't the nice guy I'd thought him to be. Just doing bad things in your life didn't make you a bad person. I believed that firmly. But how could I tell the difference? I couldn't trust him. I couldn't even trust myself.

"You're breaking up with me, aren't you?" An undercurrent of steel in his voice was the only sign of his displeasure.

"It's not like we're going steady. We've had one date and two fucks. That does not make a relationship."

"Don't bullshit me. You and I both know it was different between us."

I paused, then said more quietly, "Why me? You could go back to that club and pick up a girl who's hotter than me, who doesn't have issues, that's for sure. I need to understand why you want me."

He shook his head, though it wasn't a refusal.

"It's not just the sex. It's...it's this." He waved his hand around my apartment.

Bare white walls, cheap ratty couch, strewn plastic toys. I just looked at him.

"I want you. I want *this*." He gestured between us in frustration, maybe at me for asking the question, maybe at himself for not being able to answer.

"Oh, Colin."

He hid behind a thicker skin than I could ever hope to breach. The only reason I was seeing this was because he'd let me in. I fell in love with him a little right then, as he sat, so large and competent yet so vulnerable. I wanted him for my own, and that wanting was like a chant in my head. A greedy, futile chant.

"Maybe there is something special between us," I finally said, "but it's just too hard. I've got so much baggage I could sink the Titanic, and you...well, you have your own baggage, don't you?"

Maybe I was being mean, I thought, as I watched his defenses tighten up again right in front of my eyes. Sometimes mean was good. Sometimes mean was the difference between survival and going under.

"Don't put this on me, Allie. I'm not the one too scared to give this a shot."

"No, you're just the one who's part of a violent, tiny mob family who goes around beating people up for fun." We had both raised our voices, angry that this wasn't going to work and yet unable to fix it.

"I can't believe you're mad about that. That guy was an asshole who hurt you. He deserved what he got."

"That's not the point. It's not up to you. Did you ever think of what would happen if he got angry with me and tried to hurt me back? I was at the clinic with Bailey when I saw him."

"I made it clear he wasn't to touch you ever again. Besides, you should have called me if you needed to go to the clinic."

I rolled my eyes. "Oh, please. I'll just call you whenever I need anything at all."

"I would have come with you."

"Yeah, unless you were doing something for your brother."

His nostrils flared, but he didn't respond.

"It seems to me like you're the one who's stuck in the past. If you want to be with me and Bailey, fine. Then stop doing dangerous things that could come back on us."

"You can't ask me to give up my family."

"I'm not asking for that. You can see him all you want, just don't do anything illegal for him, anything violent."

"It's the same thing."

"Then what kind of family is that? He just wants you for what you can do for him."

He stepped toward me. "Yeah. That's right. And you think you're better than him? We all pay for what we want, me included. You're not giving me anything for free, so don't play the martyr. You'll fuck me to get what you want, and who the fuck cares what I want?"

I stared at him in shock.

He lowered his voice, still breathing hard. "Everyone has a price, Allie. And I'm not paying yours."

Colin turned and left the apartment, the door latching quietly behind him.

Chapter Nine

"THE ANTS ARE back!" In my frustration I let my voice ring out through the bakery. It was closed at this early hour anyway.

"Jesus Christ," Rick swore from the bathroom.

With a sigh, I wiped away the ants and rolled out my dough.

A few minutes later, Rick came out. "You didn't have to scream at me. Missed the toilet."

"Well, I hope you cleaned it up, because I'm not touching your piss." I waved my flour-covered fingers at him.

He narrowed his eyes at me but returned to the bathroom. A minute later he came out.

"Did you wash your hands?"

"Yes," he snapped but then turned back to the bathroom. I heard the water run for a minute before he came out again.

He leaned against the wall by the phone. "What's up your ass?"

"It's not unreasonable to expect you to wash your hands. Clean working environment. Food preparation. Health code violations. Any of this ring a bell?" Working being a relative term for Rick, but between him and the bugs, this place was getting gross.

He shrugged. "It's not that. You've been bitchy lately."

"This is just how I am."

His expression turned mulish. "Maybe, but it's been really bad for a few weeks now."

"PMS." I gave him my best feral smile. *Drop it.*

"See?" He grinned. "Bitchy."

"Yeah, well, do me a favor and fire me." Not that he would, and not that I really wanted him to. The job sucked, but it kept Bailey in diapers and that was the important thing.

"Mmm, no thank you. Maybe if you don't get that custom cupcake order done by the end of your shift."

"Don't tempt me."

He went into his office, probably afraid he'd actually annoy me enough to bail. I was the only person he trusted enough to do the large, expensive orders. And none of the others even did fondant. If only I could use my leverage for something useful, like a raise.

Bitchy. I snorted. Hell, yes, I was bitchy.

I had literally no idea where my electricity payment was coming from. No, scratch that. I did know. Shelly. She'd offer it, and Bailey couldn't very well live in an apartment with no lights, so I'd accept. Shelly earned that money on her back. If anyone had to turn tricks to support Bailey, it should be me.

As if I wasn't feeling guilty enough, it looked as if

Shelly had a crazy client obsessed with her. The same black car parked on the street at odd hours. One bright day I caught the glare from a camera lens aimed at our apartment building. I ran inside with Bailey, and the car drove away. I considered calling the cops, but we knew they wouldn't do anything. Besides, both Shelly and I had an aversion to cops, though for a slightly different reason.

My "date nights" had gone to shit. And the man who'd done it, well, I'd broken up with him. Or maybe he'd broken up with me. Had we ever been dating? The more time passed, the hazier it became. But I did know that I needed to get fucked.

I could go to the club, but after the last trip I was gun-shy. Some slut I was—amateur.

I'd had a rough couple of weeks. Bitchy was the least I could do.

The detailed construction of gum paste calla lilies distracted me. Rick called out from his office, "Hey, get out of here, kid."

I glanced up—it was fifteen minutes past the end of my shift.

"One sec." I stroked my brush from the inner curl to the tip, leaving a striated peach coloration. Tomorrow I'd paint light pink blush onto the tips. Perfect for the wedding cupcakes they'd adorn. Once the paint dried enough to set it down, I laid the flower on the tray with the others.

The sky had darkened to dusk by the time Rick

came out of his office. "What are you still doing here?"

"Just cleaning up."

"Hey." His hand stopped mine on a package of food coloring. His eyes were missing their usual playful glint. "Are you sure everything's okay?"

I sighed. "Would it be possible for me to get a raise?" He didn't respond right away. "Or maybe just get some extra shifts?"

"Are things that bad?"

"It's just that Bailey had an ER trip a couple of weeks ago, and things are a little tight."

He ran his hand through his hair.

"Never mind," I said. "I'll work it out."

"No, you deserve a raise, but you know things have been slow around here. We're already short on staff just to stay open. But I'll take a look at the books, okay? I'll see what I can do." Maybe the bakery wasn't as busy as it once was, but I'd honestly thought he was just being cheap before. Now I felt greedy, asking more if the bakery was truly struggling. Even if he did find me an extra fifty cents an hour, it wasn't going to solve my cash-flow problems.

"Thanks, Rick. You're a good guy." I was relieved to see the creases ease from his face. Worry didn't look good on him. On a whim I kissed his cheek. He caught my arm as I pulled back.

"You smell like sugar," he murmured. My breath caught. What the hell was he doing?

I tried to laugh. "Everything here smells like sugar."

"I'm glad you told me what the problem was. I'll do what I can, but I wish it was more." *I wish it was enough* was what I heard in his voice. And sadness.

I wasn't sure I could handle the cause of it. Aiming for casual, I leaned back, and he loosened his grip on my arm.

"You do plenty," I said. "Where would I be without this job?"

"Not seeing my sorry ass every day, that's for sure." He turned and went back into his office. His words were light enough but without any real good humor.

Rick could be a jerk sometimes, but mostly he was decent. And happy. After all, a guy who owned a bakery but didn't bake, that was right out of one of Bailey's Dr. Seuss books. But money was tight, and maybe the bakery was in trouble. Colin was right—everyone had problems.

Outside the back door of the bakery, I checked left and right along the alleyway. Empty as usual. I walked along the brick wall, skirting away from the smelly Dumpsters until I reached the employee parking lot. I got in my car and breathed in some air. It was musty but safe.

I drove home on autopilot, shedding the tension of work and worry in anticipation of seeing Bailey. When I got out of the car and headed for the stairs, I had almost forgotten to check my surroundings. Out of habit, I turned my head. And froze.

"Hey, Allie." Andrew leaned against the wall.

That carefree smile. Those sparkling blue eyes. The face that was as known to me as my own. The one I saw hints of in my daughter, who was right upstairs.

My body, ever the traitor, wanted to turn and run. Get away, it shouted. As if in exclamation, chills rippled through my skin.

But I had to stay and act normal. This was the path I had chosen a very long time ago, faking it. I wasn't even sure what would happen if I ever decided to stray from it. What would honesty in this look like?

"Allie?"

"Andrew." Thank God my voice worked. It had been a crap shoot, really. "What are you doing here?"

"Just visiting an old friend."

My mind formulated insane escape routes more appropriate for an action flick than real life. "Oh, yeah?"

He pushed off from the wall. We were completely out in the open. Sure, no one was actually around, and yes, this neighborhood was shady. But nothing bad was happening. Nothing bad *would* happen. But my body didn't seem to believe that. It was shivering and sweating and clenching like a spastic marionette.

His arms came around me in a bear hug. My face smashed against his chest. I drew in a Andrew-filled breath that soothed me. How could the sight of him terrify me but the smell of him comfort me? My body was as confused as my mind.

His embrace tightened to the point of pain. Abruptly he released me, then pushed past me to my car. I spun around, watching in horror as he peered into my backseat. He looked back at me. "This is yours."

"Yes." He knew my car, of course. He'd been in it before. He'd even helped me fix it up, back in the day.

"No, that." He pointed through the window to the car seat. "You have a baby?" His voice was strained. The first crack in our shared facade.

"Andrew." So many things in that single word: *don't go there, I don't want to tell you, you don't want to know, why did you hurt me?*

But he didn't hear them, or didn't care. "How old is it?"

"Please. Just go."

"Answer the question."

"It's none of your business. There. How about that for an answer?"

"Don't bullshit me. You were never good at it."

"I'm not bullshitting you. That's the truth. Bailey's not your business."

"Bailey." He said it slowly, weighing the name. It made me angry. His eyes faded from anger into wonder. "A girl?"

"She's mine. You have nothing to do with her."

"Really? Is that true?" His tone called me a liar.

I said nothing, just narrowed my eyes at him in impotent rage and fear.

"Tell me who her father is, if not me? Is it Kyle, from third period? You went out once, right? Did you see him again? Or was it that guy where you work? Or are you hooking like Shelly, and you got knocked up? Whose is it, if it's not mine?"

I hated, *hated*, the stinging warmth in my eyes. I blinked, but it only made it worse. Weak. Stupid girl, never learns.

"Let's not fight."

Andrew's voice turned soft, a supplication I'd interpreted as affection back then. Now I wondered whether it had always been a front. Or was it sometimes true? Either way he couldn't be trusted.

"It doesn't have to be like this. We were friends once. I want to be your friend again. I've been looking for you everywhere. And now I find you, and we have a…a kid together. Jesus. It's crazy. I mean, I'm in shock. But it's good, right? You and me, it's always been you and me."

Somehow during his speech he'd moved forward, and I'd moved back until my back was against the wall. "No. I don't want to be friends. I can't do that."

"I know that you're…angry at me." It was the closest he'd come to referencing what had happened that night. "But we can work through it. I know we can."

"I don't want to, don't you get that? If you cared, you wouldn't even ask me."

"You're wrong, Allie. It's because I care about you that I'm here. I made a mistake when I left before. I should have stayed and fought for you, but I've always cared about you. You have to know that."

"It's not going to happen between us, not ever."

"You can't just throw this away. You can't just ignore me because you're angry." His voice was rising now. I hoped Shelly would know to stay inside, to keep her and Bailey out of sight rather than check on me if she heard him. In this neighborhood, staying inside was the default thing to do.

I kept thinking that if I just told him no, in clear terms, that maybe he would walk away. But that was stupid. It hadn't worked before. I tried a new tactic. "She's not your kid. You're right. I got knocked up by some guy I met at the bakery. So don't worry."

"I don't believe you. I told you, you never lied good. She is my kid. I want to see her."

"Just stop." My voice came out so shrill that it shocked me into silence. I took a deep breath. "I swear to God, Andrew, you will not get to see her. I am her mother, and you are not her father. You did not make that baby in any way that counts, and I am not going to let you in our lives. Do you hear me?"

"Yeah," he said. "I hear you."

His words barely registered as I went on. "You will not touch her. You will not touch me, not ever again. Do you understand that? Are you hearing me? Are you listening to me tell you no, because goddammit, Andrew, I said it before and you didn't listen. I need you to hear me now."

He grabbed my wrist and twisted. My whole body followed. The wall stopped me, but I wished it hadn't.

I wanted to melt into it, to just fade away. All my hard-fought words of power, obliterated with the grip of his fist.

Where was the boy who'd chased me on the pier or filched my books, only to return them just as stealthily? I wanted to ask him that and so much more, but the cold brick muzzled me. "I do hear you," he said behind my ear. "And I…I want to listen to you."

"But you won't." My shoulders slumped against the wall like a cold embrace.

"It was a mistake to walk away before," he said. "And it was a mistake…what happened. I want to make it right with you. And now, with her. It's a lot to take in, but I feel like I owe her something. And I already know I owe you."

"Why don't you start by letting me go?"

He released me. I rolled against the wall to face him but still leaned against it. It was so blessedly vertical.

"I don't think I can walk away this time," he said.

I was too tired to fight, and I already knew I'd lose. He'd proven that handily. "You wanted to leave, so you left. You want to stay, so you will." *You wanted to fuck me, so you did,* but I didn't say that. "What about what I want?"

"Tell me what you want. Tell me how I can help you."

He didn't get it. He could help me by leaving. But he wouldn't go.

I shook my head. "Go away, Andrew. Go away, or

I'll call the cops and they'll make you." It was risky, to bring up the cops. Andrew wouldn't want them involved, would think he might get in trouble if they were called. He didn't know the cops didn't care, but he didn't call my bluff.

"I'll go," he said. "But I'm staying in town. I'm going to give you some time to cool down, think things through. Then we'll talk again. We're going to work this out, whether you believe that right now or not."

Chapter Ten

Once his car was out of sight, I ran up the steps. Shelly took one look at my face, said, "Shit," and pulled me inside. "What happened?"

I walked past her to Bailey, who saw me and held out her arms for me to pick her up. Squeezing her close to me, I buried my face in her downy hair. She gurgled a protest and squirmed.

"You're scaring me," Shelly said. "Tell me what happened. Is it Rick?"

"What? Why would it be Rick?"

"I thought maybe…I don't know. You're just not giving me much to go on. You come back late from work, and now you look like you've seen a ghost."

"I'm sorry I was late." I set Bailey down, and she immediately went back to her toys.

I sat down on Shelly's couch. My fingers stroked the soft leather. It was so out of place in this crappy apartment, but I knew why she was here. It was for me. For Bailey. Oh God, what would I do? She reached for my hands, and I jerked back without thinking.

"Jesus, Allie. Tell me what's going on."

"It's Andrew." I waved my hand. "He was here."

"Where? In Chicago?"

"No, *here*. At our apartment. Just outside. I watched him drive away, but he said he'll be back. He's coming back."

"Oh, shit."

"And he saw Bailey's car seat. He knows about her. I need to go. I need to take her and leave."

"That's crazy. Where will you go?"

"I don't know. Maybe I'll track down my dad. Ride in his truck for a while." It was mostly a joke. My dad may not have been a stellar example of fatherhood, but he'd help me if I were in trouble. Still, riding around in the cab of a semitruck with a baby wasn't a realistic plan.

But what could I do other than run? The law wouldn't be on my side. I'd found that out two years ago.

It would only take a DNA test to confirm what Andrew already suspected. He was the biological father of Bailey. And if he pursued it, he could be her father legally too. At one time I would've thought those were the only ways that counted, but not now.

I didn't think of him as Bailey's father. I couldn't. She was mine.

If I stayed, he could compel me to let him near Bailey. Hell, to let him near *me*. The court system, the authorities, they would support him.

But if I ran, what kind of life would that be for Bailey? When would it end? I had trouble enough keeping her stocked in diapers and secondhand plastic toys even with a reasonably steady job at the bakery. On the run, even that would be in jeopardy, and who would watch Bailey when I worked? I wasn't sure I could hold up without Shelly.

"Hey, there," she said. "I know this is bad, but we'll work it out. You're not in this alone."

"Ah, God." I put my head in my hands. "I'm not trying to be a whiny bitch here, but sometimes it feels like the cards are stacked against us, you know?"

"Yeah," she said. "I know. Do you think…?"

"You know the police won't help. And I don't have money for a lawyer, much less a good one."

"I wasn't going to say that." At her pause I looked up to see Shelly tracing her fingernails in the woodlike grooves of the plastic coffee table. "What about that guy?"

I blinked. "Colin? What about him?"

"Don't say you haven't thought of it."

I hadn't thought of it, but I was now. To send Colin like he was some goon to shake Andrew up. To fuck him up. After all, Colin had already shown a willingness to protect me in the physical capacity. "You're crazy."

She pressed her lips together and refused to look me in the eye.

I shook my head. "No. Freaking. Way."

"Okay, okay," she conceded. "I wasn't saying it was a great plan. Listen, do you want me to talk to him?"

And the way she said the word "talk" made it clear what she really meant. Persuade him. Maybe even whore herself out for me.

"Shelly," I said; then I couldn't get any more words past the lump in my throat. I couldn't let her do that. But God, that she would even do something like that for me. For Bailey. She was my daughter. I should be able to protect her, but I couldn't even protect myself.

"Come here, sweetie." She folded me in her arms. Between the two of us, I was the mother. I was responsible for Bailey and myself. And I felt responsible for Shelly too. She was only a few months younger than I, and prettier and probably smarter than me as well. But somehow she'd always trailed after me through middle and high school. I'd always suspected she'd had a crush on Andrew. But when he'd fucked me over, both literally and otherwise, she'd been there to help me. She'd continued to help me all this time, even now offering her body in exchange for what? For friendship? For this pale imitation of a family?

I didn't deserve her loyalty.

Straightening my back, I pulled away from her warmth. "Thanks, Shelly. Don't worry. I'm not going to do anything crazy. He said he'd give me some time, so I'll think of something. Everything will be fine."

Of course she didn't believe it. I didn't either, but she let me go.

I carried Bailey down to our apartment and put her in her high chair. I set down a jar of sweet peas and let

Bailey go to town with a plastic spoon. It felt weird to do something as mundane as mealtime when my world was being ripped apart. But that's the thing about kids—they make you practical.

A stronger mom, a better mom, would probably have chastised her for the mess. But it was easier to let her make a mess and then clean it up after. Green mush sprayed across the linoleum floor wiped clean in a single swipe.

If only all my problems could be cleared with such ease.

After Bailey ate, I peeled off her clothes and diaper and carried a pea-spattered baby to the tub. After washing her, I let her sit for a few minutes in the warm water while she splashed around with some foam alphabet letters. To say she was my everything wasn't giving her enough credit. I didn't know how I would have gotten through those dark months back then without her inside me. Even now my composure had all the sturdiness of a house of cards. I'd just as soon lie down and let Andrew have his way with me than fight him again. And Colin. Well, Colin. But always there was Bailey to consider, and so I had to be strong.

Bailey was rough to put down to bed that night, probably feeding off my nervous energy. I sang her all the lullabies in my arsenal three times before her eyes drifted shut.

I took a shower and slipped on a ratty T-shirt. Then paced. I couldn't go anywhere, for obvious reasons, and besides, there was nowhere to go. I considered watching TV, reading a book, but nothing could hold my focus.

My mind ran like a hamster on a wheel.

What a relief it must be for a rape victim to hate her rapist. But even if I hated Andrew, I also loved him. Not the way he'd wanted me to. I loved him as a friend, a brother. It may have been chaste, but it was real. Maybe the most I'd ever loved anyone, at least before Bailey.

And that old love was still inside me like a cancer.

Maybe if I could believe what I'd told myself all those nights at the club, that I didn't really have the right to say no, that all guys were assholes, I could find some kind of peace. Then, at least, what Andrew had done would make sense.

I had thought I was over it. It wasn't even rape, right? Sure I'd said no, but men didn't listen. Now, though, with Colin waiting in the wings, tempting me and respecting my refusal, I had to wonder if I'd just been fooling myself.

And that begged the question—what would it take to truly get over it? Was it even possible? The thought of being broken forever was a scarier thought than anything Andrew could do to my body.

It wasn't the first night I'd baked in lieu of sleep. The methodical measuring of ingredients and the steady rhythm of mixing never failed to soothe me. During the day I played with recipes, taking delight in creating something new. But night baking was about comfort. All I had to do was follow the formula, and everything would turn out okay. Better than okay, considering double chocolate brownies came out of the chasm.

Chapter Eleven

The drive only took twenty minutes, as loitering teens and half-empty strip malls gave way to artistic cafés and pocketed neighborhoods. My would-be Prince Charming's castle turned out to be a white, bungalow-style house with a front porch. It was small compared to some of the others, but still much too big for a bachelor. Too domestic.

Colin had called this morning, asking me to come over and talk. I owed him that much. It was more of a meeting than a date. More of a breaking up than an opening.

I told myself that, again, fussing over my meeting-date outfit as I sat in the front seat of my car. But I didn't really believe it. I wanted to make it right with Colin.

The heart wants what it wants, even if that means fucking over the people it loves. Because it really wasn't fair to drag Colin into this. Bad enough I was so messed up, and that I was broke and had a kid and all the other things that were wrong with me. All the things that made me a poor candidate for a girlfriend, as if this were a job interview, an audition.

After the new troubles with Andrew, I should leave Colin well enough alone. It was impossible to say how it would affect him, impossible that it *wouldn't* affect him, indirectly somehow.

Or maybe directly, by me running to him for help, like now.

I fidgeted in the car for ten minutes, parked a bit too far away from the curb as if those extra few inches could keep me from arriving. I caught movement out of the corner of my eye and looked over to see Colin open the front door. I couldn't see his expression, but I read the lines of his body as he leaned against the door frame. Just waiting. His stillness poured through my body like steamy coffee on a winter day. That's why I was here: he was different.

It wasn't that Colin was never pushy or controlling, because he excelled at both those skills. The difference was that, whatever he did, he wouldn't harm me. Not ever. I couldn't even make him do it. I should know—I had tried. It was as if I'd been searching for him without even knowing it, trying out random men at a bar in the world's stupidest litmus test.

And now that I'd found him, the trick was how not to lose him. I got out of the car and strode up the sidewalk. He stepped aside and, with a nod of his head, invited me in. As I passed, I could feel the tension vibrating within him—curiosity, frustration, maybe lust—carefully caged within thick walls of patience.

He took my coat. I followed the trail of savory

aromas to the kitchen and set the dessert I'd brought on the counter.

"Drink?" he asked.

"Sure. That would be… Thanks."

"Wine? Beer?"

"Oh." I didn't usually drink alcohol except for my club nights. The numbing effects would be welcomed now, except I needed to keep it together tonight. Didn't want to go spilling secrets, after all. "Maybe just water."

He handed me a glass. "We've got a few minutes before the pot roast is done."

"Mmm, pot roast." It had been forever since I'd had real meat, not the rubbery stuff that came in canned soup. Since my last date with Colin, actually. "It smells amazing."

"It's from the restaurant." He quirked his lips. "With scalloped potatoes."

I grinned. "So you're a meat and potatoes kind of guy."

He shrugged. "I'm pretty simple."

I snorted. Simple as a Rubik's Cube. But all I said was, "Maybe."

The white cabinets, Formica countertops, and tiled backsplash matched the quaintness of the house but looked new. The stainless-steel appliances and fixtures completed the picture of a modern kitchen. But I'd expect nothing less from the owner of a restaurant. I might have been envious if I had ever imagined such things for myself.

I peered back the way we'd come, through the dining room.

"Did you want me to show you around?" he asked.

"Yes." I smiled. I noted his hesitation and his stiffness, but I did want to see his house. Every little detail, from the green splash of color from the tea towel to the prickly aloe plant that sat on the counter, was a piece of Colin. I would hoard that knowledge like a miser collects coins and later strums through them with his fingers just for the pleasure of it.

Despite the coziness of the house, there was a definite sparseness to its furnishing. So male. So Colin. Plush seating and dark wood furniture stood so perfectly in place, without clutter, that I half expected to see price tags hanging on them.

Colin was quiet, even for him. And watchful. He walked ahead of me, leading me to the different rooms—the living room, the dining room, a study. And outside, the back porch overlooking a small but lush lawn. I oohed and ahhed. It came naturally, this admiration, because his house was beautiful and stark, like him. The place was large enough to be roomy, but small enough to be cozy. It was, as Goldilocks would say in Bailey's book, just right. But I felt like he was waiting for something specific in my responses.

I leaned my elbows on the wood rail of the back patio as if I belonged. "It's a great house."

"Do you think so?" he asked. It didn't sound like

the idle question it should have been.

"Absolutely. It's perfect. Why? You aren't thinking of selling it, are you?"

"If I did, would you buy it?"

I laughed. "There's no way I could afford this house. How much does something like this run? One hundred thousand?"

A faint blush tinted his cheeks, and I knew it had cost more. Not that I could even afford a fraction of that. It might as well have been a castle for all that it was accessible to me.

"The food's probably ready," he said, and we went back inside the house.

I found the dishes while he transferred the food from metal pots to ceramic platters. We met at the dining table amid clanking utensils. I set a place for him at the head of the table and sat next to him. That left five empty chairs and a wide expanse of cherry wood table.

"Do you have company often?" I asked.

His eyes flicked over the table, all those empty chairs. "No."

I took a bite of the pot roast. The juices exploded in my mouth, and I released a soft moan. "God, this is good."

A quick smile. "I'm glad you like it."

"I bet you get that all the time."

He shrugged. "It's nice to eat a meal here, for once. And to have company." My face heated. "How's

Bailey?"

I blinked. "She's fine. And your brother?"

"Also fine."

Have you talked to him lately? I wanted to ask. *Done anything illegal? Dangerous?* But his eyes warned me away. I wouldn't like the answer.

We moved on to safer topics. My work at the bakery and his at his restaurant. We both worked with food—something so elemental, providing sustenance, health. In my case, not so much health, but there's a special intimacy that comes from preparing food for someone, as he had cooked this dinner and I had baked that pie.

We ate and were merry, as merry as Colin ever was. It was a last meal, of sorts. When we'd both eaten too much, Colin took me to the living room.

His hand caught mine, tender, and his eyes captured mine, intent. "What's wrong?"

"Nothing," I said in a falsetto.

"Tell me," he said.

I sighed. The man was a walking lie detector. Either that or I was transparent as fuck. "Something happened," I said. "Bailey...well, her father has come back."

His face showed no reaction.

I averted my eyes before continuing. An omission was still a lie. "He was a friend of mine. From school. And we...hooked up. And then he left town. Now he's back, and he wants to see Bailey. At least that's what he said, but I don't trust him. He doesn't care about her. He's just using her to get to me."

Those dark brown eyes revealed nothing. "What are you going to do?"

"I don't really know what I *can* do. I guess visitation is something that would have to be figured out in court. But I would… *strongly prefer*… that he not get to see us at all."

Colin's eyes sharpened. "What's wrong with him?"

I blinked away the answering thoughts. "Nothing. I mean, it's not like he's ready to be a father. He just wants to mess with me, but he…he had a rough childhood. I mean, really bad."

"He ever hit you?" His voice was soft, but even if I couldn't have sensed the banked fury within him, I knew from experience what he could do to a man who hurt me. Even if I could've gotten the words out, I couldn't tell him, not without risking Colin going after Andrew, hurting them both.

I was grateful that the phrasing of the question allowed my "no" to be the truth. He hadn't hit me, not exactly. But I knew I had to be more specific if I wanted Colin's help. "He's just not completely…stable. He drinks too much, and he uses. He picks up and leaves whenever he wants. And when he's angry…well, I don't want Bailey around him."

"You need money," he said.

"Sort of. I have money…" Not enough, probably, but that wasn't what I wanted. I wanted safety. And him. "I mean, I'm not sure how much it'll be, but—"

"I'm not rich, but I have enough for this." He looked like a man calculating the odds. Unnecessary, really, since I was woefully out of my league. This wasn't a negotiation as much as total surrender. "I'll help you."

I gave Colin a look.

He raised his eyebrows, all innocence. "I meant the right way. I can find a decent lawyer. We'll fight him, legally. In the meantime, move in with me."

"What?" Hadn't seen that one coming. "That's...that's insane."

He actually rolled his eyes, making him look more like the twentysomething that he was. "People move in together all the time."

"Not after dating for a week," I said.

"I'm counting since the first time."

"In case you forgot," I said, "I have a baby. A kid."

"I didn't forget. There's room for her. Besides, your apartment is a shithole."

Harsh. Even worse, he was right. "You're completely frustrating."

He raised one eyebrow, which somehow proved my words irrelevant in one smooth swoop.

I set down my fork, taking his offer seriously. "We barely know each other."

"We know each other enough," he said. "From the first it was different."

It was only the truth. Ever since my sordid proposition at the bar, there had been something between us. A spark, or maybe just recognition that he could handle my brand of crazy. I'd tried to ignore it and had even gone back to the bar to disprove it, but nothing had worked. What was this thing that felt like trust but looked like lust?

"But why?" I said, desperate to deny him or find some excuse to accept. "Just tell me why you'd even want that?"

"I have reasons."

"But you aren't going to tell them to me."

"It's okay, what happened before." He pulled me close. "You're with me now."

The words were pitched perfectly, but they bounced off the wall of secrets I kept between us. I'd left out the most important part. What would he do if he found out?

I shivered, and he encircled me in his arms. Keeping me, for now.

"Can you spend the night?" he asked.

"Yes." I had already put Bailey to sleep in Shelly's bed. This was the third time in as many weeks, but Shelly graciously claimed not to mind about the loss of income.

"Good," he murmured.

He took me to his bedroom upstairs. It was just as plain as all the other rooms, just as casual. Home, but I couldn't think about that. Instead I tried to psych myself up. Please him, pay my dues, when all I really wanted to do was have sex with him. I wanted to rip off my clothes and his. In my wildest thoughts I wanted to push his face down between my legs and tell him to do that thing again.

Instead I just stood there in his bedroom like I'd never been inside a man's bedroom before. Which was almost true, except for Andrew's.

He turned down the sheets. When he glanced back, his eyes softened. "Come here."

I averted my eyes while he tugged my dress over my head. He gestured to the bed, and I kicked off my shoes and climbed in, still in my underwear and bra. After stripping down to his boxers, he followed me in.

I wished I didn't feel this strange nervousness. It felt almost like a wedding night. How awful.

Colin turned me away from him. I expected him to take off my bra or fuck me from behind, but he was working from a totally different playbook, because what he did was pull me in close to his body and *cuddle*. Christ, we were spooning. And not as a sexual position. Although there was a certain hardness pressing into my ass, it was doing absolutely no nudging, no rocking, and no thrusting. Whoever heard of a hard, docile cock?

Ah, hell. We'd skipped the wedding night and gone straight to married.

Well.

I pushed my ass back slightly, gratified by the catch in his breath. His arm tightened around my waist, but his hips remained still. Another nudge of my ass, this time triggering a twitch of that hardness.

Yes, that's it. I rocked back into him. He had wanted me, the slut. And sluts were for sex. No more thinking, no more feeling. No more worry. At least for tonight, I got to play the slut and still be safe.

When I felt his hand drift around to my hips, my lips curved into a smile. *Gotcha.* Then his hands skimmed over my stomach and beneath my panties, and my smile slipped and my eyelids lowered.

Rough fingers prodded me open. One finger worked inside me, a little deeper each time my hips rocked into his hand. And thank God—finally!—his hips pushed against mine. At the knowledge that he was into this, a participant, my mind slipped a little closer into that blissful space of submission. But God, I wanted so much more. He was capable of more.

"What's wrong?" I whispered.

"You want this, don't you?" He repeated his words from earlier, still worrying over my consent. No, nothing like the others. Tears sprung into my eyes, and I was grateful he couldn't see them.

"I want this. I want you." I could only hope he took the thickness of my voice for arousal. "I want you to give it to me hard. Be rough, Colin. Do it." Even before I'd finished speaking, his fingers inside me and his cock rubbing against my ass sped up, roughened.

His other arm slipped under me, holding me flush against him. As if I was going anywhere. But I was totally cocooned now, at his mercy. His fingers hit a certain spot inside me, and a soft cry escaped me. My hips jerked in a frantic rhythm, reaching for it, begging.

But it wasn't his fingers rubbing me that took me over. It was the sharp pant of his breath on my neck. His excitement, mine. And as my climax took me, I shook in his arms, falling apart, held together.

As I collapsed into his hardness, my heart felt overfull. Desperate to turn this into something familiar, something sexual, I grabbed his wrist and sucked his wet fingers.

I swirled my tongue around his fingers like a cock, offering.

He shifted on the bed so that he lay flat, accepting.

I crawled—prowled, really—on my hands and knees between his legs. The tense arousal on his face made me feel sensual, powerful. There *was* a certain power to my role, that I could incite this man to lust. He pulled down his boxers, and, with his hands in my hair, slipped my mouth over his cock. That'd been the shortest power trip ever.

Down and up, he directed me. Steadily, inexorably forcing more of his smooth, hard skin into me. My focus narrowed to my senses, what I could see or taste or feel. Every time I lost my way, he brought me back with his fingers at my neck, a soft grunt or a tensing of his thighs beneath my hands.

It wasn't about sucking cock. This was Colin guiding, and me yielding. Colin giving, and me receiving.

Or was it the other way around? It didn't matter, so long as it never ended. There was a certain urgency about him, more than a man wanting to come, and I answered it by taking him deeper.

Even as my jaw tired and my eyes watered, I felt his pleasure like it was my own. His labored breathing, his fingers tightening in my hair, the small thrust of his hips—I wanted it all. My fingers fumbled, wrapping around him, stroking him below, fondling delicate skin.

Suddenly he surged up. Next thing I knew I was on my back, knees bent, and Colin deep inside me.

I gasped, belated.

"Fuck," he said.

He wrenched back, then fished a condom out of the nightstand. A few seconds respite and then he thrust back inside me. He was too deep to move. Too deep to breathe.

"Colin." Pleas had never worked, but he stilled.

With his nostrils flaring and a light sheen of sweat on his face, Colin looked savage. "Hurt you?"

"No, I…"

He rocked against me slightly, straining. "You what?"

I want you. Don't leave me. "Fuck me."

He did.

And then I feel asleep, enfolded in thick arms, feeling like Alice falling down the rabbit hole.

Chapter Twelve

SUNLIGHT BEAMED DIRECTLY into my closed eyes, but how? Cheap vinyl blinds provided little relief, but my window backed up directly to the next apartment building. Besides which, it was coated in decades of goop.

My nose tickled. I took a deep breath and smelled—a man. Shit.

I snapped my eyes open. Chest hair. A familiar face. Ah, Colin. Safe. I shut my eyes again, fully intending to employ a fake-it-till-you-make-it approach to sleep.

The brightness pricked behind my eyelids. I peeked one eye open and glared at the big bay window with no curtains. This house needed a woman's touch.

The night rushed back to me like the pop of a balloon. Well, damn. Looked like that was my job now.

Speaking of which, a certain piece of hot, hard flesh pressed into my hip.

Last night was the first time I hadn't showered shortly after sex. I always had done so immediately after my date nights, even with Colin. Despite the fact that he'd used a condom, I felt surprisingly sticky—everywhere. I supposed it should be hot, the remains of sex, the morning after, but it was…awkward.

Naked, I slipped from Colin's unconscious grip.

The bathroom held only the basics: a bar of soap, a bottle of shampoo-conditioner, shaving supplies. The shiny surfaces shone, too clean for a bachelor's place. Had he just moved in? That would explain the minimalist but catalog-perfect furniture and lack of decor. I made a mental note to ask him and decided he wouldn't mind if I took a shower.

I stood under the spray and flipped the tap all the way to hot, relishing the biting cold that steeped into a blissful scald. As I lathered myself using the minty bar of soap, I heard a snick from the door and Colin's voice. "Excuse me." Excuse what? I peered around the shower curtain to see two pale, *tight* ass cheeks, then snatched the curtain back in place with a squeak.

Damn.

He was using the potty. No, the toilet. Fuck! I was an adult. It was called a toilet.

"You okay?" He sounded amused.

"I'm fine." I clutched the soap, which slipped from my hands onto the tub with a thud.

"Sure?"

I picked up the soap. "Never better."

"Can you move today?"

I dropped the soap again. "Fuck!"

"What?"

"Nothing. Ahhh, moving. Hmm…" To be honest I hadn't been entirely sure we were doing that, or whether the whole thing had been some weird date dream. And I really hadn't expected it so soon, but leave it to Colin to be expedient.

"I don't know," I said. "Can we talk about it later? I have to go in to work this afternoon."

"About that," he said.

I didn't like his tone. I poked my head out of the shower. Colin leaned against the bathroom counter, somehow looking not at all silly while totally naked—and hard.

"I was thinking you could quit," he said.

I gaped but managed to eke out a, "What?"

He shrugged in the face of my shock. "It sucks. The pay is shit, and so are the hours. You don't even like it."

He added that as an afterthought, but of course, I *didn't* like it. Damn him for knowing that. "Wait a minute. How do you know how much I make?"

His eyes flickered. "You work shifts in a low-end bakery. How much can it pay? Besides, I'm in the industry."

That made sense, I supposed. But still... "It would take time to find a better job. How would I pay my share?"

"I didn't ask you to move in because I need a roommate, Allie."

The effect of his sarcasm was offset by the teasing light in his eyes. I tightened my grip on the shower curtain to shield myself from the cold air and his hotness. "How will I pay you back for the lawyer?"

He snorted. "It wasn't going to be a loan. Besides…there won't really be a regular bill."

That alarmed me.

"Relax," he said. "He's a real lawyer. He's already on retainer, that's all, with my brother."

I wanted nothing to do with his brother, and Colin knew it. I especially didn't like the idea of using his lawyer, someone who might have a different agenda. And worse, if the lawyer was paid by Colin's brother, I'd owe *him*.

"No," I said.

Colin didn't look the least bit perturbed, as if he'd known I'd say that.

"It's not about the money. He's good at what he does." Colin paused to give me a look, confirming that yes, the guy had gotten them out of illegal shit before. "I wouldn't trust just any lawyer to help with this, seeing as, well…fathers have legal rights. Visitation, joint custody." He shrugged away the awful words.

"I see," I said through clenched teeth. "If you think he deserves visitation and…custody, why are you helping me?"

Colin looked me straight in the eyes. "I don't think he deserves anything. I don't give a fuck about him. I'm doing this because you want it, and I'm going to get it for you." Then he turned and walked out of the bathroom.

My heart beat against my chest, hard and fierce.

It was a rather dark shade of gray, his declaration,

but I didn't think I'd ever heard anything more romantic than Colin telling me he'd spend his money, break laws, do anything he had to, to give me what I wanted. He was the man I'd been looking for without even trying. The man I hadn't believed existed, one who'd fight for me. One who'd win.

Chapter Thirteen

My best friend in fifth grade was my neighbor two doors down, Leslie Pritchard. We didn't like each other all that much, but absentee parenting made for strange bedfellows.

Leslie was lonely on nights her mom worked, and so she got a kitten. Leslie and I would sit around in the evenings playing with him, and as if the kitten were our campfire, he would jump in the air and flick his frizzy orange tail.

She'd toss a string, and he would leap with abandon only to come crashing down to the thin carpet in a tumble of tiny limbs. Bug—that was his name—didn't know that cats should always land on their feet, and he remained staunchly flippant throughout his adolescent years up until he got run over by my dad's truck. That day marked the end of my friendship with Leslie Pritchard.

The cats around my old apartment were nothing like Bug. They scattered as I climbed the steps, Bailey in one hand, a double-layer cake in the other. All I needed was a handless trombone and I could star in a Dr. Seuss book.

I slid Bailey down my leg so I could knock.

My gaze traced the lines of peeling paint on the door, maroon with white underneath and a trace of blue between them. Like the rings in a tree, marking the time. It had been two days since I'd fled Colin's house, making empty promises about *calling him* and *soon*. I knew what I had to do, but it could be hard to leave home, even if home was a shitty apartment in the scary side of town.

Shelly opened the door.

"Hey, ladies." Her voice was hoarse, and her smile didn't quite reach her bloodshot eyes.

Shit, shit, shit. Maybe it was just the tiredness resulting from staying up late. But this was Tuesday, and she usually didn't have a client on Monday. In fact, I left her alone most of the time on Mondays to let her sleep it off. Besides, lack of sleep wasn't enough to affect her like this. Shelly was like a prey animal. Her problems never manifested in her appearance. If she looked like this, then things had truly gone to shit.

"Shelly?"

Her eyes slid away. She opened her mouth, to answer maybe, but then clapped a hand over it. Leaving the door open for us, she stumbled back through the hallway. The thud of the bathroom door punctuated her departure.

I found Shelly curled up on her bed on top of the covers. Bailey tried to go to her, but I distracted her with a chunk of cake that would be hell to clean up later.

I returned to the bedside. "Jesus, Shelly. Which one?"

"Things just got out of hand," she mumbled, her eyes closed.

It had been a stupid question, because the answer didn't matter. She could hardly go to the police. I'd been too afraid to ask the important question, but I asked it now. "How bad is it?"

"Not bad."

I sighed. "Just tell me. I'm going to find out anyway."

She looked so thin. When she swaggered around, dressed provocatively and with that half smile, she looked every inch the femme fatale. But lying there, she seemed almost childlike. I reached for her, my hand hovering in the air as if she might break if I touched her. Except she'd already been broken. I gingerly pulled up her shirt to reveal angry, red welts that streaked the length of her back and down under her jeans. I'd seen them before, back when Shelly had first started in the life, before she had regulars to keep her safe.

"He did this," I said, my voice detached from my head as if I had a cold. I meant the one who liked to rough her up. I told her not to see him, and usually she didn't take on clients like him, but there was something about him that kept her going back.

"It wasn't him. I took on a new client."

"Why? Why would you do that?"

She gestured toward the nightstand, and I opened the drawer. On top of the mess of beauty products and a few books was a single white envelope. A thick one.

I looked inside. Money, and lots of it.

"Shit," came out on my exhale.

"Five thousand." Pride colored her voice—I didn't know whether that was a good sign or bad. Five thousand fucking dollars. That was ten times her regular nightly rate, as much money as she made in a month. Of course, she wouldn't be able to work now for the next couple of weeks, with her back all torn up.

"But why? We agreed you wouldn't do shit like this. Christ, Shelly. You could have been really hurt. You *are* really hurt."

"It's for the lawyer," she said. "A retainer or some shit."

Oh, fuck. No.

I threw the envelope into the open drawer, hundred dollar bills spilling out in a vulgar array.

"We need a lawyer. You know that. You can't run from this. Where would you go? A lawyer will figure this out. Make it right."

I couldn't even think about that, not in the face of her gory sacrifice. "You did not do that for me. Tell me you didn't do that."

She sighed like I was the irresponsible one. I wanted to rail at her, except she'd already been beaten, hadn't she? And for me.

I thought I'd known what my own stupidity would

cost the people I loved, but I'd been wrong. My father had been doubtful of my future, but I'd cinched the deal when I'd ended up pregnant and alone. Parenting was a laughable term for the desperation with which I kept Bailey in generic-brand baby food.

I'd even failed Andrew. No one understood, not even Shelly. He had lusted after me, wanted me, all that time, not that I'd deserved such devotion. I should have walked away from our friendship once I found out. Or maybe just sucked it up and been with him. Anything other than remain friends but without fucking him. That was my mistake.

And that night. I'd done a million things wrong that night. I shouldn't have worn that dress or hung out with him alone or stayed there with him when he'd been drinking. But most of all I shouldn't have said no, because then it would have just been sex. It would have been a hookup, not rape. And right now I wouldn't be a victim.

I'd allowed Shelly to be an escort—no, a prostitute—all this time. Not that it was my prerogative strictly, but I could've made her stop. I should have found a way to make her stop.

Bailey fussed, mashing the last bit of frosting into the carpet, but I stood rooted to the spot, my eyes stinging.

"Hey," Shelly said softly. "You didn't ask me to do it. Don't take that on yourself. I want this fixed as much as you do, okay? It was for me. You have to take it."

I took the money. I had to, because she'd given up strips of her skin for it, and the very least I could do was make it worth something.

With dry eyes I washed Bailey up and brought her into the room. In that age-old way of children she seemed to recognize Shelly was hurt. She curled up in Shelly's arms and planted a sloppy, wet kiss on her cheek. I circled the bed and crawled in from the other side.

I wanted to hold Shelly, to be the big spoon, but she wouldn't appreciate being touched like that, especially not now with her back torn up. So I settled for facing her back on my side, like a sentry, until she settled into sleep.

Some preternatural sense told me to stay. Not to protect her from the men who hit her—as if I could—but instead from the monsters that haunted her. Or maybe just to protect her from herself.

Downstairs seemed too far, too risky, when her hand clutched the pillow so tightly. So I tucked Bailey into the bed right in the middle and watched over them. There was a peace in the dark, in the quiet, where even my thoughts could still.

I didn't want to be like the alley cats, terrified of everything. They'd rather live wretchedly than take a chance. A leap of faith. I had spent a lot of time fighting men—and fighting myself. I'd managed to hurt myself over and over again, all to prove I didn't need to trust a man.

Except I did trust a man. *Colin.*

It came from deep inside, that trust, unexpected and even unwanted. He slipped under my defenses with his quiet solidity. If a man had tried to persuade me, to cajole me into moving in with him, I never could have. It was only his bluntness, his cold and steady regard that could have swayed me.

He said he'd protect me, and for some reason I believed him.

He could protect Bailey, and she deserved that.

I slipped from the bed and called Colin. Then I tucked myself back in beside Bailey and went to sleep.

Chapter Fourteen

The only fanfare for my grand dive into trust was a soft knock on Shelly's door. I opened it and gave him a half smile, uncertain how to treat him.

"Hey," I said softly.

"Hello," he said, and I was struck by the formality until Shelly answered from behind me.

"Colin—nice to meet you," she said.

Bailey burbled a greeting.

"I brought boxes," Colin said, nodding to the parking lot.

"Boxes?" Shelly asked with a lilt of accusation.

"Yes, well." I cleared my throat. "Colin asked me to move in with him, and…I agreed."

I held my breath. If she hated me, if I'd hurt her, I'd never forgive myself.

Shelly smiled. Not the perfect, blinding, fake one she got paid for, but a real, lopsided grin that made her a million times prettier. "That's great."

I smiled back, relieved. "You're not upset?"

She patted my hand. "About time we got out of this rat's nest."

Of course. She only lived in this dump because it

was all I could afford. She deserved better, and that alone was enough to convince me that I was making the right choice. It felt like giving up control—my apartment, my job, my fight with Andrew—but I'd been treading water on my own for too long. If I could make this better for Bailey, for Shelly, then it was worth the risk.

"Now go on," she said. "You pack. I'll watch Bailey."

Relieved, I gave her a peck on the cheek, which she accepted with the forbearance of a queen. I practically skipped down the steps with Colin at my heels. We each grabbed a handful of flattened boxes from the back of his truck before going to my apartment door.

As I put the key to the lock, the door swung open an inch. The lock itself cocked, exposing the circular hole it occupied in the door. I stood there blankly until Colin shook me.

"Go upstairs," he said. "Now."

It registered then—my apartment had been broken into. I ran upstairs and back into Shelly's place, where I snatched Bailey up. She was safe. She squirmed, but I held her even tighter. Shelly questioned me, and I must have said something. What if Bailey had been there?

Shelly opened the door to Colin.

"They're gone," he said.

"Who could have…?" Shelly trailed off. It was better unfinished.

"Pack quickly," Colin said.

I went cautiously back downstairs, as if I were going to survey the aftermath of a hurricane. But there was no disaster, not outwardly. Nothing had been taken—not that I had anything valuable—and nothing had been destroyed. Just the lock on the door, broken by some faceless person.

A violation. I should be used to them by now.

It was probably just a prank. Or a robbery that ended in disappointment when all they found were dolls and toys.

This place was crappy, but it had been home—mine. It shouldn't matter because we were going to a place that was so much better—Colin's. I tried to focus my thoughts on the practical, like throwing clothes into trash bags.

Colin loaded the crib and high chair and other furniture into his truck. That meant leaving behind my bed, my dishes, my dinette. Colin said he would come back later and take whatever was left to Goodwill. We filled up his truck and my car trunk, and I realized just how few material possessions I had.

Shelly brought Bailey down when we were finished.

She paused for another hug as she handed Bailey over. I glanced at Colin. He was strapping down the stuff in his truck.

"The lock—" I started.

"Don't think about it," she said.

She was right of course, but... "Am I making a mistake?"

"Of course not." Her face was perfectly smooth, gaze clear, completely giving herself away, the faker.

"You're a horrible liar."

She raised two perfectly groomed eyebrows. "I have a buttload of clients who say otherwise."

"Yeah, well, I know you too well." I lowered my voice. "I'm scared."

"What's the worst that could happen?" she said.

We both laughed. She always knew how to cheer me up.

Because, well, the worst was pretty bad, but then we'd both been through bad. What Shelly meant was that bad things happen, but we couldn't let them rule us. Living was a choice.

Colin slammed the tailgate shut and turned to me. He raised his eyebrow. *You still in?*

Yes, I answered silently.

BAILEY DUG THROUGH my box of clothes while I hung them up in the closet. The room had two closets, so this one had been empty when we got here. Still, it was already stocked with hangers, and that had to count for something.

Colin stepped in. "I've got the last of it downstairs."

"Thanks." I wiped my palms on my jeans.

Christ, how awkward. Why had no one ever given me lessons on how to handle moving in with a guy I barely knew? Suddenly that seemed like a vital life skill.

"So." I took one of my high heels out of Bailey's hands and replaced it with an innocuous sweater. "It's official."

"Yeah." He had an almost cautious expression, as if I was freaking out.

Was I freaking out? Possibly a little. "We're cool, right?"

Humor glinted in his eyes, turning them from glacial to just chilly. "We're good. But listen, I've got to head out."

Alarm streaked through me. "You're leaving?"

He frowned, just a crease of his forehead, but I didn't think it was directed at me. "It just came up." He shook his head as if to negate the importance. "I'll be back by dinner."

"Right, okay."

He gave me a speculative look. I strove for casual and failed. With a grimace I took as an attempted smile, he left the room. A few minutes later I heard his truck bump out of the driveway.

"Bye-bye," Bailey said.

"That's right!" I winced as my feigned cheerfulness came out louder than anticipated. "He's gone bye-bye. But he'll be back soon, promise!"

Back by dinner, apparently. Should I make dinner? I made dinner for Bailey and myself every day, of course, but I wouldn't feel right serving Colin spaghetti from a can. He probably thought I could cook, seeing as I baked, but it wasn't the same. Give me flour and sugar over turmeric any day.

I quickly finished up with the clothes; then Bailey and I forged into the kitchen. I expected a barren refrigerator, save for lumpy milk and beer. There'd be stale chips in the cupboard for sure. Instead what I found was a chef's paradise. A fully stocked fridge with vegetables. A pantry with buckets of grains I couldn't even name.

He *did* own a restaurant. I was so fucked.

But I didn't have a choice. Most likely he did expect dinner, and besides, it seemed fair and right. Even with my income from the bakery, I couldn't cover a fraction of the costs of this place. Of course I should contribute this way.

I rummaged through the fridge, past fancy cheeses and free-range eggs and vegetables that just reeked of organic, when I heard the crash behind me. Bailey had helped herself to the pantry, her chubby arm jammed in a box of whole wheat graham crackers. She fished out a still-wrapped plastic package and held it up triumphantly.

"Crackers," she said with a baby chuckle.

"Glad one of us is already at home."

She fussed at the plastic until I pulled it open for her. That pantry would need reorganization—namely, the entire bottom shelf should be empty—but that would wait for another day.

I foraged for something easy, like pasta, and came

up empty until I found the lasagna slices. Sure enough, there was marinara among the sauces, ricotta among the cheeses, and grass-fed ground beef in the freezer. Hell, I'd eaten lasagna before. Mostly frozen, but it was self-explanatory, what with those layers.

I even got fancy, sautéing onions and chopping parsley, while Bailey built a sand castle on the once-gleaming kitchen floor. I did a double take. Yes, she had crumbled what was probably an entire box of graham crackers into some sort of sandlike state. She sat in the middle, gleefully trailing her grubby fingers through the layer like it was her personal zen garden.

"Oh, Bailey," I groaned.

She sucked on her crumb-coated fingers, but I couldn't even be upset about the mess when the state of the entire kitchen smacked me like a frying pan. It was a disaster. The counters were piled with food in varying states of cooked.

I laid the layers of lasagna and stuck it in the oven, then set about cleaning. First I put away all the produce and ingredients. Then I grabbed the pan to wash it and burned my hand in the process.

Ouch. Leave it to some fancy brand of cookware to actually have fewer features than a cheapo knockoff, like say, plastic handles for safety. Probably they were expecting rich people not to be idiots and spring for pot holders. Fair enough.

Bailey watched me curiously as I ran my hand under the cold water, and I realized I'd been making monkeylike sounds in my pain.

A smile slid across my face. "Mommy silly?"

In response she puffed up proudly and presented her hand, covered in crumbs. "Cracker!"

My shoulders slumped. "Right."

Although I had plenty left to do cleaning my own mess, I figured I'd fix the floor first. For all I knew, he'd take one look at the nuclear wasteland that was his kitchen and order us out into the street. Okay, probably not that drastic, but it wouldn't be good.

He wasn't used to living with a kid. Even if he was, graham cracker snowfall was not an everyday occurrence. So I cleaned like a woman possessed. I would not even mention that regular graham crackers did not crumble on touching them. It was probably the grains, being whole as they were, but he wouldn't hear that from me.

Possibly I was becoming unhinged. A hysterical laugh bubbled up, but I ruthlessly forced it down. I was going to make this work. Everything was going to be fine, and if it wasn't…well. Well.

I swept up the crumbs, though the wet ones got caught in the broom's bristles and had to be washed out. Then I went back over the floor with paper towels, but the particles had wormed their way into the grout, as if it could camouflage itself with cement. I scrubbed until my hand was tired, but this called for stronger stuff.

I ducked my head into the cabinet under the sink,

rummaging for some harsh chemical shit to wipe those suckers out.

"Uh, Allie?"

In a knee-jerk reaction, I banged my head into the wood above me. A cry escaped me as tears sprang to my eyes. A sense of utter failure assailed me, and I contemplated just how long I could keep my head buried in the cupboard before it got weird. Not very long, it turned out, because Colin dragged me off the floor and into a kitchen chair with such horribly insensitive commentary as "Jesus" and "Are you okay?"

"I made a mess," I said flatly.

In acknowledgment he gently pressed an ice pack to my head.

I flinched, then let him hold me steady. "I'm sorry."

"Hey." That was all he said, his chiding tone tempered with concern.

The tears fell in streams then, making my voice all high and wavery as I tried to explain. "I'm sorry. I know you said dinner, and I tried to make it, but I just didn't... I didn't have *time*, you know? Or the ability to cook, either. I'm so sorry."

"Stop apologizing," he cut in.

"But—"

"No, listen. I didn't mean you'd have to cook. I can cook, or we can go out. Don't stress out."

"I am so beyond stressed," I said, watery.

"Let's order a pizza."

The consideration and utter simplicity of the gesture touched me. "Really?"

He handed the ice pack off to me and pulled out his cell phone. "Ordering now. What do you want?"

"But the organic," I said. "And the grass feeding. I know you don't just order pizza."

"Pepperoni with extra chemicals? Got it," he said to me before he turned to the phone to place a real order.

I swiped at the tears, but they didn't want to stop. While relief flooded me, I toyed with the empty box of lasagna noodles on the kitchen table. Idly I read the fine print.

"Hell," I said. "You're supposed to boil these first?"

"Silly mommy," Bailey said.

Chapter Fifteen

If I thought I'd made a mess in Colin's kitchen, it was nothing compared to the bakery.

Cabinet doors were open, pans littered the countertops, and a fine layer of flour coated the entire room. It hadn't even been this messy that time a hailstorm had knocked in the front windows.

I stepped inside, my mouth open. No one was in the back. The restroom was dark. I peeked into the storefront. Empty.

That left Rick's office. The door was shut, and I was almost afraid to knock. The place looked like a crime scene. First-degree baking by an idiot, maybe. I couldn't muster up the proper seriousness when the place looked like a supersized snow globe.

A deep breath. Knowing Rick, this was going to get strange. Well, stranger than usual.

I knocked. "Rick?"

Scuffling sounds from within. Then Rick poked his head out the door. "Allie. What are you doing here?"

"It's my shift. What happened?"

"What happened?" he repeated.

I closed my eyes tight, prayed for patience, then

opened them. "Here. In the kitchen. It's like a flour bomb went off."

"Oh, right." He glanced past me as if just noticing the mess.

I narrowed my eyes. "Seriously, what happened?"

"Nothing. No work today. Bakery's closed. Go home." And he shut the door in my face.

Oh man, I would love nothing better than to go home, to pick up Bailey from Shelly's and maybe even convince Shelly to spend the afternoon out with us. But even as I planned my afternoon off, I stomped my foot. A cloud of flour rose up, and I sneezed. I couldn't leave. Rick was a friend. An annoying, clearly deranged friend, but there was no way I could walk away from this. Whatever this was.

I knocked again, harder. "Rick!"

A thud and then a curse. He opened the door. "Why did you yell?"

"Let me in."

A pause. "No."

"Then come out here."

"Definitely no."

"You have exactly three seconds to open this door, or I swear to God I will…"

Before I had to make up a false threat, he opened the door. Files and papers flooded the small office. The cheap wood furniture peeked out between crumpled pages. I shouldn't have even been surprised.

Rick turned away and squatted to rifle through a

bookcase. Rather halfheartedly, considering the magnitude of disarray.

"What the hell, Rick? Now."

He stopped and bowed his head. Then he turned and stood, with so much raw emotion on his face that my breath caught. In the year and a half that I'd worked here, I'd never figured him out, but in this moment his eyes told the whole story.

Nothing so mundane as details. The broken, raw, painful part of me recognized the same thing in him. We stood there, connected by this nothing, and everything. It was uncomfortably intimate. More intimate than sex, but I'd learned long ago that the recognition of pain was so much more potent than the sharing of pleasure.

He leaned in, his intent clear. I didn't want to kiss him. He was a friend to me. Maybe even a surrogate father, since mine never came around. And there was Colin.

I jerked back, just slightly.

He froze, and then smiled a small, sad good-bye. It was a relief, to see he understood and accepted it, and a confirmation that we'd been real friends. A small rush of air escaped me. It was a miserable thing, not knowing a friend from an enemy.

"Allie," he whispered. "Come with me."

"Where are you going?"

"Away. Let's leave this place. I've got a little money saved up. It'll be just us."

Even if there wasn't Colin or Shelly, I wouldn't

have. Probably not. But stupidly, the first thing that popped into my head was, "What about Bailey?"

"She'll come, too, of course."

I shook my head against the crazy. "What are you saying? We aren't going anywhere. You have the bakery. And I have…well, I have roots here." That was an exaggeration. I had history here, in this city, which wasn't quite the same. And I had Shelly, who'd just as soon transplant with me.

Colin counted as roots, however young and tender they may be.

I had to see him again. Right now.

Rick was searching again, picking through the papers like they were rubble from an explosion and babbling about finding things and running out of time. I wanted to help him, but sometimes I had to learn when to walk away. When I wasn't really wanted or needed. And Rick, for all that he cared about me in his own way and had asked me to go away with him, was in his own world. I was a prop, not a player.

I put a hand on Rick's arm, and he stopped moving. He looked up at me, lost.

"I'm going to go now. I've moved in with someone."

"Okay," he said. "I'm sorry."

"You have nothing to be sorry for," I told him. "But…I quit."

The relief on his face was answered by gratitude within me. There weren't words, so I pressed a soft kiss to his lips before leaving the bakery for the last time.

Chapter Sixteen

"Is living with a man all it's cracked up to be?" Shelly asked as she examined her nails.

I studied her, unsure if she was being sarcastic or not. A mist of caution had risen between us in the few days I'd been at Colin's. "Oh, you know. The toilet seat's up, and there's extra laundry. That's about it."

She glanced up, a small curve to her lips. "You do his laundry?"

My lips answered hers in a smile. "Yeah."

"Isn't it sort of...weird? I mean, *underwear*." She lowered her voice—this from the girl who'd taught me everything I knew about how to give great head.

I ducked behind my pizza slice as I took a bite. It *was* weird. Blowing a guy was one thing, folding his underwear seemed so...personal.

Still, I'd insisted. I picked up all the housework and even got a cookbook. It was the least I could do, considering I wasn't contributing financially.

Speaking of which. "Where've you been staying? I stopped by the other day."

Shelly grabbed another slice from the box and began picking off the toppings. She always picked everything off, though she insisted on ordering supreme. It added variety, she always said. "At a friend's place."

"A friend?" I didn't mean to sound so skeptical, but she and I weren't exactly the book club type. It had just been me and her. At least since Andrew had…well, since Andrew.

"A client," she said.

That was new. Brand, spanking, completely against the rules new. I opened my mouth—to warn her, to chastise her—but she was a big girl, and I wasn't quite that much of a hypocrite. In fact, that meant she was now living with a guy too, although I doubted he could pay her enough to do his laundry.

"So, did you bring me something fancy?" I asked.

"Some of my best stuff," she said. "What's it for?"

I sighed. "Colin's taking me to the ballet."

"Seriously?" She whistled. "Classy."

"You see the problem."

She laughed. "What—is he trying to impress you?"

"Not exactly. His sister is in the ballet. A dancer. We're going to opening night, and then we're going to meet her and Colin's brother after."

She whistled. "He doesn't do anything half-assed, does he? Well, I brought three different options. Come on."

We crept up the creaking stairs, past Bailey's half-open door, and into the bedroom.

I immediately rejected the elegant, black, form-fitting dress, knowing it wouldn't flatter my lack of curves. Shelly and I were the same size, but if her body type was Tinkerbell, mine was Peter Pan.

Next was a gown with a sequined silver bodice and gray, gauzy skirts. I'd been pregnant during my prom and felt no need to re-create the experience now. Pass.

The last one I had never seen before. Pink and silky with a modest neckline, the fabric gathered below the bust and then flared out into asymmetrical curves ending below my knees, almost like petals.

"Oh," I said, awestruck.

"You like it?" Shelly asked.

"I do, but—" I glanced at her, a bit surprised. It was so bright, so flirty, and she hated to be the cliché of her profession.

She looked pleased. "It's for you."

I opened my mouth, but she cut my protests short. "No complaining. And no calculating how many bags of diapers this dress could pay for. You don't need to worry about that anymore, remember?"

"Well, she still needs to poop," I muttered, but it did nothing to mask my delight. How long had it been since I'd had new clothes? Plastic flip-flops from Target didn't quite count.

I put it on—perfection. It was pretty and feminine and everything I'd always wanted to be but wasn't. Of course Shelly had known. I wanted to hug her, but she wasn't really a fan of touching.

"Thank you." I gave my skirts a flick, enjoying the

way they swished against my bare legs. "You're like my fairy godmother. Now I can go to the ball."

"But you already bagged the prince," she said lightly.

Dismayed, I said, "You *are* mad."

"I'm not." She put her hand on my forearm and looked me in the eyes. "I'm not."

A slam of the door alerted us to Colin's arrival. By the time steady footsteps trekked up the stairs and to the doorway, I'd already fled to the bathroom.

"Just a minute," I called out. I wanted to brush away my pizza breath and freshen up my makeup before Colin saw me. Tonight had to be perfect.

Through the door, I heard the murmurs of Shelly and Colin, and I stepped up the pace. They'd gotten along well so far, but no need to press my luck.

When I opened the bathroom door, Shelly and the other dresses had vanished. She was probably already curled up in the armchair in Bailey's room with a book.

Colin stood at the window, looking out at the street. He still wore his jeans and T-shirt from work at the restaurant. His suit was laid out on the bed where I'd left it.

He turned, saw me, and froze. Framed by the soft evening glow, I couldn't see his face. I swayed, swishing softly. "Do you like it?" I asked.

A slight nod.

That left something to be desired.

"Are you sure?" What if he really didn't like the

dress? What if it wasn't the right thing to wear to the ballet? What if he was tired of me? For all I knew, I was just the flavor of the week. Intuition was nice, but it wasn't security.

Sometimes his terseness could be downright unnerving. I didn't want to mess this up, but at this point how would I even know until he kicked my ass to the curb?

I took a deep breath and approached him, all timidity. "Are you sure this is okay?" I asked.

He nodded.

"Tell me the truth," I said.

"It's a nice dress." His leashed body and hot eyes said he liked it very much.

I blinked up at him. "Really?"

"Yes."

A smile spread across my face. "You're sweet."

I threw my arms around him. He stiffened and then put his arms around me too. And wow, I guess it *was* okay, considering the thickness I felt press against my hip.

"Hey." I put my hand on his cock through his jeans. "I can take care of that."

His hips backed away. "After the ballet, or we're never getting out of here."

"Are you sure?" I mused. "You don't want me to kneel down right here in front of you, with my new dress on, and make you feel better?"

I would've sworn I had him, but he tightened—all

over—and then shook his head on a long exhale. "Later," he said.

Then he went into the bathroom to put on his suit. He looked just like I knew he would. Perfect.

✧   ✧   ✧

WE DROVE TO the theater in silence. I rehearsed sophisticated-sounding things to say to his brother and sister. When we arrived, seating hadn't begun yet, so Colin got us drinks from the bar. Turned out rich people liked to get drunk too. Same beer, triple the price. None of the cocktail tables had any chairs, so we found an empty one to stand around. As soon as we'd settled, Colin got a call on his cell. He stepped off to the side, just out of earshot, but not so far that I couldn't hear his voice rise. I still couldn't make out his words, but I felt his anger. One word slipped through a few times: "No."

Colin returned to the table, frustration seeping through his stoic mask.

"Who was that?" I asked.

"My brother."

I tensed. He and his hold on Colin were still a sore subject for me, but I knew I had to make nice. "He's on his way?"

Colin shook his head. "He doesn't like crowds. We'll stop by his house after."

We drank. My mind scrambled desperately for a topic but came up empty. The solemnity was unnatural for me, and the more desperate I became for a topic, the more inappropriate the suggestions in my mind became. Finally the tension got to be too much, and I burst out, "I've never been to a ballet before. It's weird walking on carpet in high heels."

He said nothing.

"You've been before…right?" I asked.

"Just to see Rose." His sister.

"I'm worried I'll do something stupid."

"You won't," he said.

I bit my lip. "We got a book about the ballet from the library. I promised to tell Bailey all about the real thing later."

We fell into silence, with my lame words echoing in my head.

Then Colin said, "One day we'll bring her with us."

I curled against his side in answer, my chest feeling too full. The awkwardness fell away, and everything was perfect again.

Chapter Seventeen

I HADN'T REALIZED exactly how long ballets were. Angelina the ballet-dancing rat from Bailey's books left something to be desired in her descriptions. Okay, so I hadn't really known what to expect, but too many people dancing in repetitive swirls for two and a half hours wasn't it. Colin's brother had the right idea after all. Crowds, my ass.

After the curtains closed, we waited backstage.

"Your sister looked really great," I said.

Colin nodded. He'd pointed her out to me, though I had no idea how he'd been able to tell her apart.

A beautiful woman with stark black hair, dark eyes, and a stunning smile emerged from the crowd.

Colin gave her a brief hug. "You were great."

So this was Rose. She looked glamorous, almost ethereal, and I felt incredibly awkward. "That was beautiful," I said. "You looked great."

Rose smiled at me with open curiosity and appraisal in her eyes. "Thank you. Colin told me about you. I'm glad to finally meet you."

"Thanks. You too." Though that wasn't entirely true. Colin hadn't told me much of anything about her.

I only hoped she didn't ask for specifics.

"You have a…baby, don't you?"

"Yes." I couldn't get a read on the undercurrent, whether it was the standard weirdness about my obvious age or whether she didn't want her brother dating someone with a child. "A girl. She's twenty months."

"Where's her father?" Rose asked. I knew she didn't mean where he was physically. She meant, where was he while me and my child were freeloading off her brother.

"Rose," Colin warned.

I put my hand on his arm. "It's a fair question, but it's kind of a long story." A long story, starting with "No" and ending with a plus sign on a stick.

"I see." Rose glanced at Colin's glowering face—not that she looked particularly cowed—before shrugging. "Just looking out for my little brother."

I blinked, then looked over and up at her little brother, all five feet ten inches and one hundred and eighty pounds of him.

"Stop," he said. I could feel his tension under my hand.

Crap, starting a fight between them was the last thing I needed to do tonight. I didn't need him to take offense for me, not for this. "It's okay," I said to Colin.

He glanced down at me and then, with a deep breath, visibly relaxed.

Rose's eyebrows rose as she watched our interactions. "You know," she said. "I just might end up liking you after all."

It was hardly the ringing endorsement I'd hoped for at the beginning of the night. But then again, it was better than how things could have gone, considering how she'd been gunning for me at the start.

Once we made our good-byes, I was ready to drag Colin out of there. But he was even more eager than I, his long strides pulling ahead of my hurried steps. Once we were back in the comfort of his truck, I sank into the faded fabric of the seats, soft in a way that can only come from wear, and breathed a sigh of relief.

✧ ✧ ✧

Colin's brother, Philip, lived in a mansion.

I wasn't sure what I'd been expecting. With Colin's modest home, casual clothes, and rough build, maybe a tight-knit little family. I gaped at the sprawling building, probably in some sort of architectural style that had a name, like deco or postmodern or something, and started to doubt the tight-knit family scenario.

It dawned on me how incredibly, impossibly Colin was beyond my reach. His house was beautiful but normal. But his family. Shit. His sister in the ballet. His brother with a mansion and a lawyer on tap.

What the hell was I doing here?

Oh, right. Saving my ass. From Andrew. Like a total user.

No wonder Rose had been suspicious of me. I was

everything she feared.

Despite the chilly night air, warmth invaded my hands, and I glanced down to see Colin's large hands rubbing mine between his own. I looked up at him. "I don't…"

He cocked his head. "What's wrong?"

"I just… It's so big."

"Yeah." He shrugged. "It's mostly for show. Don't worry."

He squeezed my hands. I wished I could believe him. I trusted Colin. But he hadn't seen how his brother was using him. And Colin hadn't expected his sister to confront me. It seemed to me that he had a blind spot where his family was concerned.

But we needed Philip for the lawyer, and besides, I had hopes that I could get in his family's good graces. It was clearly important to Colin. I would do this for him.

I squeezed his hands back, and we walked up the steps.

We were let in by a man who seemed to know Colin but who didn't look or speak to me directly. I looked to Colin for an introduction, but he seemed not to notice.

Surely Colin would know the way. It was clear he'd been there many times. But the man led us to an empty room and then left. A butler, of sorts.

The room screamed masculinity, a portrait of brown tones lined in black. I squinted at the framed sepia photograph nearest me—a matador and a bull.

Very subtle.

"Colin. Are you sure…?" I didn't even know how to end the sentence. This felt all wrong.

"Trust me," he said.

I couldn't tell him no. Over the warning bells clanging in my head and through the tense knot in my stomach, I trusted Colin. So I sat down in one of the chairs, the plush leather welcoming my body like a bed of quicksand.

Colin sat in the chair next to me, also sinking low.

Neither of us spoke, but I was determined not to second-guess him again tonight. He didn't deserve that from me.

The click of shoes on wood announced the arrival of a tall man, leaner than Colin, and darker. He was dressed in a white dress shirt and black slacks, but he wore them as effortlessly as sweats. And when he stepped forward into the lamplight, I saw that his face was disfigured on one side, but it was hard to say what exactly was wrong with it. At least without staring, which I tried hard not to do.

I must have failed, though, because the sharpness in his voice held a reprimand. "You must be Allison Winters."

"Allie," I offered, shrinking into the chair even as I told my feet to stand. Colin was made of sterner stuff and stood.

"Philip," Colin greeted.

Philip swung his gaze to Colin and raised his eyebrows. "You've been absent." Every word was clipped, like it was cut off a second too soon.

"You know why." Colin spoke evenly. "Where's Laramie?"

"Late, as usual. I'd love to fire him for it if he wasn't so fucking useful." Philip grimaced and threw a nod in my direction. "Pardon my language."

Ha! That was a trip. If he thought I was a lady enough to watch his speech, then maybe there was hope for me yet. But this was stupid. I'd been silent this entire time.

"Nice to meet you." It came out as a croak. Neither man acknowledged me.

"Any news?" Colin asked, his demeanor excluding me.

"A few packages arrived last week," Philip replied, "but we're seeing delays all over the place. I'll need you to look into it."

Colin nodded as if he'd expected as much.

"Bad enough the quality issues," Philip said. "Now with shipping trouble too. It's gotta be a setup."

"I'll take care of it," Colin said.

Philip inclined his head as if that settled things. I wondered if I could have as much trust in Colin as that.

I let my mind drift while they talked shop. I'd gone to the parenting clinic for testing and contraception earlier today. The doctor had been different, but the nurse had been the same as two years ago. She hadn't recognized me. I'd gritted my teeth against their vacant expressions and impersonal touches in my most private areas, but at least that was better than the alternative.

Laramie joined us soon after. Laramie the Lawyer, though I kept that moniker to myself. He had soft features and kind eyes, all the better to trust him with. He, at least, was introduced formally to me. This was Drew Laramie, attorney-at-law and family friend. I was Allie Winters, the one with "the problem."

I had a short speech prepared. What I'd told Colin but with details. When Bailey was born, what her birth certificate read, how I'd supported her all this time. These things had seemed important in the light of day when I'd anticipated and dreaded this meeting.

But here, in the dark, with the men settling in and throwing their words above my head, my planned words seemed superfluous, as if the details hardly mattered. Laramie sat across from Colin. Philip served us all drinks, somehow managing to not look the least bit subservient. He served me first, as the lady, I supposed. I brooded into my glass of water while the men were given an amber liquid.

"It looks like he hasn't filed yet, but that doesn't mean anything," Laramie said, finally addressing the case. "These things take time."

"And you know we'd rather avoid that altogether," said Philip.

"I understand. I have Roark looking into his background. If we can find something appropriate…" Laramie let the sentence die as he took a sip from the drink Philip handed him.

"That's risky," Colin said.

Laramie nodded. "Hard to say how a man'll react until he's pressed into a corner. You mentioned paying him off, but that carries its own risks. Technically there'd be no guarantee he wouldn't file at some future date or press for more money."

"Oh, he'll stick to the deal," Philip said.

Laramie smiled without humor. "There's persuasion, but you don't need me for that."

God, no more violence. *Please.*

"She doesn't want that," Colin said.

They paused in unison and looked at me.

"Definitely not," I said. Which seemed to work, because they resumed talking around me, about negotiations and agreements. Riddles cloaked in ordinary words. At least there was no more talk of persuasion.

It was like I'd stumbled into some sort of Mad Hatter's tea party. I should speak up, I knew. I should advocate for Bailey, but despite the questionable ethics of some of their suggestions, they seemed to have a much better grasp on the possible solutions than I did.

If only Philip would look at me when he talked about me.

Laramie did, giving the occasional sympathetic glance, particularly when he mentioned Bailey specifically. Colin also looked at me with his usual impassivity, though he directed his comments at the other men.

Philip looked at the other men and, on occasion, at the air beside me. Never at me. After Andrew, I'd lost any claim to be a great judge of character, but everything about Philip made me nervous.

I trusted Colin, and he trusted Philip. Colin seemed to think that was enough, but I was starting to realize trust didn't work by proxy.

Laramie's eyes caught mine, an apology in them. "This man, did he ever hurt you?"

"What?" The very worst liar in the world, my eyes widened and my hands clenched.

"If he did," Laramie said carefully, "it would certainly help our case. Give us leverage."

I stared into his gentle eyes with my mouth open.

"Allie?" Colin said, but I couldn't look at him.

Laramie was silent, watching me.

I'd thought about confessing all to Colin, but it wouldn't be like this. I couldn't possibly bare all my sins, all my shame in this room full of strangers. A room full of men. I was already the gold digger, the slut, the problem. I wouldn't also be the victim.

Besides, violence had already been discussed once tonight. I didn't want Andrew hurt, though I wouldn't let myself think too hard on that. And I certainly didn't want Colin picking a fight, possibly injuring himself, possibly in trouble with the law. Hurting himself in the process because he thought he needed to fight to keep the people he cared about near him.

"No," I said.

And then stronger, turning to look at Colin. "No. He didn't hurt me."

The lie was a small stab to my stomach, which was good. I deserved no less for deceiving Colin, even if it was for his own good. Or maybe it wasn't a lie, if I thought of all my date nights. Asking for sex, for pain, in a sick bid for control, but that was an illusion. I'd never had control, and this farce of a consultation only underscored it. Those men hadn't hurt me, Andrew hadn't hurt me, not nearly so much as I'd hurt myself.

Chapter Eighteen

Colin's house was quiet. After I shut the door behind a groggy Shelly, Colin reached back behind my neck and pulled me in for a kiss. He backed me up right there, the cool wall against my shoulders a contrast from his hot hands gripping my hips and his tongue invading my mouth.

My mind reeled from the earlier conversation. Like the flashing pictures in a slot machine, my emotions ran from guilt to fear to anger. And then frustration with myself. I was getting what I wanted; I should be happy. He pressed his mouth down the side of my neck. Should be happy.

"God," he muttered. "This dress."

Pride sparked in me, a welcomed respite. His arousal was thick, insistent. I struggled to catch up as we all but mated in the hallway, minus the intercourse.

Colin's hand parted my legs and stroked me.

I shut my eyes tight as if I could lock out my thoughts and just feel. His fingers were thick at my entrance, the calluses providing a delicious friction. His body loomed large around me, shielding me from the outside world. His lips on mine were hot and hungry.

I slickened below, just a bit. Thank God. I could do this.

I wasn't quite ready. Not physically. I was barely wet; nothing close to what Colin could bring me to, drenched and supple. Not mentally. My mind was still running replays from earlier. I wasn't in the mood right now, and my body had only begun to recognize what Colin wanted.

Colin shook with his arousal. He intimidated me with it, looking angry and intense, though I knew by now that was eagerness. I tugged him up the stairs, past the room where Bailey slept, and into his bedroom—our bedroom—and shut the door. I slipped off my panties and kicked them aside, then bent over the bed and looked back. He understood. With quick, jerky movements, he lifted my skirt and entered me.

I gasped as his cock stretched me. He paused. I wanted to do this for him. I needed to. I tilted my hips back to allow him deeper access, accepting the sharp pain without further sound.

He pulled out, almost completely, and then rammed back in. My teeth gritted together and my fingers whitened on the bedspread, but I would take it. He grabbed my shoulders and set up a rhythm of deep, punishing thrusts. He seemed lost in his pleasure, unable to notice my confusion, which I was grateful for. The air was too thick to breathe. My thoughts too murky to pierce. I didn't think I could talk—or orgasm, for that matter—if he had wanted something more than my compliance.

Colin flipped me over. I spread my legs wide, and he entered me again with deep, rooting thrusts. He slammed into me, pushing me up the bed. His wrists were beside my shoulders, and I reached up to grasp them, to anchor myself.

The pillow smashed between my head and the headboard. It was just a pillow. A soft pressure, especially considering the force of Colin's thrusts. But it triggered something in me, something hard.

Cold washed over my body. My skin prickled into goose bumps. My nipples were oversensitive, abraded against his chest. My cunt felt sore, like pulverized meat. My clit felt smashed under the thrusts of his pubic bone.

I made no move to stop the sex. This was just a way for my body to service his. My discomfort was small and well earned.

He noticed, though, and reached down to touch my clit. I jumped. "No. Don't," slipped out.

His hand stilled, and he slowed his hips to a gentle rocking. "What's wrong?"

"Just keep going."

He narrowed his eyes. "Something's wrong."

"Don't worry about it. Just…just finish."

Damned if the man wasn't as contrary as I was. He froze, still inside.

"Tell me," he demanded.

"It's nothing." As if we could have an actual conversation while his stiff cock was still lodged deep inside me. "Just do it." I put a challenge in my voice and my eyes. "Fuck me."

I knew he wanted to by the way his hips rocked forward as if testing the waters. Coming up dry, he pulled out and sprawled across the bed, catching his breath.

I felt hot and cold at the same time. And raw. As if the physical barricades had been burned away, leaving me exposed. Helpless. All I could think about was ending this night so we could get back to normal—at least our version of normalcy.

The room was silent except for our breathing, and I had the inappropriate urge to giggle. I managed to restrain myself. All I needed was another bout of hysteria for him to peg me as crazy, not that he'd be wrong.

Colin broke the silence. "Was I too rough?"

"No." And before he could ask anything else, "I don't want to talk about it."

For the second time in our relationship, I retreated to the bathroom after sex. I slammed the door to let him know he wasn't invited this time. To ask him to follow me again.

From on top of the toilet seat, I watched the doorknob. My ears listened for footsteps or the turn of the knob, but none came. I wanted for him to come, but he never did.

I should be grateful that he'd listened to me. After

feeling invisible at Philip's, after raging for control over my body for years, the fact that he'd granted my request should be bliss.

For the first time since I'd met him, I felt truly alone.

Hard

Chapter One

"Do you want pancakes?" I asked Colin, imploring him with my eyes. *Let's be normal. Just pretend.*

His eyes narrowed, but he nodded.

Thank you.

I couldn't talk about what had happened last night, not when it was so fresh. More than that, I wasn't even sure what had happened.

I'd gone cold during sex before. In fact, I'd been cold during every sexual encounter I'd ever had, except with Colin. Never with Colin, until last night.

I piled three pancakes, the top one fresh off the skillet, onto a plate and carried it into the dining room. Colin sat, not at the head of the table, but near the foot, next to Bailey. Right in the syrup splash zone.

"Waka!" said Bailey. She was coated in syrup and pancake crumbs, from the tips of her sticky hair to her grubby, outstretched fingers.

"Good morning," Colin replied to her, with the same gravity with which he'd accepted my offer of pancakes and peace. Satisfied, Bailey returned to sculpting her soggy pile of pancake. I set the plate down in front of Colin.

"Coffee?" I offered.

"Please," he answered.

I returned to the kitchen, which I already knew like my own, and brewed the coffee. More baby talk trilled from the dining room, but I figured I'd best let them get on without me. I would try my hardest to keep Bailey in line, but if Colin was truly averse to the mess or the noise of a child, then this wasn't going to work.

A string of warbled sounds. Low tones. The bang of tiny fists on the high chair tray punctuated with a shriek.

I rushed into the dining room, prepared for the worst. Bailey fussing or throwing a tantrum. Colin angry and splashed with syrup.

What I found was Colin sliding a handful of pancake squares onto Bailey's tray. A slice of the pancakes from his plate was missing, now replaced with Bailey's pancake lump.

He turned to look at me, all seriousness. "She wanted to trade."

Bailey giggled.

How in the hell he'd understood that from her garbled syllables, I didn't know, but it didn't matter. Bailey was happy. Colin seemed happy enough. And, dammit, if I could just figure out the trick, surely I could be happy too.

After breakfast Colin headed out to run some "errands." His restaurant had a general manager, but

Colin still checked in, preferably around peak mealtimes. He also spent a fair amount of time at home with me and Bailey, but the rest of his time was unaccounted for. He went out, and I wouldn't be the nagging woman to demand to know where he was going and when he'd return.

We both knew that at least some of his time was spent working for his brother, but we didn't talk about it. Avoidance may not be a psychotherapist-certified coping technique, but it worked for me. I wasn't trying to get fancy. This wasn't about true love. I didn't need Colin to complete me. I just wanted some security, and he was it.

An hour later Bailey and I were rescuing the doll princess from the foam block castle. The doorbell rang. I'd told Shelly to just come around back. I stood and opened the door, but it wasn't her.

Two men stood on the porch, dressed in identical brown suits. Cops. I knew this from years of avoiding them, not because I was a consummate lawbreaker, but because it was a well-known fact, in my neighborhood, at least, that cops only brought trouble. They'd brought a whole lot of nothing back when I'd needed them, but I suspected this was trouble.

I tightened my fingers on the door and hugged it close to my body.

"Allison Winters?" His face had the look of an overweight person, though he wasn't really, and it was mottled red. It took me a second to place it—the look of an alcoholic. "We're with the Chicago Police Department. I'm Detective Shaw, and this is Detective Cameron. We'd like to have a word with you."

How the hell did they know who I was? Or where to find me? "What is this about?"

"It'll be best if we come inside."

I glanced back at Bailey on the floor. I hated the thought of these men, with their weapons and condescension, being around her. My long-practiced avoidance demanded I slam the door on whatever bad news they brought, but it seemed that lately the cockroaches crawled out into the sunlight. There was nowhere to go. No place was safe.

The cops accepted my deliberation without surprise. The second cop, with a surprisingly respectful demeanor and startling blue eyes, offered his badge and prodded, "Ma'am."

"Yes. Come in." I opened the door wide and allowed them into the living room.

How would someone act if she'd done nothing wrong? That's the part I had to play. I hadn't actually done anything wrong, but that didn't seem to matter when my heart was hammering in my chest. Keeping secrets had turned me into a skittish creature.

I gestured them to the couch away from where Bailey sat on the rug. She regarded them with a serenity I envied. I tried to don the confidence of my slut persona, but the props and setting were all wrong.

"How can I help you?" I asked, a touch too loud.

Damn.

"You've been seeing Colin Murphy," Blue Eyes said, more a statement than question.

I snorted. "I'm living in his house. Yeah, we may have run into each other a time or two."

A slight smile tugged at his mouth—gone just as quickly. "Mr. Murphy is a person of interest in a number of ongoing investigations with the CPD."

My heart beat faster, mostly with worry for Colin and whatever trouble he may be in, but, to my shame, there were other emotions too. Relief that they weren't here about Andrew. And, because I guess I'd always been selfish, fear of what this would mean for me and Bailey.

"He's not here," I hedged.

A note of smugness marred the other one's face. "We know that."

I affected an amused look, as if I'd thought of something naughty. "Were you *watching* us?"

Blue Eyes remained impassive. What was his name? Detective Cameron. "We know his schedule."

"He's not usually out of the house by now." I clamped my mouth shut. Could not believe I'd just said that. Even if it was something they could easily find out, I didn't have to *help* them.

Shaw's eyes glittered with triumph at the slip. He knew he could play me now. This Detective Shaw was stockier than the other guy, coarser, and an asshole besides. Like the kind of guy I'd pick at the club if he wasn't hiding behind a badge. Cameron was leaner, quieter, with those watchful blue eyes. Both dangerous in their own ways.

Detective Cameron leaned forward, just a smidge, but immediately Shaw subsided. So, we had a leader. And it wasn't the mouthy one either. Interesting.

"Are you aware of what he does for a living?" Cameron asked.

"He owns a restaurant."

"He does own a restaurant," he agreed. "It's a very nice restaurant that he spends a few hours a week on. What does he do the rest of the time?"

"Knitting?" I suggested.

"You think this is funny," Shaw snapped.

Dick. "No, I don't think it's funny that you're in *his* house and making accusations."

"We haven't made any accusations," Cameron said. Crystal blue eyes scanned me, cataloging my words, my reactions. I straightened.

"Where does Colin go out at night?" Shaw asked.

"He's with me."

"Every night?" he prodded.

"Pretty much. Is this some sort of interrogation technique? Divide and conquer. It won't work."

"There's been an increase in illegal trafficking the last couple of months," Cameron said, interrupting Shaw's words. "Shipments at night, that sort of thing."

"Then Colin's not your guy." I let suggestiveness color my next words. "He's with me all night."

Shaw opened his mouth, but Cameron cleared his throat.

"Why don't you leave your cards? I'll let him know you stopped by." I gave them my best smile, otherwise known as a baring of teeth. I may not like what Colin did for Philip, but let there be no confusion about whose side I was on. If they came here looking for an in, a mole, thinking because I was new here, I wouldn't know what was up, then they were shit out of luck.

Shaw sneered, but Cameron stood. I stood myself, aiming for nonchalance but failing miserably as they paraded out the front door to the porch.

The quiet one turned back, a card between his forefingers. "I'll be around if you ever want to talk." He glanced past me toward Bailey. "You may not be safe here."

A shiver wormed through me, and I took the card.

"Nice cat," I heard just as I slammed the door shut.

What cat?

I glanced back at Bailey, whose fingers were clamped around the tail of a big orange cat. Must've slipped in when those idiots had taken forever to leave.

"Shit," I said.

"Sit," said Bailey.

Double shit. I stomped around toward Bailey, and the cat darted away. Apparently Bailey had chosen that moment to let go. Of course she'd side with the litter pooper.

I tiptoed into the kitchen where the big cat was

licking a sticky spot of syrup on the counter that had escaped my morning cleanup.

"Bad cat," I said. Which turned out to be stupid, because the cat leaped off the counter—with surprising grace for his size—and ran back into the living room.

"Sit!" cried Bailey as I made a wide dash around her toys to follow the cat up the stairs.

Fifteen minutes later, panting and sneezing, I tumbled the cat out of my arms and onto the front porch.

"This isn't a shelter," I told those big, glassy eyes.

I shut the door.

That wasn't quite true. It was a shelter, but it was full. No vacancies.

I turned around and shrieked. "What are you doing here?"

Shelly pushed off from the wall she'd been leaning against. "You said to go around back."

"I know. I meant how long have you been there. You could have helped."

She shuddered. "I don't do cats."

I rolled my eyes—and shuddered a bit myself—at her double entendre. "Yeah, well. Neither do I." I shook my hands free of the imaginary cat hair. "What's up?"

Shelly lifted Bailey and gurgled on her belly. "Just checking on the happy couple. You looked kinda freaked out last night."

For a second I thought she'd meant at *night*, when I had indeed freaked out. Right in the middle of Colin fucking me. But then I realized she meant after the ballet. Yup, still freaked out. I made a habit of it, apparently.

"Never mind that," I said. "Did you see who just stopped by for a chat?"

"Rick?" she asked.

"What? No. It was *cops*."

"Oh," she said. "Shit."

"Sit," said Bailey.

Shelly met my eyes. Double shit.

"What did they want?" she asked.

"It's a long story," I sighed. "So I don't think I ever told you, but…Colin's brother is…I'm not sure."

She raised her eyebrow.

"A criminal," I said.

She thought for a second, unfazed. "Like, what? A thief?"

"Maybe."

"A drug dealer."

"Probably."

"Worse?" Now she was interested.

"I think yes."

"And the cops were looking for him?"

"No, they were looking for Colin. Actually they came to talk to me. Because Colin is involved in the whole thing. And that means…"

"Bad shi—stuff," she finished.

I nodded.

"Do they have anything?" she asked.

"Hell if I know." I glanced at Bailey as if that absolved me of my swearing sins.

"How bad are we talking?"

"Don't know that either. Colin was pretty vague. He made it sound like some sort of business. Crime business. What the hell is that? Anyways, Philip looked like the—"

"Wait. Philip? Philip Murphy?"

Oh, no. No no no. The only thing that could possibly make this bad situation worse was if Shelly were involved.

"You know him?" I choked on the words.

"I know him," she confirmed, her face grim. "I've gotta run."

"What? Now?"

"Yup." She plopped a fussing Bailey into my arms and vanished out the back door as quickly as she'd appeared.

Well, shit.

I gave myself a tacit pat on the back for keeping that swear to myself. It was hard as hell, but I was learning. It twisted me up inside to want something better, but when I looked at Bailey, I couldn't help but hope. It would hurt like hell to face my past—to start to heal—but being with Colin almost made it seem possible.

Chapter Two

I DECIDED TO tell Colin about the cops. After dinner.

It didn't take a domestic goddess to realize a man was more amenable on a full stomach. Plus, spazzing out as soon as he got home just reeked of insecurity. However accurate that might have been, I wanted to show him I could deal with this. No problem. Detectives questioning me before snack time? Easy.

So when Colin came through the back door, I just called over my shoulder. "Hey, you. How was your day?" I dropped a spoonful of cookie dough onto the sheet. *Look at me, so domestic.*

"Not great," he answered.

I froze, but the lump of dough slid from the spoon and landed on the tray with a plop. Colin was like Shelly. A faker. He said great when he meant fine, and fine when he meant total suckage. Not great was practically a cry for help.

I turned around. He looked like…Colin. Sturdy, steady. Dependable. Or maybe it's just that I had depended on him so much that I wanted him to be that way for me.

I walked over to him and reached up to cup his jaw.

"What's wrong?"

"Where's Bailey?"

"Napping." I smiled. Physical comfort, I could give.

"We need to talk."

My smile fell. So much talking today and none of it good.

"Is there something you didn't tell me about Andrew?" he asked.

Alarm bells clanged. There was a lot I hadn't told him about Andrew, actually, but I had a feeling I knew exactly which thing he was talking about. The question was, how could he know? "Like what?"

"How long did you and Andrew date?"

Shit. He knew. But how? And perhaps more importantly, how the hell could I get around this? I tried to collect my thoughts, my lies. Lying about this felt more natural than not, but I wasn't prepared for this direct questioning out of the blue. I wasn't prepared for all this fucking *security* to shatter. It was too soon. I'd had just a taste, and it was too fucking soon.

"Colin," I tried. "Has something happened?"

"Answer the question."

I felt panic rise in my chest, and I tamped it down. "I'm not going to answer the question until you tell me what is going on. Something had to have happened. You're acting weird."

"I spoke to Andrew today."

"You did *what*?" Jesus Christ. Colin and Andrew together. This was a cluster fuck of the first order.

Fuck, fuck, fuck. "Why would you do that? What did he say?"

"We had to find out if he was going to pursue this."

I tensed. "What did he say?"

"He said he was sorry." He paused. "He acted like I was going to hurt him before I even threatened him. Why would he think that, Allie?"

The room blurred. "Because…you're a mean son of a bitch?" I hoped repeating his own words back to him would distract him. At least enough so I could breathe again. Actually the whole not breathing thing was good. Kind of dimmed the panic of the whole Colin and Andrew thing when I thought I might pass out.

"I don't think that's why," he said, so far away.

"I don't…" My voice faded, and so did I. I wasn't sure how I'd finish that thought anyway. *I don't know why Andrew does anything. I don't want to think about that. Don't make me tell you. Don't hurt me.*

I was nothing good or special. I had never deserved this knight-in-shining-armor treatment. I knew it, and now Colin would too. I felt his touch on my arms, warm and sure. The next thing I knew, I was sitting down on the couch with Colin beside me.

The stillness in the room belied the way my world was crashing down around me. I hadn't wanted this moment to come, but it had. Of course it had.

The sound of my breathing roared in my ears. Colin's warmth seeped into my skin, but not deep enough. I wasn't stalling. I was bracing myself.

"If I tell you," I said, "you have to promise me something. You can't hurt him."

"Fuck no," Colin said.

"I'm serious. I can't…I can't deal with that too. You have to promise. And you can't ask anyone else to hurt him either. Swear it to me."

He looked down, and I heard him swallow. I knew he wouldn't want to. I thought maybe he'd refuse and just go beat Andrew up anyway, knowing that if I feared it, it would probably be deserved in his eyes.

"Please." I put my hand on his arm. "Please."

He looked up. "Okay. I promise."

Thank God.

"I didn't exactly tell you the truth." What a way to start. God, I really deserved what was coming to me.

I turned to face him and pulled my leg up underneath me. Might as well be comfortable for this. There would be few enough comforts left afterward.

I told him everything. Or really I'm not sure what I told him, so lost was I in my story, my shame.

Andrew and I were best friends. It wasn't Shelly I called to chat about nothing for hours as I painted my nails or lay on my bed, but Andrew. And it wasn't his buddies he confided in about the nights his father had drunk too much, but me.

His father was away, had been for days, leaving Andrew without any way to contact him and no food. As usual. We hung out in his basement and ordered a pizza from the money my dad had left me. There was a movie playing on the TV, but neither of us were interested.

"Allie," he said. "I've got to get out of here."

"Okay. Let's go," I said.

"No. I mean, out of here. This whole city. The fucking country, maybe."

It wasn't the first time he'd expressed discontent. More than anyone, I knew what he risked, what he tolerated to stay in this shithole of a house, but there was an edge in his voice tonight. And that bottle of rum we'd jacked from his dad's stash had run awfully low.

"Where would you go?"

"Anywhere," he said. "Maybe I'll join the army."

I snickered. "You wouldn't last two seconds. You don't follow orders well."

He laughed, a hollow sound. "You're probably right." He looked over at me. "Come with me. We'll find someplace to go. Anywhere's gotta be better than here."

I shifted on the couch. That was true enough for him, but not for me. I wasn't sure I loved my dad, that guy who stopped in with his semi between long-distance routes every couple of months, but it was comfortable.

"Come on," he said. His eyes turned stormy. "Do you want me to stay here? You think I deserve this?"

"What? No. Of course not."

"Are you sure?" he said in a singsong voice. "I might deserve it. Maybe I should tell you what he did, and then you can decide."

Selfishly I didn't want to know. It was easier to pretend his dad was an ass. The ordinary kind. I didn't want to see the remembered pain in the eyes of the boy I loved, not when I'd be helpless against it.

"Stop it," I said. "Just stop."

"Maybe I should show you," he went on. There was a strange glint in his eye, and I couldn't tell if he was teasing me or was angry with me. Maybe both. "Then you would have all the facts. What do you say?"

"Please stop. I'm sorry."

That only made him angrier. "You're sorry," he spat. "I don't want your fucking sorries."

He crawled over me on the sofa, and I shrank back into the thin cushions until the springs pushed into my back. I was afraid of him, afraid he'd yell at me, or afraid he'd say something mean. So when he tilted my head up and pinched my chin hard, I was more surprised than anything.

"What the hell are you doing?" I asked, pushing his hand away. But he still crouched over me.

"First, he was drunk." Andrew glanced at the empty bottle of alcohol. "Done that. Then he started yelling, you know, that I'd never be anything but a loser, that sort of thing."

A funny feeling tickled my nose. "Oh, Andrew. Fuck him."

"Yes," he said. "That's pretty much what happened."

And he smiled. Something *had* happened. The man-boy hovering above me wasn't Andrew, my friend, the person I loved and trusted. He'd been replaced by an echo of his father, sick and sadistic.

It wasn't exactly the same, he said. Because I was a girl, it would hurt less. That's what he told me anyway, but with my wrists in his hand and my body forced open, it hurt a whole hell of a lot. And then it was over, but the pain never stopped.

Chapter Three

My heart thudded, in that moment long past but never forgotten, and here in the present. Colin pulled me closer. I wouldn't have thought I'd like to be touched right then, but it calmed me.

"I said no, but he didn't listen. It…happened anyway."

"He raped you," Colin said in a flat tone.

"No," I said. "It wasn't like that. We were friends."

Colin just looked at me.

Tears blurred his image. "We were best friends. I…loved him."

Colin's arm tightened around me.

"Why didn't he stop?" I whispered. It wasn't a rhetorical question. I'd been searching for that answer, desperate to understand, ever since it'd happened. Maybe Colin would know.

"I'm sorry," he said.

I understood why Andrew got so angry when I'd asked that. I didn't want to hear that. It wasn't an answer to the question. What did "I'm sorry" really mean, anyway? *I'm sorry this happened to you, but I'm glad it wasn't me. I'm sorry you're broken, but life goes on.*

It wasn't anything good or anything helpful; it was just pity. Fucking pity.

I took a deep breath. "After that, he drove me home. I just sat there. I didn't know what to say. I should have screamed or cried or *something*, but I couldn't. Why couldn't I cry then, but I can't stop crying now? He was my friend, but I hate him. So much. You don't understand how much I hate him."

"I think I do," Colin said. He was squeezing me almost to the point where I couldn't breathe. I doubted he even realized it, but I wanted more. There's a certain magic to being held. No one could hurt me there.

"I heard he left town right after that. I didn't see him again." Not until a week ago, when he showed up at my apartment.

"Why didn't you call the cops?" Colin asked. His voice was even, without the judging lilt I'd expected, but I didn't want to talk about that. There was enough bitterness in the room to choke on without adding more.

I shook my head and tried to blot the tears out of my eyes. "It wasn't really…"

"Rape? Yes. It was."

"I know," I whispered. "I know, but I just… It's better if I don't think about it like that. I know I never should have gone out with him or let him kiss me. I should have fought harder. I should have—"

"No." I winced at his raised voice, and he lowered it. "God, is that what you think?"

"I don't know. I'm sorry." Christ, now I was doing it. "I just…I don't want him to know Bailey. I know that fathers"—I practically choked on the word—"have rights and that Bailey deserves a father, but he isn't…he's not…" My voice broke, and I bit into my lip hard to stem the tears. I also clutched Colin's hand a little too hard, but I couldn't seem to let go.

"I don't want him near Bailey." I was babbling. "I can't be near him, either, but it's not just for me. He doesn't care about her. He doesn't even know her. What if he takes her away from me?"

"No. He's not getting anywhere near you or Bailey."

Colin held me while the threat of tears passed. The rhythm of our breathing synced, as if to steady us both.

The quietude was interrupted by the ringing of Colin's cell phone. Without releasing me, he reached into his pocket.

"Yeah," he said quietly.

The faint buzz of another person speaking.

"I can't come now," he said.

More buzzing, slightly louder this time.

"I'll talk to you later." He hung up.

"If you need to go…" I said. Hell, my problems had stewed for this long. It was hardly an emergency.

"It's fine," he said, stroking my hair.

"There's something else I have to tell you," I said into his shirt. "Earlier today, some cops came by. Detectives, I mean. They were asking about you."

His grip tightened to just this side of bruising before subsiding. "What did they say?"

They said I wasn't safe. Bailey wasn't safe here. "Nothing."

"Don't talk to them again."

I should have bristled at the command, but I really had no desire to ever talk to them again. And I was drained. "Okay."

Bailey's soft cry crackled from the baby monitor. Up from her nap, and life goes on. I pulled away. Colin clung to me for a beat and then released me.

In that sort of dulled state that comes from falling apart, I retrieved Bailey from her bed and set her up with a bowl of watermelon chunks in the kitchen as I finished baking the cookies. Dinner was a quiet affair. Neither Colin nor I had any words left. Bailey seemed to take her cue from him, peppering the silence with subdued grunts and eating little. I regaled Bailey with outrageous stories, slapstick versions of her favorite books complete with silly voices, through dinner. I put her to bed early, which of course only made her stay up extra late, tossing restlessly in her bed until sleep overcame her.

Colin was somewhere in the house but not in his room. *Our* room, I reminded myself. Exhausted, I stripped down to my underwear and collapsed on the bed.

When I woke, it was dark in the room. Strong hands cradled me, and I cuddled up to a hard chest. I craved Colin for the reassurance that he was here, that he would stay. I trailed my hand down, but he caught it in his.

"Not tonight."

"You don't want me?"

"Always, Allie, but...it's not right. Later." Even though he was right, I felt the sting of rejection. He pulled me close to him, holding my hand. I closed my eyes and drifted off to sleep.

I didn't have nightmares about what had happened with Andrew, not even right after it happened. Or maybe I did, but I never remembered any of my dreams. So I wasn't really prepared for when Colin started tossing around in the middle of the night.

He jerked against the tangled sheets and mumbled, "No...leave her..."

I'd done this. I shook his shoulder firmly to wake him.

"Colin. It's all right. Wake up. Everyone is fine."

He blinked up at me blearily. "Allie?"

"Yeah, it's me. You were dreaming."

"Won't let him hurt you again."

"I know. I know. Shhh."

Then he crushed me to him with both arms and slipped right back to sleep. I wasn't sure he had woken at all, even though he spoke to me. My arms were trapped by my sides, and my neck was tilted awkwardly, but I held myself still. This was the way he'd put me. I needed to be able to do this small thing for him, have my body be the way he wanted it. I just closed my eyes and tried to will comfort from my body into his.

When I woke up again, it was still dark in the night that would never end. Colin thrust between my legs. He was inside me and over me and everywhere. It wasn't fear or discomfort I felt, but relief. Gratitude that he was letting me do this for him. But he was muttering, "I'm sorry. Sorry." I roused myself enough to mumble, "It's okay," and spread my legs wider, and he quieted. I understood why he was apologizing, though, because he didn't even seem to have control of his own body. It was like his hips were thrusting of their own accord, and the rest of his body just had to go along with it. Each thrust was deep and strong, and with an unsteady but deliberate rhythm. It felt like being claimed, like being marked, protected, and I could hardly describe how that felt different from regular sex, except that I knew it when I felt it.

The irony is that I felt more owned, more controlled, than I ever had during the rough sex I'd craved with other men. He was telling me that I was his—that he couldn't stop it and neither could I, so it was damned convenient that neither one of us wanted to. I don't know how long he went on this way, but I could have taken him forever. My body was already relaxed and pliant from sleep, and I made no effort to change that.

When he came, he groaned my name and then

shuddered over me, clutching me to him. I didn't try to push into him, or away, just yielded completely to whatever shape he gave me.

Chapter Four

The light of the morning teased me, shadows dancing from behind my closed eyelids. Still feeling the lethargy from the night, I opened my eyes to…orange.

Orange fur.

"Goddamn it." I bolted up from the bed, away from the orange hairball curled up on the pillow next to me. I was still gaping at the cat when Colin walked in and stroked my ass. Only then did I realize I was completely naked in the middle of the bedroom while Colin had dressed.

He fitted his body to mine, my back to his front, and nuzzled his face into my hair.

I pointed at the intruder. "The cat. It's yours?"

Colin didn't even look up before he murmured into the side of my neck. "Figured it was yours."

"So, wait. Did you let it in?"

He nodded.

I pulled away from Colin, and he groaned in protest. "Sorry," I said. "But this cat is leaving."

I wrapped the sheet around me and picked up the cat, who'd now gone deadweight. His heft proclaimed that this was no starving kitty. "Absolutely, positively no cats allowed," I said as I carried him down the stairs. Then I set him down outside the door and shut it with a satisfying *click*.

My confessions weighed on me, but the important thing was that Colin was still here. He still wanted me, and that was enough. I'd make it enough. I'd make us a family if it fucking killed me.

Chapter Five

I PEEKED UNDER the blanket draped over the stroller. A cherub with chubby cheeks and tawny curls slept peacefully, in direct contrast to the little devil who'd shattered my eardrums in the house earlier. Bailey had begun insisting, quite loudly, that she was finished with naps. Droopy eyelids at the dinner table and cranky bath times proved otherwise, though. The battles were epic until I found a secret weapon: the cracked, slanted sidewalks of Colin's neighborhood. A few minutes in her stroller, and Bailey was out like…well, like a baby.

I didn't mind the walks. I enjoyed them. Would have done them before, had I not been likely to pass a streetwalker and two drug dealers on a trip around the block. It was like a bad "three guys walked into a bar" joke, but with needles.

Here, there were houses instead of boarded-up storefronts and trees instead of broken streetlamps. I even passed the occasional jogger, a pastime that I'd never understand, or another mom pushing her kid. They'd wave, and I'd wave back. So neighborly.

But I missed my neighbor of almost two years. Shelly hadn't come around since the revelation about

Philip, when she'd said his last name unbidden, and I feared I knew exactly what that meant. Her client, the rich one, the one who liked to hurt her, the one she lived with, was Philip. I already disliked Philip for how he treated Colin—shitty—and how he treated me— like I was invisible. But if I were right, I'd despise him for what he did to Shelly.

I didn't really understand it. She was beautiful, and she'd had long-term clients. With me and Bailey out of the woods financially, at least for now, she didn't need a whole lot of money. So why would she live with him? Did he have something on her? Because he sure as hell held something over me. Oh, just my entire future. All because Colin trusted him, and so I had to by default. No biggie.

A cool breeze whistled through the trees. I leaned over to make sure the blanket was still in place, tenting Bailey in her own warmth. The blanket was fine, but from this angle, reflected sunlight glinted at me from the street. I glanced over.

A parked car, black, vaguely familiar. Was it possible that was the same car Shelly and I had watched from her apartment windows, watching us back?

It had to be a coincidence. I hadn't been close enough to that car, or even this one, to get the exact model. The shape looked similar, but it was common. And so was the color and dark, tinted windows.

What were the odds?

I walked faster than before.

It was silly, I knew, but my heart raced. My body was always betraying me.

Could it be Andrew? He shouldn't even know where we were. And if he did, would he really watch instead of just approaching us? Then again, it hadn't worked so well for him before. Maybe he was waiting for something. Or gathering evidence to use against me.

I sped up.

As I reached Colin's street, I heard the low rumble of an engine. I glanced back as I rounded the corner and saw the car moving away. Good.

I wished I could laugh it off, but my breath was still coming too fast. I paused only at the bigger bumps, not wanting to jar Bailey out of sleep but still needing to get home now. Home, yes. I'd be safe there.

Turning the stroller onto Colin's driveway, I saw the same black sedan pull onto the street from the other side. It had circled the block in the opposite direction I'd gone. And arrived here. A handful of houses down from Colin's house. Within viewing distance. Fuck.

No longer concerned for Bailey's nap, I raced the stroller inside through the back door and slammed it shut. And locked it.

A quick glance; Bailey was still asleep. Normally I would push her into the dining room so she could finish her nap while I got dinner started, but the bay windows in the dining room didn't have curtains. Neither did the cupboard window in the kitchen. None of the windows in this house did—goddamn bachelor pad—making me feel like a bug in a jar.

Who could they be?

Then I realized—cops.

Fucking cops. Of course. They knew about me and Bailey. They knew about Colin and Philip. And they wanted to know more. Stakeout seemed too strong a word, when the most dramatic thing that might happen on our walk was a poopy in Bailey's diaper. Surveillance, though. That made sense. Learning our routines. Trying to get something on us. On Colin.

Protectiveness was a welcome feeling, anger even more so, but it didn't distract from my discomfiture in this house. An hour ago it had been home. Now it was a goddamn evidence storage facility. What secrets did he hide here? Besides me and Bailey, that was.

I had to get out of here. I packed a still-sleeping Bailey into her car seat and drove to the grocery store. I'd put this trip off for a couple of days now, making meals that taxed my creativity with whatever I'd found in the pantry because I had eighteen dollars in my bank account. The credit card Colin had given me only two days after I moved in, all officially printed with my name, had rested unused in my purse. This day had loomed, of course, ever since I'd traded in my apartment and my job for this security. The day when I'd surrendered Bailey and myself completely to Colin's care. Now it was here, when that very security was suspect.

Bailey woke up on the way and fussed. I sang to her

from the limited selection of nursery rhymes I knew. She, thank goodness, turned a deaf ear to the tinny waver of my voice today and settled down.

At the store I distracted myself with price comparisons and Bailey with produce. Bell peppers in particular made excellent toy doubles with their stoplight colors, hardy shape, and ability to go into a stir-fry at the end.

We'd made it through the pantry aisles and were just approaching the dairy section when I heard my name in a hiss. Startled, I glanced behind a display of chocolate syrup to see Rick.

Christ, he'd scared me, huddled behind there like some sort of mugger of perishables. "What are you doing here?" I asked.

He glanced behind him, toward the meat counter, and then back at me. "Come here."

"What? Why?"

"Just...come back here. I need to talk to you." Then he turned and went down a fluorescent-lighted hallway.

Goddammit. Rick always brought the weird. But he was my friend, of a sort, and I couldn't just continue shopping as if I hadn't heard him. I backed up my cart and then pushed it after him. I caught sight of his boot just as some maroon loading doors swung shut. We shouldn't be back here. And I had Bailey with me. I paused.

Rick poked his head out. "Come on."

"All right, all right," I grumbled. This had better be good.

Chapter Six

I PUSHED THE cart through the doors into a large, shadowed room. Stacks of crates sprouted haphazardly from the cold, concrete floor.

The atmosphere of the room demanded I whisper. "What is it?"

"She's so big," Rick said, looking at Bailey.

Well, yeah. It'd been about a year since he'd last seen her, and then only for a brief hello one time when Shelly'd gotten an "emergency" call from a client and had dropped Bailey off at the bakery on her way. Which served to point out that the word "friends" was a bit of an exaggeration for the boss-employee relationship we'd had.

I cleared my throat and spoke normally. "We needed privacy for that?"

"Ah, no. It's about your new guy."

"Colin?" Damn. I had to stop volunteering information, especially with the cops nosing around.

"Yeah, Colin Murphy."

I narrowed my eyes. I wasn't even sure I'd said Colin's first name when I told Rick about him, but I definitely wouldn't have said his last. It hadn't been a secret at the time, but it wasn't Rick's business.

"What about him?" I asked.

"I don't know how much you know about him, but he runs some dirty shit. Anyway, he..." Rick trailed off.

"Spit it out," I said.

"Well, I had some debts. You know, gambling, shit like that. Just around town, but he bought them up. Then he said I had to pay up."

I glanced at Bailey, who'd managed to pull the stem off a red pepper, the use of swear words around her registering distantly in my mind. "Okay...did you want me to talk to him about it? Because I don't really know if—"

"No, not like that," he said. "He didn't want the money."

He looked at me expectantly. I didn't get it. "But you just said..."

"He wanted the bakery shut down," Rick said. "He wanted you out of a job."

More crazy. Shouldn't be surprised. "Why would Colin want me to be out of a job?"

He shook his head. "I'm not explaining this well. He wanted you out of a job so that you'd be dependent on him. For money. And since I was in a shitty situation, he could just make it go away. He knew I couldn't pay up, but he didn't care."

"Wait. Colin came and said all this to you."

"No, no. It was just one of their players. One of his brother's guys."

Yeah, Philip. It seemed as if everything circled back to him, and not in a good way. "But if it wasn't Colin, then it could have just been…"

"He said I had to leave town," Rick said. "And I wasn't allowed to tell you why or give you anything or talk to you after that."

I raised my eyebrows. Of course the thing I'd latched on to would be the useless piece of information, that he wasn't exactly following the rules if he was talking to me now, was he?

Rick flushed. "I left, but I couldn't stay away without you knowing what you're getting yourself into with him."

"Well, it's a little late for warnings now. Jesus, Rick."

"I'm sorry," he said, and I was gratified that at least he did look sorry.

But fuck, I was still annoyed at him. To tell me this at all. To tell me this *now*, when it was clearly too late for caution. I was entirely moved in and financially dependent on Colin, I was a known associate of his and Philip's according to the cops, and Philip and Colin were now, independent of me, it seemed, handling my situation with Andrew. The cart of groceries that Bailey sat in, the groceries I couldn't pay for without Colin's money, underlined the entirety of my dependence.

Bailey picked that moment to throw the stemless pepper at Rick. I wanted to do that too. He caught it and tossed it back, where it hit her in the chest with a soft thud and fell to her lap.

Her eyes widened, and her lips quivered.

Rick gave me a panicked look.

I stared back at him stonily.

"I'm so sorry," he said with his hands up. "I thought she could catch."

All I could think was that men really sucked. Bailey wailed her agreement.

✧ ✧ ✧

I SLAMMED A jar of tomato sauce down, then rethought the object of my aggression when the shelf rattled ominously. From the living room Bailey banged her block down on the floor in solidarity.

The *snick* of the back door let me know Shelly had responded to my summons. I'd left a brief voice mail for her on the drive back from the grocery store. *"We need to talk,"* was all I'd said.

She paused to kiss Bailey on the forehead and then entered the kitchen with a rush of crisp winter air.

I pounced on her. "Who's the guy, Shelly?"

"Okay." She didn't play dumb. "It's Philip. Don't be angry."

"Don't be angry? This guy is like…I don't know! Something bad."

"He's not so bad."

How dare she side with him? "I saw what he did to you."

"He didn't do anything I didn't agree to," she

countered.

Damn. A low blow.

"I'm sorry." She stepped toward me. "I didn't mean it like that."

"No, you're right," I managed to get out.

"No, I wasn't." She reached out her hands for mine. "I'm really sorry. At first I didn't know, and then by the time you told me, there was the thing with the cops, and I knew you'd be upset about it, so…"

I sighed. "Avoidance."

"Learned from the best," she said with a small smile.

That pulled a smile from me. I kept my voice down. "Bitch."

"You love me anyway."

My eyes prickled. "Is this the part where we hug?"

"Let's not," she said.

And I was fine again. I picked up a can of soup from the bag. "I can't believe you're seeing that asshole."

She just gave me a wry look—*I see who pays me*—and crossed to the coffee machine.

Fair enough, but there were limits. Or there should be. "Have you seen his study?"

She started the brew, then turned around and leaned against the counter. "The bullfighter," she said. We both laughed.

But maybe it didn't have to be like this. I wasn't sure how much, but Colin had money. And I knew

Shelly had some saved. "Maybe Colin could…"

"No," she said. "You know how I feel about it." I did. Honest pay for honest work. Besides, I wasn't totally sure Colin would be okay with stealing away Philip's live-in prostitute.

"So if you live with him, is he like your sugar daddy?"

She crunched up her nose. "I hate that term."

"This from the girl who prefers the word 'whore' to 'escort.'"

She laughed. "It's for the same reason. Girls want to act all uppity, but it's all the same."

"Colin is like my sugar daddy, you think?"

She shook her head at me—not "no," but more like it didn't matter. "You did the right thing. We all make deals to get what we need. Everyone has a price."

Colin had once said the same thing to me. Everyone did, and I suppose it was a small comfort that mine was high. Oh, not as high as Shelly's, especially not in terms of hard cash, but choosing me with all my issues, taking in a little girl, spending time with us, that all counted for a lot.

And even when I tried to box it into a neat little agreement, it didn't fit. He could get straight sex from Shelly or someone like her, or just one of those other girls at the club. No, somehow he actually liked me. And I liked him right back, despite his gender. Fucking complications, feelings.

Shelly handed me one of the mugs she'd been preparing.

"I need a favor," I said.

"Anything," she said.

"They've been in contact with Andrew. I need you to find out where he is."

Chapter Seven

An hour. That's how long I'd been in bed staring at the ceiling while Colin was downstairs, "finishing up a few things."

My thoughts were not friendly company tonight.

Rick's accusations stung. More information than I'd wanted, and yet less than I really needed to act on. I wasn't in a position to have any leverage with Colin.

And while I was glad that I'd cleared the air with Shelly, our conversation had dredged up more memories. What I'd told Colin was true; I'd sat there, almost comatose, when Andrew had driven me home.

The weight of what had happened, of what Andrew had done, had sat between us like another passenger in the car. I hadn't dared look at him, afraid I'd see the face of my friend masking a violent stranger. Or maybe I was more afraid that Andrew—sane, safe Andrew—had returned and I'd have to deal with his horror at his own actions.

Before we had even slowed to a stop, I bolted out of the car and ran into my house. I wasn't sure how long I lay there on my bed. Movies showed rape victims rushing to take a shower, to wash it all away, but I just lay there. As if the water would make it real. Or maybe if I scrubbed hard enough, there'd be nothing left. I already knew the important things could never be rinsed off. The shame, the fear. The pain. So it was better not to feel.

I might have stayed there forever, slowly withering away, only found two weeks later when my dad returned from his route. But Shelly had come.

She'd taken one look at my torn clothes and discolored wrists, and she'd *known*. God, the horror of *that*, of someone else knowing about that dark moment, was like another thrust of the rape.

"Who did this?" she'd asked.

I couldn't tell her. I'd seen the way she looked at Andrew when she thought I wasn't looking. The way she invited him to everything, the way she asked after him if I'd seen him without her. I hadn't even been able to tell her that he *liked* me, that he had asked me out, again and again. How could I tell her this?

As it turned out, I didn't have to.

My silence gave it away. *"No,"* she'd gasped.

But she'd brought something new to the table: anger.

Anger was good. I felt it burble in me now, hot springs of wrath. Manipulative. Controlling. Asshole. This had started about Andrew, but now it was about Colin.

Why did Colin have to force things? Well, I answered my own question there. Because I'd told him no, repeatedly. To men, *no* just meant *make me*.

I *had* wanted Colin, but by taking away my choice, he'd degraded me as much as Andrew had. Colin hadn't even had to do it, because I'd needed more money than I could make at the bakery. Because of Andrew. Andrew, who pushed me for custody and then disappeared. Andrew, who Colin had spoken with, but not me.

Was it possible Colin had used Andrew the same way he'd used Rick—to try and force my hand into coming to him? No, that seemed beyond even him. Still, though, the lines had utterly blurred. We'd moved from shades of gray into hot mess.

I couldn't stand the cool sheets, the drafty room, the black, yawning bay windows. There was only one thing to do at a time like this. Night baking. I tiptoed from the bedroom, so as not to disturb the slumbering child across the hall, crept down the stairs, so as not to disturb the hibernating man in the study, and into the kitchen.

I opened the pantry door with a sort of reverence and fingered the packages, like a painter might before selecting his materials. A cheesecake, maybe? I'd gotten enough cream cheese for it. It would have to harden overnight, but in the morning I'd drizzle it with melted chocolate and some of those raspberries.

Or maybe something chocolaty. What was I thinking? Definitely something chocolaty.

A tart. A light chocolate crust, a smooth truffle filling, and a shiny chocolate topping. A bit more foreplay, what with the three separate components, but—ah—the payoff. My eyes glazed at the thought. It was an orgasm in cake form. Really, no one could pamper themselves better than a baker.

I crushed graham crackers for the crust, then pressed the mix into the tart mold I'd bought from Goodwill a year ago. While that hardened in the oven, I whisked eggs and melted chocolate to make my filling. Once the tart itself had baked, I poured a thin layer of glaze over the top, forming a black, glossy surface.

It would take a while to set, so I wandered through the quiet house. There wasn't anything to see, nothing to touch, so my hands rested behind my back.

Light peeked out from under the study door.

I knocked, my timidity downgrading it into more of a tap.

"Come in," he said from inside, and I opened the door.

This study was nothing like Philip's. It was open and airy, matching the minimalism in the rest of the house. A desk and chair filled out one end of the room. A small sofa sat in the other, and that's where Colin lay. He shut the drawer on the side table just as I entered.

"Can I talk to you?" I asked.

"Sure." He rubbed a hand over his face. Dark shadows etched under his eyes, and I felt guilty for my earlier doubt. Not that I was convinced he'd done nothing wrong, but he'd also done plenty right. And at the time he'd been little more than a stranger.

Colin resettled in the corner of the sofa, his arm out. I closed the door behind me and joined him, curling into his side. He wrapped his arm around me, pulling me in tight.

I could have this forever. All I had to do was wait, the perfect, placid little girlfriend, for Colin to solve my problems. Let him control me—trust he wouldn't betray me.

But what would the cost be if I was wrong? If he was?

And Bailey would be the one to pay.

"I'm going to talk to Andrew," I said.

My words kicked him into standing.

"No," he said, sounding exactly like I did when Bailey shoved peas up her nose.

I tried to remain calm. "It's not up to you. He's *my...*"

"Rapist?" he scoffed.

That stung. "My friend."

"And what am I?" he said.

"You're my...lover." My voice broke.

He raised an eyebrow. *Is that all?*

"Well, what are you, then?" Calm was over. His silence infuriated me. "What do you want to be? I don't even know, because you won't...fucking...talk!"

He glared at me. Then a flicker—a small, reluctant smile cracked.

I laugh-cried back at him. Goddamned, fucking, adorable man.

It wasn't just about trust. Living here, I'd started having little daydreams about what it would be like to stay. There wasn't an exit date planned, not that I knew of, but this was hardly a permanent arrangement. Maybe I wanted it to be.

But if I was going to be worthy of that, I'd have to handle my own shit. Whether Colin liked it or not.

"I have to do this. For Bailey and for myself." I pulled out my trump card. "Would you let Philip handle it if someone hurt you?"

His eyes flashed. That was all. Just a small visual sign, but I felt the jolt through his body. Maybe I'd hit a little too hard.

"Actually," he said. "Laramie found a loophole."

Heh, Laramie the lawyer found a loop—and then the meaning of the words registered. Relief was there, but I didn't like his tone. "What is it?"

"If you get him on the rape, then he won't have a legal claim on Bailey."

I blinked. Nope, still didn't get it. Didn't want to understand.

"What does that mean—get him?"

He seemed to choose his words carefully. "If you press charges, prosecute him, and he's convicted, then legally—"

"No fucking way." I'd practically shit myself telling Colin. There was no fucking chance I was going to say it in public. And that's assuming they even *would* prosecute. And that I'd win.

"Allie," he said.

"Colin," I said. "How would Laramie know?"

He didn't meet my eyes.

"No," I whispered. "Tell me you didn't."

His lips firmed.

It was a small comfort that he didn't give me excuses. That it was for the best, or that he had a right to share my secrets. Rage would be great, but all I had left was a whisper. "Fuck you."

I ran from the room, stumbled up the stairs, unseen through my tears, and huddled under the covers. The feeling of my heart being ripped out slipped on like an old shoe. God, the betrayal.

The pain echoed from past wounds, but not just from Andrew.

I remembered my shock at Shelly's furor. I was grateful for her anger on my behalf, but she was more than that. She'd been spitting mad. She'd called Andrew every swear word I'd ever heard, and a few I hadn't, and she never swore. Then she'd insisted I tell the authorities. He couldn't get away with this, she said.

I was confused. Even through my own hurt and anger, I didn't want anything bad to happen to Andrew. He'd been my friend for so much longer than he'd been my rapist. It wasn't a switch I could turn off.

But Shelly's arguments made sense. He deserved

whatever punishment he got for what he'd done. And if I didn't say anything, he might hurt someone else.

A woman on a mission, she kept at me until whatever sanity was left in me wore down.

When I finally wanted to shower, she blocked me. Evidence, she said.

My bruised, sticky body was evidence.

Shelly drove me to the hospital herself. We waited for hours—I wasn't an emergency. She stayed with me until they took me into the exam room. They wouldn't let her come with me.

In a room full of strangers, wearing a small, paper gown that gaped open in front, I was made to lie down on a hard table. There were stirrups there—I'd never seen anything like it before.

"Put your feet here," the doctor said.

I wouldn't do it. The doctor, the nurses, the police officer all coaxed me, but finally they just lifted my legs and put them in. They didn't need my consent either.

They poked me and prodded, ferreted out all the bruises and a few cuts. Cold gloves caught on my flesh. A camera flashed, memorializing my shame. They put their fingers and instruments inside me, where nothing had ever been until a few hours before. They hurt me there too. Everything down there hurt.

The doctor stopped once, to take a phone call. I thought it was his wife, because of the way he kept saying he'd call back soon so many times before he could hang up.

I stared up at the ceiling. First I tried to find shapes in the bumpy ceiling tiles, like the game children play with clouds. But all I found were faces. Inhuman faces, with wide, blank eyes and gaping mouths, swirled above me. I closed my eyes, but that was worse—they could come and get me. So I stared up blankly.

I was waiting for it to be over. Little did I know it would never end.

I'd trusted Andrew, sure. My friend, my pal. But even my adolescent mind knew he was fucked up, and with good reason, and we were both just stupid kids. I'd outwardly agreed with Shelly's venom, but inside, in that part of me as confused and as hurt as Andrew was, I understood him.

I'd trusted these strangers far more. These helpers in the community, these pillars of society—doctors, nurses, policemen. They weren't supposed to touch me, hurt me, humiliate me. At least Andrew had cared enough to hate me while he hurt me. These people were thinking about their shift ending, even while they had their fingers inside me.

When Andrew had touched me, I'd burned from the pain and the fear. When those men had touched me, I'd grown cold. Frozen to ice, never thawed.

In the present I felt the warmth of Colin's touch at my back.

"I'm sorry," he whispered.

I still felt the anger, the hurt, but those things were impotent. At least when you were small like me. So tired. And hell, I didn't want to be mad at him. It probably made me weak, but that was nothing new.

I fought past the lump in my throat. "Give it to me."

He paused. "What?"

"The way I want it. You know."

I felt his indecision as my breath caught. He didn't want to hurt me, I knew, but he'd want to do as I asked, because he'd fucked up. I didn't even know if I wanted him to say yes or no.

"Okay," he finally said, resigned.

Relief and panic warred within me, but both emotions were muted by the sharp pain on my wrist. Why did men always go for the wrist? They wanted to immobilize women, I supposed. Immobilize our hands, at least—were hands really so powerful? Then he tightened his other hand in my hair and yanked. Fuck. Yes, they were.

I slid down the side of the bed, where the hardwood floor slapped my face. My knees jolted as they hit the floor, and then again with the impact of Colin's weight from behind.

All over, my body was twisted or crushed. It was perfect.

I surrendered. There's a freedom in not having to move, not having to think, but knowing it would happen anyway.

My clothes were yanked out of the way, and then he was fucking me.

Each thrust slammed my head into the ground and my shoulders from their sockets. Ah, bliss.

My mind took up a chant. *Hurt me, hurt me, hurt me. Make me hurt, cry, bleed. Make my outside match my inside. Help me get it out, because I can't cry on my own.*

And then my plea escaped my mind. "Hurt me, hurt me."

"Oh, God," Colin groaned.

"Hurt me."

He reached around and pinched my nipple. I gasped. He pressed harder. *Yes.*

"Allie," he said. It sounded like a warning. I couldn't think.

The initial pain of his cock stretching me had passed. I wanted more. I tilted my hips back to meet him. He took the cue and grasped my bare hips with both hands. His fingers dug into me as he rammed my body onto his cock. Fuck, it hurt. *Yes, more.*

My mouth formed the words, but no sound came out. "Hurt me."

"Fuck!" With a final, erratic surge and a long, almost painful moan, he climaxed. He slumped over me, crushing me.

He was right. Fuck.

What had I done? I couldn't face him.

A tear slid down my face. That wasn't strange. My face was wet—I'd been crying before we even started. But this one came from near my ear and slid down to my nose.

It wasn't mine.

I jerked up, which only succeeded in slamming my body against his and then back into the floor. I finally threw him off, heavy and limp as he was, but he covered his face.

"Oh, Colin," I said.

He was dressed, only his fly open. Like a drunkard staggering from a bar, he managed to stand and stumble into the bathroom. He slammed the door in a sick reversal of the scene in the motel that first night with him.

I just sat there on the cold floor, absently rubbing my bruised knees. What had I done? This was so much worse than I'd thought. It wasn't just about turning myself into a whore.

I'd wanted to be hurt, but I'd hurt him.

Chapter Eight

SOMEONE WAS WATCHING me. I could feel it.

If it was that damned cat in here again…

I opened my eyes to round, mischievous blue eyes. "Bailey!"

She blew out her lips, and wetness sprayed me. Nice.

I wiped my face with the sheet, wincing at the contact of fabric on abraded skin. "How did you get in here?"

"My fault," Colin said.

I looked over at the bathroom where he was shaving with the door open. In jeans and nothing else, he looked delicious. How the hell did men get hip bones like that? Even though Colin was not skinny, nor really even lean, there they were. Mine were all padding.

"It's no problem," I said, pulling Bailey under the covers with me. She squirmed and kicked until she was free, lounging on Colin's pillow like a princess.

I stretched, and my muscles screamed a protest. No, last night wasn't a dream. Damn. I looked at Colin again, who was now pulling on a T-shirt, facing away. He headed for the door.

"Colin?"

"Yeah?" He definitely wasn't looking at me.

I wasn't sure what to say. *I'm sorry for being so fucked-up, but you knew that when you signed up with me.* Yeah, that'd go over great. They should print that on greeting cards. So I settled on, "What are you doing today? Want to hang out?"

"I've got to work. Early meeting."

"Oh," I said. "Okay."

A beat passed. "If you want, you guys could come for lunch."

"At the restaurant?"

He nodded.

The only time I'd ever been there was when I'd asked him out. He hadn't asked me back. But here was an invitation, almost engraved. "Yes! We'd love to. Wouldn't we, Bailey?"

"No," she said.

"She means yes," I told him.

"No, no!" she said. Goddammit.

Colin smiled faintly, I could see from the side, and then left the room. With a heave, I sat up and settled the pillows around Bailey. Then I went into the bathroom.

Oh, shit. That explained why Colin wasn't looking at me. The left side of my face was…wrecked. It was all black, a little bit green, and my eye was puffy. Christ, it hurt more to look at me than it had last night. Maybe. I'd been pretty zoned out. He hadn't hit me. More like the floor had hit me, slowly, in a long, painful punch that had pushed harder with each thrust from behind.

I'd be able to patch this up some—some ice and a heavy foundation job would do wonders. But for now I looked hideous. I fretted about whether to say something about it to Colin while I got ready, but when Bailey and I went downstairs, he'd already gone. Ugh, avoidance was contagious.

I puttered around the house, making breakfast and doing some chores, mostly waiting for lunchtime. My face was a half an hour project, so that was a nice distraction. In the right light I looked like someone who'd done a horrible job with her makeup. Looking like an idiot was preferable to looking hurt.

I packed up Bailey's lunch in the kitchen. Hmm, dessert. I eyed the chocolate tart that I'd taken out of the fridge earlier. I did want some. Badly.

More importantly Colin might like it. He was freaked, justifiably, and possibly mad at me—also justifiably. It would be a peace offering, even if I'd initially made it for myself. I mean, if I gave it to him, he'd still share, wouldn't he? Two birds with one stone and all that.

I wrapped the tart in plastic wrap and then bundled us into the car. It only took ten minutes to arrive at the restaurant, and then the unbundling process commenced. Finally Bailey and I sat at a table in the corner near the office hallway. I was debating whether to knock at the door when he emerged.

"You came," he said, sounding surprised. That gave me pause. Did he think me so unreliable? Or worse, did he think our relationship was irreparable after last night? Please, no.

"Of course," I said. "And I brought a cake. You do like chocolate?"

"You made it?"

"Yes…did you notice the bowls and pots covered in black goo in the kitchen?"

He considered. "No."

"Okay, that's…disturbing. But yes, I made it. Do you have a fridge or something where it can sit?"

"Sure." He took the tart from me and disappeared into the kitchen. I returned to Bailey and pulled out her lunch. I hadn't been sure what they'd have here for her, so I'd packed the full complement—pasta, mixed veggies, and milk to drink. We hadn't had much opportunity for eating out, but we'd been here before, at least. Bailey took to her restaurant high chair with aplomb. It was the eating part she struggled with. In minutes the floor around her was littered with lunch. So much for planning.

Colin returned and took a seat across from me. "I ordered for us already. Hope you don't mind."

"No, not at all." I smiled, fishing for one from him. "I bet you know what's best here, don't you?"

He gave a short nod. He looked out the window, at the table, at Bailey crunching carrots—anywhere but my face.

I sighed. "Is it that bad?"

"Is what bad?" he said.

"My face."

He looked at me, and then away. A muscle in his jaw ticked. "Yes."

Well, damn.

Our food came shortly. I suppose since he owned the place, he'd better get prompt service. So we busied ourselves with eating. When we were done, I offered to go back and find the tart, but he went into the back himself. I liked the way the employees looked at him, both with respect and a sort of affection that I recognized in my dealings with Rick. It was a contrast to the formality he'd been dealt at Philip's house.

He returned and, for the first time that day, looked me in the eye. "I'm sorry."

Crap, it'd probably ended up sitting on a lukewarm burner and melted or something. "It's ruined?"

"Sort of. I put it in the back, and my manager thought it was available. He moved it to the front case." He paused. "It's gone."

"Wait, like sold?"

"I'm sorry," he said.

"Well." So much for my apology cake. "That's okay, I guess. At least someone enjoyed it."

"Several someones," he said. There was a note in his voice. Pride? "At eight dollars a slice and ten slices, your cake was eighty bucks."

Shit. Eighty bucks. That was more than the bakery

would charge, though I guessed that by-the-slice was the way to higher profits than selling full cakes.

Yes! There was a smile, however small. "Do you want it?" he asked.

"Want what?"

"Your money."

"Uh, no thanks." That barely covered the grocery bill from yesterday. Plus, it'd been made with ingredients bought with his money. "But I was just thinking. Do you think they liked it?"

"It was gone in twenty minutes."

Okay. "Could I bring in more?"

He paused. "Yes, but you don't have to do that."

"I want to. It will give me something useful to do, and besides, I love to bake." And this could be just what I was looking for—a way to pay Colin back, at least a little.

He looked doubtful.

"I really will enjoy it," I said. "And I won't let it interfere with the house cleaning or anything."

He scowled. This wasn't helping.

I made big eyes, wishing I had Bailey's baby blues. "Please?"

"Don't work too hard," he said.

Score! "I'll be the laziest supplier you ever had," I promised.

A smile flickered on his face. His smiles were like a collector's item for me.

We said our good-byes, veiled in politeness.

Chapter Nine

Back at the house I declared Quiet Time, my nap replacement therapy while Bailey had her midtoddler crisis. She got a couple of plastic books I'd borrowed from the library. I pulled out a magazine—something I'd thrown onto the conveyor at the grocery store on a whim. Who had $3.99 to spend on articles about sex? That would be me, apparently. I opened to "Ten Ways to Blow His Mind with Your Thumb."

I'd only gotten to "deep tissue massage" when Shelly showed up. She should write for Cosmo. Her tips blew more than just minds, I felt sure. She wore a gauzy blue dress that looked at once both naive and flat-out sexual. That contradiction was her specialty.

As she gave Bailey a kiss, I dropped the magazine onto the coffee table. "Do you think Colin wants me to put my thumb in his mouth?"

"Maybe." She sat down, flipping her hair back. "But he'd like it better if you put it in his—"

"Okay." I glanced pointedly at Bailey to stop her. "That's what I figured."

She grinned. "You're cute."

I scowled. "Shut up. It's not like I'm innocent or

something."

"Compared to me, honey, everyone's innocent."

I wasn't so sure about that. "What did you want to talk to me about?"

She examined her nails.

"You got it, didn't you?" A way to contact Andrew.

"I don't think this is a good idea."

"Shelly, I have to," I said. "It's the best way."

"You don't just have a conversation with your rapist."

"It's something I have to do. And I think maybe I can even convince him to walk away. Now that he's had time to really think about it, to get over the shock."

She traced the wood knot on the side table with her fingertip. "Philip says if you press charges, that he wouldn't have a legal claim."

"I can't believe you talked with him about it."

"He brought it up," she said. "I figured I might as well hear what he had to say."

"Well, it's more complicated than that."

"I'm not saying it would be easy, but…" She'd always wanted me to report it, to press charges. And I'd tried, she knew that much. She looked up, anguish in her eyes. "At the hospital. What happened with that cop?"

The lunch in my stomach threatened revolt. The doctors and nurses had left, leaving only the two cops to question me. I could smell the alcohol and sickly hospital smell.

I shook my head to clear the memories. "Why did you push so hard?"

She demurred and sat back. I'd hit my mark.

I'd guessed long ago why she had been so ferocious toward Andrew. A friend would have supported me, but she'd practically taken up a war cry. She was a victim too; that was why. I didn't know the details, but it explained a lot. Not just her reaction that day, but her subsequent profession. One day while I was nursing Bailey, she announced that she was an escort, as easily as if she'd gotten a paper route. It had been part of our tacit pact. She never brought up the rape—or the hospital—and I never questioned her work. She pretended like my "date nights" were normal, and I pretended like selling her body on a nightly basis was A-OK. We were enablers of the best sort.

"Give me the number." My gaze held hers, willing her to do what I asked.

She pressed a few buttons on her phone, then slid it across the table to me. It was opened to a contact—*JW*, it said. Andrew Williams. We used to joke about the fact that our last names started with the same letter. Said I wouldn't have to change my initials when…

I hit the Call button and waited.

"Hello," and just like that, I was back in my childhood room, calling to tell him about the drama of second period. It took a second to return to the present.

"Hello," I said. "It's me."

"Allie? Are you okay?"

I almost laughed at the concern. It felt real. No, it probably *was* real. Our friendship had been real, except for that one time when it wasn't. "I'm okay. I think we need to talk."

"Yeah," he said. "Remember Pop Rocks?"

I smiled at the memory. There was a diner where we'd hung out and gorged on cheap cheese fries and free refills of soda. Then Andrew had made a miniature explosion with his drink and the fizzy candy, and we'd been banned. Not that it mattered now—only two years later and we were both unrecognizable. "I remember."

"Meet me there in thirty," he said.

"Okay." I hung up the phone and handed it back to Shelly. "Can you watch Bailey?"

"Of course," she said. "I miss my girl."

My head was blissfully empty as I drove into that crappy part of town.

The diner was the same, still dirty but somehow smaller. I sat down in a creaky vinyl booth. The lamination was peeling off the tabletop. I rested my hands there, but it was sticky to the touch, so I put them in my lap.

The worst part of waiting was the thinking. What would I tell Andrew? It depended on his mood. He'd become increasingly capricious, up until *that* day—the emotional equivalent of an atomic bomb. It wasn't personal; at least, I thought not. I just happened to be in the vicinity at the time—a casualty.

Thinking, thinking. I heard Shelly's voice, *What happened with that cop?*

Then again in her voice, *Don't think about it.*

I was trying, dammit. I really was.

But the alternative was to contemplate this sticky stuff on the table. No, seriously—what was it? I prayed it was some sort of food product, at least. Ugh, I couldn't keep thinking about it. I reached for the menu the server had dropped off. I was hardly in the mood for eating. I'd already eaten lunch, and plus it was pretty gross in here. But, well, I was desperate.

I ordered chocolate pie. It took about ten minutes, and then the server reappeared with a slice of pie and a glass of water. I cut a small bite from the corner and tasted it. It was good. A bit too sweet. Oh, yuck. A kind of clay aftertaste. I took a gulp to wash it down—metallic water.

I coughed and sputtered. Andrew chose that moment to appear. I clapped my hand over my mouth as he folded his long body into the booth across from me.

"Not as good as you remember it?" He smirked.

I pushed the plate away and shuddered. "I don't know how I ever ate that."

He eyed the slice of pie. "We had a strict fries-only rule, if I remember right. And always order pop."

Our eyes met. "Don't drink the water," we said at the same time. We smiled.

How strange, this camaraderie. Perhaps it had something to do with the location. We'd been friends here, so it was easy to fall into that role now.

We both stilled.

This wasn't the paralyzing panic of our last meeting, after two years of snowballing fear and apprehension. For all I'd known at the time, he could have raped me where I stood. Of course, he'd done worse. He'd threatened to take Bailey from me.

Even as I marveled at my ease, cold fingers of remembrance clenched my insides. No, this grimy diner had been only a very temporary sort of amnesia. Memories assaulted my calm: flashes of pain, the blue eyes flashing darkly, almost too black.

"I missed you," Andrew said softly.

I'd missed him too. My friend, Andrew, I'd missed. The guy he'd turned into that last night, not so much. In the past two years he'd filled out from a lanky teenager, but he was still lean. Probably would always be. I'd filled out too. From skinny girl to pregnant to young woman.

Andrew looked down. "I guess I fucked up pretty bad."

It was both an understatement and stunningly accurate. It also stoppered any recriminations I might have thought to serve him. He knew what he'd done, and he knew it was wrong. What was the point of an accusation, when he'd already accepted the verdict? But there was one thing I wanted to know. "Why, Andrew?"

Remorse was in his eyes when he glanced up at me,

but also confusion. He shook his head as he spoke, as if to negate his words. "I never would have thought… It wasn't planned. I went a little crazy, I guess. More than a little."

That was the rub of it. There was no magic answer.

He wasn't the stereotypical rapist. He wasn't a mean person. He wasn't one of the guys I picked up at the bar. If he'd passed out from the alcohol that night, or if I'd left early, or if so many things, then it might never have happened. Our lives would have been so different, never knowing how close we'd come to breaking.

And I knew all about doing things that were out of character, that went against our ideals, that hurt people. I'd done it once a month, and I'd done it last night. I didn't even have the luxury of them being spur-of-the-moment. Mine were so deliberate.

"Where have you been?" I asked, because it seemed like the thing to say. And maybe I was curious.

"Marines." He grinned, and little-boy Andrew peeked out at me. "You didn't think I could do it."

"Did they kick your ass?"

He made a solemn face, but his eyes still twinkled. "Absolutely."

Idiot. "Good."

"What about you?" *And our daughter* was unspoken.

"Nothing much. I worked in a bakery." I wondered if he thought back to when I'd brought over chocolate-chip cookies, his favorite. Or when I'd made cupcakes as both our contributions to the school bake fair, since neither of us had mothers to do it for us. Or when I'd made brownies, laced with more adult things. I wondered but didn't ask. The pain mixed with nostalgia—bittersweet.

"And now?" he asked.

I blushed.

"Ah," he said. "Colin Murphy, right?"

Something flickered—had I told him Colin's name? I must have. "Something like that."

His eyes darkened as his gaze raked down the side of my bruised face. "He's treating you right?"

I raised an eyebrow. As if he were one to worry about my well-being. He hadn't only hurt me, but he'd kicked off the chain of events that had *hurt* me. The doctors and nurses, then the… *Don't think about that.* "What're you going to do if he's not?"

"Hey, it's not all sunshine and candy in the military."

I gave him a full-body perusal back. He'd clearly gotten built since years ago, but he didn't have Colin's bulk. Nor did he have Colin's determination, no matter if he'd matured in the past two years. I had the feeling Colin's fortitude had been forged early, making him a lot older than the six years that separated us.

"Still," I said. "I wouldn't pick a fight with the guy, if I were you."

"Wouldn't dream of it. I'm still recovering." He

touched the corner of his eye.

Now that I looked—yes, there were some shadows there, maybe even discoloration. "He hit you?"

"Just once, and it was way less than I deserved," he said. Hadn't Colin promised not to hurt him? Or had that just been me? Either way I couldn't be too hard on him for showing restraint. In the wilds of the Chicago underground, a black eye was more a warning shot than punishment. I couldn't deny that a very small sense of satisfaction welled inside me. As he said, it was the least Andrew deserved, but all he would get.

"We make quite a pair." Both bruised by Colin but loving him anyway. That last part was probably just me.

"I always thought it would be me and you, in the end." He sighed. "Tell me about her."

Bailey. The longing in his eyes pierced me, but I shook my head. "It will only make it real, and it can't work like that."

I expected the questions—why not?—or for the demands to start, but he looked as solemn as I'd ever seen him. And despite the conflict that warred in his eyes, he said, "I know."

My heart leaped in hope. "So you'll leave us alone?"

A wry smile, then, "You charmer, you." He grew serious. "Yes, I'll leave you alone. I stayed away because I couldn't trust myself around you. I didn't want to hurt you again. But I think I also didn't want to see you suffering. I told myself you could pretend it was bad sex and move on. I didn't know about…her. I wouldn't have left you to deal with it alone."

"We did okay," I said, thinking it was probably true. "And I had Shelly."

"She had a few words for me when I called her. Between her and *him*, you've got a nice little army at your back."

A slow smile spread on my face. It was a nice thought, anyway.

"I just wish I'd been one of them," he said. "You have to call me if you need something, though. If things don't work out with what's his face."

"Colin."

"Whatever," he said. "Promise me."

"Maybe."

"Good. I'm only on leave, but if you need me, call the base." He pulled a thick envelope from his pocket and slid it across the table. "That was my retainer for the lawyer. It's yours. And I'd like to send more if you'll let me."

I recoiled at the pile of money in front of me. I didn't want his money, but this was for Bailey. It could pay for things she needed, and I was supposed to be a grown-up. "Okay."

He eyed me curiously. "I'm surprised he let you off his leash enough to see me. He was very close-lipped about where you were."

I feigned interest in the pie. Colin would be beyond pissed.

"Ah, he doesn't know." He tapped the table, then rubbed his fingers together. "What the fuck is on this table? Whatever. Here's what I'll do. I'll sign those papers he gave me, giving up any paternal rights that might now, or forever in the future, be established against one Bailey Allison Winters, and send them to him. We don't have to mention this meeting."

"You'd do that for me?" I asked.

"Anything," he said.

Shelly had once said that to me too—anything. Maybe Andrew was part of my army, after all. An unexpected ally.

"Thank you," I told him and meant it. His debt to me wasn't so great that I couldn't still feel gratitude.

He dropped a twenty on the table and walked away, murmuring. "Bye, Alice."

The nickname stung. He used to call me that, back when we were kids. Alice in Wonderland, he'd say. I'd protest, because she was dumb and I wasn't. He'd proved me right, of course. I just hadn't known the only mirror I'd fall into would be him.

I tucked the money he'd given me in my purse and left the diner, vowing not to go out to eat again for a year. It was a nice gift he'd given me, letting Bailey and me walk away. Or rather, doing the walking away himself. Sure, it'd been a problem that he'd started, first by *that* and second by coming in and threatening me, but I could still appreciate what it meant for him to sign those papers. Or maybe I was just a sentimental dumbass.

I drove home, struggling to tamp down my elation. No need to tempt fate by getting hopeful.

"Colin called while you were out," Shelly said as soon as I walked through the back door.

"Hey, baby girl," I said to Bailey, picking her up and nuzzling her tummy. Then to Shelly, "Damn, what did you say?"

She looked apologetic. "I said you were out jogging."

I shot her an exasperated glance as I dislodged Bailey's fist from my hair. "I don't jog."

"I know. I'm sorry. It was all I could think of."

I still hadn't been sure I would keep my visit with Andrew from Colin, but this would make telling the truth more awkward. Still, my worry over Colin couldn't conceal my thrill over the result.

"So tell me what happened," she said.

My voice muffled from beneath Bailey's clinging arms, I said, "It's over. He said he's going to sign away his parental rights and leave us alone."

"Just like that?"

"Yep," I said.

She collapsed on the other end of the sofa, still managing to do it with grace. After a moment she said, "Then you didn't really need Colin."

Hell, I hadn't even thought of that, but it wasn't true. He provided financial support, physical protection, and stability. He cared for me and, I thought, even for Bailey, rounding out our little family. And, though it now seemed a small thing in light of his contributions, "He got the lawyer who's doing the custody paperwork."

She seemed to hear what I'd left unsaid, though, because she weighed it thoughtfully. "Will you stay here?"

"I want to."

She nodded. "I'll go now, but I think I'll be seeing you soon." With that cryptic note and a wink, she went out the back.

Left holding a wriggly Bailey, I laughed aloud at Andrew's assessment of Shelly as my soldier. She may help me—a lot—but I had no illusions that she took orders from me.

Chapter Ten

Bailey was fed and—hallelujah—sleeping. I was halfway asleep too, but this laundry wouldn't fold itself. It was a load of linens, though. No Colin underwear tonight. I stifled the urge to giggle. It really was getting late.

A soft scratching came from the front door. I tensed. More shuffling. The break-in at my apartment flashed through my mind. Worse things than random junkie burglars lurked as well. It could be something mixed up with Philip's business. Plus, threats could come with badges and warrants.

I tiptoed over to the window and peeked around the side. I had a clear view of the front of the door. Nothing.

That was worse.

This was the part in the scary movie where the girl did something stupid while the audience groaned. She would open the door and let the bad guy in. No, she'd open the door, and it would turn out the bad guy was already in the house. Shit, I was scaring myself. I could suddenly understand her compulsion to find out. Knowing had to be better than sitting here pissing myself.

I opened the door a crack—chain firmly in place—and the orange cat squeezed through the gap and into the house.

I sighed in relief. "Stupid cat."

The cat leaped onto the coffee table and curled up amid the stacks of sheets and towels.

"Make yourself at home," I said, but cats don't care about sarcasm, and I didn't have the heart to throw him out. This night was dark and scary. Or at least lonely.

"If you shit on the towels," I told him, "I will turn you into a shag rug." He seemed unconcerned. I took this to mean he was potty trained.

Headlights swerving against the wall and a low rumble told me Colin was home. He unlocked the back door and then was in front of me. "Sorry I'm late."

I should tell him I saw Andrew. Now, before I lost the chance. "I worried about you."

He ran his thumb across my lips. "Pretty girl."

"Are you…drunk?"

He shook his head slowly. "A little bit."

"You shouldn't drive like this." I didn't want to nag, but it was only the truth. I wrapped my arms around his waist.

He pulled me close and rested his face in my hair. He smelled like smoke. "I like you."

Wow, he really shouldn't have driven. Clearly it would do no good to talk about it now. "Come on," I said. "To bed with you."

His arms tightened. Seemed no one was much for sleep in this household.

"You'll feel better in the morning," I said.

"Feel good now." His voice was muffled in my hair.

"That was a lie anyway," I said. "You'll feel worse in the morning, but you still have to sleep."

I pulled back, and this time he let me go. Leading him by the hand, we went upstairs. I pushed him into the bathroom and shut the door, then listened until I heard the water running before changing into a nightshirt.

Ten minutes passed, and I debated knocking when he opened the door. Completely naked.

Though—and I double-checked—not aroused. I didn't think I'd ever seen him that way, except for right after sex. And even then it was more of a half-mast situation. It was oddly deflating to my ego, even though I knew it was most likely whiskey dick.

"Well," I said.

But it wasn't the time for talking or for turning off the bathroom light, because he grabbed my hand as he walked by me, dragged me into bed with him, and wrapped his arms and legs around me like a Colin-shaped straitjacket.

Okay. I guess I was going to sleep.

"Good night," I said.

"Don't want to hurt you," he mumbled. Then nothing.

No, he didn't want to. I was the one doing any hurting here, even if the one in pain was me.

I hadn't told him about Andrew, and it was becoming increasingly difficult to do so. I should just let it go, I knew. I had been given a free pass by Andrew not to tell Colin, and that should be good enough.

In fact, his arms, which had once been snug, now felt stifling. A literal weight of guilt.

Even if I were to tell him, I should wait until morning when he was awake. In fact, I should wait until tomorrow afternoon when his hangover had passed, but I had a feeling that if I didn't tell him now, I never would. I'd ruined many good things in my youth and stupidity—often one and the same—but I desperately wanted to make this work.

"Colin." I nudged him.

A quiet snore emerged. Silly man.

I pushed harder. "Colin!"

"What's it?" he mumbled, without opening his eyes.

"I have good news," I said. That was preframing, something I'd learned in one of the books from the library about parenting toddlers.

No response.

"I talked to Andrew," I whispered, "and he's going to sign the papers."

"No," he said, startlingly clear. "It's a trap."

And then as far as I could tell, he slept on. It took me a long time to fall asleep after that.

Chapter Eleven

When I woke up, a note was on Colin's pillow. In bold, block letters: *Call me.*

So he was as terse in writing as he was in speech. He'd never left this early, but if he'd received a call, I had a suspicion I knew what it was about. I dialed his cell number—he answered on the first ring.

"Good news," he said.

Shit. He didn't remember my confession from the night before. What to do? I opened my mouth to interrupt, to tell him the truth.

"Andrew's taken care of," he said. "I'm with Laramie now."

The words caught in my throat. Over the phone and with Colin sitting in his brother's house most likely, was not the time or place to tell him, but I had to say *something*. I pushed past the panic lodged in my throat. "Oh," I said, my voice hoarse. "That's good."

A short pause. "It's going to be okay."

"Yeah," I said, my voice breaking on my agreement.

"I'll be home soon. We'll celebrate." He hung up.

Oh God, he was so horribly perfect. All concerned for my state of mind and trying to reassure me. Dealing with my shit, and for what? I couldn't even have sex right. I would've thought two years was enough time to heal, but it was abundantly clear that I wasn't okay. I was as messed up as ever, and worse, it was infecting Colin.

If he were just a little less wonderful, then my brokenness wouldn't seem so bad. As it was, we fit together like a diamond in the gutter. On the outside we were well matched, but on the inside he was slumming with me. What would happen when he realized it? I'd be alone again, and Bailey would be back in that shit-poor apartment. At least the problem with Andrew had been resolved, I was thankful for that, but I didn't want to go back to the way things were.

I couldn't let that happen. I wouldn't.

I'd glimpsed happiness here. I might not deserve it, but Bailey did.

No, I wouldn't even put this on her. I wanted this for myself. Living all ghetto had one major benefit—it had molded me this way. Ruthless.

From somewhere deep inside I dredged up the will to fight. A low-down, dirty street fight between me and, well, the other me. The stupid one who lied and fucked and hurt but had no business in Colin's life. Her death was a worthy sacrifice so that Bailey and Colin and I could be a family.

And when Colin came home, offering a bouquet of daisies, I accepted them as my right. I thanked him as was appropriate. And I kissed him as I really wanted to—hard and deep.

It almost felt real. Maybe it was.

I felt fidgety, bursty, like I might explode but laugh right on through it. Was this happiness?

I wanted to jump Colin, though that feeling wasn't new. But I didn't want him to hurt me. I didn't want him to hold me down or berate me. I wanted him to touch me, hold me, *love* me. I wanted to hear his voice again telling me everything would be okay. And, because happiness made me horny, I wanted his tongue on my clit. *Pretty, pretty please.*

But life intruded. I had Bailey, and that meant no midday sex romps.

"Let's go out," Colin murmured.

"Okay." Think, think. Where did people go? None of our usual haunts—the library, the city park, the local playground—seemed adequate for this day when Colin would spend the day with us. A day of celebration.

And then it came to me—the zoo! We'd gone there once, but it had been so crowded and Bailey so young. A family thing, a real outing.

"What do you think of the zoo?" I asked Colin, trying to keep the excitement out of my voice in case he hated it.

"The zoo." He nodded.

Bailey had been crawling figure eights around our feet, but now she stopped to look up. "Baba?" she asked.

Colin knelt down where he stood. Bailey pulled

herself up by his knee to a stand.

"Want to go to the zoo?" he asked her.

She tapped his knee.

"She probably doesn't know what that means," I said.

"Giraffes," he said. "Elephants."

"Elphhhhhh," Bailey said, spraying baby drool into his face.

"Oh!" I grabbed a nearby cloth and wiped him dry. "I'm sorry. I think she's getting a tooth."

He looked alarmed.

"Makes her drooly," I said. "Plus the 'phhh' sound."

"Ah," he said. He didn't sound too upset about the baby bath, for which I was thankful.

"Would it be at all possible for you to hang out with her while I get ready?"

At Colin's nod, I hurried into the kitchen. Packing her bag for a long outing like this would take a while. I needed food and drinks and diapers and wipes and a change of clothes. Oh, and the camera. Crap, was it charged? Had I even unpacked it?

On a whim, I raced up the stairs to get Bailey's animal flash cards. I handed them to Colin and said, out of breath, "You could show her these if you want."

Then I was gone, loading the stroller and diaper bag into the car. And I was done. Bravo to me. Already feeling worn-out, I found Colin and Bailey on the living room floor where I'd left them.

"Phant," Colin said. "El-e-*phant*."

"Phhhhhhhhh," Bailey said. Prepared this time, Colin blocked her easily with a cloth to catch the spray. She giggled.

"Phhhant," he said.

"Phhhhhooey," she said, then broke into peals of laughter when he wiped his hand.

"She's playing you," I said from the doorway.

He glanced back at me and winked. "I'm a sucker for that laugh."

Ah, shit.

Stick a fork in me, I was done. Completely, positively, irrevocably in love with him. That too-full feeling closed in on my heart, and my eyes pricked. I turned to face the coat closet just to catch my breath. Oh God, I wanted to keep him.

Bundled and packed, we set off on our zoo adventure. Or as Bailey called it, the "phoooo" with a sprayed exclamation point. I would not be sad when she learned a new sound.

The Lincoln Park Zoo was packed with families. Today was one of the first days of the year that we could spend time outdoors without freezing our fingers off. We wandered over to the lions—"Kitty!"—and then to the seal enclosure. The seals did tricks: clapping, diving, and barking, but there were too many people lined up against the railing to see.

"Up," Bailey demanded, tugging on a lock of my hair.

"No." I shook my head.

Colin looked at me in question.

"She wants to sit on my shoulders," I explained. "I tried that only once. It was the Fourth of July, and she was wrapped around me like a cobra"—I mimed a choking motion with my free hand—"and then a BOOM went off"—I mimicked the struggle—"and, well, never again."

"I can try," he said.

I looked at him dubiously. Not that the guy wasn't tough, but he'd never seen her go full turbo. As if sensing her impending triumph, Bailey wriggled furiously.

"Fine." I handed her over with a sigh.

He lifted her and—BAM!—tiny elbow to the eye.

"I'm sorry," I said, though I couldn't sound too sorry. I *had* warned him.

"She does have an arm on her," he said but managed to wrangle her onto his shoulders.

Bailey squealed in what I guessed was both excitement and fear of her new height. Her legs crossed tightly around his neck, and her arms wrapped around his forehead, leaving only a slit for his eyes.

I bit my lip to avoid laughing. "Having fun yet?"

"I'm okay," he wheezed.

He wasn't the only one. Around us a sea of men held children on their shoulders or in their arms. Fathers, one could assume. Though in our case they'd be wrong. How many of these men were the biological fathers of these children, and how many were just father figures? Because that's what Colin was to Bailey, a father figure, even if it had only been for a short time.

This was a side of men that had been unfathomable during my monthly date nights at the club. How many of these men had once been, or even now were, the guys at the club? How many of them were like Andrew, with a horrible mistake in their past? For that matter, did Colin have a mistake like that in his?

There was nothing for it but to wonder. The smiling faces and caring gestures painted only happy portraits. I wanted to believe in it. Here, amid the laughter and shouts of children, I almost could.

Before the show was over, Bailey grew fidgety, and we wandered over to the children's section. She let out a shriek. I followed her reaching hands to the carousel.

With a groan, I wondered how I could get out of this without a screaming fit. Even if I let her have a ride, she'd only want to go again and again.

It turned out that Colin had the answer to that. When he left to go get tickets, I figured he'd get two, one for me and one for her. He came back with twenty.

"What are we going to do with twenty tickets? That's ten rides."

He shrugged. "If she doesn't want to, we can save some for later."

Of course she wanted to. By the third ride I was ready to throw up, so Colin offered to take her. While I had firmly insisted she pick an animal to ride and stick with it, Colin helped her bounce from horse to zebra to otter in the minutes before the ride started. She chattered endlessly to him while he danced attendance.

Good Lord, was that how he and I looked together? For all his trouble, that man needed to get laid way more often.

They went round and round and round, until both Colin and Bailey had turned a sickly green. Turns out when you gave her exactly what she wanted, she didn't want it anymore. She was her mother's daughter.

Two hours and a detour through the petting zoo later, it was past time to leave. Despite the brisk air, the smell of sweat and tiredness trailed us. Bailey was coated with sticky residue from a slush drink and peppered with salt from a soft pretzel. I might as well have tried to scrub off the city's graffiti for all the good the baby wipes did.

Bailey cried all the way to the car. Actually the parking lot was filled with screaming children. There was probably no better torture device invented for children than a superfun outing. No matter what, it always ended in tears.

Chapter Twelve

At home I gave her a rushed dinner and warm bath. And the very good, somewhat unexpected benefit to the whole excursion was that she fell asleep almost immediately. I was still gross and exhausted, but it was freeing, nonetheless, to have her down so early.

I found Colin in his bedroom. "You hungry?"

"A little bit," he said. "Come here."

He drew me to him and pressed a soft kiss to my lips. I pulled back and made a face. "I'm gross."

He pulled me back and kissed me harder. Well, okay, if he wanted me this way, he'd have me. I wouldn't say no. I'd learned long ago what a mistake that was.

"Shower?" he asked.

"Um," I said. "You or me?"

His lips curved into a smile against mine. "Both."

Oh. Of course. Not that I had ever done that before, but even I knew that's what lovers did. I suppose it was because I'd never had a lover before, not really. Andrew had been my first, and then the date nights had been about the opposite of cleanliness. I knew Shelly would laugh at me now and call me innocent, and maybe she'd be right, but I wanted to learn. I wanted to experience everything with Colin.

"Come on, then," I replied, donning my slutty persona. She'd know what to do.

He cocked his head as if I puzzled him.

Time to distract him. I pulled off my shirt with a small flourish. Then my jeans with a shimmy, until I stood in only my bra and panties. It worked—he came at me.

"Uh-uh." I stopped him. "I thought we were going to shower."

He reined himself in with a small shudder.

I turned on my heels and sauntered into the bathroom, satisfied when I heard him enter behind me. Still facing the shower, I undid the clasp of my bra at the back and let it drop before me. Then I wriggled the panties down my legs. At last I threw a glance over my shoulder, letting him see the arousal on my face.

He'd somehow beat me to naked. God, that body. I wanted to eat it up, and if this night went the way I wanted it to, I would. Lines of muscles crossed with male hair. And that cock, long and hard. The complement to my body. I'd never been a religious person and probably never would be, but if there was anything that could convert me, it would be this. That much perfection couldn't be an accident.

I wasn't sure what should happen next. My whorishness failed me, eclipsed by inexperience. Should I start the water? And what did we do while it turned to hot? All of a sudden I was awkward and gangly, the virgin teenager again.

Impervious to my quivery indecision, Colin reached around me and turned the shower on, testing the water until it was the right temperature. Then he stepped under the spray and put his hand out. I followed him in and shivered under the warm water. The dampened skin of our bodies kissed tentatively, while our lips above remained parted. Steam encased us, muting the outside world and hiding us from it.

Our eyes met. I breathed and felt his breath on my lips. Something passed between us, a tether that both sides grabbed hold of, never to let go. Silly thoughts. I'd turned soft and without even the excuse of alcohol. It was all me. Stupid, vulnerable, loving me.

My throat tightened.

Don't let me fall.

And then he was kissing me, holding me—no, he wouldn't drop me. He turned me around, so that the spray of the shower fell on my breasts. From behind he roamed the curves and dips of my body. I reached my arms up to rest in his hair, anchoring myself to him.

Both his hands cupped my breasts, his fingers massaging my nipples. They felt swollen and sensitive, like they had after Bailey had been born. The tap, tap, tap of the water on my breasts fused with his touch. Pleasure tipped over into almost pain and wrung low moans from me. His cock lay slick and warm against my ass, but it never pressed me. No, it was my hips that rocked back, desperate and wanting.

Please, they begged.

Have patience, his leisurely caresses admonished.

His fingertips traced the lines of my belly and down. Down across the crease where the gentle curves of femininity leveled into the velvety skin of sex. I was bare. I'd shaved myself every day since I'd moved in, instead of just in preparation for my date nights. I'd had more sex here with Colin than I'd had in the sum of all my date nights. Years' worth of sexual experience overwritten in a week.

His hands on my sex were familiar now. They knew me, what rhythms pleased me, and how I liked to be touched. The knowledge was an intimacy so much greater than the fitting together of bodies.

The shower decorated my skin with droplets. Colin lapped them up with openmouthed kisses to my neck and shoulders. I felt luxurious, sensations assailing me from both sides. I felt worshipped, Colin's hands and mouth revering my skin. I felt protected, wrapped tightly in his arms, his shower, his home. God, I felt loved. This was love. Fuck.

Suddenly that bursting feeling felt all too literal. There was too much. Too much happiness, too much love. Too much fear. My body shook as it struggled to contain the explosion. However it would come, it wouldn't be pretty—I never was.

I turned in his arms, needing the intimacy of face-to-face. He resisted at first, wanting to continue his assault on me, but I was insistent. It was his turn. Or really it was mine. Nothing felt better than pleasuring this man.

The air was thick with moisture—that had to be why my breaths were shallow and my eyelashes wet. His eyes were the potent black of a lake, drowning me, but his arms rested at his sides. I surveyed his body like an explorer does a map. I wanted to visit each place if only I could decide where to go first.

I sprinkled my fingertips across his shoulders, then trailed them lower to his flat, brown nipples. Leaning forward, I licked one of them, then nibbled across to the other. I started to kiss my way down. I knew where he wanted my mouth, of course. I wanted it there too.

I flashed back to when I'd tried to go down on him the very first time we'd had sex. He'd stopped me. I hadn't understood what he was about, then. He'd wanted to give me pleasure; that was nice. But he didn't want to receive pleasure, and that was just perverse, especially for a man.

I realized something. He'd been respectful and generous, not things I'd expected nor even wanted from a guy at the club. But something he hadn't been was open. He'd kept himself closed off from me, piercing my walls but not letting me in himself. I'd been so distracted by his invasion, his domination of me, that I hadn't noticed his own reserve. It had been okay, then. We'd been strangers.

But not now. Oh, he'd let me blow him now. I'd

already done it several times, and I was sure I'd do it again tonight, but he still held himself back from me. As horrible as the last time we'd had sex had been, at least I had reached him inside then. Of course, I'd reached him through pain and shame in a way that neither of us wanted to repeat. Could I reach him this way, through pleasure? I could try.

Tugging on his arm, I made him turn around. He looked a little bit confused and a little more frustrated he wouldn't be getting what he wanted. *Have patience.* I grinned at him.

I placed his hands against the wall at the back of the shower so that his body canted forward. And then I did what I wanted to do, hoping it would please him too. I licked along the seams of his muscles, starting on his back as high as I could reach on my tiptoes, and making my way down. I took my time, stopping to explore every path, every route, sometimes backing up to taste another. I used my hands to mark my progress along his backside, occasionally slipping them around front to stroke his erection, like an erotic compass.

I roved over his ass, tracing the indents at his side and even slipping my tongue in the crease. Then lower, across the backs of his thighs. I knelt behind him, a supplicant with all the power. Above me he shook and groaned into the wall, but I barely heard him over the rush of water in my ears.

I had just reached his calves when he snapped.

Without warning he turned. One hand behind my

head and the other on his cock, he guided my mouth to him. He pushed his cock inside, held it there, and then pulled back. Then again. In and out, he thrust. I rested my hands on his thighs and let him use my mouth.

And Colin, my taciturn, reserved Colin, spoke to me in words of sex and love. "Fuck, yes," he said. "I love your mouth. Jesus…Fucking…Christ, take me. That's right. Deeper. Christ, Allie. Fuck!"

I could feel the shudders that worked through him, telling of restraint, but he wasn't gentle. I felt no respect or generosity, kneeling here on the hard tub bottom as he fucked my mouth, but he'd let me in. This was Colin, harsh and demanding. Open and beautiful.

"You're so fucking sexy," he said. "Jesus! Beautiful. There, suck on the tip. Now open, deeper. All the way, hold it. *Yes.*"

The words tumbled out of his mouth. I'd opened the floodgates. Even though I knew they'd close again eventually, this was as close as I'd ever be to him, here with his cock in my mouth.

"I want to hold it in," he said. "Just for a little while. Take a deep breath. Now, there. Ahhh, Jesus. You're okay. I've got you. Fuck…fuck."

He pulled me back, and I sucked in breaths. I'd gagged, and tears had streamed down my cheeks, but thank God, he hadn't stopped. We did it twice more, my nose to his groin while his cock pulsed inside my throat. There could be no greater gift than my breaths.

No greater sign of trust than my life in his hands.

Then he was pulling me up and out of the shower. We both dripped buckets onto the floor, but neither of us cared. He tossed me onto the bed, and I laughed. Then he spread my legs and put his mouth on me—yes, there, down, lower, *yes!*—and I forgot everything.

He'd lost any tenderness, but with rough strokes and kisses edged with teeth, he made me violently come. Before I could even see again, breathe again, he was over me and inside me. Our still-wet bodies rammed together, too hard and too fast, making squishy sounds that would have been embarrassing if I could think.

He fucked me so hard I couldn't have said a word, but he was talking again. In between thrusts and on his exhales, he gave me more.

"Allie…you're…so…fucking…beautiful…I…never…want…to…stop…fucking… you."

The only response I could muster was to relax my hips even more so that my thighs spread open farther. It was more than an invitation; it was a plea. The pressure built until I came. He rode it out, and I waited, blissfully mindless for him to come.

But he didn't.

He thrust into me again and again until I lost track of the hour or the day. I came again.

And he didn't stop.

"Can't," I gasped. "Can't…anymore."

"Yes," he said. "You can. I'll show you."

And fuck, he did. I lost count, but by the end my orgasms were nothing more than a small spark. He groaned long and hard, and I thought then that if there were anything left in me, I would come just from the sound.

His body collapsed over mine, the only movements between us his heaving chest and the small twitches of his cock as it settled.

I couldn't breathe, but then I'd already decided to give it all to him, even my breath. I'd been so sure I would never trust a man again, and here I'd trusted Colin more than should be possible. With my life and my future, even with Bailey. I trusted him more than I trusted myself, though that wasn't much of a compliment.

He rolled off me but kept me with him, pulling me into a tangle of limbs. We shared the same air as we both caught our breath, neither of us willing to relinquish the intimacy for space.

Chapter Thirteen

I OPENED MY eyes to find him watching me. I watched him back. Neither of us said anything. Sex was a pure form of communication, maybe the only honest one. I'd known that from my first time, painful as the lesson had been, and I'd sought the same honesty from each date night. But what we'd unveiled here tonight was so much more lovely than anything I'd found on my date nights, more than anything I'd imagined. I came for the adventure but found a bounty at the end.

His stomach grumbled. I smiled, and he smiled back. I'd learned he got hungry after sex that very first time. Only this time we wouldn't be driving away from a motel separately but sharing a late meal in Colin's home. My home too.

"I'll get us something." My voice resounded through the quiet. "Stay here."

I slipped on a T-shirt and then realized it wasn't my nightshirt but one of his white undershirts. It was shorter, almost to the top of my thighs, and my still-hard nipples poked out indecently, but it matched my mood. I padded downstairs, flipping on only a lamp in the living room so as not to disturb the night too much.

The refrigerator shone brightly, and I blinked until I could see the contents. Leftover chicken potpie from last night. An uncooked lasagna I had put together in anticipation for tonight. Ingredients for sandwiches. It was all wrong. The blackberry cheesecake beckoned, but it was for the restaurant. And besides, I couldn't get away with eating sweets on an empty stomach. I wasn't a kid anymore.

The squeak of the pantry door alerted me that Colin hadn't listened. That wasn't a surprise, of course. Colin could be extremely obedient…so long as he wanted to be. Any docility he displayed, it wasn't so much an act as much as it was a complete lack of show. He'd do what he wanted. Sometimes the rest of us would like it, sometimes we wouldn't, but his actions were his own, without any of the pomp and circumstance of rebellion or pride.

I liked to think we had that in common. I was happy to obey him when I could.

That he'd pressured Rick because of me, well, I didn't like that. But that was Colin, and I had to accept it if I wanted him. I wouldn't be so vulgar as to try to change him.

And me talking to Andrew, well, Colin wouldn't like that. But I'd had to do that, and I wished he could accept that too. If only he'd heard me when I'd had the courage to tell him.

He held up a box of pancake mix and quirked his eyebrow in question. I supposed he'd used up his allotment of words.

"Sure." I held out my hand.

He walked past me and got a bowl. I rolled my eyes. Stubborn man.

I heated the griddle and greased it with butter—liberally, because these hips didn't fill themselves out—while he mixed the ingredients. He poured the batter, and when it was time, I flipped them over.

We made six pancakes, split two for me and four for Colin, and had just sat down to eat when Colin's phone rang. I pushed back the resentment. At ten at night, it would only be Philip.

"Hi," he said. "No, not sleeping."

I made a face at him.

"Mmm-hmm," he said.

With a wicked smile, I trailed my foot up the inside of his leg. If he was going to take calls during dinner, at least I could have a little fun.

"I'm not sure," he said. "You can ask her."

He handed me the phone, paying me back twofold for my little tease. *Damn.*

Not really having a choice, I took the phone. "Hello?"

"Hi, Allie. This is Rose."

My eyes flew to Colin's, but I said, "Oh. Hi there."

"Listen. I wanted to apologize for giving you a hard time when we met. And I was hoping you'd all come over for dinner. Bailey too."

I opened my mouth and then shut it. How could I get out of this? It wasn't a rhetorical question. My eyes beseeched Colin. He shrugged. Useless, stubborn man.

"I'd love to," I said.

She laughed. "It won't be that bad. I promise."

I didn't quite believe her, but it didn't matter. "I'll be fine." Pray that it was true.

"Okay," she said. "You'll see. How about next Saturday night at seven?"

"Sure. Sounds great."

"Perfect," she said. "Oh, and I'll host it at Philip's. You've already been there, and it encourages him to come if we have it in his house." She laughed. "See you there."

"Bye," I choked out.

"She wants to have dinner," I told Colin.

He nodded slowly.

"At Philip's house," I said.

He gave me a sympathetic grimace.

I suppose that was the best I could hope for. Perhaps this "meet the family" would go better than the first time around, but it could hardly be worse. My issues with Philip were mostly over now that Andrew was out of the picture. And besides, I doubted he would spend much time talking to me, judging by last time. Rose had apologized and offered this dinner as an olive branch, if I'd understood correctly. Maybe it was even a sort of welcome.

It wouldn't exactly be fun, but this was part of a real relationship. A family dinner, I mused. It was almost quaint in its normalcy.

I narrowed my eyes at Colin. "If I'm going to deal with all that," I said, "you'd better put out."

He gave me a small, mysterious smile before he took a bite of his pancakes.

Chapter Fourteen

The week that followed was a honeymoon of sorts…if you subtracted wedding vows and an exotic locale and added a toddler. But then I'd always done things ass backward.

Colin took us to Navy Pier, where we visited the children's museum and gorged ourselves on corn dogs and ice cream. A fearless Bailey demanded we ride the giant Ferris wheel, and Colin indulged her. Only after the pair emerged from the cab covered in upchucked corn dog did he admit that perhaps I'd been right after all. We visited the aquarium, where Bailey squealed as she touched a prickly starfish and dragged us all to the splash zone. Colin even got us tickets to a community theater production of *Mary Poppins*, though we discovered Bailey preferred to sing her own soundtrack and left at intermission.

It was amazing. Really, it was. If I felt an undercurrent of frantic energy, then it was just relief at my newfound freedom. And if it seemed that Colin was desperate to experience everything, to give us everything we wanted, it was just due to the newness of our happiness. It had to be.

Philip called constantly. At first Colin would answer, excusing himself to speak in tense, hushed tones. After a while he turned his phone off.

"Will it be okay?" I didn't know how much we really relied on Philip, especially financially. "I know you do work for him…"

"Don't worry," Colin said. "He'll get over it."

When I looked at him for more, he ran his thumb along my lips. A tender *shut up*.

That eased my worry—somewhat. It seemed we could get along just fine without Philip, but if there was major damage to their sibling relationship, Colin might regret his time with me.

The dinner party was still set for tomorrow, so we'd see then just how angry Philip was. I doubted he took well to being ignored.

I'd offered to make a dessert to bring with us. Colin suggested wine, but I thought dessert would be more personal. Make it clear I was willing to put in an effort. Besides, that way Rose wouldn't have to worry about making it. Colin had chuckled at me then, but he'd agreed to text Rose and let her know.

I pulled the packages of fresh strawberries from the paper grocery bag. Since we'd witnessed the first tendrils of spring, I'd decided on a strawberry-rhubarb crumble.

From her high chair Bailey chomped on a bowl of diced strawberries while I went to work on the rest. A knock on the door stopped me midchop.

I peeked out the window beside the door and saw a short, wide person standing there. I unlatched the chain, flipped the dead bolt, and opened the door a foot. "Hello?"

"Oh, *hi*." The woman wore an overlarge white shirt with a picture of a kitten on it and tight, black leggings. Her hair was in disarray, a mop of ringlets, and her face crinkly. Despite all that she managed to look fresh and bright, her cheeks rosy and her eyes sparkling merrily like some ginger-haired Mrs. Claus. "I'm looking for Mouse, my cat Mouse. I haven't seen him in…oh, it's been a full day now, and—"

She paused when I opened the door wider to reveal the orange cat sprawled on our ottoman.

"Mouse," she cried. "You horrible cat, look at you, making yourself right at home."

Ah, so Mouse had a home, and it wasn't here. That couldn't be disappointment. I had no desire to keep a cat, and definitely not this one, so presumptuous and rotund. Not very mousy, either. Well, I told myself, thank God for that. To the woman I said, "He just started coming around, so—"

"Of *course*," she said. "You wouldn't know he was ours, what with us being so new here. I haven't even had time to come around and say hello to you guys. Oh! What am I saying? I haven't even introduced myself. I'm Linda. What was your name, dear?"

"Allie," I said quickly, feeling like I'd been sent to the nurse's office. Not that she was examining me or sending me home or anything, just that was the last time a woman had really spoken to me.

"Allie," she said. "You don't mind if I call you that, do you? I hope you don't think I was too rude, just moving in and not saying a word, and then coming around to find my cat on your furniture. He knows better than that. You know better than that, Mousy! That's what cat trees are for."

She paused for breath, watching me expectantly.

"No, it's not rude at all. I just…actually I'm new here too."

"Are you? Well, that's great! We can get settled in together. It's a very nice neighborhood, don't you think? Yes, very quiet. No bad happenings go on, that sort of thing. Did you know? At my last house the person across the street from me rode a motorcycle."

I paused, unable to come up with a suitable reply to that. I liked things quiet too, but if ever Colin or I brought trouble to the neighborhood, it would be a lot messier than a motorcycle.

"Well, don't worry your young head about that," she said. "This is a nice, *safe* place. And you have a man to watch after you. Yes, that's right, I've seen him coming and going. And what a man, if you don't mind me saying so."

I shook my head, but she spoke before I could.

"Yes, he looks very strong, which is always good in a man, I should think. My William was strong too, don't you know? Well, until the very end, bless his heart. Thirty-two years, it was. Now tell me, how long have you been married?"

She tilted her head at me, her eyes bright with expectation. *Motherfucking hell.*

Lies ran through my head, as stupid as that would be. Of course she'd find out, and what was the point of that? I couldn't be ashamed of this. I'd done a lot worse in my life than live with a man who wasn't my husband.

"I'm sorry," I said. "We aren't married."

"Oh." Now it was her turn to gape like a fish. To her credit she recovered quickly. "You know, that is *okay.* Don't you worry your pretty head about that. I know how young people carry on these days."

I had a strong suspicion she had no fucking clue how young people carried on these days, but I wasn't going to tell her that.

A squawk from the kitchen knocked me from my daze, and I rushed in with Linda on my heels. Bailey just squealed and kicked, eager to join the conversation. Linda blinked a few times, and then must have decided this was all part of the carrying on.

"Oh, you pretty girl," she exclaimed to Bailey. "And what is your name?"

Somewhat awkwardly, as if I were interrupting the conversation, I said, "Her name's Bailey."

Linda didn't miss a beat. "Bailey! Beautiful Bailey, is that what they call you? Yes, you are. Yes, you are. Oh, yes, you are."

Bailey preened.

"You sweet thing. You pretty girl," Linda cooed.

Bailey offered up a smooshed strawberry chunk atop a chubby palm. I rolled my eyes. The girl sure knew how to work an audience.

"Oh, thank you. Yes, thank you." Linda accepted the strawberry chunk and held it behind her, where I slipped it from her hand and into the trash can. We grown-ups had to stick together.

Linda turned to me. "Listen, sweetie. I'd love to stay and chat, but I've got to run. But you know you can come and stop by anytime. I'm a great listener, you know, if you're ever having problems. Not that you would. You're such a dear. I'll see you around."

As she went through the living room she picked up Mouse, whose long, thick body hung like a pendulum from where she'd clasped him to her chest. And then she was gone through the front door in a *whoosh* of bouncing auburn-gray curls and fresh air.

"Wow," I said to Bailey. "That was new."

"Baba?" She offered me another strawberry bit in her palm, which I accepted and plopped in my mouth.

"Thanks," I told her, "but I'm much harder to impress. Poop in the potty; then we'll talk."

I wiped the red strawberry film off a sleepy baby and carted her upstairs. She drifted off to sleep after the fourteenth verse of "Hush, Little Baby." And thank goodness too. I'd already promised to buy her a tutu, a tricycle, and a host of other things well beyond her pay grade. Not that Colin would mind. He'd probably buy her a castle if she crooked her pudgy little finger at it.

I shook my head. It wasn't that he didn't understand about spoiling her. He *wanted* to spoil her. It was like some little-boy-lost redemption drama playing out in our own home. The worst thing was that I was probably part of it. Somehow his white-knight radar had settled on the two of us. We made a quaint picture, this family, and I only hoped it would last. However it had started, on a whim or just an accident of fate, I liked to think we'd built something real by now.

Things were good, very good.

Chapter Fifteen

Back downstairs, I prepped the strawberry-rhubarb filling and crumble topping and set it to bake. Then I pulled the clothes from the dryer and into the basket, the warm scent of spring filling the laundry room. A shuffle behind me caught my attention, but before I could turn, I was spun around and slammed into the wall. Struggling to gasp for air, I saw the sneering face of a cop. One of the cops who'd come around earlier, poking around about Colin. Shay, Shat, Shaw—that was it. Detective Fucking Shaw, the asshole.

How did he get in? The front door. I probably hadn't locked it after Linda left. Too damned complacent. Should've known better.

"Hi, Allie." He smiled an ugly smile.

"Where's your partner?" I gasped. Despite his quiet intensity, I'd trusted the other guy much more.

"Oh, just on a break," he said. My mind flashed to Bailey sleeping upstairs, and I prayed she kept sleeping. "Thought we'd just have a little talk, you and me." He waved a manila folder that I hadn't noticed before in my face. "Take a look."

Hesitantly I accepted the folder from his hands.

A picture of Rick leaving, swinging loading doors behind him. The next one was me pushing Bailey through that same door in an overfull grocery cart, glancing behind me. The last picture was me and Andrew sitting across from each other, the broken blinds of the diner window behind us.

My mind latched onto inane details first. How had they even known about these meetings? I suppose they were following me. Where had the photographer been sitting in the diner? From that angle it looked to be a booth across the restaurant. Maybe a cell phone camera, although I'd been so wrapped up in the conversation, I probably wouldn't have noticed full-fledged paparazzi.

But none of that mattered, because it was clear what these were—leverage. They'd wanted information on Colin and Philip, and I'd refused. Now he was back, bringing pictures that threatened to tear Colin and me apart.

"That's right," he said, nodding approvingly like I'd done a neat trick. "Your little sugar daddy wouldn't be too pleased to see these, would he? Doesn't allow you to sleep around, does he?"

It didn't matter that Colin meant so much more to me than a sugar daddy; that actually made it worse. And it didn't matter that I hadn't slept with these guys; if Colin saw them, he would be extremely and rightfully pissed. I damned myself a million times for not telling him. Rather, for not telling him again, when he was sober and awake. And still I thought I should do just that. I had some hope that it wouldn't mean the end of us. Maybe he could understand why I'd had to meet Andrew and why I'd kept it from him. It was worth a shot and definitely better than whoring for this guy.

He must have taken my silence for acquiescence. "I need information on shipping routes," he said. "Only Philip Murphy will have that, understand? I need you to get close to him and give me the dates and locations of the drops, see?"

I handed the pictures back. "No."

"Now, now, don't be stupid. I could have you written up for conspiracy, drug trafficking, anything I fucking want. Hell, I could even say you propositioned me and arrest you for prostitution."

He leaned close. There was nowhere to go. "Who would take care of your little girl, then?" he asked.

I shut my eyes against the wash of rancid breath. Oh fuck, oh fuck, that wasn't helping. I needed to fucking think. What could I do? I wasn't sure if he was right, but it sounded pretty convincing, and I really didn't want to test it out. If I got arrested, Bailey would go into the system. They wouldn't grant custody to Shelly or Colin, either, but put her in a group home. Or worse, give her to some stranger who might do God knows what with her. Fuck. Even Andrew would have been better than that, but he'd already signed away any legal claim to her.

I felt a hand on my neck, and I stopped breathing. I held it even as that hand traveled lower.

"I just want to help you," he whispered.

No, no, this couldn't be happening. Not again.

It didn't seem possible, and I held on to that thought. If this wasn't happening…fuck, let this not be happening. Both his hands touched me. There, on my breasts, and down lower, to my jeans. Just over my clothes, the thick barrier of my jeans, but it was enough.

I felt like I was underwater, hearing and feeling everything through deep waters. Maybe it was better this way.

He touched me for an eternity, or maybe just a few minutes, before he stopped. I didn't know why he stopped. In that objective sort of detachment, my mind wondered at it. What made a bad man stop when he could go further? Was it just that this left no marks, no bruises, or fluids or anything else, and so made it easy to get away with?

He muttered into my ear, "I know about the little Murphy family dinner. Get me what I need, and you'll be free."

Then he was away from me, though my eyes were strangely fuzzy. The slam of the door and boot steps down the stairs signaled his retreat, if I could call it that. More like a victory dance, I thought. Tires squealed from the front of the house as he drove away.

I slid to the ground.

What a lie. I'd never be free.

I would have lost it completely, right then. It was close, hovering right there on the precipice. Even in my breakdown I was practical. Even broken and insane with my private grief, I loved Bailey. So I crawled across the floor to the phone on the side table.

I heard Shelly's voice. "Hello?"

"Can you come?" I heard myself ask in a hoarse voice.

"Allie? What's wrong? Allie! Okay, I'm coming over," and then a *click*. It was good to have a friend.

A shout and rattle of the baby gate told me Bailey was up. I was a mother first. No rest for the wicked. I dragged myself up the stairs, brought her down, and plopped her in front of the television. I figured impending mental collapse was as good of an excuse as any for bad parenting.

I curled up on the couch, watching the dancing letters. Sanity slid away like a balloon lost at a carnival. I felt its loss with relief.

"Allie? What happened?" Shelly's voice, garbled and distant. She was still above the surface, but I was down, down, down. Thank God she was here, I thought, someone to watch over Bailey. Because down here it was black.

The doctors and nurses left, leaving only the two cops on either side of my hospital bed. The woman cop shifted on her feet, very pregnant.

"Go on down," the man told her. "I'll wrap up and meet you there."

She bit her lip, deliberating. She probably didn't want to appear weak, like she wasn't holding her weight against a man. Then again, she looked very uncomfortable. That appeared to win out, because she nodded and said, "I'll see you in the cafeteria."

"You'll be okay," she said, squeezing my hand. "It wasn't your fault." Practiced words, probably recited to all the rape victims, but they warmed me. Maybe there was hope.

After she left the room, the man took off his jacket and draped it across the foot of the bed. He questioned me, scribbling my answers on a notepad.

Yes, I knew my assailant. We'd been friends.

No, I hadn't had sex with him before. Not with anyone.

Yes, I told him no. I'm sure he heard me.

The cop had just been a person-shaped blob to me in that room full of people. But he'd come closer to the bed, and only then did I notice his eyes were green. Green eyes, so rare. I wasn't sure I'd ever seen them before in real life. At least not ones so brilliant, so bright. The green eyes were narrowed.

"Reporting a rape is an important matter, Ms. Winters."

I said nothing. He shifted closer to the bed.

"I can see that you're upset," he said. "But false accusations of rape have serious implications."

I sucked in a breath. False accusations?

He pushed aside the flimsy paper that clothed me, exposing my breasts. "I wouldn't want anyone to get the wrong idea about you."

No, I'd been wrong. There wasn't any hope.

He pulled out a condom, speaking calmly while he put it on. "I wouldn't want anyone to think you're a slut."

She'd been wrong too, the other cop. I wouldn't be okay.

"Look at me," he said. I refused, but his hand firmly turned my head toward him.

He pulled my face closer, until I looked him right in the eye. I shut my eyes.

"Nobody likes a tease," he said. "But don't worry. I can get you through this."

I wanted to die. I prayed that I would, that second, but no one heard me. No one cared.

It was my fault. It had to be, or why else would this be happening? It didn't make sense. Make it stop.

And I thought, then, in the absence of any fucking clue of what to do, I would do as I was told. I'd said no before, and it hadn't worked. It had only made him angry. With my eyes tightly shut, I opened my mouth to protest, to scream, but nothing came out.

"That's right," he whispered. "I can help you."

I tried to open my eyes, but they were weighted shut. No, they were already open; it was just dark in here. It hadn't been dark when I'd last been awake. What time was it?

I rustled in the linens. Bed. I was in bed. And it was

night.

Fuck it all to hell.

That meant Colin would have come home. What had Shelly told him?

I had to think of some sort of excuse, something Colin would believe. I sure as hell wasn't telling him the truth, not about what happened today, and not where it had taken my mind. *Wouldn't believe me anyway...*

Don't think about it. It was too late.

Chapter Sixteen

My mouth felt thick, my head too large, and my limbs sluggish. It was all the pain of a hangover but without the bliss of forgetfulness. No, I remembered every fucking detail from earlier today. Even things that hadn't registered in that strange moment of disconnect came to me now. The smell of the cop's aftershave, the rasp of the hair on the back of his hands, the harshness of his breaths. *Make it stop.*

I had to even my breathing. If I was going to play this off as a stomach bug or something, then I shouldn't be in the middle of a panic attack. That was it, rational thoughts. *Keep breathing.*

Ever the coward, I wondered how long I could stay here. I heard faint clinking in the kitchen—someone was cooking dinner. That was good. Someone had Bailey. Someone was in control of the situation. How long could I lie here before that someone came to find me? It was a very nice cocoon, Colin's bedroom.

Staring into the darkness, I heard soft thumps up the steps. Then whispers outside the door. Without moving I tried to make them out.

"…still sleeping…"

"...shouldn't wake...rest."

"...been four hours..."

The door creaked, and a band of yellow light fell across the bed. I shut my eyes. The floor creaked as someone walked toward the bed. I steadied my breathing. The floor creaked again as someone walked out. Then a soft *click* as the door shut.

I opened my eyes again to the dark. I couldn't sleep. I wouldn't. It would just invite the nightmare back. That was the one that came to me—not what happened with Andrew. And even then it was a rare thing. Usually only after seeing a cop. Sometimes even seeing a cop car would trigger me.

There'd been a neat row of cop cars when I'd gone to the police station to withdraw my complaint the next week. I'd worried myself into vomiting, thinking I'd have to see him there. But I hadn't. It had all been very formal, very bureaucratic. There were forms to fill out, and a statement to sign. It had been a misunderstanding, that night with Andrew. I'd been drunk and hadn't really said no, and so it wasn't really rape, after all. The cops there, in uniform instead of in a suit like *he* had been, looked at me blankly. They did not judge me when I was a rape victim, and they did not judge me when I was a false accuser, recanting her statement. They just didn't care.

But it was in those days that I'd formed my crazy ideas. Even then I knew they were crazy. All men couldn't be bad. My dad wasn't bad, even if he was gone a lot. Besides that, there had to be plenty of examples of good guys if I'd cared to look. But I hadn't wanted to look, not at all.

I'd made the decision then never to have sex with a guy. More than that, I wouldn't even put myself in a situation where I'd be *near* a guy.

Then I'd found out I was pregnant. Holy fuck.

I'd thought about trying to reach Andrew. His dad was a fucker of the worst sort, but he might have Andrew's phone number or a way to reach him. In the end I didn't do anything.

My dad probably guessed who the father was. Andrew had been my best friend, and then he was gone and I was pregnant. It was an age-old story, right? But he never said anything. He just gave me some cash and told me he'd send what he could.

After I'd had Bailey, it had taken a few months to heal, physically at least. Only after that had I come up with the idea of date nights. I'd thought it ingenious. Now I knew I'd been an idiot.

I'd hurt myself on those date nights, over and over again.

It hadn't been about those guys, not really. They'd been props, whips used for self-flagellation. I thought maybe Shelly's deals were flays of her own whip and that was troubling, but we'd agreed not to interfere. After they'd let her into the hospital room with me and I'd dry heaved for an hour, she'd apologized to me in whispered tones for making me do this. She hadn't protested when I'd gone into the police station to withdraw my statement. She hadn't guessed what had happened, I thought, not then nor ever, but she saw what it did to me. She didn't understand why, but she didn't want me to be hurt.

The cocoon grew stifling. Suddenly I wanted to see people, these people who cared about me, God knew why. I still didn't know what excuse I would make, but surely I could think of something. I wanted to leech their comfort, their normalcy.

I descended the stairs, feeling an odd remoteness. There should be pictures here, I thought, as I trailed my finger along the blank stairway wall. At the bottom I found Shelly and Bailey on the couch in the living room, playing a game of cards. I paused there in the corner, watching.

I knew from experience how Bailey played. We would deal the cards, in whatever number and setup we wanted, and Bailey would grab for the face cards—the kings, queens and jacks—and collect them. I always figured it was a pretty decent strategy for a toddler.

She'd probably grow up a card shark and best us all. I could only hope as much. Maybe it wasn't the doctor or president that other moms hoped for, but it was all about power in the end. The money, the respect, and not having to take shit from no one. That power came in different forms in my world, but no less potent.

A soft clang from the kitchen caught my attention. Colin. I floated past Shelly and Bailey—not sure if they greeted me or not—and leaned against the kitchen door. Colin looked up from the oven, lines of worry on his face. I felt a pang of guilt at that, like someone watching herself be mourned.

He straightened and came to me. "How are you feeling?"

It startled me out of my trance, that he could speak to me. Not dead yet after all.

I had no fake story prepared, no blithe comeback to deliver. In fact, as I opened my mouth to offer one of those practiced platitudes—*It's okay, I'm fine*—I found I couldn't speak at all.

"Hey." He pulled me against him in a tight embrace. "Everything will be okay. You'll be fine."

And damn me, even knowing it was a mirage, I believed him.

Chapter Seventeen

The doorbell rang like a gong in a cavern.

I shifted on my feet in front of the wide door. Colin stood like a pillar beside me, holding the cobbler. Bailey waved her hand futilely for the doorbell, trying to press it again. Muffled footsteps approached, and then the large carved door swung open, spraying light onto the front step.

"Won't you come in?" It was the same guy as before, wearing the same stuffy suit. I wondered if he got days off. What was the pay like for door answering these days?

He led us down a hallway, past the closed double doors of the study I'd seen before, and into a very large room. A dark, curved leather sectional took up more square footage than my entire old apartment. Low lighting and groups of candles were—what was the word?—*ambient*. Soft music played in the background, something on the piano. I did a double take. No, there wasn't music playing, like from a CD. There was a piano player in the corner. Fuck.

I could see Rose and Shelly seated at a bar at the other side of the room. I trailed behind Colin as we crossed over an inky black floor. Surely it was tile, though I couldn't see the cracks.

"Hi, Allie." Rose smiled and stood, her slinky black dress sliding into place. "I'm so glad you came. Colin. And who's this little one?"

"This is Bailey," I said, looking at her. She promptly shoved her face into my hair, dampening my freshly straightened hair.

"Aw, that's okay," Rose said. "Why don't you come sit here? What would you like to drink?"

"Thanks," I said, scooting onto the bar chair with a clinging Bailey. "Just water."

As Rose accepted the cobbler from Colin, I nudged Shelly with my foot.

"I like your hair," Shelly said with a smile. More of a smirk, really. She knew how long it took me to straighten it. She also knew I only did it because I so wanted to make a good impression.

"Bite me," I muttered but without heat.

"Don't worry," she said softly. "I softened him up for you."

I threw her a look. I had no desire to hear the details of *that*.

She put up her hands. "Just trying to help."

Yeah, yeah, everyone wanted to help. I might just keel over and die from all the goddamn help. I didn't really mean it, though. I wasn't mad at Shelly, just nervous as hell. Before we'd left, Colin had told me again that it would be okay, that whatever his brother thought of me didn't matter. I knew he meant to be reassuring, but that just freaked me out even more. Thinking about them talking about me, about Philip cataloging all my faults for Colin, made me sweat. It wasn't like it would be hard for Philip to think of ways to put me down.

"I'm sorry," I said to Shelly. "I'm a dumb-ass."

Colin came to stand next to me, bringing the glass of water Rose poured for me and his own drink. I almost dropped the heavy crystal cup, surprised by its weight, but dug my fingertips into the carved grooves just in time. Even water was different here.

Shelly gave me a covert sympathetic look that said she understood my nervousness. I wondered if that meant Shelly and Philip had talked about me too. I didn't doubt Shelly's loyalty to me, even if she did have to listen to him talk bad about me or even agree with him. It was just odd to think of my best friend and the person who hated me together that way. Me and Colin, Shelly and Philip. This had to be the weirdest double date ever.

Except it wasn't, because Rose was here, and just then Philip and Laramie entered the room. I hadn't expected Laramie to be here, but I supposed he was a friend. It made sense, since he was exposed to the inner workings of Philip's business. And it made me feel a little better that Colin had entrusted this man with our situation. He wasn't just a hired guy, but someone who attended a family dinner. Then again, I was here, and

Shelly, Philip's prostitute, was as well, so maybe it didn't take much.

"Ah, Allie." Laramie spoke to me first. "It's good to meet you again." He lowered his voice as he shook my hand in both of his. "And congratulations, young lady."

"Thank you," I said, suddenly feeling shy.

Laramie released my hand, and I was left face-to-face with Philip. "Ms. Winters," he said distinctly.

"Please," I said. "Call me Allie."

"Allie." He grimaced, though I thought it was meant to be a smile. "You made it."

Then he turned away and resumed his conversation with Laramie. Damn, that was cold. I noticed he didn't say he was glad to see me, or that he was happy I could make it. He'd just stated the obvious—I was here. I shifted my gaze to Shelly, who rolled hers.

"Ignore him," she said. "That's what I do."

I didn't think that was true, not at all, but I was reassured that she seemed so blasé about Philip.

I'd been worried about her, locked up here in a tower like some damsel in distress. I worried that Philip was hurting her, that he was cruel to her, but she didn't seem hurt or scared, not in the least. She sparkled. She could have been faking it, but I liked to think I knew her well enough to see through that. She seemed at ease here. Not happy, necessarily—had I ever seen her happy?—but content.

The idea that I could snoop here, that I could *spy* here, seemed laughable. This place was huge, and the information well secured. They'd given me a glass of water, not the combination to the vault, but I had to try.

I wasn't sure whether I would help that asshole cop. I thought not, actually, but knowledge was power, or so said my third-grade teacher. If I at least had the information, I could bargain if it came to that. And there was no doubt in my mind that if it was between me and Philip, or even Colin and Philip, that I'd sell Philip out. I wanted to ingratiate myself with Philip, just for Colin, but not so much that I'd let him endanger my family.

"Sorry." I interrupted Philip. Oops. "Bailey made a mess. Could you point me to the bathroom?"

"Down there." Rose pointed back where we'd come from. "Third door on the right."

"Thanks," I said. "Shelly, can you come help me a sec?"

Shelly slipped off the bar chair and grabbed the diaper bag. She wasn't even surprised, probably expecting some sort of scoop. Well, she'd get it and then some.

I'd thought we could slip into one of the other rooms to talk, but it turned out my request for her to join us wasn't as ridiculous as I'd thought. This bathroom didn't have a bathtub or shower. Instead it had several sinks spread across a long counter, a love seat, and a door opening to a toilet. It was like the bathroom at the swanky mall, before it had gotten ghetto.

"What's up?" she asked.

I sat Bailey on the love seat and handed her the tube of diaper rash cream to occupy her while I told Shelly what the cop had said. I left out the part about the groping, but Shelly was a smart girl. She'd put together his visit with my breakdown yesterday. She still may not know why exactly, but it probably wouldn't take her long to connect it back to that time in the hospital either.

Shelly shook her head. "You're crazy, sweetheart."

"I know," I agreed. "But I have to do something. Colin doesn't keep anything around the house." I knew that, not from snooping but just from trying to do a kick-ass job at cleaning. There weren't any papers in the study. The computer was password protected, and I wasn't so skilled a spy that I could break into that. Besides, I felt oddly better about poking around in Philip's home than in Colin's. Even though Colin might see it as the same thing, it sort of wasn't. I wouldn't let my actions harm Colin.

"Well," Shelly said. "Philip doesn't leave stuff around either. He's kind of paranoid. If there's anything important, it'll be in his study. And there wouldn't be much online either. From what I've seen, he's real old-fashioned. Likes to do things by paper. No chance of backups or hackers or anything."

"Paper?" I asked. "Isn't that less secure? I'd expect a fancy dude like him to have high-tech security and shit."

"Oh, he does," she said. "The whole house is rigged

to burn if the security gets tripped. No paper trail, just ashes."

Great, we were having dinner in a matchbox. Paranoid was right. "So what do I have to do to make sure we don't all fry?"

"You're sure you want to do this?"

"Yes," I said.

"All right." She reached between her breasts and pulled out a key.

I accepted the key, still warm from her body, and gave her a wry look. "Really?"

"I make it work," she said airily. I didn't even want to know how she had this key. Even if Philip trusted her, why would she need it? She wouldn't. I narrowed my eyes. She gave me her best "I'm a dumb blonde" smile. Not that I bought it for a second, but I also knew when I was beat. And running out of time.

"Okay," I said. "You go back to the group. I need to freshen up."

"Sure thing," she said, playing along. "I'll take Bailey. She doesn't get enough time with Aunt Shelly."

She trooped out the bathroom door with the diaper bag and Bailey. I used the bathroom. Well, I had to pee. And I was already nervous enough to piss myself as it was. I washed up and then peeked out the door. No one.

Feeling very suave and very terrified, I slipped into the hallway and down to the double doors that I recognized from the study.

What if he was in there? Or someone else could be. I rapped lightly. Nothing.

The lock was a monster of a dead bolt, but the key slid in and turned easily. I pushed the door open just a crack, waiting for flames. Then I laughed at myself. It would be a fitting way to go for my sins.

After I slipped inside, I left the door ajar to listen for anyone approaching. The thin band of light from the hall illuminated the deep leather armchairs we'd sat in last time. The desk waited for me in the dark side of the room. I crossed to it and flipped on a small lamp. I sifted through a few papers right on top: documents, maps, schematics.

In a side drawer I found a leather binder so thick my hand could barely grasp it. The smell of ink wafted up from the pages when I opened the flap. It was a ledger of some sort. Thin green lines demarcated entries that provided a long space for description, an amount, a few columns for balance adjustments from different accounts. The descriptions varied from initials to long scrawls, followed by symbols and letters. This wasn't what I needed. I returned it to the drawer.

Atop the desk, underneath the scattered papers, I hit the jackpot. It was one of those desk calendars, the kind a secretary might use to schedule meetings. In thick black lettering, an address and time were written into two days from now. There were a few other notes made, but that one was the most conspicuous. It had to be what the cop was looking for. I scribbled it onto a blank scrap of paper I found. I stared at it for a second, then tucked it into my bra. Time to go.

I paused on a whim. What might be in that ledger? Something about Rick, maybe. I could find out whether there'd been any truth to his words before confronting Colin, but that was greedy. I really needed to get back. I flipped off the lamp, slipped back out the door, and locked it. I shoved the key down next to the slip of paper. The paper was itchy, the key cold against my skin.

I glanced both ways as if crossing the street. Which way?

I went down the hallway. Hmm.

This was ridiculous. The house wasn't *that* big.

Okay. It was.

I saw the tall archway that had led into the large room from earlier. Thank God. I rushed in and froze. This was not the right room.

Rose and Laramie sprang apart. Laramie cleared his throat. Rose looked down and smoothed her dress out.

"I was wondering," I said, "which way led back to the group."

A red-faced Rose gestured through the room to another large archway. "In there."

I started to walk through, averting my eyes, when Laramie cleared his throat again. "Allie, I—"

"I never saw a thing," I said without turning.

"Thank you," he said behind me.

I sailed through the archway and stumbled into the

room, this time from the other side, so that I was right next to the bar.

"Ah, there you are," Philip said. "I feared we'd lost you."

"Sorry," I said. "I just…got a bit lost." Fuck, that sounded ridiculous, but it was true.

Shelly coughed and did this little shimmy that dragged his attention away from me. Really, thank God for boobs. I stood next to Colin, who'd been speaking in low tones with Philip. When I got to his side, though, he stopped talking and pulled me close. Rose entered a few minutes later, looking no worse for wear. A few minutes after that, Laramie came in and joined Philip.

A woman in a white shirt and black slacks entered and announced dinner was ready. En masse we stood and migrated over. As I walked by the woman, she looked right past me as if I were invisible. I thought that if things had happened differently, if I'd happened to hear about her job, I could be her coworker. I could be the one calling the fancy people in to a fancy dinner, but it was her and I was the outsider now.

The table was set with white dishes with gold-plated trim. That couldn't be real gold, could it? Bowls were set upon plates, which sat upon chargers, making me wonder exactly how much food would be served. Little placards assigned the seats, but the high chair made it obvious where Bailey was to sit.

"Oh, thank you," I said. "I was thinking I'd just

hold her, but this is better."

"It's no problem," Rose assured me.

"Do you have a baby?" I asked and then cringed at myself.

"No." Rose laughed. "We rented that. The caterer had them."

Oh, a caterer. Well, now I knew why Colin had laughed when I'd told him I'd bring dessert.

I cringed again at the thought of my rustic cobbler dish. I should have made something better. Something more upscale. Fancy desserts raced through my head. The chocolate tart, sure, but other things too. Things with French names that I could barely pronounce but I could *make*. Too late. Damn.

I set Bailey up in the high chair and sat down at the seat labeled "Allie."

Soup was brought out, and servers ladled it into our bowls. No one spoke, the only sound the rush of edible liquid. Everyone, even Shelly, watched their bowls, like it was some sort of prayer ritual. That thought surprised me. Maybe it was. Like a moment of silence. Wasn't that a thing? No, that was for observing dead people. Shit, I didn't belong here.

When the servers left the room, we all reached for our spoons. The soft clangs of those spoons against the table or against the bowl filled the air, and then quiet slurps of soup.

I took a sip of my own. It was some sort of seafood dish. It tasted kind of like this chowder they served down the street from my old apartment. Damn, that had been some good gumbo. This one was smooth, like one of Bailey's baby food purees, and had sprigs of green, but it was basically the same. I tried to entice Bailey with the fruit I'd brought her, but she squirmed for the soup. I brought the spoon to her lips.

She took a sip. Then another. Then—*pffft*—she spit it out.

"Yucky," she said.

My face burned. I turned to face Rose, an apology on my lips, but she was biting her lips against a smile.

"Don't worry about it," she said. "Honestly."

"I'm sorry," I said anyway. "I really like it."

I looked around and noticed Colin looking down and Shelly covering her mouth. Okay, amusement would be had at my expense tonight. I chanced a glance at Philip, but even his expression seemed to have softened under Bailey's spell.

Until he spoke. "Allie," he said. "I heard you're working in Colin's restaurant."

I glanced at Colin. I could tell from the way his eyes had clouded over that he'd caught the edge to Philip's tone, but I wasn't sure what he thought about it. Colin didn't meet my eyes.

"Not working there, exactly," I said. "Just sending over a couple of cakes or pies every few days."

"I see." Philip's tone said he found that doubtful, though I didn't see why.

"I like to bake, so it's just a little extra. And you

know, or maybe you don't, but I did that before." I caught Shelly's eye as she sipped from her spoon, and that bolstered me some. I took a deep breath.

Philip took a drink and over the rim said, "Mmm-hmm." He set the glass down with a thud. "I imagine you're very busy"—he nodded toward Bailey—"taking care of your daughter."

"Oh, sure," I said. "We stay busy. I mean, not too busy, but we get along fine, between that, and…the baking."

Jesus, why couldn't I shut up? It was like watching a train wreck, but I was on the train.

Philip looked at me expectantly. Hadn't I answered the question? What was the fucking question?

Maybe this was about Colin taking time off. Did Philip think he'd had to do that to watch Bailey for me? "I mean, I take care of her, if that's what you mean. Colin doesn't have to—"

"That's enough," Colin said sharply.

I looked down at my soup, feeling ridiculous but relieved. Philip said nothing.

A few minutes later our soup bowls were taken away and replaced with a plate of…what? I poked it with my fork. Round fish pieces. Ah, scallops. And even a corn mixture. I picked out the greens and fed them to Bailey.

Rose broke the silence. "The company's going to New York next month."

"Oh," said Colin. "For how long?"

"Just a week," she said.

Nothing, then Shelly said, "How exciting. Have you been?"

"Oh, yeah," Rose said. "I love it there."

She paused. We all did.

"The nightlife," she added, "the shopping…" Then she trailed off.

Belatedly Shelly said, "Ah."

We all ate.

I'd expected as much from myself, but Shelly and even Rose were good conversationalists. It shouldn't be this awkward.

I scowled into my plate. The cloud of Philip's derision had dampened any real gaiety. Even the white lily centerpieces seemed to wilt under his wrath.

The paper in my bra started to itch. I wriggled to surreptitiously fix it, but that only succeeded in getting Colin's attention. The heat in his eyes would be fantastic later tonight. But for now I could hardly reach in my bra and remove a slip of paper with his eyes boring into me.

"So," Shelly broke in. "You guys were raised in Chicago?"

I'd thought this was a nice neutral topic until I saw the glances exchanged between the three siblings.

"Yes," Rose finally said. "We were raised in Chicago."

Hmm, that wasn't really a mystery. Why the sudden tension?

"Ah," said Shelly. "Did you—"

"Next course," Philip said flatly. Shelly's eyes flared in surprise at the unsubtle change of subject, but she let it go.

The servers exchanged our empty plates for large plates of thinly sliced smoked beef and a small chopped salad of carrots and potatoes and green herbs. It was pot roast done fancy. It smelled divine.

But then another smell wafted to me, this one putrid. What the hell…oh no. I'd been caught in my own lie. Bailey had pooped, for real this time. And it would look weird that she'd gone twice so soon. Assuming they knew about babies, which they probably didn't.

My palms itched. I glanced over and saw Shelly's eyes widen as the smell hit her.

One by one they all turned to me. I tried for a smile.

"Sorry, guys," I said in a small voice. "Turns out she's got the runs."

Shelly coughed into her napkin, but I was pretty sure it was only hiding a laugh. The bitch. *This is serious*, I should tell her. But, well, damn me, at least someone could enjoy this night. There was a reason we never saw spies with toddlers, I thought, and it started with what went *in* and ended with what came *out*.

I grabbed the diaper bag and one seriously stinky child and headed toward the bathroom. I hadn't been entirely lying about the runs, turned out. Rich food didn't agree with her tummy.

We worked our way through a bag of wipes to a clean, shiny bum, and were ready to head out. In the hallway I paused again. I glanced longingly at the study door. I really wanted to see that file.

Chapter Eighteen

It seemed like a detour like this was only asking for trouble, but then I'd never really found all that much luck on the straight and narrow either.

That decided it.

I used the key again to get into the room and set Bailey down on the rug by the chairs. I'd probably go to hell for using her in this farce, but she'd act as a distraction if anyone came in here. If we were caught, having her might actually be a great excuse—I could say I needed to give her a break from the high chair and that's why I was in here. That wouldn't really explain how we'd unlocked the door, especially without triggering his alarm.

Bailey pulled herself up using the leather armrest and gnawed on the corner. I turned on the lamp and went straight for the ledger. I flipped through the pages dating back before I'd moved in with Colin. Farther and farther back I went. They'd started to blur together, but suddenly some pages caught my eye because they all looked alike.

They all started with *R. Sanders*—Rick's name. There were five different entries, for amounts ranging from $3,000 to $13,000. Holy shit. Rick had been playing around with a lot of money. And for some reason Colin had bought up these debts...and traded them in for me. I snorted. He'd got the bad end of that deal.

It didn't mean that for sure. There could be other reasons Rick's name was in this book. Maybe he'd come to Philip and gotten five different loans on the same day. I huffed a breath. Not likely.

I figured Colin had done it after our date at the restaurant. We'd gotten to know each other, at least. Maybe I'd demonstrated some sort of datable qualities that night. Or maybe someone had roofied his drink or he'd hit his head or...well, something. Because guys did not pay to be with me, not for sex, not for anything.

But no, the date of these entries was before that. I thought for one scary moment that they were from before I'd even met Colin, which would have been truly confusing, but they weren't. They were a week after the night I'd picked him up at the club, and we'd had anonymous motel sex. What had made him decide to seek out my boss and try to manipulate me—so early?

Colin had asked me out that night, I remembered, and given me a way to contact him. But that was a far cry from taking on thousands of dollars in a bad debt that could never be paid.

I flipped through the next few pages. I didn't have a suspicion, not really, but something drew me on. And only a week after the Rick entries, I found this one: *A.*

Winters TY. It had to be me. What could *TY* mean? Thank you? Hah! The amount was for one thousand dollars. I certainly hadn't received a thousand bucks, as a thank-you or otherwise. I checked a few pages forward and found nothing else I recognized.

Bailey crawled around the desk and stood up at my knee. I sat her in the chair and twirled her gently around. She giggled softly, and I glanced at the door. I should go, but something anchored me here. As I turned the chair with one hand, I slid open the file cabinet. Names mostly, a few other code names I recognized from the ledger.

Colin had a file. Interesting.

A birth certificate. Colin was twenty-eight, born in Chicago proper to Philip Murphy Sr. and Louisa James Murphy. More paperwork. Hmm, custody something or other. I'd known he had a rough childhood, mostly from his refusal to discuss it, but I hadn't known he'd been in the system.

I had a file: *Winters, Allison*. And it was thick. I thumbed through the contents. The information about Andrew was in here, as well as the papers that Laramie had filed for custody.

I slowed when I found the pictures. They were of my apartment. My mind immediately ran to reasons why Philip would have these. Laramie may have wanted them to show where I was living as part of a custody assignment. No, that wasn't right. I'd already lived with Colin by then. I glanced at them again. Both

Shelly's and my car were in some of the pictures, meaning we both still lived there, so this wasn't some after-the-fact thing.

Actually, from that angle…it looked like they were taken from the street. The same place we'd seen the car sitting and watching. We'd assumed they had been watching Shelly. She was the one in the dangerous profession, but it looked like they'd been watching me. If Philip had these prints, then he must have been the one spying on me. Just because Colin liked me? But I knew. Philip didn't act like an overprotective brother, more like a dog with a bone. He didn't act like he loved Colin as much as owned him.

I flipped through them, even catching one of me loading Bailey into the car. Only after seeing these photos, how we'd looked through the eyes of an outsider, a *man*, did I realize just how vulnerable we'd been. Shelly and I had always known that, to some extent, and that our anonymity was our greatest protection. So long as we stayed under the radar, no one would *want* to hurt us. That was the goal, but it looked like someone had known after all.

Agitated, I moved Bailey back to the floor and opened the last drawer. *Wozney, Wride, Wu. Yates, Tony.* Those letters could have meant anything, but that was the only *TY* name here. I pulled out the file and opened it. A violent shiver racked my body. Someone stepping over my grave, Shelly would say. No, this was worse.

I sat down. Right there on the Persian rug next to the dark oak filing cabinets, I sat. Bailey crawled over, and I had enough presence of mind to lift the papers up out of her reach.

The arrest records of Tony Yates had two pictures on it, one facing the camera, one profile. I recognized that man. That was the man who'd fucked me, who'd *hurt* me, that night I'd gone to the club. The one Colin had stopped, the one Colin had *known*. The receipt dated before I'd even met the guy.

What did it mean? My mind couldn't make sense of it, or maybe it just refused to, knowing it wouldn't be good.

I slipped the contents of Tony Yates' folder back into the cabinet and shut it. I tucked the other scrap of paper from my bra deep inside the diaper bag.

Time to go.

In the dining room the plates were being cleared.

"There you are," Rose said warmly. "I was just going to get your cobbler."

Jesus, the fucking cobbler. The fucking ridiculous cobbler with its fucking ridiculous hope of making a good impression.

"I'm sorry, I—" My breath stuttered.

Colin stood. "What's wrong?"

I blinked rapidly. *Don't cry, you fucking idiot.*

"Bailey wasn't doing so well," I heard Shelly say. "Allie mentioned they might have to leave early because of it."

I couldn't say a word. I needed to get out of this house, or I was liable to do something really ridiculous, like sob or scream or tell the fucking truth.

Colin was talking, then Rose. False words, all of them. *Yes, of course we can go. Oh, I hope you feel better. Let's pretend we care while we pay people to hurt you.*

I was bundled into the car. Shelly tried whispering to me, asking me what had happened as I slipped her back the key, but I couldn't tell her. I barely knew myself.

The drive home was quiet, thank God. I was the chatty one between us, and I was struck mute. Colin didn't seem to know what to do with that. I couldn't help him.

I tried to think rationally, as if I'd ever been any good at it. The guy had approached me, out of nowhere, but that wasn't unusual for the club. I'd gone with him, hadn't I? Or had he forced me? It had felt forced, but then at the time I'd wanted it that way. I'd said no, I knew that for sure. He hadn't listened or cared, but that wasn't all that strange at the club either. Wasn't it supposed to be, though? Guys were supposed to stop when I said no. I didn't know where I'd learned that from, but it seemed like it should be true. They should listen. But they didn't, they didn't. A sob escaped me.

"Tell me," Colin said. "What's wrong?"

I buried my face in my hands. I couldn't talk, not without breaking apart. And this would be the kind of fracture that couldn't be taped back together with a fake smile and a smart mouth.

No matter whether it had been rape or not, the guy had singled me out. He had hurt me. And before he'd done those things, he'd been paid by Philip.

Colin's shock had been real, though. And he *had* beat the guy up afterward. Both the guy and Colin had confirmed that to me. It had scared me then, the violence, but it comforted me now. Surely Colin hadn't been involved in hurting me.

Back in Colin's house, I went on autopilot. A bath first. Then a snack, because Bailey hadn't gotten enough to eat at dinner. Then bedtime stories. I couldn't read the words, my eyes weren't working properly, but I knew them by heart. A few songs and then sleep.

I wanted a shower, but Colin stopped me on the way into the restroom.

"We need to talk," he said.

Yes, we did.

"Did you mess with Rick?" I asked.

The shock on his face wasn't that of a man confused but of one caught.

"Allie, I can explain—"

"No," I said. "Don't bother. What I want to know is—that guy at the club, the one who fucked me in the parking lot, did you know him?"

"I knew who he was, that's it. He did some work for Philip, all low-level muscle shit. I barely knew him."

He must be really worried, I thought acidly, using all those words that sounded like apology but spoke of betrayal.

"Did you pay him to hurt me?" I asked.

"What? No! Jesus, Allie—"

"Did you *ask* him to hurt me? Did you know he would?"

"No." Colin held me by the arms and shook me. "Stop this."

"What was he supposed to do to me?" I asked.

Colin's hands tightened and then released. It was only a very small hurt, but it was a reminder that he was still a man, after all. I'd do better not to trust him so much.

"I had no idea you even knew that guy until Jim told me someone had taken you out," Colin said, his voice ragged. "I followed and found...well, fuck. I found him later and roughed him up a little. Told him not to come back around. And I've never seen him since."

His brown eyes implored me, so fucking trustworthy.

What did it mean if he was telling the truth? It meant his brother, Philip, was a lot more of an asshole than I'd previously thought. And a whole lot more dangerous too. Even more so, because Colin seemed to have no idea.

"Allie," Colin said, a quiet plea.

"I believe you," I said. "I'm sorry. I just...I've been

having a rough couple of days."

I reached my hand out, unsure of my reception, but he took it and pressed it to his face, breathing in my skin.

"I'm sorry," I repeated. "Let me just shower, and it will be over."

Now I was the liar, because it would never be over.

But I did shower and climb into bed, where Colin lay still and quiet. He wasn't sleeping, but we didn't touch and we didn't fuck. We lay side by side with our words between us.

The worst part, I feared, was that I could not walk away. Not that I even could leave Colin now, but it was more than that. It wasn't just a question of whether I'd tell the cop to go take a hike. Philip had sought me out for something, and it was clear that the animosity he felt toward me ran deep. All of a sudden the information I'd stolen seemed a lot more valuable.

It was leverage, just like the photos the cops had of me. Except this was leverage against a guy who wanted me hurt.

I wouldn't do anything as obvious as blackmail with my leverage, though. For one thing I didn't think it would work. There'd be nothing stopping him from telling Colin what I was doing, and that I'd snooped to get information. Even if Colin were surprised to find out about Tony Yates, I doubted he would trust me much after that.

No, I had to bring the cops down on Philip. I told

myself it was about distracting him, about destroying the business that held Colin captive, but it felt more like payback for what Philip had done with Tony Yates.

The cops and Philip—the proverbial rock and hard place. What I needed was for them to go at each other. I wasn't sure which side would crack first, maybe they both would, but I needed them to hammer each other, not me. I just had to make sure to step out of the way; otherwise, I'd get smashed right in the middle.

Fierce

Prologue

COLIN SLAMMED THE bathroom door shut, and I winced. He was still mad about last night. Maybe because I'd accused him of paying someone to rape me.

Okay, probably that.

And maybe he was also pissed because I'd obviously spoken with Rick, since I knew about the debt and the closing of the bakery. Well, I hadn't broken the agreement not to communicate with him—Rick had. I'd never even made such an agreement. Besides, Colin was the one who'd fucked up, manipulating Rick and me. Being controlling. Being a hard ass.

Shouldn't he forfeit his right to be pissed off?

Rick carried some fault as well, risking the bakery by racking up all those debts. Still, it wouldn't do to forgive Colin so easily. He'd taken away my choice. My *consent*, really. With a baby and no job, I could hardly have refused his offer to move in. I would have consented anyway—I *did* actually, not yet knowing the truth—but that wasn't the point. Driving me to desperation was just as bad as holding my wrists above my head. Almost.

Colin stomped out of the bathroom. The man could really throw a tantrum—quietly, though, like he did everything else. I got up to brush my teeth and get ready.

Once downstairs, Bailey fussed for breakfast. I gave her sliced bananas while I made pancakes. She was still making up for last night's diet and didn't mind letting me know it.

According to the calendar the next drop wasn't until tomorrow. I had no doubt that I'd see the cop again before then, probably today. I didn't want Bailey to be here for that.

Colin joined Bailey at the table and plowed through his pancakes in brittle silence.

I finally cracked. "What are you doing tomorrow night?"

He didn't look up. "No plans."

So he wasn't going to the drop. Good. I'd pay special attention tomorrow to make sure he stayed home, even if I had to deep throat him for hours.

"Let's have movie night," I offered.

He shrugged his shoulders just a smidge as he took a bite. Stubborn man.

The difference between his amiable silences and his angry one was like the difference between a chilly day and a hailstorm. I didn't enjoy the animosity between us, but I wasn't ready to call a truce. The only thing I'd done wrong, the snooping, he didn't even know about. Okay, so that wasn't the best defense, but I still felt indignant.

For the first time in weeks he left right after breakfast.

Chapter One

I called Shelly.

"Hey, girl," she said.

"Can you take Bailey out today?" I needed to make a stand, for all of us, but I could hardly do it while Bailey was here.

"You aren't going to do anything stupid, are you?" she asked.

"Of course," I said lightly. "You know me."

She sighed. "I haven't seen her in a while anyway."

"I'll owe you forever."

"You already do." She hung up.

After Shelly picked Bailey up, I settled in to wait. I had kept the card that first cop had given me, tucked between my clothes and next to the money from Andrew. My little stash of secrets. I could call the number, but on the small chance they had forgotten about me, I had no desire to remind them.

From beneath the coffee table I took out the yards of upholstery fabric and basic sewing kit I'd purchased earlier. The place was in desperate need of curtains, but one glance at the prices in the local home decor store had me bolting for the door. It cost more than Bailey's car seat to cover half of a bay window. He had told me to spend anything, buy anything, but years of thriftiness didn't just dissolve because my boyfriend was a successful small business owner and the brother of a wealthy crime lord.

At first I was nervous, constantly glancing out the window and having to redo my measurements. Maybe I was a little afraid that I'd be caught unaware again, even though I'd checked the locks three times.

Two hours later I had a matching pair of lined, navy curtains. These would go in the bedroom. For someone who'd repeatedly had sex in alleys and cars, I felt remarkably skittish about the yawning bay window there. Anonymous sex was one thing—it practically counted as public already with just the stranger I was fucking. Sex with Colin was the very opposite of anonymous. The opposite of a hookup—a mating. Love and sex, together. I was so fucked.

I heard a rap on the back door. I peeked around the window. The cop was here.

I grabbed my props: a paring knife slipped into my back pocket, an old broken cell phone that still did voice recordings, and an index card. Through the window in the door, he waved a manila folder at me. The pictures. He was probably worried I wouldn't let him in. Little did he know I expected him.

I opened the door.

He leaned casually against the doorjamb. "Hey, honey."

So tempting to slam the door in his face, smashing it. Maybe later.

"Philip Murphy's shipping routes, and *you* agree not to arrest me on false charges." I held up the index card, and a twisted smile spread across his face. It occurred to me that this guy might actually be considered handsome. His features were fine, and his eyes that rare green. Never to me, though. There was something in his eyes that I knew enough to fear. The kid who pulled bugs apart just to watch them writhe.

"Good girl," he said, reaching for the card.

I held it away. "I have a few more conditions."

He laughed. "And I give a shit, why?"

"Because I'm the one with the information you need, for one. I'm also the girl *you* molested while my daughter slept upstairs. I doubt your boss would be thrilled to hear about that, especially on prime-time news."

He licked his lips, taken aback; then he regrouped. "I could take that from you—easy." His gaze raked my body, a sneer on his face. "And you liked what I did to you."

"I don't think so," I said, but I let my eyes blink wide. A fake, seductive innocence.

He grinned. "Girls like you play hard to get."

"Maybe," I said with exaggerated thoughtfulness. "Why don't you come here and find out?"

I lay back against the wall, feigning submission. My acting skills left something to be desired, but he went for the bait. They always did.

As he leaned toward me, I smoothed my hand down over his bulge and cupped his balls. And wrenched them, hard. In a second I had our positions reversed—him slumped against the wall, me holding him by the balls.

I put the knife to his throat. "Touch me again, and I'll fucking kill you."

He swallowed hard, and his Adam's apple bobbed against the point of the blade. "Don't do anything stupid," he ground out through barely parted lips. "You'll have to let me up sometime."

"Hurt me, and I'll go to the news. Your boss. I've got a recording of this conversation, where you just admitted to blackmail, among other things."

He curled his lip. "And you'd let Colin find out about your little boyfriend?"

I shrugged as if unconcerned. "Go ahead and show him. If he gets mad, that's my problem. He'll still protect his own. All I'd have to do was point you out, and your partner would be picking your broken bones up off the street."

His eyes glittered emerald. "You stupid bitch. I could kill you right now."

I jammed the knife into his skin, and a small prick of blood trailed down his neck. "I've left a message for Colin with your name. Anything happens to me, and you're dead."

That wasn't quite true, but I had given Shelly

enough of a clue that she'd probably figure it out. I could see this man thinking it over, realizing I had him.

"Don't do anything stupid," I mocked.

He gritted his teeth and emitted a low growl. I liked him better this way, panting, feral. It was more honest. "What are the conditions?"

"You never come back here again, understand? No matter what happens. If I see you around here, I'll speed-dial Colin, and Philip's weight comes down on you. Anything happens to me, same thing. Either way you'd be fucked. You go away and never come back. Deal?"

A pause, with only his harsh breaths and the sound of my blood pumping to fill the silence.

"Deal," he ground out.

I pushed away from him but kept the knife pointing at his jugular. I had him, but animals behaved stupidly sometimes, especially in captivity.

He didn't attack, though, but held out his hand for the card.

I gave it to him, the index card with the address of my old apartment scribbled on it. A useless piece of paper, a misdirection. "Tomorrow night at ten."

He turned and slipped through the open back door. I locked the door and, just as when he'd left last time, slid down the wall, but this was nothing like last time. He hadn't touched me—or just barely—and I'd turned the tables on him. And I wasn't going to let him push me around. If he tried to fuck things up with Colin, I'd deal with it.

A new Allie had emerged, neither slutty nor cowardly. A kick-ass Allie. Or a squeeze-balls Allie, at least. I hadn't been afraid. All right, I'd been fucking terrified, but I was also angry and powerful and *giddy*. If only I could start breathing again, I wouldn't pass out.

I'd figured out over the past couple of sleepless nights that I couldn't betray Philip. I had no love for the man, none at all, but he was Colin's brother. If the law came after Philip, they'd come after Colin too. There was no way I could protect Colin against that. Besides, I couldn't ignore that Philip had helped me with Andrew. Sure, Colin had made him do it, but he'd still helped me. I wouldn't bite the hand that fed me. These were street rules. Revenge was fair play, but going to the cops was always bad form. Whatever had happened with Tony Yates, I wasn't going to let it go. I'd find out more and then decide what to do, but it wouldn't endanger Colin.

Footsteps sounded outside, and I tensed. Shit, I was still on the floor, my teeth rattling like the crappy dryer in the Laundromat.

"Hello?" Linda's cheery voice preceded the rattling of the locked door.

I let her in, still breathing hard, and the next thing I knew, I was slumped in strong arms and a plush chest.

"Oh dear," she was saying. "It must be the heat, tiring you out."

It was a breezy eighty degrees out, I wanted to say,

but it didn't matter. Besides, I rather liked this embrace. So different, so much softer than Colin's, but just as warm.

She half carried me to the couch. I blinked at the ceiling until it stopped spinning.

I sat up. "I'm sorry."

She patted my knee. I jumped, unused to touch that wasn't sexual or violent. I wanted to pull away even as I wanted more. How very perverse of me.

"I'm sorry," I repeated.

"Young lady, don't you apologize to me. I'll have none of that. Now, you need a drink of water. You sit right there, just sit."

Sitting sounded great to me.

She disappeared into the kitchen and came back with a mug. I took a sip and spewed cold coffee across the coffee table. The grossest water ever.

"Oh!" she said. "Sorry, dear. I probably should have mentioned I found the coffee in the pot."

"No," I told her with a smack of my lips to hide my revulsion. "It was good. I needed a wake-up call."

She beamed. "That's what I thought. Where is the little darling?"

"She's with her aunt." I took another sip of the coffee and shuddered.

"Good, then." She settled across from me. "Let me tell you a story."

Yes, story time. I leaned back and closed my eyes, ready to hear about litter box antics or about an anniversary cruise to Alaska. Anything to distract me.

"When I was a young girl—oh, about ten or so—there was this boy that I liked very much. William was fourteen but small for his age, very quiet. He followed his two older brothers around wherever they went. It was a quiet town, it was, just west of the Adirondacks, and they were the troublemakers."

This was even better. An honest-to-God, how-they-met story, complete with a happy ending. And a shy, little pseudo bad boy too. My whole body sighed into the cushions.

"The boys were fixing their usual, you know, tormenting this old mountain dog. They'd shove him in an old barrel and roll him down the hill, they did, and it showed. Messed him up in the head. He couldn't even walk a straight line, and he'd pee himself. It wasn't right, but who could stop them?"

Jesus Christ. My eyes had popped open over the course of this recitation. No, I hadn't quite been expecting it. I wanted initials carved into an old oak tree that they later got married under, not psychopathic animal abuse.

"One day I get all riled up," she continued, "saying how they can't mess with the dog no more, no sir. Of course, they just pushed me around a bit and got right back to it, but then William let loose the dog and said that no, he wouldn't let them hurt that dog no more and they couldn't touch me neither."

Oh. I sighed again. How romantic. Well, it was sad

about the dog, but what a moment.

"You know what they did?" she said. "They put him in the barrel, William, they did, and rolled him down the hill."

"What? Christ, tell me you're joking!"

She gave me a reproving look. "Who would joke about that? Anyhow, that's not the end of the story. Poor William was in the hospital for three weeks and then stuck in bed for longer. He'd never been first in class, you know, and after that it was just downhill." She paused. "Pardon the pun."

"We stayed in that town just until he was eighteen," she said, "and then we moved as far away as possible. Here, to Chicago. He got a job fixing elevators, because it wasn't so complicated he couldn't understand it. And it turned out to be a good thing, because there's been lots of elevators since then, and he was never out of work, not once. So you see, everything turns out for the best."

Holy fuck. I was pretty sure that was the saddest story I'd ever heard in my life, and I'd heard some bad shit. Honestly I'd been feeling pretty good about my encounter, if a little shaken, but now I just wanted to crawl into a hole in the ground. Not that I'd ever been to the country or the mountains, as she'd said, but I guessed I'd always expected it to by idyllic. Backward maybe, slow definitely, but *nice*. That story had not been nice.

"Linda," I said. "I don't know how to tell you this.

But that story is depressing."

"No, it's not," she said, all surprised. "Thirty-two years we were married before he passed over. And sure, he'd get confused sometimes. You know, I'd walk into a room, but he was already talking to me. But that's not the important thing, is it?"

"I'm sorry. You're right." I agreed, because it was her life and William's, and so I could hardly disparage the story without insulting her. Besides, I was afraid she'd keep talking. Jesus.

I took another sip of the cold coffee and pretended my shiver was from that and not foreboding.

Chapter Two

Colin didn't come back until late.

In those dark, lonely hours I mulled over his actions. He had manipulated me in the worst way, cutting off my livelihood. I had a child, after all. What if I hadn't called him? What if I'd taken to whoring myself to cover the bills? Would he have come after me at all if I'd never called him, or was this just a game to him?

I still couldn't be sure that he'd had no part in Tony Yates. I had to believe he hadn't, though, or I couldn't even lie here in his bed.

He smelled of alcohol but not smoke as he settled beside me, in the black of night.

"What made you ask those questions?" he suddenly asked.

I thought about pretending to be asleep, but instead I stalled. "What questions?"

"You know damn well what questions. Did you talk to Rick?"

The way he said Rick's name made it sound like betrayal. It wasn't, and I wanted to tell him that and that Rick had been the one to approach me, but I realized that would only get Rick in trouble. "He's my friend," I said. "So yes, I talked to him."

"I don't want you to see him again," he said tightly.

It was weird to have a conversation in the dark, both of us facing the ceiling. I turned my head on the pillow to see his profile. "You don't get to tell me that. Or is it because I live in your house and eat your food, you get to tell me who I see?"

"Yes," he said. "No! He's a loser, and he wants to fuck you. That's why you can't see him."

Okay, maybe in my most uncharitable moments, Rick was somewhat of a loser. And I thought that maybe he had a point about the other part. I didn't think girlfriends were really allowed to hang out with guys who wanted to fuck them or offered to take them away to some tropical place. At least not girlfriends of guys like Colin.

"I didn't even want to see him," I mumbled. "I just don't see why you had to do that. It's really fucked up."

"I'm sorry," he said, sounding calmer if not actually sorry.

We were silent for a moment, and then he spoke again, sounding almost cautious. "What about the other thing? That night?"

I know someone paid Tony Yates to hurt me because I was snooping in your brother's records as a spy for the cops. No, that would not go over well.

"I can't tell you," I finally said.

"What does that mean?" He sounded incredulous.

"Just what I said. You don't tell me everything you do or everywhere you go, hardly anything. I tell you everything, even my secrets, just not this."

The other reassurances, that this wasn't a big deal, that it wasn't anything he needed to worry about, died in my throat. I wanted to get through this without actually lying. Maybe someday when I'd figured this out, I could tell him. And maybe somehow he'd understand, but it would be better if I didn't lie to him now.

Or maybe not, because he'd sat up, practically vibrating with anger.

"This isn't just anything," he said. "This is you accusing me of raping you."

"You didn't rape me," I said, rather calmly, I thought. "I asked if you paid that guy to rape me or hurt me or anything at all. You said you didn't, and well, I believe you." *So that's that*, my tone said.

He made a disbelieving sound.

We paused with only the sound of his harsh breathing and mine to fill the air.

"I mentioned it to Philip," Colin said.

I sat up too. I hadn't expected Colin to figure it out, but of course he would. It only made sense that if someone paid Tony Yates, and if it wasn't Colin, that Philip might know something about it. That was the same conclusion I'd come to, only I saw Philip as the enemy and Colin didn't.

"What did he say?" I asked, dreading the answer.

With good cause, it turned out, because Colin answered, "He said you were an informant for the cops. That you were digging around for information about his guys."

I held my breath as if my very exhale could incriminate me. "What did you say?"

"I said he was full of shit and punched him in the face."

A sharp laugh escaped me. I clamped my lips shut. *Very inappropriate*, I scolded myself. Still, a small smile curled my lips. He'd believed in me. He'd defended me. And Philip had gotten what was coming to him.

"I hit my *brother*."

I sobered. "I'm sorry, Colin. Even if he deserved it, I'm sorry."

"Allie." *Are you*, his tone asked, *an informant? Did I turn on my own family in defense of a traitor?*

"Are you going to make me answer the question?"

"Are you going to make me ask?" he said.

I sighed. "I can promise you this. I have never given the cops any information about you or Philip or anyone, okay? I never have and never will. I'm on your side. Do you believe me?"

"Yes," he said, and only then did I breathe normally.

His long, large body sat sprawled on the bed, its indolent pose belying his intensity. And, in fact, as we sat there, I felt his breathing change. The air shifted even as we sat very still. Turned out anger was a powerful aphrodisiac once we'd gotten over the fighting part.

Except for the first time with Colin, I wasn't sure if I wanted it. I wasn't sure I *didn't* want it either—fickle me—but I was nervous. My mind flashed to the ridiculous bullfighting photographs in Philip's study. This must be how a bullfighter felt, standing in front of a raging force over which he had no control, waving his red flag, even as he wondered what the fuck he'd gotten himself into.

I'd had sex how many times? Almost a dozen, over the months. All with mean, angry strangers. Bullies, really, but that wasn't Colin. He wasn't a stranger or mean or a bully. He was an angry Colin, and that made him entirely unknown.

I'd let him fuck me, even let him hurt me, but what if he went too far? An even scarier idea occurred to me. What if I didn't want it? I didn't want him to hurt me. Maybe I didn't even want him to fuck me.

What then?

I pictured myself, cowering behind the red flag, scuffing my boots on the dirt. I couldn't run—he'd only chase me. I couldn't fight him—he'd only beat me. As laughable an idea as it was, the only thing left to do was tame him.

I reached out and cupped his cheek. His breath puffed against the inside of my wrist in time with my pulse. I curled my fingers in and stroked the backs of my knuckles up along his temple. He tilted his head into my caress, and I caught my breath. He stayed my wrist in his hand.

He tugged, and I fell over his lap, facedown. He held me there by my wrist while his other hand slid up the back of my thigh. His fingers explored between my legs, not teasing or asking but feeling and taking.

The pleasure was there, but I didn't like it. His legs under my stomach, the bed pressed against my face, my ass exposed. What a whore. No more, *please*.

I made a small sound in my throat, maybe a refusal, definitely a complaint. I didn't know what he made of it, but he rolled me off him. Then he was on me, kissing me. When I didn't open my mouth, he moved down, down.

His hands were rough, pulling off my shirt, touching my body, pulling me apart. His mouth was demanding. He wanted everything, but I couldn't give it to him. No, that wasn't true. I could give in to him. My body was wet with anticipation, my mind slipping to that dark, quiet place, but I didn't want to. *No.*

He tried to kiss me again, and I turned my face away. He made a low sound like a growl, and then flipped me over onto a pillow. I knew what would happen next. The way he pushed apart my knees and tilted my hips and parted me there, it all meant I was going to get fucked. *No!*

"No," I whispered.

He thrust inside me, hot and thick.

"No," I said.

He pulled back. I thought he would pull out.

"Yes," he grunted, and then he thrust again, and again, deeper each time, filling me, invading me—*Get it out!*

"Stop," I said. "Colin!"

He froze. "Allie?"

It was his name that had caught his attention, so I used it again. "Colin, stop."

In a heartbeat he was out of me. I was whipped around onto my back, and he was crouching over me. "What's wrong?" he asked. "Did I hurt you?

"No, I just—" I was fucking this up, that's what I was doing. I'd done this before, in the alley, in my car, once in the bathroom of the club, what was one more time? But I couldn't. I just couldn't.

"I'm sorry," I said. "I don't want to. Not right now. I'm sorry."

"Jesus, Allie." He rolled down to the bed beside me, breathing hard.

We lay there side by side, both flat on the bed, with only his cock standing up, gently waving in rhythm with his breaths, as if to say *don't forget about me!* Neither of us had forgotten, I was sure.

"I thought it was…fuck, I thought it was a game," he said in low tones. "I thought that's what you wanted. I'm sorry."

"No, don't be," I said, my voice small and stupid. "I know that's what I asked for before, but that's not…I didn't want it now."

"Okay," he said, but he sounded confused.

"I'm sorry."

"Allie," he said, then paused. "You're allowed to say no. You know that, right?"

"Of course I know that," I said, too quickly and too brightly.

"Fuck!"

"I'm sorry," I practically wailed. "I'm so messed up."

"Shh," he said, pulling me into his arms. He whispered things into my hair to quiet me while his hands stroked down my back, while we both ignored the thick, damp cock bobbing between us. Damned insistent things, cocks.

It was okay, though, because he didn't freak out or get mad, but of course not. He'd always been tender with me, but there was this block built up in my mind. It wasn't even about men, like I'd thought, or cocks or fucking, but about saying *no*.

I ignored the urge to tell him I was sorry, *again*, or to offer to make him come. It was hard to do, with his cock practically begging for my hand or my mouth, and I so wanted to make him feel good. That way we wouldn't have to lie here thinking about me and my ridiculous issues. Yes, pleasing him was so much better, but if I did that, I'd have nothing. I'd gained one small thing by saying no, by meaning it, by insisting it. I'd gotten my consent back, and I wasn't about to give it away so easily. Not ever again if I could help it.

Men could take my body if they were stronger than me, and they usually were. I never fooled myself about those women's self-defense classes or mace cans. Where I came from, pulling shit like that got you killed. The important thing was to be able to get up and walk away from it after.

I'd given away so much more than that, though. The physical pain had been over in a week. But I'd made it all worse when I gave away my consent, when I'd set out to prove that sex didn't matter, that getting raped was the same thing, and that men didn't listen to *no*.

But not today. Today I'd said no, and he hadn't forced me. He hadn't left. Not even when the air cooled my skin, still damp with a sheen of sweat. His breathing evened out, and with his arm still wrapped around me, he slept.

Chapter Three

With my hand shielding Bailey's eyes, I poured water over her soapy head. I only had to finish up her bath and put her down to bed before I could join Colin downstairs to watch the movie. I'd left him in his study after dinner. It was half past eight, and I was eager to pin him down, safe and secure from the looming drop across town.

Nothing would happen. Nothing *should* happen, after all. Philip's drop should go down as planned, and the cops, if they'd heeded my note, would stake out my empty apartment. Still, I couldn't shake the bad feeling that had shrouded me all day.

By the time I slipped from her room, frazzled, it was past nine o'clock.

I checked the study first. He wasn't there. I strode through the living room, kitchen—no Colin. I peeked out of the burnished amber curtains I'd made for the living room. His truck was gone.

Surely he'd only left to grab some popcorn or drinks or something. Or maybe he really hadn't liked my movie selections. Feeling antsy, I went into the kitchen, where I saw a note sitting on the small stack of

DVDs I'd rented.

Raincheck. Business. Don't wait up.—C

Well, shit. It didn't take a genius to figure out what business stuff he could be up to tonight. Sure, there was the restaurant, but somehow I just knew it was Philip. It wasn't like Colin to ditch me when we'd had plans, but he would go running if his brother called him.

I paced around the kitchen. Something might have gone wrong for Philip to call so last minute, and I worried it was a green-eyed cop in a tweed brown suit.

I hadn't interfered with Colin's business before, not since that night in my apartment when he'd made his stand clear. It required a certain amount of trust that he knew what he was doing. I wasn't his keeper, and he didn't need one. Then again, maybe I'd fucked up. I had thought I was doing him a favor by leading the cop in the wrong direction, but I hadn't been brave enough to tell Colin they were trying to bust him. If he knew, he could be more cautious. If he'd known, he might have stayed with me or canceled the drop or so many other things. What if the cops had found the correct information, or hell, staked out this house and followed Colin when he'd left tonight?

That cop, he was dirty. The fact that he'd tried to blackmail me and hurt me was proof enough of that. He might not even arrest Colin. He could shoot first and ask questions later. If Colin ended up dead tonight…

Resolved, I called Colin's cell. It rang and rang. Voice mail.

I hung up and glared at the phone.

I called again. Still voice mail. This time I left a message, babbling about calling me back right away, that I needed to talk to him, it was *important*, but that wasn't good enough. He may not check his messages until after. He might be in trouble right now.

I did know where the drop was happening, the real one.

That was a bad idea, very bad. But as bad ideas tend to do, this one sprouted up like a weed, strangling all the others.

Picking up the phone again, I dialed Shelly.

"Hello?" She sounded anxious, which matched my mood.

"Shelly. I love you, sweetie, but can you please, *please* come watch Bailey?"

"I can't, not now," she said, sounding distracted. "Some bad shit is going down."

"That's what I'm worried about. There's this drop, and Colin just left, and—"

"Wait a minute. Colin's going tonight? He wasn't supposed to." The sharp edge to her voice startled me. Almost panicky.

"What's going on? What do you know?" I demanded.

"Nothing," she said, but I knew her too well.

"Shelly," I warned. "Tell me what you know."

"The cops," she said. "They're going to be there tonight."

"No, they're not," I said. "I gave the guy a fake address."

Silence on the line.

"Shelly?"

"I gave it to them," she finally said.

"What? Why? No, never mind. Shit! I can't even—I have to get to Colin. I'm going to call him again, but if he doesn't answer, I need to go there."

"I can't come over," she was saying over me. "I'm sorry, but I have to go. Philip's missing. I thought he'd just gone out. I mean, he never goes to the drops personally. I didn't think—"

"Shelly," I interrupted her. "Call Philip. Get them both out of there."

I hung up on her babbling and called Colin, only to cuss out his voice mail.

Deliberating only a second, I ran across the yard to Linda's house and banged on the door. She opened the door wearing a robe and a face mask of white. It startled me momentarily, not that it was scary, despite its skull shape, but how ordinary it was to run through a nighttime beauty regimen. A contrast to the shit storm that was tonight.

"Hi, Linda. I'm so sorry to impose on you, so sorry, but would it be at all possible for you to come watch Bailey for an hour? She's already asleep, so really you'd just have to sit there and—"

"Of course!" she said. "Don't even worry about it."

"Thank you so much. An emergency came up, a family emergency, so that's—"

"Stop, dear. You don't have to explain it all now. I can see you're in a way. Now, you get back to her, and I'll be right there."

Thank God someone could think, because I probably would have babbled half the night away, just like Shelly had done. And, damn! I couldn't believe Shelly had told the cops anything. It didn't make sense. I should have known they'd be pushing for information from all angles, but why would Shelly talk to the cops? Maybe they'd threatened her. Well, of course they had. They'd threatened me, and Shelly was a prostitute, for God's sake. Like taking candy from a baby, that's how easy it would be for them to threaten her with arrest or worse.

I practically dug tracks into the hardwood as I waited for Linda to come over. I remembered the business card that the other detective had given me. What could I say if I called him? *I know my hooker friend gave you intel, but could you please do me a favor and not arrest my boyfriend?* Really I was the epitome of class and grace.

But maybe I could find out something. I darted upstairs and into the closet, where I searched through the folded shirts, looking for the envelope of money Andrew had given me, where I'd stored the business card. They weren't related in any way except that they were things I'd hidden from Colin.

They were gone.

I flipped through the shirts again, then dumped them all out on the closet floor. No cards, no money, nothing. Then for good measure, I rifled through all the drawers. Nothing. It was like the Grinch had taken my Christmas, not even leaving the empty envelope behind.

I had a crazy thought that I'd imagined all of it. Colin was safe, and I'd only imagined my meeting with Andrew and the cops in some sort of housewife hallucinations. I indulged in those fantasies for half a second before snapping back to reality. Colin needed me.

Except Colin must have found the money and the business card. I rolled that over in my mind—he found them together. Would he have thought, was it possible he might think they were connected? That I'd gotten the money from the cops? And there was only one reason the cops would give me money like that: to betray Colin.

No, he'd know better. I wouldn't betray him—I hadn't—and he trusted me. He'd said as much to his brother when Philip had accused me of being an informant. But the money—fuck! And of course Colin had no idea that I'd even met with Andrew, much less that he'd given me money. This looked bad.

The discovery compounded the cluster fuck, but it didn't change my purpose. If anything, it strengthened it. I couldn't sit on my hands at home while Colin did God knew what with the wrong information. It could get him hurt—or arrested.

I peeked in on Bailey, sending up a quick prayer for her safety here at home. Back downstairs, Linda came in carrying a thick book. She hugged me hard, clasping me to her round body. I resisted as if a hug was a threat to me, but she held on until I slumped in her arms.

"Don't worry, hon. Whatever happens, you'll be okay, you know. Go on now."

The words helped, which was strange, because they never had before. I stumbled from the house, hoping I was doing the right thing, hoping I wouldn't be Colin's downfall.

Chapter Four

Some of my panic morphed into frustration as I circled the warehouses that huddled the one I was looking for. For blocks they went on, all large gray boxes, and none of them labeled. Around I went, peering at the tiny block numbers on the street signs, trying to make out the right section of street. Christ, if I was too late because of a fucking street sign...well, that would just be hilarious.

The streetlamps glowed meekly, suspended in the thick of the night. No grassy plots or stick-thin trees dotted this concrete landscape. They'd done away with any pretense that this place was natural.

Cars whirred by, oblivious to my worry. The people inside them surely had worries of their own, but to me those cars were just two bright lights tacked onto metal freight, part of the machinery. All backdrop.

I hadn't identified the warehouse, but I found my stop anyway. Shelly's car. Parked on the side of the road behind a long line of cars, innocuously dark. I pulled in behind her and cut the engine. We were in this together, after all.

The cars zoomed past my door, shaking my car like

a bobblehead. At a break in the line, I opened the car door and clipped around to the curb. I started down the sidewalk when I heard a car door open behind me. My breath stuttered, and I whirled.

Shelly sat in the shadows of the backseat, head bent low.

"Christ, Shelly! You scared me."

She scared me still, unmoving. I walked back toward her, or at least I tried to, but ended up making an arc on the sidewalk, keeping my distance. I squinted into the car—it was empty.

I approached cautiously and squatted in front of her. "Shelly? What's going on?"

She lifted her face, streaked with tear tracks. "I made a mistake."

"I know, shhh." I tried to soothe. "Did you get ahold of Philip?"

She shook her head, and fresh tears spilled over.

"It's okay. We'll find them. We'll fix this."

"It's too late," she said.

"No," I said, feeling clumsy. I wished I had a large, soft body made for comfort and the courage to give her a hug. "Whatever happens, we'll be okay."

I expected her to blow me off with an *I'm always okay, honey*, but she sniffled and wiped her face with her forearms like a child. We were too young for this. Not the skulking around at night—that was the propriety of youth. We were too young for our lives. Selling our bodies and making babies. But then again, when was anyone really ready to do those things?

It had felt like a betrayal when we'd grown up into the bodies and minds of adults but with all the cluelessness of children. Why had they—those *adults*—snapped at us to eat our vegetables and do our homework as if it mattered? When Shelly lay down and spread her legs, it sure as shit didn't matter. And what could I teach Bailey about this world? Nothing I wanted her to know.

I pulled Shelly from the car and towed her behind me, looking for the right gray box. She followed, docile. Little girls do what we're told. We learned that lesson early. Little boys pull our hair and run away, but only a tattletale tells.

This building was barren like all the rest, the rectangular gray walls cutouts against the dark. The door was just a regular door, undersized compared to the massive building.

There was nothing and no one. Hope thumped, that they must have changed the location or canceled the whole thing. We'd come all this way for no reason. Worried little wives…or whatever we were. I would go back home, and Colin would be there. I'd explain everything. Colin would be angry, but at least he'd know I hadn't betrayed him.

A rustle sounded from around the side of the warehouse. The wind lapped against my face, but there weren't bushes or anything else to make that shuffling sound. And I doubted there were animals around here, at least of the inhuman variety.

"Go back to the car," I told Shelly. She was almost catatonic with her quietness and downcast eyes. If something went down here, she'd get hurt.

The low murmur of voices carried on the wind.

"Go," I hissed.

Shelly tightened her hand on mine.

The voices grew louder, and I dragged her toward the other side of the warehouse, thinking at least we'd stay out of sight. There was a long truck planted there, like one of the rigs my dad had driven. The back of the truck was rolled up, caught with its pants down, but no one was around. A stage with no actors, except for us.

I pulled us both back flat against the front of the warehouse. My instincts screamed to get us both back to my car. I would be able to breathe again when we were doing sixty on the highway, any direction that was away. But I'd come here to find Colin. What had I expected—concierge service?

I edged down the wall to the door. The handle actually turned, just like that, but perhaps when you had big enough guns, locks became superfluous.

Peeking inside the door, I saw only shadows and darkness. Nothing but a big, empty room, I told myself. Only children are afraid of the dark.

I didn't really want to bring Shelly in with me, but I couldn't leave her out here alone. We slipped inside.

The warehouse was cavernous, with supports and ducts protruding from the ceiling. Huge crates splayed across the floor at odd angles as if they'd drifted, glaciers. An eerie glow from the rafters lit the space.

An imaginary block of ice slid down my spine. This was all wrong. If they'd moved or canceled the drop, as I'd hoped, then there'd be no one, not even the voices I heard around the side. If they hadn't and the drop was still here and such a big fucking deal, then there should be more people, more activity.

I heard Colin's voice in my head. *"No,"* he had said in his dreams. *"It's a trap."*

We had to get out of here. At the very least I should bundle Shelly up in her car and send her off, assuming she was good to drive. As selfish as it felt, I decided to get out of there. I would have to hope Colin could take care of himself. I had Shelly to worry about now.

I turned back to the door as it swung shut. It was just the wind, had to be.

I put my hand on the knob. It didn't turn. I jiggled it again, then yanked, then banged, but the door stayed shut. It was locked—someone was out there.

I stared at the door, breathing heavily.

Shelly broke her silence. "He must have found out."

I barely processed her words, my mind banging against the futility of our situation.

"It's for the best." Shelly heaved a sigh. "I wish you weren't here, though."

Who would lock us in? Was it better to try and wait them out, maybe arm ourselves with whatever we could find? Or should we call out to them, try to reason or bluff our way out?

"Do you think," she said musingly, "they'll give Bailey to your dad?"

"What?" Her words sank in. I backed Shelly up against the ribbed metal wall, shaking her, bullying her, furious that she would even say such a thing. "Have you gone insane? You have, haven't you? I could kill you! We aren't going to die. We *aren't*. We're getting out of here, and I'm going home to Bailey. You can do whatever crazy shit floats your fucking boat, but leave me out of it. Do you understand? Do you?"

I was the crazy one, raging with impotence and venting fury at my best friend.

Shelly looked past me, her glassy eyes reflecting red and orange flames.

I glanced behind me. "Shit."

A fire spread nimbly along the perimeter of the back of the warehouse, following the path of a metal wall that shouldn't burn. It came around the sides, and I yanked us both away from the wall just as it came around and engulfed the front. Panting on the ground, we were trapped in a rectangle of fire.

Shelly's words came back to me. *"The whole house is rigged to burn if the security gets tripped. No paper trail, just ashes."*

Philip liked fire. Philip was paranoid. One of us here had betrayed him.

Now I understood what Shelly was saying. Philip

must have known someone had betrayed him and set a trap. He'd probably thought it was me, though I doubted he really cared that much about Shelly either.

There was no way we could get out of a locked warehouse. There was sure as hell no way we could get out of walls of flame. I glanced up at the ceiling. No way.

I was really going to die here.

The flames leaped from the far corner onto a crate, which burned around the edges before it puffed into an oversize torch. It was only a matter of time.

Already my breathing was labored. Some of it was panic, but probably the fire was using up the oxygen. Would we suffocate first or would we burn? What a choice.

Oh, Bailey. Now that I'd caught up to Shelly's line of thought, my question was the same. Would they give her to my dad? He'd raised me alone, after all, though he was twenty years older now. It wasn't so bad a fate for Bailey, I told myself, trying to ignore the sickness in my stomach. If I was upset that I couldn't see her again, didn't get to watch her grow, that was my own selfishness talking. I'd brought this on myself when I hadn't trusted Colin.

Oh God, did Colin know Philip had done this? For all I knew, he was the one who'd watched us enter and locked us inside. He'd found the money, the cop's business card, so he had every reason to believe I had betrayed him. I wanted to believe he wouldn't have done this. He would have confronted me, let me explain. Anything other than kill me—and like *this*.

But I'd always been a realist, and Colin was a hardened criminal, after all. A mean son of a bitch, he'd once told me. I'd denied it then, but it might be true after all. He beat up a man just for messing with me when he'd barely known me. He'd probably killed before. Just because he'd let me live with him, just because he'd fucked me didn't mean I got special treatment.

Or maybe this was the special treatment. Maybe regular enemies got a bullet to the head, but traitors like Shelly and me got punished. Not just killed but burned, like fucking witches with a phony trial.

God, I needed to do something. I couldn't just sit here and wait.

I ran to the nearest crate, one standing near the middle that hadn't yet caught fire. My eyes burned from the heat and the smoke. I groped at the sides, searching for a latch. I moved around the crate, leaving a trail of blood as the coarse wood scraped open my fingertips. Finally I caught on a padlock.

It wasn't any good. I couldn't budge it. Then Shelly's hands pushed me aside. She reached to the top and pulled herself up as if to climb it, but then stomped down on the padlock, and it broke apart.

Together we pulled aside the opening to reveal large black containers stacked up like legos.

"Help me up," I said. My voice came out scratchy,

but she heard me and bent to give my foot a lift. I caught hold of the second to highest container by its top, and my feet found holds on the lower ones. Slowly and with Shelly's support behind me, I dragged myself up to the top.

The smoke was thicker up here, and I could barely open my eyes. I waved Shelly away, and she disappeared into a cloud of smoke. I rocked, gently at first and then harder, until the containers toppled onto the concrete.

When I opened my eyes, I saw one of the containers had cracked open, spilling large, gleaming guns like a macabre treasure chest. I forced myself up, but Shelly had already picked up one of the guns. She aimed it at the fire and pulled the trigger—nothing happened.

"Bullets?" she asked hoarsely.

We looked through the rest of the guns, crouching low to avoid the worst of the smoke, but there were no bullets packed with them. That would be too convenient.

Fuck.

Through my fear and despair, anger surged. Okay, so I should have trusted Colin. He'd given me so much, all on faith, and I should have told him everything, but I hadn't betrayed him. I'd had the opportunity to strike back at Philip—and every reason to do so, considering Tony Yates—but I hadn't. And I was only here in this godforsaken warehouse because I was worried about Colin. I hadn't betrayed him. I didn't deserve this from him, assuming he'd known about it.

I picked up one of the guns and dipped low. It was heavier than I'd thought, which was good. I stormed back to the door. The flames hadn't actually caught on to the door. Whatever they'd put on the walls to make them burn, the door seemed to be resistant. But the flames still crowded in from the walls, heating my skin and making it itch.

I raised the gun above my head and slammed it down on the doorknob, a shiny beacon through the flames. The shock from the impact traveled through the gun to my arms. Christ, that hurt. Was it possible to get bruised by *vibrating*?

But pain hardly mattered when I was about to get fried. I picked up the gun and brought it down on the door again. I wasn't even aiming for the handle anymore, just hitting the door with my everything. Maybe it would somehow be enough, and it would open. Even if it didn't, I'd go down fighting.

"Allie!"

I paused with the gun raised above my head, panting. I must have imagined it. It didn't come from behind me, from Shelly, but in front of me, from outside the door. And the voice, though distant, sounded male.

"Allie!" Closer now and definitely Colin.

Yes! My first thought wasn't even that we would be saved, but that he hadn't done this. If he was here looking for me, he must not have left me here to die. A weight lifted, and I breathed easier despite the thick, gritty air. It would have been almost the worst part of dying, aside from not seeing Bailey again, to think Colin had done this to me.

"I'm here." There was no way he could hear my croak through the metal door, above the dull roar of the fire, so I banged against the door with the gun again. Not as hard now, but faster. *I'm here!*

"Hang on," he said.

I stood there, because where else could I go? I could only hope I'd live long enough to have nightmares about this scene.

Then the door banged back at me, hit from the other side. I backed up into Shelly, and we both moved out of the way. Whatever he' used, or maybe just his stronger swing dislodged the door handle, and just that small sliver of escape sucked in fresh air.

"Get back," he yelled, his voice clearer now.

We were already standing away, but we backed up even farther, to the spill of guns.

Two shots and another loud bang and the door creaked open. The top side of it had pulled down and out, but the rest of the door seemed to have melted into the frame. The space should be large enough to squeeze through, but it was too high.

Colin appeared in the space and saw that we couldn't reach. "I'm coming in," he said.

"No," I tried to yell. Then he'd be trapped. "Wait a minute. Shelly, help me."

We dragged one of the open containers over to the door. I let Shelly go first, practically pushing her out of the hole. Then I dragged myself through, ignoring the sharp pain of the too-hot metal against my skin.

I collapsed next to Shelly on the concrete, gasping for the air of the city.

"We've got to move," Colin panted. "This place'll blow when the fire hits the ammo."

Oh good. He was planning to blow us up, not burn us to death. How comforting.

I dragged Shelly up, both of us wheezing, almost choking on the thick smoke inside our lungs.

Colin pulled us all along somehow. I couldn't quite see yet, at least not beyond a few feet, and followed him blindly. He slowed, and Shelly dropped to the ground. I fell beside her again, my muscles like jelly, while Colin put his hands on his knees and head down.

Staring up at the sky, I saw only black.

My breaths rattled in my chest as I heaved on the ground, but it seemed that Colin was recovered. "Get up," he said. "You need to get out of here."

"Me?" I asked. "You're not coming with us?" I was mostly offended that he'd let me leave like this, though in truth I probably couldn't drive as I was.

"No," he said. "Take Bailey and leave."

He'd put something in my hand. It was the envelope of money from Andrew, the same fucking envelope of money. It felt different, lighter. Not that I should care about such a thing as some missing money, but I was struck dumb by the whole experience, and I looked inside. The thick wad of hundreds seemed to have grown even thicker.

I looked up at Colin. He towered over me, chest heaving, eyes flashing.

"You still think I did this," I whispered.

"I don't care," he said, the acid in his voice burning me anew. "It's not safe for you. Just go."

"Did you do this?" I stood and listed to the side, where he caught me. "Did you leave me in there to die?"

"Then why would I get you out?"

"I don't know," I asked, my voice breaking in fits and starts, like the worst case of puberty. "A change of heart, maybe?"

"I didn't know it would be you," he said, looking me straight in the eye. "When I called home and that neighbor picked up, I came here." So he hadn't meant to kill me, not exactly. It was a test, one I'd failed. Not for the reasons he thought, though. I'd come for him.

"Colin," I said. "You have to believe me. I didn't do it. I didn't tell the cops about this—"

"Don't." He looked offended.

"I'm not lying! That money wasn't from them. They were together—it was just a coincidence. They came around a couple times, but I just gave them a fake address."

"Philip said someone broke into his study."

I had to tell the truth. He'd know it if I lied. Besides, not telling Colin the truth was what had gotten me into this in the first place. I had to trust him. I'd trust him to keep me safe with the truth. If he wasn't what I thought, I was fucked anyway. "I did that. I went into his study. The cops said they'd arrest me or take Bailey away if I didn't help them. So I found out about this drop, but I didn't tell the cop, I swear. And they were going to tell you about—well, I met with Andrew. That's where I got the money. I wanted to ask him to leave Bailey and me alone, and he did. I'm sorry I didn't tell you. I just didn't want to fuck it up, but that's the truth. That's the whole fucking truth. I swear it, okay?"

He said nothing.

"I swear it on Bailey's life."

I implored him with my eyes, hoping I didn't look quite as out of my mind as I felt. It would also have helped if I could have made out his face, but my vision was still fuzzy for anything more than a foot away.

"Do you believe me?" My voice cracked.

Colin's harsh breath sawed through the night. "Yes."

"Forgive me?" I whispered.

He nodded shortly.

"How kind of him." I heard Philip's voice and looked over to see his leaning form against a concrete wall. "But that's only fair, considering he was keeping secrets for far longer."

Chapter Five

"SHUT THE FUCK up," Colin growled.

"I told you to tell her yourself," Philip said, his tone bloated with pleasant inevitability.

"Another word and I'll quit," Colin said. "Don't test me."

Even though I knew it was in Philip's best interest to stir up trouble between us, I couldn't help but ask, "What are you talking about?"

Philip smiled, the cat got the cream. "Didn't you ever wonder how you ended up with him that night? A man so ready to take on your baggage, almost as if he'd already known."

Colin's low, rumbling response reminded me of a dog I'd once seen chained to the front of a broken-down house. It sounded like fear.

"Colin?" I asked.

"Ignore him," Colin ground out.

"I don't understand," I whispered, waiting for him to say Philip was crazy, that he was *wrong*, but Colin just stood there, glaring impotent wrath at his brother.

"I own that club," Philip said, then nodded at whatever he saw on my face. "One night we hear there's a disturbance out in the alley." He shrugged. "Some people having sex."

My breath caught. Suddenly I wished I'd listened to Colin, who vibrated with anger but made no move to stop Philip. Why should he? I'd asked for it.

I didn't want to hear my shame described in cool, clipped tones, but Philip continued inexorably. "Normally I don't care what people do, but I discourage public displays of prostitution. I don't need the cops breathing down my neck. My bouncer's tied up, and Colin was visiting to talk about business, so I send him out. He comes back, says it's not a problem, but next thing I know, he's looking through receipts and spending every Saturday night at the club. It wasn't hard to figure out he had a little crush."

A small sob escaped me, cementing my humiliation.

"Your lover's drama is fascinating," Philip continued, "but if you didn't tell the cop, then who did?"

Shelly staggered up like a baby doe, ready to take responsibility for giving information to the police about Philip. He would kill her.

I stepped in front of her. "Why did you pay Tony Yates to fuck me?"

"What?" Colin and Shelly asked at the same time.

Philip strolled forward. "So you admit to snooping in my study."

Colin inched in front of me. We were like a line of dominoes: Philip, Colin, me, and Shelly. The only question was who'd fall first.

"What are you talking about?" Colin asked me without turning.

"Tell him," I said to Philip.

"You'd protect her?" Philip asked Colin, his disdain clear. "Even knowing she betrayed you?"

"What is she talking about?" Colin asked him.

Philip's face came into focus as my vision cleared, lined with fury. "She's just some girl you picked up at the bar, nothing but a little slut, and you wanted to throw away thousands of dollars for her."

"That was my call," Colin said.

"Bullshit," Philip said. "I'm the head of this family, and she was taking you for a ride. She wanted it. It's not like he had to go to her house to do it. Just wait for her to come back around the club, slumming for another fuck—"

Colin slammed his fist into Philip's gut. Philip bent over and then fell sideways to the ground, making gasping noises that rivaled our own when we'd emerged.

Colin picked Philip up off the ground and slammed him down onto his knee. Colin dragged him up again and waited while he caught his breath.

"Fight back," Colin said, shaking him.

"Colin, no." I reached out but didn't touch.

"Let them," Shelly said. "It's long overdue."

Philip threw a punch at his head. Colin blocked it, but Philip grabbed him around the neck and swung them both to the ground.

A blast from the warehouse sprayed light down on us like fireworks. Between my shock and the tremors on the ground, I wobbled on my feet.

That was enough to knock the brothers apart, thank God. Colin rolled to a stand, breathing hard. Philip, battered and disheveled, lounged on the ground like he'd just sat down for a picnic. Fucking Philip, with his clipped, almost accented words, even though I knew he was from here, and his fancy clothes and house. He thought he had power, but he was just a fucking poser. True power was Colin protecting me. Colin *believing* in me, seeing me fuck a guy in an alley and thinking I was worth more than my dirty actions.

When my ears stopped ringing from the boom, I heard sirens.

"If they didn't know where we were before," Philip said, "they do now. Let's wrap this up, shall we?"

"Fuck you," Colin spat.

Philip affected a bored look, but I wasn't fooled. His eyes shot daggers at me. Mine shot them right back. The man had just tried to kill me. I wasn't inclined to be polite anymore.

"Fine," he said. "I'd hate for the cops to catch us with our pants down, so to speak. We can fight over the bitch later."

Colin growled at Philip's reference to me, looking almost ready to pounce.

"Guys," Shelly said in a singsong voice. "I think we

have bigger problems."

I looked at her, and then I saw them. Surrounding us were three thugs and the cop, my own personal nightmare come true. No one had weapons drawn, but these weren't the sort to bring a knife to a gunfight. This was what I'd come here to avert—Colin caught, Colin endangered—but here we were.

Because of me, Colin was here. Because of me, we were all fucked. The story of my life.

Philip stood and brushed himself off, then gave an ironic bow to Shaw. "Hello, Detective."

Clearly no introductions were necessary.

"You're under arrest," Shaw said with a smirk. "You have the right to remain silent. Should I go on? I know you've heard it before."

"If you're going to arrest me, then by all means, continue." Philip shrugged, the picture of a man unconcerned. "But I think we both know that's not what's going to happen."

"I might," Shaw murmured. "I just might. Or maybe one of your whores." He eyed Shelly.

"I don't share," Philip said.

"That's not what she says," Shaw taunted. It was a schoolyard insult, but somehow it rang true. "She's been talking to the cops."

Philip's facade paused in a freeze-frame; then he turned slowly to Shelly, who shrank from him.

"You," he said incredulously. Every muscle tensed as I watched him for the rage that would come. An asshole like him wouldn't take well to one of his own betraying him, but oddly he looked more confused than furious. Hurt, almost.

Shelly put her hands up like she was apologizing for forgetting to pick up milk at the damn grocery store. She actually took a step *toward* him. I wanted to shout at her to get away, but it caught in my throat. Why wasn't she afraid of him?

"I'm sorry, Philip." Her mouth tightened as she looked Shaw over. "It wasn't him, though."

Shaw flicked his gaze to me, and his eyes hardened. "No, someone gave *me* some misinformation. I figured that out soon enough. It was my partner, but I'm afraid he's been unavoidably detained at the moment." He sighed with exaggerated forbearance. "I'll have to clean up this mess by myself."

"What do you want?" Philip said as if bored. "More money? How trite."

Shaw's forehead ridged in anger. He couldn't act even half as cool as Philip. I had to give Philip credit for that much. He played his part well, even when he was outgunned.

"I already have a friend with deep pockets," Shaw said. "Turns out you aren't that popular. Dimitri Golastov wants you dead."

Philip snorted. "A street dealer who pretends he's playing in the big leagues. Buying up cops with his daddy's money."

Shaw looked briefly disconcerted, but only for a

moment. "Yeah, well, there's a lot of it, and cash rules the street. He's got all the players in place. Now all he needs to do is knock out the competition."

"You're the one who's been fucking with the shipments," Colin said.

Shaw shrugged. "When I could find them, and assuming I could keep my snotty little partner away. I knew it would only be a matter of time before you came to one of these drops yourself." He nodded toward one of his men. "Put the girls in the car. We'll deal with these two here."

When one of the men made a move toward me, Colin stepped between us. "I don't think so."

"Let's do them all," one of the men said.

Shaw's eyes slid to me, then down my body. "I'd hoped for a little more time with you, but I don't want this to get messy." His gaze lingered on my breasts. I resisted the urge to cover them with my hands. Then he nodded to the one who'd spoken. "Do it."

An efficient one, he was, because he lifted his gun and aimed it straight at Philip's chest. The money shot.

The bang sounded just as Shelly flew in front of him. Even before they'd collapsed in a heap, Colin had knocked down the guy nearest us. He pushed me down. My cheek hit the concrete with an alarming crack. Dazed, I heard more gunshots, but all I could think of was Shelly. What the hell had she been thinking to do that, any of it? God, let her be okay.

I looked up to see the first shooter fall back. The

sirens whined closer. Shaw took off at a sprint in the opposite direction. Once he'd lost his goons, he was toothless. Colin took off after him.

Philip was crouched over Shelly. He would hurt her. Hit her, choke her; there were a million ways a man's body could hurt a woman's. He could do it because he wanted to, because he paid her, and most definitely because she'd betrayed him.

Ignoring the throbbing in my head, I crawled over to them. And then stopped in horror.

Shelly lay flat on the ground, a circle of blood spreading across her stomach. Her eyes blinked wide in her face, her skin pale under a layer of soot.

"Don't move." Philip pulled off his jacket and pushed it into the wound. "We'll get you to the hospital. You'll be fine."

She tried to sit up.

"No," he said, pushing her gently down. "Stay still." He wasn't hurting her; he was helping her.

A shudder ran through her, and then she lay still. He looked up at me, eyes bewildered. "I don't know what to do," he said.

I shook my head. I didn't either, and terror gripped me. This was *Shelly*.

She smiled faintly up at me, ever on display. "Ouch."

My laugh came out watery. "I don't understand. Did they threaten you? Why did you do it?"

She blinked in slow motion. "Worse than that. I

broke the rules. I fell for..."

I looked at Philip and then back at her. It didn't make sense. If she'd fallen for Philip, why would she betray him?

"Not him," she said, her breaths coming faster.

I looked at Philip. He looked as confused as I was. Then who?

Shelly squeezed her eyes shut as another shudder racked her body.

"Shh," he soothed, tucking a hair back from her face. "Just rest. It's okay."

A car pulled to a screeching halt, dousing us in red-and-blue lights. A door slammed, but neither Philip nor I moved from Shelly's side. I hadn't expected this kind of self-sacrifice from Philip, to give himself up just to see that Shelly was okay. He seemed to be in shock.

I hadn't realized he'd actually cared, but he'd definitely been shocked and hurt when he'd realized she'd betrayed him. He looked devastated now that she was injured. He cared about her, but she'd fallen for someone else.

The cop didn't tell us to put our hands up or read us our rights. He didn't even acknowledge us except to shove us out of his way to Shelly.

He bent over her and ran his hands along her arms, frantically checking for more injuries. Shelly's eyes were still closed, but I felt her tacit acknowledgment of him.

"The ambulance is on its way," he told her in a gruff voice that I recognized. His name I remembered well—Detective Lucas Cameron. It had been on the card he'd given me.

"Doesn't even hurt," she murmured.

"That's not good," he said, clasping her hand between his. "Stay with me."

"I'm here."

They spoke quietly, intimately. Lover's voices. I felt like a voyeur watching them. I looked again at Philip, whose ass was planted on the concrete. He looked like he'd just been steamrolled. I could almost feel bad for him. Almost.

Oh, she'd gotten him good. Moving in with him, pretending to like him, getting him to care for her. Meanwhile she'd just been pumping him for information to feed to this guy. Except she did like Philip. I hadn't misread that. She'd taken a bullet for him.

More cops arrived. They went through the formalities, questioning both of us, and arresting me in relation to the explosion. Philip, who'd only arrived later, was allowed to go. Yeah, that stung like a motherfucker. I knew what my sins were, but I hadn't done anything wrong here. Definitely nothing illegal, but somehow I ended up in the backseat of a car with flashing lights. Philip, with his money and his arrogance, got to walk away.

I'd been playing a game without knowing the rules. I hadn't even seen the board. Meanwhile Philip was arranging shit, and Shelly was turning on him, none of which I had any clue about, and Colin. Colin had been playing the middle, trying to appease both Philip and me, more fool him.

I rested my face against the cool window of the police cruiser. I hoped Colin was okay, at least, wherever he was. I made excuses for why he didn't come back, ones that didn't involve him getting injured or him abandoning me. After all, it didn't make much sense for a criminal to walk into a cop's nest. He couldn't have known they'd let Philip go, and besides, if Colin had shown up, they might have done something different. Police were dangerous because they were an unknown quantity. They could be working for the moral superiority or taking kickbacks or just trying to get a paycheck. At least the bad guys had a clear objective.

I understood why he'd gone, but it still hurt. With Shelly sent off in the ambulance and Colin off to parts unknown, I was completely alone. It must have started raining, because a droplet wove down the glass and pooled at the bottom. One, then another. I'd watched them just like this when I rode in my dad's truck. They never went in a straight path. That would have made the most sense, straight down. Instead they turned and curved and angled, taking a long, circuitous route to the end. It would be scary, I thought, to be that drop. To know she was going down, but not know how or when it would happen.

My gaze flicked up to where Shelly was being loaded into the ambulance, Detective Cameron at her side. No, it wasn't raining. It was me.

God. *Bailey.*

Chapter Six

EVEN THOUGH WE'D taken different vehicles, Shelly and I ended up at the same place. The county hospital was surprisingly cheery, for all that it was populated with the no-healthcare segment of the population. The blinding yellow lights and ridiculous sea-green walls said we might die here, but we'd die brightly.

Although it looked like we wouldn't die. Shelly had gotten out of surgery and was stable. The bullet had missed her major organs, only nicking her intestines. She'd been lucky.

They'd patched up my scrapes and treated me for smoke inhalation, but it was my head that was the problem. I had a Grade III concussion, they said, and I'd stay in the hospital in case I kicked the bucket overnight. Ironic that my main injury was sustained when Colin had pushed me down out of the gunfire to protect me.

They knew about Bailey, and a social worker was to check on her and decide what to do. Supposedly, but no one knew anything, and I wasn't allowed to use the phone. Trust the system, the nurse said. I laughed aloud, an ugly sound. That had been two hours ago. It would be breaking dawn soon, and I still hadn't heard anything.

Oh, and that guard at the door would make sure I didn't get any bright ideas. *Thanks, system.*

My head pounded as if my old upstairs neighbor's music was blaring into my brain. I was afraid to tell them, though, in case they'd give me something that would knock me out before I heard from the social worker.

The door clicked open, and I tensed.

Philip walked in, looking aggravatingly clean and fresh in a suit despite his black eye.

"You bastard," I said. The gravity of the night had settled in. I'd almost died because of *him*. I swung out of bed, ready for what would have surely been the feeblest ass-kicking ever. But it was worse than expected, because I hadn't counted on the dizziness, despite the nurse's warnings, and I ended up in a tangled heap on the floor.

He was at my side, lifting me, and I took full advantage, swinging my fists. They glanced off the slick, tailored fabric with no injury to him, though I felt every blow reverberate in my skull. "You stupid, sick bastard. I hate you. You're such a fucking bastard."

He dropped me back onto the bed and gave me a raised eyebrow that questioned my skills at insults. "Are you finished?"

I glared at him. Bastard. "What are you doing

here?"

"Came to check on you," he replied smoothly.

"Uh-huh, and the guard just let you walk in here?"

"He's there to keep you in, not others out. Besides, despite what happened earlier, most of the cops are my friends."

"Friends or employees?" I asked.

"What's the difference?"

I snorted, and a small smile cracked on his face.

"Actually," he said, "I thought you'd be glad to see me, since I bring news of Bailey."

I sat up so hard my head spun. "How is she?"

"She's fine. Relax. She's with Colin back at home. I just came from there, and she's still sleeping. When she wakes up, she'll stay with him."

"Really?" I narrowed my eyes. "Is that what the social worker said?"

"Absolutely."

"Don't mess with me," I warned.

He nodded. "At first she had other ideas, but then...let's just say we became friends. Colin assumed that's what you would want, rather than her being placed—"

"That's what I want." I should no longer be surprised at the problems that could be solved with money. But well, the world had looked very different when I didn't have any. I was glad of it now, though I still didn't trust Philip. "Why didn't Colin come himself?"

Philip looked down, kicking his Italian leather shoes into the gray rubber tiles. He looked suddenly like a little boy who'd gotten in trouble, overgrown and overdressed. "He didn't want to leave in case Bailey woke up. She knows him, so she wouldn't be scared. And also…well, I am supposed to apologize."

The silence stretched.

"So," he said. "I'm sorry."

"For?" I asked.

"For getting you almost raped and almost killed," he mumbled. Then he added quickly, "I didn't know he would hurt you. He was just supposed to pick you up. And the explosion, you weren't supposed to even know about it if you weren't spying on us—"

"I just don't understand *why*," I said, baffled. "I didn't do anything to you."

"I suppose I owe you an explanation." He paused, a long, reluctant minute. "Our childhood wasn't…easy. The three of us, we weren't always together back then. And later I considered it my responsibility to make sure it stayed that way, no matter what. I'm sure that sounds like an excuse, because it is. It was wrong and paranoid, but it's just that once a woman knows his name, what he's worth…"

He seemed to be waiting for me, reassurance maybe. "It's a nice restaurant," I finally said. "Seems like it's doing very well, but that's not why I was with him."

He looked faintly puzzled. "It does okay, sure, but where do you think he got the money to build it in the first place?"

Ah, more guilt. "From you?"

Definitely confused now. "No. From us, from what we—" Suddenly he laughed. "He didn't even tell you, did he? He was in business with me. He's probably got more banked than I do."

I frowned. "He said he did work for you."

Philip snorted. "We went into business together. I didn't even come up with most of the ideas; he did. I was the strategist, but he was the dreamer. He was the one who wanted to get out. Settle down, he said, try to be normal. Then he hooks up with some girl from a nightclub, and she happens to have a baby but no father for it. A ready-made family, no offense."

"None taken."

"So you can see why I was worried. And then I hear that someone's talking to the cops, giving them information, and I assumed it was you." He sighed. "I'm truly sorry."

If he was lying, I couldn't tell. The normally harsh lines of his face had smoothed, making him look so much younger. I felt very motherly, then, having to put aside my righteous anger in the face of a sincere apology. It sucked.

"Are you going to throw money at someone so I can get out of here?" I asked crossly.

He looked relieved I'd changed the subject and snapped back into his usual, brusque self. "We're working on it. The cops want to hold on to somebody just so they can look like they're doing their jobs. Laramie's on it, and we should have you out of here in a few days—tops."

"Days?"

"Tops," he repeated. I rocked my head back onto the bed in frustration and immediately regretted it as my head throbbed in retaliation.

He turned to leave.

"Wait," I said, and he looked back. I'd been hesitant to bring her up, but he was my only source of information. "Have you seen Shelly?"

His eyes flashed briefly before they chilled. "No," he said, like ice. He paused at the door, sighed. "Room 504," he muttered before slipping out.

I could have laughed. Why have her room number if he wasn't going to see her?

I was sure everyone thought I'd be comfortable enough here. Colin and Philip and even the cops probably thought it was a favor that I was here and not in jail, but I'd have preferred that. This room upturned too many memories. The smell, the thin, rough fabrics, and, when I forgot myself and looked up, the same bumpy ceiling tiles.

I fell into a fitful sleep and woke up huddled against the cold plastic railing, drenched in sweat. The clock said it was morning. Muffled footsteps and voices came from outside the door, doctors and nurses bustling about their day. I got up and used the bathroom, then wrapped the sheet around me like a robe.

I poked my head out. The guard stood up when he saw me. The skin on his face was as smooth as Bailey's bottom. He had to be around my age, but he seemed so young. Had I ever been that wide-eyed?

"Hi," he said. "Are you okay? Do you need something?"

"Actually," I said in a low tone, and he leaned forward. "I need you to go and get me the morning-after pill."

"What?" he practically squeaked. He glanced to the nurse's station, which was empty.

"Yeah," I said. "There was a little accident last night."

"But"—he swallowed hard—"shouldn't the doctors be the ones to…you know…"

"They could," I said. "But they'd ask all sorts of questions. I figured you wouldn't want that. What with—well, considering it was your colleague and all."

His eyes bulged. "My colleague?"

"What did his badge say?" I pretended to think. "Sham. No, Shaw."

His mouth worked, but nothing came out.

"Yeah, so I just figured you guys wouldn't want that going around. About a cop and all. Well, it's up to you. I'll just be inside."

I shut the door and waited five minutes, then poked my head out. He was gone.

With my sheet trailing behind me like a robe, I strode through the hallway. So long as I looked like I knew where I was going, no one would bother me. I passed a few people in regular clothes and scrubs, but they only spared me a glance, despite my hospital gown and bare feet.

Room 504.

I slipped inside and saw why Philip may not have stayed, if he'd come by at all. Detective Cameron sat on the bed, his hair mussed and suit rumpled.

He looked up at me with bloodshot eyes.

"How is she?" I asked, letting the door fall shut behind me.

He tried to speak, but nothing came out. He cleared his throat and tried again. "She's doing well. Unless she gets an infection, she should make a full recovery."

I nodded, hanging back near the door. He was a cop. He might just send me back to my room. "That's what they told me."

"Here," he said. "You can sit."

He got up and stood by the window. I went to stand by the bed.

Shelly lay there, sleeping. Her skin was pale, with a flat, grayish tint. The only movement was a slight rise and fall of her chest under the blankets. More blankets than I'd had, and I supposed she could thank her cop for that.

Shelly had fallen for a cop. And if the way he looked at her was any indication, he'd fallen right back. It stung that she hadn't told me, but I understood.

What a match. A modern-day tragedy.

The chair behind me felt too far away. I climbed in beside her. The hospital bed groaned ominously, but it would just have to deal with it. I wrapped my arm across her from atop the blankets. Her body felt so slight, almost childlike. I rested my chin on her shoulder. She slept on.

Wind whispered across me, followed by a blanket, and I was covered up too.

"Thanks," I whispered, without turning my head.

He grunted his welcome, then pulled the chair around to the other side of the bed and even farther away, and sat down. Somehow he knew he made me uncomfortable. More than that, he felt inclined to help me, stepping away so that I could be near Shelly without fearing his proximity. He was a strange one, this cop.

I rested that way, calmed by the scent of Shelly's peach shampoo and the steady thump of her heartbeat. A nurse came in to check Shelly's machines. She started to ask me to move, but Cameron cleared his throat, and she worked around me. Then it was the three of us and the machinery, steadily beeping away.

"Shelly said you had a problem with a cop," he said.

I tensed. *The smell of alcohol and sickness. Rough hands pulling, prodding.*

"She said someone threatened you. I'd like to hear what happened if you'll tell me."

Ah. She'd told him about his partner, or the gist of

it, anyway. Not *that*.

Still, I wasn't sure I could. It was too raw, too related.

Maybe Colin or Shelly, *maybe*. I trusted them, but I barely knew this guy. He seemed nice enough for a cop. And the way he'd been with Shelly, that counted for something. But trust was a rare and precious thing, like a jewel. When I found it, the thing to do was lock it up tight, where it would be safe. The very worst thing was to lose it. It would have been better not to have it at all.

He stood slightly and took off his jacket, then draped it over the back of the chair.

He removed his jacket and pulled out his notepad. Then he came to stand by the bed.

Shelly whimpered in her sleep, and I realized I had tightened my arm around her. I loosened it and moved it close to my body, resting at her side.

"It will be okay," he said. "I just want to help."

"That's right. I can help you."

I shuddered.

What would happen if I told? It was such a foreign idea.

Almost like thinking, what if I jump off a cliff and try to fly? After all, it might work.

I opened my mouth to tell him nothing happened or, hell, to tell him the truth about his partner, but something else came out. Everything.

I told him how I'd grown up riding in the cab with my dad. While my dad was in the bathroom, one of the other truckers called me a "little lot lizard." I'd thought it was funny, but when I'd told my dad about it, he'd beat the guy up. I didn't know then it meant a hooker.

I told him I'd met Andrew in third grade. This one boy had kept picking on me. It even got physical, pulling my hair, pinning me down. Well, I'd always been small. One day at recess Andrew shoved a handful of poison ivy leaves down the boy's pants. Andrew ended up getting the rash all over his hand, and he got detention too, but the other boy never messed with me after that.

I kept talking, lost in my own world. I said what Andrew had done. What the cop at the hospital had done. And then finding out about Bailey. How I'd raised her, and how Shelly had helped me do it.

I talked about Colin and that first night. I'd have blushed if I'd been thinking, telling this guy about our sex, but I wasn't thinking, I was talking.

I told him about how Andrew came back and my fear and about Colin and Philip and, finally, about Detective Shaw. All the way up until last night. I told him everything dark and shameful, and probably even incriminating.

It wasn't really a conscious choice. Something about this place, this cop, my fear for Shelly, had destroyed my barriers. The dam had broken, the one that was supposed to keep me from spilling my soul to people I didn't know and who didn't care.

Maybe also it was a kind of therapy. I'd wondered

before how people ever talked. How did someone share something dark, something secret, with a stranger? Now I knew. When the time was right, it just came spilling out, unstoppable.

It did help. He hadn't given me any psychobabble or cop talk. He hadn't said anything throughout my monologue of a regular girl's life, but it had helped to let it out. Someone knew now. Someone knew it all. I felt lighter, like I'd given a bit of it away.

When I got the courage to open my eyes, his head was in his hands. I thought he might have fallen asleep. It would be for the best. I almost giggled, that's how giddy I felt.

He looked up, and his bloodshot eyes looked haunted. My spirits fell. Of course I felt lighter. I'd just dumped it on him. He'd only asked what had happened with his partner, and I'd given him my life story.

"I'm sorry," I said. "I don't know why I did that."

"No, don't be sorry," he said. "I just—I think that might be the saddest story I've heard."

Then I did laugh. "I know a better one, but I'll spare you for now."

It was quiet. I drifted into a dream state. I'd lost everything, at least for the moment: Bailey, Colin, almost Shelly. I was stuck in a hospital room with a cop—a nightmare if there ever was one. But somehow, strangely, there was peace.

Chapter Seven

I WOKE UP to the soft sounds of the nurse fussing over Shelly's bandage.

"Good morning, sleepyhead," Shelly said quietly from beside me.

I rubbed my eyes. I'd fallen asleep in Shelly's bed and had one hell of a crick in my neck. I glanced around the room. Her detective was gone, his jacket missing from the chair. "Sorry," I muttered. "I don't think these beds were made for two."

"I'm glad you came, though," she said.

She looked better. Still wan compared to her usual self, but it seemed the indomitable Shelly could bounce back from even a bullet.

I slid from the bed and wobbled on my feet.

Shelly snickered softly. "Nice ass."

I waved my hand at her, leaving my hospital gown to gape open as I shuffled to the bathroom and shut the door. I only came in to use the toilet, but now that I was here, a shower seemed even nicer. I should probably have gone back to my own room, but walking was so hard today.

I stood under the hot spray for a long time. Just

how big was the water heater of a hospital? It was a question that needed an answer, I decided. So I stood under the steamy spray even longer, letting the warmth seep into my bruises.

The hot water hadn't run out when I heard voices murmuring outside. A knock sounded on the bathroom door. I shut off the water and wrapped myself in a thin towel small enough to be a hand towel for Colin.

Ah, my jailer, come to cart me back to my cell.

He stared at my body. His gaze lifted, paused, drifted down, then snapped up to my face. Red bloomed across his smooth cheeks when he saw me watching him.

"I, ah, Detective Cameron told me you were here," he stammered. "And…I thought you might need this." He waved a small brown bag, presumably containing a morning-after pill I didn't need, but just as quickly withdrew, as if realizing the proximity of his hand to my almost naked body.

It was cute, really, but I yearned for Colin's unshakeable composure. "Thank you. I'll also probably need clothes."

I took the bag from him. "Bye, Shelly."

"Bye, hon." She waved me away.

I walked through the hospital halls in the thin, short towel. My personal cop danced attendance behind me, making strangled sounds of protest at my state of undress.

Inside my room I paused, forcing myself to appear

steady. A bag lay on the side table, one that hadn't been there before. Rape Victim Advocates, it said. Gee, what rape victim wouldn't want to carry this around? At least the puffy shape of the bag meant it contained clothes.

"Ask and you shall receive," I said to him where he hovered at the open door. I held the bag up to show him.

His cheeks flaming red, he shut the door just before I let the towel drop.

I dressed in the oversize sweats from the bag, trying not to let the memories take me. My little therapy session with the good detective had helped, but it wasn't magic.

After a meek knock, the cop outside my room, still looking a tad pink, informed me I was to be released. A credible witness had come forward and accounted for my whereabouts in the hours before the blast, though not directly during, which means I likely did not set up the explosion. I refrained from saying I'd already told them that, because it appeared that *credible* meant someone not affiliated with Philip.

Linda wrapped me in a big bear hug before I could even process her appearance. Her perfume gripped my lungs in a vise even as her arms squeezed my body, but I welcomed it all. When she finally pulled back, I gasped. And then coughed as I inhaled a fog of perfume.

She wore a wine-colored suit with a rose-blush blouse and matching heels. Her hair had been pulled back into some sort of updo and topped with a maroon cap. Between her clothes and her makeup, she exuded glamour, like some sort of old-fashioned movie star.

"You look fabulous," I said. "Don't tell me you got all dolled up for me."

"Of course not," she said as she ushered me down the hallway. She lowered her voice as if to impart a secret. "It's the policemen, dear. I know it goes against all those *liberation* ideas you young girls have, but sometimes you have to work what you got."

Linked arm in arm, we took the elevator down. "How did you know to come get me?"

"A little birdie called and told me to go down to the station and make a statement. He told me who to talk to, what to say, and he was very specific. After that I came here to bring you home."

A little birdie named Detective Cameron was my guess.

The sliding doors opened, and we entered the parking lot. Her necklace glinted in the sunlight, almost blinding me. "Are those real diamonds?" I asked, gawking at the rocks the size of dimes.

"Of course," she said. "I told you William did well doing elevator service. When he died, his company had contracts with all the big skyscraper buildings and just a whole bunch of employees. I sold it then, of course, but he did real well for himself, he did."

I could only laugh at that. Done well, my ass. Maybe it was, like she'd said, a happy story after all.

On the ride home Linda said, "Let me tell you a story."

I shot her a dubious look.

"Now, now," she said. "Don't you worry. This story *does* have a happy ending. It's not even a real story, it's made-up. Like a fairy tale, only shorter."

"All right," I fake grumbled.

"So one day there was this fox, see, and a scorpion," she said.

I groaned. I knew this story already. And it did *not* have a happy ending.

"Hush, now," she admonished. "Well, the scorpion, she wants to cross the river, but she can't swim. So the fox, being a gentleman fox, offers to take her across. But he's worried, you know, because she stings. But she says, now, you'll be doing me a favor by taking me across, so why would I sting you?"

She paused the story to accelerate through a yellow-red light. I gripped the leather seats, probably leaving permanent nail marks.

"So the scorpion gets on the fox's back," she continued. "And they're going across the river, when the scorpion stings the fox! And the fox says, why did you do that? And she says, because I'm a scorpion. And every day after that the fox knew what to expect from the scorpion."

I stared at her.

She smiled.

"I don't know how to tell you this," I said, "but

that's not how the story goes."

"What are you talking about?"

"The fox dies, Linda. And the scorpion. They both drown—that's the ending."

"That's ridiculous," she said. "If they drowned, then how could the fox ask the scorpion a question?"

"Well." I considered. "I suppose it's *as* they're drowning."

"*As* they're drowning," she repeated indignantly. "How long could it take? And why is the fox using his energy chatting when he's about to drown? Besides, if he died, how could the fox learn his lesson?"

"It was just right then, in those moments, that's when he—you know what? Never mind. I'm sorry. I think you had it right."

"Damn straight," she said as she gunned the accelerator.

It had taken me a minute to catch on, but I hadn't been lying. I thought Linda had the right of it. It wasn't the original version. It was better.

Chapter Eight

Linda barely pulled into her driveway when I jettisoned from the car, raced across the lawn, and into Colin's house. Bailey shrieked, and I cried as I scooped her up into a bear hug of my own. It had only been sixteen hours since we'd parted, but they'd been a hellish sixteen hours, and I never wanted to repeat it.

I breathed in her baby scent and didn't complain one bit as she ran her sticky hands all over my face. Linda came in for one last group hug before she patted both our heads and left. I collapsed on the couch with Bailey and smothered her with kisses. One for every hour I'd been away seemed reasonable to me.

In my rush to find Bailey, to hold her, I'd barely registered that Colin was in the room. Now I looked over at him, to find him watching us intently. He didn't look away—which was good, right?—but he didn't say anything. I couldn't read him. I usually could, at least a little, but now his eyes were frozen over, so cold, so remote, like they'd been on that very first night in the club. He'd been a stranger, then. He looked like a stranger now.

"Colin?" I asked.

Only the slightest twitch of his eyebrow as acknowledgment.

"Don't look at me like that. You're freaking me out. I know you're angry. That's okay—you can be angry. But I'm home, and that's…that's good, right?"

A long pause, then he said, "Yes."

I hadn't necessarily been expecting a parade or anything, but what a welcome.

"Okay," I said. "So how was Bailey for you? I mean, I know it's only been a few hours. What time did she wake up?"

"She's been fine. She woke up at eight and had watermelon for breakfast."

My face fell. He was so distant. "Colin, talk to me."

He shook his head, though it wasn't quite a refusal. His throat worked. Oh no, he wasn't uncaring. He was upset. I set Bailey, who'd recovered from my absence with somewhat insulting speed, down and went over to him.

"Hey," I said, touching his cheek. "I know things were bad last night. But we'll get through this, right?"

"You shouldn't be standing," he said gruffly.

It wasn't the reassurance I'd been hoping for, but at least he cared. I let him maneuver me onto the couch. I also let him serve me the lunch he'd had delivered from his restaurant, *without* helping clean up afterward. Then I lay down for Bailey's nap with her. He tucked us both into his bed, settling the blanket around us before shutting off the light and closing the door.

Throughout it all, he barely said a word to me.

No, things weren't great between us, but they would get better.

After the nap Colin insisted I lie down on the sofa while Bailey played in front of me. Since I was, in fact, tired, I allowed him to coddle me. Besides, about the only time he talked to me was to tell me to eat or sit or lie down, so I figured I might as well encourage him with my obedience. I wished he'd open up to me, but that wouldn't be Colin.

Oh, I figured he'd crack one of these days. I'd learned that much, at least, from our drama about Rick. He kept quiet, but if I waited long enough, he'd be the one to bring it up. That's what I told myself.

Like that night I'd been sick in my apartment, he even put Bailey down for bed.

I lay across the hall, listening to him read *Goodnight Moon*. There was murmuring back and forth and a song. Then he trekked down the stairs and back up, for a glass of water was my guess. And so forth.

Late, past Bailey's normal bedtime routine, Colin came into our bedroom.

"Ready to shower?" he asked.

I raised my eyebrows, amused. "Are you telling me I stink?"

"You'll need help," he said as he walked into his closet.

Hmm, help in the shower. I did need one, and bonus—we'd be naked. I desperately needed to reconnect with Colin, and sex was the one way that had always worked. My head kind of hurt, and my body rather ached, but I could do this. It would be worth it, not to have Colin holding himself so still and tense whenever I was near.

He came out of the closet wearing only boxers. He pulled me off the bed and undressed me, reminding me of that night in my apartment. That night he had kissed every bruise. Would he now? I had plenty of bruises in all kinds of interesting places. And if I didn't, I'd fake it.

Colin held my hand as I stepped into the shower; then he came in after me. He didn't take off his boxers, though. He just walked right in and soaked them through.

He gently soaped me, starting at my neck and working down my back, down my legs and then up my front. His blunt fingers ran the soap between my legs and then up to my breasts, reminiscent of our last time in the shower together. My body remembered, getting hot and wet. That had been good, if a little too acrobatic for my current physical state. We would just have to move slower, maybe find a nice position that involved sitting completely still.

I slid my hand down to the wet fabric of his boxers and gripped his cock. He moved my hand away.

"You don't want me?" I pouted. It was a game.

He shook his head. "Not now."

And then it wasn't. "Are you serious?"

"I don't always have to want sex."

I narrowed my gaze to his erection, covered in wet cloth but obvious. "I think you do."

"I said I don't."

"Then why did you come in here with me?" I asked, honestly confused.

"You had a concussion. You might be unsteady and slip."

"Fine," I said. "So this isn't about sex. You're mad at me. I know you're mad. Can we just talk about it?"

He turned off the water. Cold air sucked into the stall, pebbling my skin. "Christ," I said.

Colin stepped from the shower and helped me out. Then he tossed a towel in my arms and stalked out, still dripping water, his wet boxers sagging from his hips.

Okay, I supposed we were done talking. I dried off and put on one of my oversize sleep shirts. The bed was plush and warm and wonderful. I'd wanted to wait for him, I'd wanted to fix this, but I fell asleep.

We slept in the same bed, as usual. Side by side, though, not touching.

The next morning was the same, or maybe even worse. Colin made breakfast. He cleared the table. He even took Bailey for a walk. Anything but talk to me.

And the next day Colin catered to my every need, still managing to maintain his silent treatment. The day after, Colin went to the restaurant for a few hours, but only while Bailey and I were napping. The rest of the time was spent covering me with blankets or handing me new things to read, but he seemed to be talking *less* as the days went by.

Somehow he'd managed to punish and care for me at the same time. The more I pushed him to talk, the quieter and the more helpful he would become. It would be impressive if it weren't so frustrating.

Chapter Nine

"So let me get this straight," Shelly said. "He's making you meals, doing all the housework, and not even asking for sex, and you're complaining."

"I actually *like* sex with him," I said. "But okay, when you put it like that, it sounds stupid."

I pulled out a vase from the box and held it up. "This definitely isn't yours."

She shrugged. "Just stick it on the mantel."

"You're in a downtown loft. There's no fireplace."

"Whatever."

I set it down on the dining table, next to the growing collection of rich-ass things Philip had packed in Shelly's boxes. So far I'd found a heavy crystal clock, a figurine of a dolphin, and an oriental fan folded accordion-style. Leave it to Philip to do the breakup box backward, putting in extra stuff rather than leaving a few things out. I was surprised he'd even packed them himself, but I figured if anyone was giving away hundreds of dollars' worth of junk from Philip's place, it was Philip. No one else would dare.

Shelly had been released from the hospital yesterday. I'd picked her up with Bailey. Colin hadn't wanted me out of the house yet, hadn't thought I was ready, but I insisted. Poor Rose had suffered the position of in-between as we'd had Shelly's belongings brought to Colin's house and then forwarded on to her new condo.

No way was she going back to the mansion, not being suicidal and all. Philip had helped her after she'd been shot, sure. She *had* saved his life, after all. But since then, he'd had time to think, maybe about how she'd betrayed him while living under his roof and on his dime. There was no reason to press her luck.

It had surprised me, though, that she hadn't moved in with her cop. Sure, I had only just found out about them, but they'd seemed…intimate. But no, she told me when I asked, they weren't a couple. They'd never even had sex, paid or otherwise. There was *something* there, of course, but it wasn't enough.

We stood in the fancy furnished apartment, boxes piled high in the large foyer.

"Bailey, no!" I grabbed the painting, but she'd already torn the corner.

I shoved the canvas back into place. It curled up. I stared at the ruined painting of geometrical shapes.

"Please tell me Philip likes to paint. Or he's one of those guys who likes to support local college kids by buying cheap art."

"Nope," Shelly said, sounding almost pleased. "He's got an art dealer. All famous stuff."

"Damn," I said.

Bailey toddled over to Shelly, who handed her a golf-ball-sized rock that looked suspiciously like an emerald.

"Tell me again why we aren't taking this stuff back," I said.

"It's part of the game," she explained. "That's why he likes me, because I know how to play."

"Only rich people would throw away expensive shit for fun," I grumbled.

"Don't judge, Allie baby. We're all mad here."

There she went again, quoting Alice in Wonderland. Using silly to cover up the serious. I moved to the kitchen and packed the plates in the cabinets.

"You know what I think?" she called from the sofa. "I think he's sulking."

I almost thought for a minute that she was talking about Philip, and then I would have agreed that yes, maybe he was. But her voice was way too contented, and that meant she wasn't talking about her man problems, but mine. I poked my head through the bar to look at her. "Colin doesn't *sulk*. He's angry at me. You know, for not telling him about the cops and Andrew and all that."

She looked puzzled. "But his brother tried to kill you. Doesn't that mean he loses his right to be mad at you anymore?"

Hmph. That's exactly what I thought, but apparently not.

I folded up the box I'd emptied and plopped down

on the armchair beside Shelly. "This chair is harder than the floor," I said.

"Rich people," she said, shaking her head.

"*You're* a rich person."

She laughed softly. "I know."

"Just how much money did Philip give you?"

"Way more than I'm worth."

My curiosity sparked—what did she *do* to him?—but no. This was Philip, who I both knew and disliked, and I didn't need the mental images.

"What do you think I should do?" I asked.

"I think you should make him talk to you," Shelly said.

"Yeah?"

"Or maybe give him time to come around," she said.

"That's the exact opposite advice."

She shrugged. "What the hell do I know about relationships?"

Point taken.

It had been a week. In only a couple of days it had been clear I was physically recovered, but we still hadn't really talked. We still hadn't had sex. He barely even acknowledged me.

He'd frozen me out for one week. Surely he couldn't last much longer.

Chapter Ten

When I woke, it was dark and still, but something prickled at my awareness. I turned my head on the pillow to see Colin standing beside the window, staring between the slit in the curtains, all big and solid and beautiful. I loved him. Well, clearly I'd hit my head. I'd turned into a sap.

But I did love him. I'd proved myself to him, when I hadn't given the cop information. And he'd proved himself to me, when he'd trusted me about it. It didn't fix everything, but it was enough. It should be.

I slipped from the bed and padded across the wood floor. He didn't move, even when I laid my head against his back.

"You never said if you liked them," I said.

There was a short pause. "Like what?"

"The curtains. I made them, so they're kinda wonky in places, but they're a hell of a lot cheaper than what they were trying to sell. If you don't like them, I can—"

"I like them fine."

I ran my hands up the smooth muscles of his back to his bunched shoulders. "You're so tense."

He said nothing, but he didn't move away, so I kneaded gently. I hated that he was so upset. If he'd just open up, I could fix it, surely I could. Maybe it was just a high, but after facing the cops, both dirty and clean, and coming out on the other end intact, I felt invincible. I could be normal. We could be together.

He sighed, and his shoulders relaxed just slightly.

"I want to tell you something," I said.

He tensed even tighter.

"No, no," I soothed. "It's nothing bad."

I waited until he'd leaned back into my hands again, urging me to continue.

"I don't expect anything from you when I say this. It's just that, after everything that's happened, I feel like I should tell you." I slipped my hands around his waist. "I love you."

He bolted away so fast I almost fell over.

"Shit," he said as he steadied me.

I tried not to be offended. And failed. "Shit? I mean, not that I expected you to say it back, but *shit*?"

He paced away from me to the other side of the bed. What was he scared of? His hard expression told me to leave it alone, that I'd never know, but I couldn't.

"Are you that mad at me? I can't even love you while you're mad at me? Well, too bad, because I do. I love you, I love you, I love you—"

He turned and left the room.

Well. That could have gone better. It didn't matter

to me that he said it. I figured a girl who deserved Colin had to learn to read his actions, not his words, but even his actions hurt at this moment.

We were so close. We had everything right there, within our grasp, but he—what? He didn't believe in it? He didn't want it?

I wasn't good enough.

No, dammit! I wouldn't go down that path again. It wasn't so much a path as a sinkhole. I'd fallen into the ice, or been pushed. I'd treaded water, stuck, as people gave me pitying looks. No one wanted to come close for fear they might fall in with me, except for Colin.

I *was* good enough. If he didn't want me…well, I would be devastated. Even my newfound confidence couldn't protect me from that. But as painful as that would be, I refused to let it define me.

That kind of confidence mumbo jumbo was easier said than done, though. I wanted him, loved him, and his rejection hit hard. I debated leaving him alone, letting him calm down, but it had been a week since the explosion, and we'd gotten no closer to getting over this. No closer to each other.

Down the stairs I went. I found Colin sitting on the couch.

I sat next to him. "Colin," I said, in my best imitation-Colin voice. "I was hoping we could be together, you know, like a happy ever after, but this doesn't bode well for my chances."

It was, of course, a mimic of what he'd said to me that first night. It was also cheesy as hell, but I wanted to make him laugh, and also to show him that he'd been right. We belonged together, and he'd insisted on it until I finally believed. This was the reverse, and to my surprise it worked.

His lips cracked just slightly. Then they slowly, reluctantly widened into a smile.

I cheered inwardly. "Oh, you like that? I've got more where that came from."

"Yeah?" he said, the grin—that sweet, sexy grin—still in place.

"No, that was a lie. Or a horrible attempt to talk dirty. I'm just happy I got you to smile."

"Hey," he said. "I'm not that bad."

He ducked his head to hide his smile. I squirmed onto my belly so I could see it, like a puppy begging for attention.

"You are that bad," I said up at him. "You're a bad boy. That's what I like about you."

"Really?" he asked skeptically.

"No, not really." My head rested on his lap. I turned to nuzzle my nose into his abs.

"So everything you're saying right now—"

"Lies, all of it. I like your smile, though. That's the truth."

He leaned back, amused. His hand came up and stroked my hair. I closed my eyes and dreamed.

When I woke up, I was in the bed. In the dark and

alone.

I sighed. That man was more obstinate than I gave him credit for. I didn't want to nag him, but I wouldn't be able to sleep. I got up and peeked in Bailey's room, but she slept on, snoring softly. I went downstairs. He wasn't in the living room, though the throw pillows were still squashed from where we'd sat on the sofa. I checked his study and the kitchen—nothing. Had I missed him upstairs? Maybe he'd decided to stand *behind* the curtains, seeing as a certain nosy girlfriend had disturbed his reflection last time. I should let him be, but a little bit of unease had wormed its way inside me.

Back upstairs I checked the bathroom, which was still open and dark. Then his closet. His clothes hung there, like always, but there was a gap. It could be a trick of the light. Or maybe it was laundry day.

It wasn't.

The sadness hit me full force then. He'd left; I knew it.

I checked behind the curtains anyway. Then I went downstairs and stared at the oil blot where his truck should have been parked, to be sure.

What did it mean? Was I supposed to move out? Was I supposed to wait for him?

I'd thought we'd stay together, I really had. And barring that, I figured we'd break up and I'd move out. Never had I really imagined that he'd leave me alone…in his house.

Chapter Eleven

The day dawned drizzly. Bailey watched morning cartoons, happily oblivious to the fact that we'd soon be leaving. I sat on the couch drinking my coffee, memorizing whatever details I could see.

When I got the energy to get up, I'd have to start packing. Then we'd have to move into a new place of our own. The details on how we'd accomplish any of that were hazy, but that didn't make them less real.

I supposed it made sense that Colin would break up this way. Quietly, the way he did everything else. And it also illustrated just how angry he was with me, that he couldn't even give me the courtesy of a *get out*.

He just slipped away, leaving me to figure it out and get myself gone. I could stay, make a fuss, but that would just be embarrassing for all of us.

I would miss this place. I would miss Colin more, but for now I soaked in the somber peace of the house. The moldings at the bottom of the wall didn't match the floorboards. They were a different kind of wood. I'd never gotten to ask Colin if he knew how that had happened.

There was a cobweb at the top of the slanted ceiling

that I'd never been able to reach, not even standing on a stool and waving a broom. It had been here before me, and it would still be there after I left.

The weather hadn't stayed warm enough to spend much time in the backyard. I would have liked a barbecue. I'd never been to one, but they sounded nice.

A knock sounded at the door.

If they were knocking, then they weren't Colin, so I didn't care.

The knocking grew more insistent. They'd wake up the neighborhood.

I got up and opened the door. It was Detective Cameron, but he didn't look like Detective Cameron, because instead of a dark suit, he wore faded jeans and a white T-shirt. His hair was jagged, and there were dark shadows under his eyes.

"Is she here?" he asked.

Oh, Shelly, what have you done to him? "She's not."

"She's with *him*, isn't she? I knew it. I just came from there, but the fucking butler insisted—"

"No, she's not with Philip either," I said. "She got her own place."

"Oh." He blinked. "She's okay?"

"She's fine. Recovering well."

He understood that I wasn't going to tell him, not that I could hold him off for long. He would track her down at some point if he wanted to. But if Shelly didn't want to be with him, what good would it do? It seemed today was the day for breakups.

"Come in if you want." I opened the door wide.

He tilted his head, trying to glance around me. "Are you sure? I figured I'd have to fight him just to talk to you."

"He's not here," I said. His eyes met mine as he caught the finality in my tone.

"Oh," he said.

"Yeah."

He glanced behind him before stepping inside. In the living room he gave Bailey a curt nod of introduction. She gave him the cryptic message, "bagel," before turning back to her show.

I poured him a cup of coffee, and we sat down at the dining room table.

He contemplated the black liquid. "Was it because of…"

"Yes," I said. Colin had left because of what had happened that night. I'd fucked up, or he just didn't trust me anymore, but either way it was over. "You really like her, huh?"

He glanced up, his eyes hooded. "Who?"

I rolled my eyes. "Whatever."

"What did she say about me?" he asked cautiously.

"She said—" *She said you two had never had sex, paid or otherwise. It made me wonder why you'd never paid for it if you like her. But then, we all have our hangups.* "She said you guys weren't a couple."

"Yeah," he said flatly. "I guess that's right."

"Did she move there for you? In with Philip?"

He paused, then shrugged. "I never know why she does what she does."

"But you think it's your fault she got shot," I mused.

The guilt that flashed in his eyes said I was right.

"If it's any consolation, I think she likes you back."

"Thanks." He grimaced. "Could be worse, right?"

We sat there, both of us rejected, trying to imagine what could be worse. Aside from death or grievous injury, there didn't seem to be much, but that was the kind of morning it was. The morning after a breakup.

"There was something else. We found this at the site. Shelly told me it was yours." He pulled an envelope from his back pocket and slid it over to me. I didn't even know how he'd sat down with that in his back pocket, it was so thick. I recognized it, of course. It was filled with money, unless someone had taken it.

"It should all be there," he said. "But you should count it."

I didn't even know how much had been in there to begin with, how much money Colin had wanted to give me so that I could run away with Bailey after betraying him. Flicking open the flap, I saw the green, crisp bills.

Blood money, or was it? No, it wasn't born of hate or violence but something nicer. Andrew had started the little fund when he'd given me the money he'd been going to use for the lawyer. Then Colin had taken it, only to return it at the warehouse with even more money. They'd both wanted me to be safe. I slapped it shut.

"I'm sorry about the way it happened," he murmured. "And about my partner. He was a troubled person. Not that I'm making excuses for him."

"What do you mean *was*? What is he now?"

He looked surprised. "You didn't hear?"

Oh God, Colin, what did you do? "Tell me."

"He got hit by a car. Dead on arrival."

"When?"

"That night. He was running across a three-lane highway. Even at night he didn't have a chance. I guess he was trying to get out of the area. He'd have been exposed after that."

Cameron took his leave after that. I didn't show him out, just sat dumbly at the table.

Explosions and gunshots and this guy ends up hit by a car. What were the odds?

Accidents happened.

But then, Colin had taken off after him. Had he caught him and fought with him? An image flashed through my mind of the man cornered, possibly injured, deliberately steered into a busy street he had no hope of crossing. Colin hadn't struck the killing blow; that had been done by a ton of steel, but he might have played a part.

Did I even care if he had? I'd been so adamant that he shouldn't be involved in anything criminal, anything violent, but I knew as well as anyone that being innocent couldn't protect us. It just made us more vulnerable. And aside from Cameron, for whom I had a grudging respect, I had no love for cops.

That guy would have killed us. He'd certainly tried and almost succeeded. I couldn't find anything inside me that minded that this guy was dead, or that Colin might have pursued him literally to death. Maybe that made me a monster, or maybe it just made me human.

I delayed packing by putting away the dishes and laundry. They had to be done, I reasoned, so I might as well do them first.

And then at noon, something happened.

The delivery arrived. Colin had the Oasis start delivering lunch for the three of us when I had first been injured. I shouldn't have to cook, and he wanted to watch over me, so we ordered in. A definite benefit to owning a restaurant.

It wasn't the delivery that surprised me. I had hardly expected Colin to run around town, letting everyone know we were through, publicly severing ties. He wouldn't even have thought of something so small as a lunch delivery.

No, I accepted the large paper bag with thanks, not surprised in the least. Since Colin had always taken the deliveries, I introduced myself to the delivery boy.

Though he had to be at least sixteen, Kai seemed more a boy than a man. He was young and black and overly polite, as if making up for any rude, young black men I'd ever encountered. I drew the line at ma'am. He refused to call me Allie, so we settled on Ms. Winters.

The surprising part was that there were only two meals in the bag, one for me and a child-sized portion for Bailey, which meant he had changed the order. Perhaps he had even been at the restaurant and sent the food himself.

A little jolt raced through me.

It felt like a message of some sort, this deliberate delivery of food from a man who'd always tried to give me food or drink even that first night. What if it was a peace offering?

It could mean nothing, but it could also mean everything. I couldn't ignore it. What if he was, at this moment, sitting in that tiny little office down the hallway of his restaurant, waiting for a response from me? I had to try.

And if he was at his restaurant, then I had the perfect excuse to go and see him. Unfortunately, since Colin had insisted on doing the grocery shopping after the injury, we had no ingredients.

Leaving the food from the restaurant to cool on the counters, I rushed to the grocery store with Bailey and threw just enough ingredients to make a double chocolate cake into a basket. The checkout lines weren't all that long, but I still tapped my foot. Bailey puttered about in the section with little toys they always used to entice small, bored children. I decided it was their own fault if she knocked them all over.

I didn't have much hope that this would solve my

problems with Colin, but at least I could do something. Baking had always served that purpose for me. Put in the right ingredients and it turned out right, not like life. And when it was done, I'd get to see Colin.

"Got a party or something?" the man behind me asked.

I turned back to see a man with his own basket, his smile kind.

"Something like that," I said. "Making a cake for a friend."

"Oh, what kind?" He peered into my basket, with special emphasis on my left ringless hand holding it.

"Nothing too fancy," I said. "A double chocolate cake."

"Sounds great. I like a woman who can bake."

I laughed at the blunt caveman statement. It was clearly a sort of pickup line, but it wasn't accompanied with a lascivious sneer or anything. *Bake* wasn't a euphemism. He just liked a woman who could bake.

"Do you want to go grab a cup of coffee sometime?" he asked.

He looked to be maybe in his midthirties, with the kind of body that had once been thick with muscle but was now thick with padding. His age didn't bother me, even though he'd be substantially older. His chubby body didn't bother me in the slightest. It was maybe what Colin would look like, several years down the road.

He just wasn't Colin.

"No, thanks," I said. "I'm...attached."

Disappointment tinged his good-natured smile. "No problem. Gave it a shot."

I returned home with Bailey, bemused. I'd never been hit on before when I'd been out with her. What man would want to take on a young woman with a young child, except a self-destructive guy with a hero complex like Colin? This guy had, though. I wondered now if maybe I hadn't been giving off a don't-fuck-with-me vibe all along. Thinking the worst of men and only seeing what fit into my ugly little expectations.

It probably also helped that the grocery store near Colin's house was quite a bit nicer than the one near my old apartment. It was clean and stocked, and I'd never yet found dirty diapers in the carts.

Over the hour it took to make the cake, let it cool, and apply the frosting, Bailey nodded off. I tucked her into bed and asked Linda to watch her for me.

I marched into the restaurant and straight back to the office. I was a woman on a mission, the cake my Trojan horse. Colin opened the door. His face was pale and drawn, older than I'd ever seen it. His appearance shocked me into forgetting my purpose.

"Are you okay?" I asked.

His tired eyes looked me over. He was ancient today. "What do you need?"

I'd made a mistake. It hadn't been a message, or if it had, the message had been to stay away. A good-bye enchilada with a side of "it's not you, it's me" rice.

I shrugged the cake box, a bulky movement. "I just brought this for the restaurant. Like we agreed, that's all. Unless you didn't want it. Then I could—"

"I'll take it," he said, taking the box from me. He didn't sound happy about it, but then he didn't sound mad. More flat, more distant, like he had a cold. Though I knew he didn't, or at least he hadn't last night.

I stood in front of him with no further reason to be there but unable to walk away. "Are you coming home?"

"No." Not anytime soon, I understood.

Why, why, why, played in my head, but this wasn't the place. He'd removed himself from the place just to avoid that discussion. Still, I was confused.

"Do you want me to move out?" I asked.

"No," he said sharply.

I waited for him to say unless I wanted to. If I wanted to leave, then I should, and that would be my cue. The way a nice guy, a guy who's unable to properly break up with me, would do it, but he didn't say it.

"Okay." Tiring, despairing, I turned to leave.

"Wait," he said. "I want you to stay there. And you…you could keep sending these. Maybe…maybe send them back with Kai."

I stopped and glanced back. "Yeah?"

He shrugged. "Nothing fancy. Don't work too hard."

I firmly resisted the urge to mimic *don't work too*

hard back to him. He was the one who looked about ready to fall over from exhaustion. Had he even slept? That wasn't my concern. He didn't want it to be.

We resolved nothing, really.

Chapter Twelve

I DRAGGED MYSELF home. The one high point was that Colin hadn't wanted me to leave, which had to mean there was some hope for us. Or maybe he just pitied me. Either way, I wasn't really up to tackling a new apartment so close on the heels of the encounter with Philip, and this was a reprieve.

Linda was reading a book to a sleepy-eyed Bailey when I got home.

"She woke up just after you left," she said apologetically.

"It's fine. Thank you."

She looked up at my dull tone. "That man of yours at work?"

A blush heated my face. "Yes." At least it was true. I left out the part about him not planning on coming home.

Her eyes narrowed. "Why don't you go on upstairs? Take a little nap or read a book or something. I've got her covered."

Grateful, I trudged up the stairs. I soaked in a hot bath, letting the sweat and steam bead on my face before I pulled myself back out. After throwing on some clothes, I looked inside his closet. Beside the space he'd emptied, there was a row of shirts. Collared things that I almost never saw him wear. And underneath, slacks and jeans. In the drawers I found undershirts and socks and underwear.

I knew all this was here, of course. He'd gratefully relinquished laundry duty to me since my first days here. I only ever looked at these sections, of course, not what was on the top shelf.

It took me a minute to find a stool downstairs and then lug it back up. Shoe boxes filled with receipts and bills. They looked like they had to do with the restaurant, which fit, since any Philip-related papers were probably in his tinderbox of a mansion.

I set that back on the high shelf and rummaged through some folded blankets and sheets. At the very end, in the corner and under some winter clothes, was a file folder marked "Marge" in Colin's square lettering.

I slid it open and found a *Registered Claim and Deed* granted to Colin James Murphy. Was this where he was staying? It didn't seem likely. Based on the zip code, I guessed it to be out by Wolf Lake, about an hour's drive from here.

I was going to find out. Maybe because I deserved answers, and Colin was too damned reserved to ever give them to me. Or maybe because I cared about him enough to push, in the same way he'd pushed me at the beginning. And plus, I was incredibly curious about the man I loved.

Even more thankful that Linda had stayed on for Bailey's dinner, I got in my car. I passed through the neighborhood streets of Oak Park, out across Chicago's urban jungle to the remote plains near the lake.

A faded sign marked my arrival. HUNTER'S GLEN TRAILER PARK. Rows of metallic and off-white trailers suffocated among the debris around them. Plots that were little more than dirt and a few stray weeds were marked by white, jagged rocks. If this was a glen, then I was a debutante, but I could believe people hunted in the swamps around the lake.

I hadn't known Chicago had anything like this, so country. But then, it was barely there at all. As my car jostled over the gravel path, I noticed several trailers had their windows smashed in to darkened rooms. Only a man slumped against the side of one told me that this place hadn't been entirely abandoned. His eyes were yellow. And his teeth, when he bared them to me. In a smile or a threat, I wasn't sure.

At the end of the path there was a smaller sign staked into the ground. EUROPEAN FORTUNE TELLING $10.

Though a few of them seemed like they might be lived in, I was hesitant to go knocking on doors. Neither did I want to check back with the man I'd seen on the way. The fortune-teller seemed like the safest bet.

I got out of the car and wove through the path of junk. The furniture and car parts made me think the plot was used as storage. The pink metal flamingos and numerous gnomes made the area seem more deliberate, more decorous, like a poor person's sculpture garden.

I knocked and was rewarded with a raspy, "Come in."

When I opened the door, I was met with a beaded curtain. Not wooden beads or jewel tones like I might have expected, but hot pink plastic beads, like the kind that go on Mardi Gras necklaces. I parted the strings to walk into the smokiest room I'd ever smelled. Piles of newspapers and dishes crowded in on me.

"You want your fortune told, missy?" came from the corner, in a voice that grated like the gravel I'd just come from.

I blinked through the mist of smoke and dust, trying to see. "No, I was looking for…well, I wasn't exactly sure, but—"

"If you don't know what you're looking for, sounds like you do need your fortune told, eh?" She cackled. I was pretty sure it was a she.

"I found out this place was owned by someone. Someone I know—"

"You know Colin?" she interrupted.

"Yes, he's—"

"What you want with the boy?"

He hadn't been a boy in some time, but the fact that she seemed to know him and thought of him that way said a lot. "Well, he's my boyfriend. Or he was. And I guess I—"

"Girl, you's barking up the wrong tree with that one."

I didn't know who this lady was, but that really wasn't the message I wanted to hear. Thank goodness I didn't believe in psychics, especially not her.

"I wonder if you could just tell me how you know him," I said quickly to ward off another interruption.

She huffed. "I know everything about him. I practically raised the boy."

Holy shit. I thought back to the papers I'd found in Philip's study. He'd been orphaned, they'd said, so she couldn't be his mother. Maybe a foster parent? If they'd been placing kids in this dump, they must have been in a bad way.

She leaned forward from the shadows. Her face was a map of neglect with its many wrinkled tributaries and sunken eyes. "I'm his aunt."

I looked around the tiny trailer. I saw two doors leading off, though one might have led to a bathroom. There definitely didn't seem to be enough room for the three siblings.

"Where did all of you stay?" I asked.

"All of us?" she barked. "I only had that one. Oh, they tried pushing the other two brats on me, but I told them, them two's too messed up in the head after what they'd been through. Ain't gonna spend my time on that, have them stealing from me. Colin, though, he was young enough, and they didn't much touch him. So I took him in, like family does."

I just stared at her, trying to find some hint of recognition, that she knew how heinous what she'd just said was, but found nothing. She'd taken Colin in, like family does, but had rejected the other two because they'd been abused? With family like that, who needed enemies?

And then I applied that story to Colin, and even Philip and Rose, and my heart broke. I couldn't even think of Philip and Rose, whatever they had been through with their parents, and then having their aunt turn them away. And Colin, trapped here in this pit of a home, without his siblings. How lonely he must have been. How miserable.

I could understand better now why a bachelor like him had such an airy, open house even when he hadn't needed it. And maybe I also understood what Bailey and I had offered him. Something he hadn't really had before—a family.

"You say you were with him, huh? What, did he leave you pregnant or something?"

"No," I ground out. "Colin's not like that."

She laughed. "I guess not. He wouldn't leave you high and dry, not my boy. He'd just pay you off probably."

A shiver took me, even though the room was burning up. That was dangerously close to what had happened. At the time I'd written it off. After all, he'd thought I had betrayed him, making his actions more a kindness than an insult.

"He's got money, I know that," she said. "He came here once a few years ago, saying I should leave here, he'd buy me a house. But what do I want a house for? My customers know me here, and I'm comfortable. Getting on in age and don't want to go nowhere, least not till I meet my Maker. So he sends me money now and again. Thought that might be why you're here, for the money, if you was pregnant."

I scowled. "I'm not pregnant."

"Don't look it, sure, but you forget I'm a fortune-teller." She thought that was hilarious.

"Okay," I said. "I'm not pregnant, but thank you for talking to me."

"That'll be ten dollars," she said.

"What?"

"Hey, I'm sure you don't want Colin to know you was sneaking around, checking up on him. Call it a keeping-quiet fee. I could probably charge you more, and you'd pay it, but you're lucky I have morals."

I pulled a twenty out of my purse and slapped it on the grimy fold-out table between us. Storming out of the little trailer, I heard her say, "Got your change," before the rickety door slammed shut. I drove out of the trailer park so fast my rear wheels spun on the gravel.

God.

I'd wanted to know more about Colin's past. I'd wished he would tell me, but it was clear that never would have happened. Bad enough that he was naturally taciturn, but telling something like this, it was impossible. There would be no way to explain the quiet horror of that place, the matter-of-fact evil of that woman, or the brokenness of his family.

But even as I ached for the boy-Colin, I worried over the man-Colin. She'd hit a little too close to home, that woman, with all her talk of paying me off. Not just that he'd done it before, but that he seemed to be doing it now. After all, he'd said I could stay in the house, that he didn't want me to go.

I'd hoped it was because he'd meant to come back, but he'd offered her a house too. He felt some obligation to her for raising him. That was so like him. Did he also feel an obligation to me? Is that why he wanted me to keep living there?

He would pay the bills or send me money. I would live in his house but never see him. Did he think I would sit meekly in his house, growing old and crazy?

Like hell.

I picked up the phone and dialed. "Rose? It's Allie. I need your help."

Chapter Thirteen

I STUMBLED IN my too-high heels as I wove my way to the bar. The thin fabric did little to shield my body from the dancers around me. Plus, it itched. I wouldn't have been surprised to find I'd broken out in hives from the stretchy synthetic stuff.

I'd even filled out a little, eating real meals instead of Bailey's leftovers. I'd plumped up too, in places that attracted attention from the men I passed.

The stools were full, so I shuffled to the side to wait for my drink. Too far over and I'd get groped. On the other side the bar was crusted with black stuff I didn't want to speculate about. It was like one of those medieval torture chambers where the person had to stand in the middle or fall on spikes.

I wouldn't leave, of course. My purpose was too important.

Between the strobing lights and grind of bodies, I'd never find him. He would already be here. What if he didn't come at all?

He had to.

"Hey, sweetheart," a low voice said. My heart thumped, and I turned. It wasn't him.

This guy wore a wifebeater and hair spiked into a Mohawk. I hadn't even known that was in style. I was too old for this scene, though that had little to do with the pitter-patter of the calendar. I'd grown into a woman, or at least my own version of that ideal. I had a ways to go, but I had the time to do it in. And hope. I had hope now.

"I'm waiting for someone," I said.

He smiled, flashing white teeth. "I can be your someone."

Ugh, what did I expect at a bar?

"Sorry," I said. And I was. There wasn't anything wrong with him. He was the kind of guy I could date, but there wasn't any chance of that.

He melted back into the throng of dancers.

A space opened at the bar, so I sat down. The bartender slid me my drink.

At least the alcohol was the same. Watery, the way I liked it. I never wanted to be out of control, never again.

A hand closed around my arm, and I jumped. The briefest of flashbacks assailed me, of another man grabbing me from behind at this bar, but it faded as I turned to Colin.

He'd come! His familiar face drowned out the rest of the club.

It had been a test, I saw now. Not that I'd wanted to hurt him or stick it to him, but I had to know how he felt about me. If he could let me come here to sleep with another guy, coupled with the fact that he'd moved out, I'd have to assume he really didn't want me. And then I'd have to move out, because I couldn't remain a squatter in his house.

Rose had done her part and told Colin that I was back on the prowl, heading to the club to pick up some random guy for rough sex. I'd played my part, but I wouldn't have followed through. If Colin hadn't shown up, I definitely wouldn't have had sex with any of these guys.

But he'd come, looking angry and fierce and everything perfect.

"What do you think you're doing?" he raged. "You're leaving. Now!"

"Thank God," I said. "Let's go."

I hopped off the stool and grabbed his hand, then beelined for the exit, practically shoving people out of my way in my haste. Once outside I put my hand against the brick wall and sucked in air, but it stank. We needed to get away from here.

"Where to?" I asked.

"Home," he practically thundered. "You're going home."

I considered that. "No," I said. "I think I told you once that I don't bring guys home."

"I'm not coming with you," he ground out. "I'm putting you in the car and sending you there."

"I'll drive to another club," I said.

"Then I'll follow you there and drag you out."

"How very stalkerish," I said. "Do you follow girls around in clubs often?"

He stopped then and closed his mouth, probably because he had followed me at the club, according to Rose.

"Do you have a motel room we could use, perhaps?" I asked.

He glared at me. I knew he wanted to tell me to go home, but he knew it wouldn't work. And perhaps it had dawned on him now what I was about in this game. Or maybe he'd known all along and come anyway, his baser instincts winning out over whatever strange logic had kept him away.

"I need it," I said. Getting fucked was the least of it. I needed him.

That seemed to decide him. Even as some of the fury faded from his eyes, lust filled them. We were going to have sex tonight.

"Follow me in your car," he said.

"I think I know the way."

His eyes promised retribution for my mocking tone. I could only hope.

I followed him anyway, not wanting to risk it, but I'd been right. We pulled into the same motel, drove to the same building near the back, and parked in front of the same motel door.

It had to come to this. We'd both fought the good fight, but it had been over since we first saw each other. All this sex and pain and love had been inevitable, almost fated. Now I was getting sappy. Maybe I did, in fact, need a good, hard fuck.

I beat him to the door, but I didn't have the key so I turned and watched him slowly leave the truck. Was he just now accepting the inevitability? Or would we fight one last battle inside that room?

I stepped aside to let him open the door. He let me in first, and I dropped my purse on the same fabric chair and strolled inside.

The room was different than before. Last time it had been all clean and musky in the blank slate of an unused hotel room. Now it was lived in, strewn with clothes on the floor and bottles on the dresser.

Paperwork was spread across the rumpled sheets as if he'd been working there. I picked a few up and found information about leases and sales and transferals of rights.

I looked up sharply. "You aren't selling the place?"

"A new location."

"Really? Like a franchise?"

"I'll still own it. Both of them." He gave me a wry look. "I found myself with too much time on my hands."

I smiled. "Give up a bad habit, did you?"

"And a good one," he said, somehow closer to me.

The answer popped into my head. *Oh? Well, we can fix that right now.* Cheesy, but then his mouth was on mine, and I'd missed it. I'd missed its warmth, its taste, its very Colin-ness. Because it was him and he knew me and he loved me. Even if he never said it, not with words, because that wasn't his style. He said it with his actions, taking care of me and getting angry when I did stupid shit. And he said it with his body.

With his tongue as it swiped along the seam of my lips and touched against my tongue. *You're mine*, it said. *If you've forgotten, I'll prove it to you.* The love words were only in my mind, but he'd put them there. I'd been too afraid to try, to even imagine this, but he'd insisted with his feeding me and bathing me and caring for me, and all I wanted to do right now was give some of it back.

I pulled his shirt up, to feel his abs and then around to his back. He ripped the shirt over his head and tossed it aside, then unbuckled his jeans and kicked them off. I'd thought we'd take it slow, let it build, but his urgency was hot, contagious.

I started to pull off my clothes, to catch up, but he stopped me.

"I want to," he said.

My lips curved. "You like to do that. Undress me, wash me, feed me."

"Mmm-hmm." He was infinitely distracted as he circled me and slid his hands up my skirt.

"I can do those things on my own, you know," I said on a gasp as his fingers found a spot. "All on my own."

"I'd rather do it," he said. "Every day."

It was the closest thing to a commitment I'd ever

heard, and I wasn't picky. I groaned as my head fell back.

He took my clothes off piece by piece until I stood bare and wanting in the middle of the motel room. We jumped onto the bed together, forgetting who was telling who what to do. It wasn't nearly so much a power struggle as it was a joining. We both wanted this, so what was the use of pretending to fight? He didn't have to order me to do anything; he only had to ask.

I tasted his body, salt and musk, down his arm and when I got to his hand, I sucked a finger into my mouth. Almost like I was avoiding the good parts, but I wasn't. I was making up for lost time with the rest of him, all the Colin that I'd taken for granted. I'd never paid nearly enough attention to his forearm, with the banded muscles and soft hair. Or his hands, with their rough calluses and scarred knuckles. I kissed them, one for every hurt.

He was half reclined on the bed as if he couldn't make up his mind whether to lie back and let me or sit up and take over. I loved that I'd made him like this, indecisive and eager. I moved sideways to the pale skin of his hip. That soft patch of skin that's not quite his ass or his front, so soft. The softest part of him.

No, that definitely wasn't true. I moved inland, to an even softer place. A soft lick along the shaft of his cock, right in the middle, another neglected spot.

His body jerked. "Fuck."

He reached for me, ready to turn me over. Probably

to lick me and make me come as he had that night. I wanted it, but I wanted this more.

"Please," I begged. "I want to make you feel good."

"That does make me feel good."

We froze for a second in an awkward tableau, each of us reared up off the bed, ready to pleasure each other but being denied.

I laughed. "We can do it at the same time."

He laughed too, as if we'd reinvented the sixty-nine position. Silly us for not thinking of it sooner. This had all been done before, but it was new to us.

He rested back on the bed, and I clambered above him. It took a minute, arranging my legs, bumping his nose with my knee, not suffocating him, and I giggled. Laughing during sex—it felt strange but exhilarating.

Then he clamped his hands around my thighs and licked me long and slow, and I wasn't laughing anymore. He looked different from this angle, all upside down, with his cock pointing at me. I walked my hands down his body until I reached it. I put my mouth to the tip, a chaste kiss.

He sucked on my clit, and my body answered with an involuntary suck. He groaned and then licked me faster, sucked me hard. It made me wild, and I just attacked his cock, just messed it all up with my lips and my face and my saliva. It was dirty but not shameful. Sexy but not scary.

We sucked on each other, taking pleasure and giving it back. The bliss of his mouth on me was only heightened by the taste of his cock in my mouth.

But he'd hit a rhythm, licking my clit, and he put two fingers inside me. I couldn't concentrate, couldn't possibly think about sucking or stroking when I was so close. I left my mouth closed around him, letting the heat and the wetness and the vibrations of my moans do what they could for him. My hips rocked, and I tried, tried to hold them still, but even then I was shaking with the effort. It wouldn't last. I couldn't take it.

He stopped for just a minute, and I almost screamed. "Ride me," he said. "Do it."

Fuck, yes, I did. I was so close already. His tongue found my clit again, and I rode it mindlessly, letting my body sway and roll and find its release so it could take me with it. And it did. I came. I came on his mouth and tried so hard not to bite down, but that was all I could think.

The pulse of his cock in my mouth was what aroused me from my stupor. I gave him one last, hard suck, swallowing the saliva that I'd left there as I came. It should have been gross, I should have been embarrassed, but it was just how I'd pleased him. I'd made him feel good and him me, and there was nothing at all gross or embarrassing about that.

I rolled off him, because as much as I wanted to keep sucking him and make him come, I couldn't even sit up. He didn't need me to sit, thank God, and he turned me over onto my stomach. I started to pull my legs under me, to prop myself up so he could take me from behind, but he stopped me. Instead he slipped between my legs, barely spread far enough to cradle his hips.

His cock dipped low and slid into me. It was the same thing, being fucked from behind, the same cock, the same hole. But it was totally different, because he wasn't riding me or pulling my hair or anything like that, but just rocking into me. It was all pleasure, his cock in me, his chest curved around my back. The only pain at all was the small bite of his fingers into my hips, anchoring me to the bed, but it was the sweetest hurt.

And, even sweeter, he began to talk to me, saying the love words he'd written with his body. "You're beautiful, baby. I missed you. You make me crazy. Fuck, you're so hot."

My mind responded to his words with hope and love and pride, but all that was drowned out when the angle of his thrusts pointed down, pinging a certain place inside me. He sped up too, both his thrusts and his words. "Allie, Allie, fuck, you're so hot and tight. Just for me. Yes, just me. Fuck."

My mouth opened against the bedspread in a soundless cry. So close, so fucking close. His words tightened and wound, almost unintelligible, except I could hear my name and *fuck* in close succession. My ass canted back, begging for it. And then he said it.

"I love you."

He froze, like he hadn't meant to, like he'd surprised himself, but it was too late. I'd heard him, and I was coming. My body pulsed and shook, and I pushed, impaling myself on him to ride out my orgasm. That was too much, even for him, and he came with a strangled, wordless shout.

He wrapped his arms and legs around my body like a cocoon, with his cock still inside me. I couldn't move, didn't want to. We panted together, using up all the air, sharing it. We stayed that way for a long, long time, neither of us wanting to separate. Whenever it was, it would be too soon.

Only finally when I couldn't breathe—I even let myself see spots—I shrugged at him, and he rolled off. But he grasped my hand, and I held his back. This was the part where I ran to the bathroom, crying, or maybe he did, but neither of us wanted that, so we held on tight.

Chapter Fourteen

OUR BREATHING EVENED out, and I felt my mind drift into that space between awake and dreams. Something held me back from sleep—it was the fear that this was a dream after all. That I'd wake up, and he'd be gone. *Nice sex, Allie. See you next month.*

That wasn't Colin, of course, but he might still leave. I had to be sure.

I squeezed slightly, just to see if he was awake. He tightened his hand on mine.

"I think we have to talk," I said.

He tensed, his whole body did, with an air of expectancy, and then said on an exhale, "I'm sorry."

Well, okay. He was sorry for leaving, that was fine. What I was more concerned with was whether he was coming home—

"I'm sorry I did this to you. You lost your job because of me. That was fucked-up, like you said, but it wasn't supposed to—you were hurt. Almost raped, almost killed, because of me."

I have an inkling that the man feels guilty as sin.

He blamed himself for all of that, everything. No wonder he was so stressed out. Next thing he'd be blaming himself for what happened with Andrew, since he wasn't there to protect me from it.

"Christ, Colin. What an ego you have."

"What?" He sounded strangled.

"You didn't make your brother hire that guy; you protected me from him. It wasn't your fault that the shit went down with the cops. It was just dirty cops and bad business and circumstance. You saved me from getting hurt and killed."

He shook his head.

"And look, the Rick thing, you did that, and it was wrong. But I could have found another job. Or I could have borrowed money from Shelly or called my dad or a bunch of other things. I went to see you because I wanted you, and that was as good of an excuse as any to have you."

I could see he wasn't going to believe me, at least not for a long time. And that was okay, he could take his time, so long as he did it with me.

I sat up and faced him. "I love you. I want you to be with me. To *live* with me. I don't want you to feel guilty, but if you do, at least stay with me. We'll work it out together."

"It can't be that simple." He said it so solemnly. My heart broke and put back together all in that moment for the boy who thought he couldn't just love and be loved.

"It won't be easy, maybe, but I want to be with you, and I think you want to be with me. You said you loved me. Did you mean it?"

"You know I did."

A smiled played on my mouth. It couldn't be held in. "Maybe so, but I want to hear you say it again." I thought he'd refuse or maybe say it begrudgingly, but he sat up with me and looked me straight in the eye and said it.

"I love you."

It was too much again, too much emotion, but I wasn't going to run into the bathroom or away or anywhere. I turned into his arms where he held me safe. There was something to be said for being able to defend myself, but I liked it better that I didn't have to.

As the night turned to early morning, I asked, "You are coming back with me, right?"

He nodded against the pillow.

"Let me just shower first," he said. "You can pack my stuff."

He looked so hopeful I didn't have the heart to tell him no. I dressed back into my club trappings and began to pick through the wreckage. What a mess he'd made. Though I couldn't even grumble about it. I liked that he could depend on me for these small things. He didn't really need me, but he could rely on me.

And the same was true for him. What I'd said back at the club, that I'd needed it, needed him, hadn't been right. I didn't need him, or even his house or any of that. I wanted it and him and everything, but I would be okay no matter what.

I threw his clothes into the one piece of luggage there. Everything else went into a large trash bag I found. I'd sort it all out later and clean all the clothes. I tossed a pair of jeans into the bag, and they thudded against the floor. I pulled them back out—maybe it was his phone or something like that.

I reached my hand into the pocket and pulled out a small velvet box.

And stared at it. Marveled at it, rejoiced, then rejected it.

It had to be jewelry. Maybe a—*No, don't even think it.* It had to be a necklace or something. Maybe an apology necklace. Or maybe it wasn't even for me, but Rose or Bailey or anyone but me.

I didn't want to know. Well, I did, but I didn't want to *guess*. Madness lay that way. It was like Pandora's box, only worse. I hadn't even opened it, and already it couldn't be put away.

If I put it back in the jeans and put the jeans back on the floor, he'd know I'd seen it. If I put the jeans in the bag, I'd only have to pull them out again to wash them, and then I'd be in the same dilemma and he'd know I'd seen it.

In a situation like this, damned if I did and damned if I didn't, there was only one thing to do. I opened the box. A big, square diamond winked at me from its satin bed.

Yes, I immediately thought, only no one had asked me a question.

"Damn," Colin said.

I hadn't even heard the water shut off. He stepped out of the bathroom with a towel wrapped around his waist and plucked the box from my hand, snapping it shut.

"Pretend you didn't see that," he said.

My jaw dropped. "You're just going to leave me hanging?"

"You're not pretending."

"Have you changed your mind?"

He shrugged. "Wait and see."

"Uh-uh." I shook my head.

He sighed, resigned. Then I saw the spark in his eyes. He was enjoying this, the sadist! I ought to say no. I ought to make him ask me and then say no, but there wasn't any chance of that.

He dropped the towel and pulled on the jeans from the floor. He was going to do it.

I clapped. "You didn't have to do that. In fact, it could have helped your case."

He gave me a look.

"Okay, I'm sorry," I said. It was all in good fun, but now wasn't the time to risk it.

He dropped to one knee and took my hand. I shivered. *Don't cry.*

I had dreamed of this, once. I'd thought all those wishes and hopes had evaporated away, but now I greeted them like an old childhood friend. It had never been like this, in those dreams, in a motel room where we'd had sex, me wearing slutty clothes and him wearing only jeans. Well, he might have been wearing only jeans in my adolescent dreams. He looked damned good that way. The packaging was different, but this was what I'd always wanted.

Not just getting married, but the forever and ever, I love you, amen.

"Allie," he said. "You told me once I had a white-knight complex. You said I saved you."

He was going to say I saved him. It was going to be so romantic.

"But the truth is," he said, "I didn't save you—I stole you. I wanted you and I knew I didn't deserve you, but I didn't care. And for some reason it seems like you don't either, so it seems to me that I should make it permanent before you come to your senses. Will you marry me?"

The whole last half of that speech, I hadn't been able to see his face, but I'd *heard* him. God, had I heard him. It was the very best possible proposal I'd ever heard. More than I'd ever imagined, but so incredibly *us*. Only Colin could have said that, and only to me. *Don't pass out.*

"Allie?"

"Yes." I sucked in a deep breath. "I do. Yes, yes."

The ring slipped on my finger. Then he was kissing me, and I tasted my tears on my tongue and then impatiently swiped my face and kissed him some more. He pulled me into his arms and kissed me harder, but I pulled away.

"No," I said. "Not until we get home."

We packed everything else up together, and then we drove separately back to our house. The sky was already in that dusky color of almost light of the very early morning. Shelly lay sleeping on the couch, and I decided not to wake her. We tiptoed past her into the bedroom like two teenagers late from curfew.

In our bedroom we pulled off our dirty clothes and jumped into bed together. We rolled and roughhoused. We played.

A spring must have squeaked or something, because Bailey began to fuss from across the hall. I threw on a nightshirt and undies before settling her back down.

She blinked at me groggily, the slight light through her curtains probably keeping her from sleep. I'd stay here by her side until she fell asleep again, whatever it took. I rubbed her back while she tossed on the bed.

A few minutes later Colin padded in wearing jeans and a T-shirt.

"I'm sorry," I whispered. "I think she'll take a while."

"It's okay," he whispered back. "I thought I'd sit with you."

We sat in a daisy chain: Colin, me, and Bailey. It turned out to be not great that Colin had come in. When Bailey saw that there were two of us, the sleeping gig was up, but I didn't mind. It was sweet that he wanted to be with me and her as a family. It had always been that way with him. From the beginning we'd had the sex, but also the closeness. The love, if I'd been able to put a name on it back then.

Bailey climbed off the bed and sat in my lap as she fully woke up. Then she moved around the room, picking up toys and discarding them, and putting some in Colin's lap until it was stacked with toys. She explained a complicated game to him involving her giving him a toy and him giving it back, and there may even have been a point system. Colin did his best, but he got scolded a few times.

The nagging part of my mother's brain knew her sleep schedule would be all messed up now. She'd fuss and be cranky, and I'd have to work extra to get her back on schedule. It could take days, really, but I couldn't be upset, not as the day dawned on our family, playing and happy. It could take days, but we had forever.

The End

Thank You

Thank you for reading Rough Hard Fierce! I hope you enjoyed Colin and Allie's story. The next book in the Chicago Underground series tells the story of Shelley and Luke—a prostitute, a cop, and a forbidden love. You can read Wild Dirty Secret now!

Be sure to sign up for my newsletter: www.skyewarren.com/newsletter

And you can discuss this book in my Facebook group for fans: Skye Warren's Dark Room

I appreciate your help in spreading the word, including telling a friend. Reviews help readers find books! Please leave a review on your favorite book site.

"This story is emotional, dark, erotic, suspenseful, traumatic and raw. It will have your heart hurting yet you will laugh plenty too. I can highly recommend this series."

~ TotallyBooked Blog

Excerpt from Wild

THE PARTY TURNED out to be a corporate affair in the penthouse of a swanky modern hotel. A bunch of high-profile CEOs getting high and horny amid miles of glass surfaces—what a brilliant idea.

The guys at the front desk checked me out, but discreetly. With furtive glances instead of leers, as befitted an escort of my price range. For all they knew, I was a spoiled girlfriend, not a prostitute. But then, what was the difference?

Outside the suite, I sank my stilettos into the carpet. The dull beat shook from behind the door, already matching the throb in my head. I had the sudden urge to call him as I brushed my fingers against the little black clutch.

What could I say? *I know I promised I wouldn't do it anymore, but I'm about to go bang assholes for money. I tried to join the regular world, but they didn't want me. I'm sorry. Don't hate me. Help me.*

The door swung open, revealing a man with a shiny forehead and a bulbous belly hanging from between his open dress shirt. "I call dibs," he shouted, spittle flying in my face.

Fabulous.

"Sure, lover." I tried to squeeze by him, but he caught me in the doorway. His hands were everywhere, his foul liquor-breath suffocated me, and the doorjamb cut into my back. "No need to rush, handsome. We've got all night."

He grunted and stuck his tongue into my cleavage. His sweat-sheened head filled my vision, and I swallowed bile.

Shit, I wasn't ready to go back. I never would be.

I had to. It was a miracle Henri had let me off so easily. The least I could do was bear my punishment gracefully.

But my new boyfriend's face felt slimy. *I* felt slimy.

I'd only been out of the game for a few months. Maybe more, if I didn't count Philip, which was debatable. Still, there was no reason to freak out over a simple groping. I'd made it through much worse.

Just let him. Let him.

Let him touch and grab and pinch. Let him slobber. Let him treat me like I was a piece of meat, no thoughts, no feelings. Let him treat me like this was all I was good for. Do it for long enough, and I might start to believe it. Lord knew I already did.

Think of something else.

Not him, the man on my speed dial I never called, not while I did this. I didn't understand why it hurt him to see what I was when he met a dozen other hookers in his daily work, each worse off than me, but it did. I couldn't think of my best friend Allie or her daughter either, because to imagine them in this position was a weight too heavy to carry.

His fingers were inside me, pumping away. Thank goodness I'd lubed up, or this would really hurt.

It still hurt. God.

Philip, now he understood me. He wouldn't mourn for me or feel guilty. We did what we had to and didn't waste time on remorse. But I'd told him I was done with the life. I'd promised I'd let him know if I needed help. I needed help, needed…

"Stop," I gasped.

He froze and then gently rocked his fingers back and forth, like a child testing his boundaries.

I lowered my voice. "Wait, lover. I just need to freshen up."

He raised his head and blinked, confused. "You look pretty to me."

My stomach twisted at the compliment. He looked so earnest, his eyes slack with lust and his mouth covered in his own spit. This wasn't a guy who got off on hurting or humiliating. He just didn't know how to deal with people, wouldn't know how to please a woman if he tried. Hell, maybe he was trying.

"Thank you." I choked on the words. "I want to look good for you. Make it good for you. Give me five minutes. Please." Because if he didn't, I would freak. If he didn't get his thick fingers out of me and off my skin this very second, I was liable to do something really stupid. Like leave and to hell with Henri and his hired fists.

The guy backed up, though. His face contorted into an uncertain composition of wounded lover and dissatisfied customer, but he released me, stepped back. I attempted a smile, ignored the pounding in my ears. I wanted to tell him that I would be right back, that everything would be fabulous, but how could I when I didn't believe it myself?

I'd forgotten how to lie. In this business, I was as good as dead.

I pushed off the wall and stumbled my way down the hall. I passed the sitting area, catching flashes of rumpled suits and one lace-clad female body straddling a guy probably twice her age. What was her name? Jenny, Janey, what the fuck ever because it was all a lie. All fake.

The bathroom was empty—thank God for small favors. The sound of the door slamming cracked loud in my head, even though surely it wouldn't be heard above the music. I locked it anyway, turning the little knob. So flimsy, an illusion of safety.

I rested my palms on the counter and stared at myself in the mirror. Blonde hair that I'd straightened this afternoon, sleek and shiny. Makeup—perfect, even though lover boy had slobbered down the side of it. Waterproof stuff, cum-proof stuff—never let them see you sweat.

Even my eyes were steady. Clear. Empty.

I searched my appearance for something, any sign of weakness—none. This was what strength looked like, then. Oh, I had confidence aplenty. I strolled and drawled and acted my fucking heart out, but that was the secret. For me, it had never been an act. I hadn't been hiding what was inside me. There was nothing inside me.

So what was one more empty promise? If he really cared, he would be here right now. He would have protected me from this. What was one more trick? If the life was all I had, I might as well live it.

I touched up my makeup, just because. My hand trembled only a little, but my face came out flawless, like always. And then there was nothing left to pretend, no way left to stall.

The hallway was still empty, and I started to head back to the sitting area. I heard a sound over the pulse of the music: a muffled cry. The hair on the back of my neck stood on end; my heart began to race.

No big deal. Of course there would be those sounds at a party like this, where women were paid to perform, to endure. Probably she had faked it on purpose. But I knew she hadn't.

Still, don't get involved. That was the first rule of staying alive. Even that pitiful kid from yesterday had instinctively understood how it worked: look away, pretend you don't see, don't start trouble.

But there it was again, that sound. It curled sharp nails into my gut, signaling danger. Get away.

I had stayed alive for years by keeping to myself. Those latent self-protective instincts were still there, still honed, and yet I couldn't walk away, couldn't leave her there without knowing.

I crept down the empty hallway and paused at one closed door. At first there was nothing. I almost turned away, left, but then I heard a moan. A female moan of fake pleasure, and that was fine, just fine. Time to go.

A thud sounded from the end of the hall and then echoed in my chest. Inexorably I walked to the last door, knowing through instinct or experience exactly what was happening here. It didn't matter the men or the woman; it was always the same. Too much, too fast, too hard. *I didn't know, wasn't expecting. Too late, bitch.*

A tear slid down my cheek. It was more than just my safety at stake here. *Get away.*

I twisted the knob and pushed the door open a crack, exposing just a sliver of the scene. The face of a girl, her face contorted in fury. The grin of a man. Hands holding down arms. The low sound of laughter. A little slice of hell, and what was I supposed to do about it?

I could do nothing.

This wasn't a young girl on an empty street corner who could be cured with a fast-food burger and a lifetime of therapy. This was one of Henri's girls, off-limits for me and mother-fucking-hen Marguerite Faust. No one could help her, just like no one could help me.

I saw her body jerk with purpose. Heard the crack as her kick landed on someone's skin. The laughter grew louder, more combative.

Shit. She was going to get herself killed that way. Beaten, at the least. Didn't she know that? Didn't she care?

But Henri didn't do hand-holding. Had he recruited this girl fresh out of high school? Given her money she desperately needed to get away, to help her friend, only to indebt herself to him forever? Dumped her at this party without any training or knowledge or a goddamned thing?

This wasn't about me. I told myself that, but it didn't help.

I pushed the door open and stepped inside. Four guys, not counting the ones out in the sitting area or my erstwhile boyfriend.

I smiled and set my hips to sway. "Hello, gentlemen. I see you've started the party without me."

Want to read more? Wild Dirty Secret is available now at Amazon.com, iBooks, BarnesAndNoble.com and other retailers.

Other Books by Skye Warren

Standalone Dark Romance
Wanderlust
On the Way Home
His for Christmas
Hear Me
Take the Heat

Stripped series
Tough Love (prequel)
Love the Way You Lie
Better When It Hurts
Even Better
Pretty When You Cry

Chicago Underground series
Rough
Hard
Fierce
Wild
Dirty
Secret
Sweet

Criminals and Captives series
Prisoner

Dark Nights series
Keep Me Safe
Trust in Me
Don't Let Go
Dark Nights Boxed Set

The Beauty series
Beauty Touched the Beast
Beneath the Beauty
Broken Beauty
Beauty Becomes You
The Beauty Series Compilation
Loving the Beauty: A Beauty Epilogue

About the Author

Skye Warren is the New York Times and USA Today Bestselling author of dark romance. Her books are raw, sexual and perversely romantic.

Sign up for Skye's newsletter:
www.skyewarren.com/newsletter

Like Skye Warren on Facebook:
facebook.com/skyewarren

Join Skye Warren's Dark Room reader group:
skyewarren.com/darkroom

Follow Skye Warren on Twitter:
twitter.com/skye_warren

Visit Skye's website for her current booklist:
www.skyewarren.com

COPYRIGHT

This is a work of fiction. Any resemblance to actual persons, living or dead, business establishments, events or locales is entirely coincidental. All rights reserved. Except for use in a review, the reproduction or use of this work in any part is forbidden without the express written permission of the author.

Rough Hard Fierce © 2015 by Skye Warren
Print Edition

Previously in Giving It Up © 2012 Amber Lin

Cover design by Book Beautiful
Formatted by BB eBooks
Edited by Ann Curtis

Printed in the USA
CPSIA information can be obtained
at www.ICGtesting.com
LVHW091154241123
764753LV00003B/278